12/19

PRAISE FOR
THE
SIMILARS

"Fascinating. I was captivated."

—Francine Pascal, bestselling author of the
Sweet Valley High and Fearless series

"A page-turner that more than delivers on its premise. Hanover takes on sci-fi and high school with equal wit and understanding. The perfect mix of achingly familiar and completely mysterious, the world of *The Similars* is one we don't want to leave."

—Allison Raskin, *New York Times*
bestselling author of *I Hate Everyone But You*

"A brilliantly imagined near-future world where six clones and their counterparts grapple with profound questions of identity and what it means to be human. Part cautionary tale, part gripping teen romance, *The Similars* is as immersive and fast-paced as it is shrewd, compelling, and heartbreaking."

—Ray Kurzweil, inventor, futurist, and
New York Times bestselling author

"Episodic and fast-moving... Plenty of twists and one very big turn that will delight mystery readers."

—*Booklist*

"A fast-paced thriller about identity and love."

—*Publishers Weekly*

ALSO BY REBECCA HANOVER

The Similars

THE
PRETENDERS

THE
PRETENDERS

REBECCA HANOVER

sourcebooks
fire

Published by Sourcebooks Fire, an imprint of Sourcebooks
P.O. Box 4410, Naperville, Illinois 60567-4410
(630) 961-3900
sourcebooks.com

Library of Congress Cataloging-in-Publication Data

Names: Hanover, Rebecca, author.
Title: The pretenders / Rebecca Hanover.
Description: Naperville, Illinois : Sourcebooks Fire, [2020] | Sequel to:
    Similars | Audience: Ages 14-17 | Audience: Grades 10-12 | Summary:
    Still reeling from the events of last year, Emma isolates herself from
    her friends and Ollie, but when Gravelle's plot is revealed, Emma
    realizes she must stop him before he destroys everyone she loves.
Identifiers: LCCN 2019031079 | (hardcover)
Subjects: CYAC: Cloning--Fiction. | Experiments--Fiction. | Science fiction.
Classification: LCC PZ7.1.H36425 Pr 2020 | DDC [Fic]--dc23
LC record available at https://lccn.loc.gov/2019031079

Printed and bound in the United States of America.
MA 10 9 8 7 6 5 4 3 2 1

For Winnie and Bill: the best of the best.

To: levigravelle@darkwoodacademy.edu
From: emmakchance@gmail.com
Date: August 29
Subject: Can't

…not write you anymore. It's been one hundred and thirty-nine days since I left the island, and you, and I told myself if I let it get to a hundred and fifty without doing something—anything… I wouldn't.

So. Levi. I hope you're safe.

I hope you receive this, and not Gravelle.

I hope when you eventually get off that island, I'm one of the people you want to see. Of course, you miss Maude and Ansel and Thea and Jago and Pippa so much, but—

I miss you too.

Can you figure out what I'm not saying? Because what I'm not saying is really kind of everything.

Yours,
Emma

RETURN

I DREAM ABOUT Levi every night.

I'm still an insomniac. That won't ever change. But when I do catch a few hours of fitful sleep, Levi is the first thing I see. His face. His hair, too long and scraggly around the edges. I hear his voice and the accent that used to sound so wrong in his mouth. I see his gray eyes and his solid arms. Those arms carried Pru to safety, and I long for them. For him.

I sent him a message five days ago.

Nothing.

Nothing to let me know that the boy who made me feel *all the things* last year is okay. Not that this radio silence on Levi's part is anything new. I haven't heard from him all summer.

Which is why I've spent the last few months running every possible scenario through my head. *Is Levi okay? IsGravelle torturing him? Has Levi thought about buzzing me? Has he even tried?*

Yes, I've considered that Levi's silence isn't Gravelle's doing at all. That maybe he just doesn't want to talk to me. Because maybe what we had—maybe we *didn't* have it, after all.

I anguished over every line of that email. Wrote fifty-seven versions before I finally sent it, then instantly second-guessed every word choice. What I said, and what I didn't.

But I don't regret sending it.

I miss Levi with an ache that takes my breath away. It's why he inhabits my thoughts even when I'm sleeping. I don't dream of Oliver. No need; I have Ollie back. He's beside me now, napping on the cool leather of the Lexus Earth that's delivering us to our senior year at Darkwood. I look over at him—at his head propped up on his hand, on the armrest—and my heart does a familiar flip. Ollie is home. Ollie is *back*.

We spent the summer together, but it wasn't the carefree reunion I'd imagined. Ollie's been different since he returned. I don't think he's changed fundamentally, but I'm still struggling to work out what's off about him on a cellular level. What's the pharmas, and what's *him*.

My father rides in front. I've placed myself strategically behind him in the back seat. It's better if we can't look at each other. Ever since I read Gravelle's letter—the one where he revealed that I might not be me, but another girl, Eden, the replacement for the daughter my father originally loved—it's been hard to face the man I call Dad. The gulf that already existed between us is now wider than ever. Every time I think about him, I wonder: Is this why he's never loved me? Why he's tolerated me, at best? Because I might not be me, but another girl? One born on a remote island. And if what Gravelle claims is really true, and my father's kept this secret from me for all these years, how can I ever trust him again?

"Darkwood campus in five! Four! Three!" chirps the virtual driver of our car. She's so peppy. Why can't bots be programmable to fit your general mood? In this case, "utter relief that your best friend is alive, with a side of total despair over the boy you love."

I know how lucky I am. Oliver is back. And for the most part, well. He's listening to music through his earbuds, dozing in and out after our flight from California, a look of contentment on his face. He shouldn't even be here right now. I spent nearly a year mourning his death. Believing he'd died by suicide. At the end of the school year, when I learned it had all been a trick, that he was alive... I fully appreciate that what I've been given is a precious gift: more time with the boy who befriended me in the third grade. Who knows I like to layer chips inside my sandwich and who teases me about all the right things: my sarcasm, the way I eat pizza—crust first—and never about the wrong things, like the fact that I'm always overcompensating. That my mother's death left a permanent scar, its edges still raw. If only Ollie's return weren't inextricably tied to leaving Levi on Castor Island, at the hands of Gravelle.

"Emmaline," the familiar voice of my bot, Dash, cuts through my tangled thoughts. "You have an incoming call. Do you wish to answer it?"

I look down at my plum. There's no number listed, but it's definitely ringing.

Could it be him? Levi?

The thought of it sends every nerve in my body tingling.

Is he okay?

That question sends fear coursing through me.

"Yes!" I whisper, frantic, as I shove my earbuds in. I don't want to wake Ollie or tip off my father, whose head is bent over a work memo. But if there's any chance this is Levi, there's no way I'm not answering.

I take in a breath. "I'm ready," I tell Dash. Then, after a click, "Um, hello?"

"Hello, Emmaline," says a familiar voice, infiltrating the quiet space in my head. "Long time, no talk."

I instantly bristle, feeling my skin growing clammy, my heartbeat quickening. I know that voice, would know it anywhere.

It's the Similars' guardian. The man who created them, and who wrote me that note back in April breaking the news that I'm a Similar.

It's Gravelle.

In seconds, his face pops up on the screen of my plum. I shiver at the sight of his sagging skin. His thin lips. His eyes that seem to bore right into my heart, squeezing it dry.

"Yes?" I'm testy, on edge. Why is Gravelle calling me? Why *now*? I have nothing to say to this man, except to rail at him for all the suffering he's caused. To demand to know why he insisted on holding Levi on that island. "What is it?" I ask, not bothering to keep the venom out of my voice.

"Emmali—rather, *Eden*." His pinched lips curl into a half smile. "You did get my letter, did you not?"

"Of course I got it," I snap at him. "Excuse me for not writing back. I didn't think your *note* warranted a response. Especially since there's a good chance you're lying to me. You didn't exactly provide proof that I'm a..." I don't say the word out loud. *A Similar.* "So who's to say you're not making the whole thing up?"

"I can see I hit a nerve." Gravelle's lips drop the pretense of a smile. "I can understand how *traumatic* the contents of my note must have been to you. But that's not the letter I'm concerned with. Not today."

It's not? Heart pounding in my chest like a brass band, I glance at Ollie. Thank goodness he's still asleep and hasn't heard a word of this conversation. My father's wearing the noise-canceling headphones he always uses while working. Good.

"Surely you know what this is about?" Gravelle prods, bringing my focus back to his soulless face.

"Of course I don't—"

"I intercepted a certain...email of yours. Not five days ago, I believe."

My heart lurches to my throat. He means my email to Levi. He read it. *He* got it. Of course he did. How could I have ever thought he wouldn't see it? The man sees everything. Controls everything.

"That jog your memory?" Gravelle asks, humorlessly.

"Where is he? How is he? What are you doing to him?" I choke out in a strained whisper.

"Ah yes, young love. You would want to know, wouldn't you?"

"Tell me what you've done to him. Or I swear—"

"What, dear Eden? What would you, what *could* you possibly do?"

I don't answer, because I have no idea. What power do I hold over Gravelle? Absolutely none at all. He holds all the cards, and he knows it.

"Don't hurt him," I whisper. "He's never done anything but try to please you. If you do, I'll tell the world what you did to us last year. Holding Pru hostage. Killing that clone of Ollie so you could traumatize the Wards. Make them believe their son had died."

Gravelle sizes me up. "Speaking of Oliver… I don't suppose he'd have any interest in seeing your email to Levi—would he? Because I'd happily forward it along. If you'd like."

I freeze. Forward that note to Ollie? I sneak another look at him, my pulse thudding. *No, no, no.* He can't see what I wrote. I haven't told Ollie about Levi, except to say we were friends. All summer I struggled with how to explain that Levi's arrival at Darkwood rewrote my entire narrative. It's impossible, and it would only hurt him.

"No. Don't send him that."

"I didn't think so," Gravelle answers silkily.

"Put Levi on the phone," I demand.

"That's impossible."

I feel my stomach lurch. Sweat forms on the back of my neck, and I feel faint. Impossible? Why—because Levi's hurt? Or worse, *dead*?

"What have you done to him?"

"Always so dramatic. It's not what *I've* done. It's Levi. He's asked me to tell you not to contact him again. I know this won't be easy to hear. Such is life… He doesn't want to see you. Now, or ever."

"I don't believe you," I snarl.

"Levi's made it clear he'll be quite content finishing up his senior year here, with me. Darkwood never was a good fit for him. He felt he was always in Oliver's shadow."

"But…but…" I stammer.

"But what about you?" Those narrow lips curl up into the first full smile I've seen on his face since he called me. "Must I spell it out? *You* were never a good fit for him, Eden. And if you need a reminder that contacting him is not in your best interests, or his—check your email. Until next time." He grins at me, and his face vanishes from my plum screen. The call cuts off.

Hands trembling, heart in my throat, I'm about to ask Dash to open Gravelle's email when I hear voices outside the car. I look up from my plum, past the leaves and branches that brush against my window on our journey up the hill to school. We should be pulling into the circular drive right now. Why are we stopped?

I press my face to the glass. A cluster of students blocks the entrance to the driveway. Eight, maybe ten kids stand in our way, holding up signs: CLONING IS A CRIME, AND SO ARE CLONES.

THE MESSAGE

THE SHOUTS FROM the protesting students grow louder, and I unbuckle my seat belt, craning to get a better view. SAY NO TO CLONES, reads a second sign. NO SIMILARS HERE, reads a third. One girl seems to be leading the charge. She's petite, with silver hair and a nose ring. I've never seen her before.

I think I'm going to be sick.

"Ollie?" I reach out and nudge him with my toe, then scramble to slip on my flip-flops. "Wake up. We're here."

He opens his eyes, furrowing his brow like he's reaching for a memory.

"There were tacos. Thousands of them, as far as the eye could see." He rubs sleep out of his eyes, then takes in the trees surrounding us. "And now, thanks to you, I'll never know the sweet euphoria of slathering them with salsa and stuffing my face until the end of time."

"Look." I point out the window, ignoring his joke. I love that his sense of humor's intact, but now's not the time. Ollie follows my gaze, then opens his window so we can get a better view of what's happening.

The chant hits our ears almost immediately.

"Say no to clones. *Say no to clones. Say no to clones!*"

It's Madison Huxley's rallying cry. But she graduated last year. I'd hoped she'd taken her bigoted anti-cloning views with her. I feel heat rising up my body, fury building within me at the sight of these students raising their signs higher in the air and joining together in unison in this offensive display.

I scan the grounds for a teacher. A parent. *Someone* to put a stop to this. But no one's doing anything.

"I'm afraid we're gridlocked," our virtual driver tells us.

"You think?" I snap.

My father turns to reprimand me. "You don't have to antagonize her, Emma."

Great. He heard that interaction. So much for his noise-canceling headphones. But the admonishment dies on his lips when he notices the protest unfolding outside our car. His eyes widen, and his mouth settles into a thin line. "I'm calling the Darkwood board this afternoon. I've stayed silent for too long."

"Do you think it will matter?" I counter. "Headmaster Ransom allowed rallies like this to go on all last year. What's different now? Nothing, except for all the new laws banning clones from citizenship. Stripping them of their rights! And anyway, no one's even stopping this… Let us out here," I instruct our driver, cutting my dad off before he can respond. "I'm not going to sit and watch this," I explain. "Ollie?"

"I'm right behind you," he answers. He's already exiting the car and grabbing our bags from the trunk.

"I love you, Dad," I say quickly before he can react. I open the door and climb out. He follows me.

"Emmaline—"

"What?" I feel myself losing patience, fast. Gravelle's call has set me on edge. And now this…

I let my father pull me into a stiff hug.

"Be careful, Emma. Please. And if you feel the need to run off to another secluded island without telling me," he adds, without a trace of humor in his voice, "don't."

"Don't worry, Mr. Chance. Sir," Oliver chimes in, right at my side. "I'll be keeping a close eye on her."

"I'm counting on it, Oliver," my dad answers before returning to the Lexus and zipping his window closed, his nose already buried in work buzzes.

"I didn't realize sucking up to my dad was your new extracurricular," I mutter.

One end of Ollie's mouth turns up, in that way he has of looking cocky and sweet and annoying as hell, all at once. "I need *something* to round out my college applications."

Normally I'd smack him, but his witty comment is nearly drowned out by the protestors. "Say no to clones! Say no to clones!" The students amp up their rallying cries.

I look angrily past the knot of kids, still searching for that teacher to intervene, when I let out an audible gasp. It's them, up ahead, maybe ten feet in front of us. I've been so focused on the rally, I almost missed them. It's the Similars. Maude, Theodora, and Jago. I haven't seen the three of them in months, since we all left for vacation. They spent the summer together in Boston, holed up in a sublet they rented with funds that their guardian had earmarked as spending money. I don't know how they arranged that without an adult's approval, but maybe Gravelle signed off on it. All I know is that they didn't return to Castor Island. They feared that if they left the country, they might never be able to return. Which is why a feeling of dread has been churning deep in my gut since we left Levi on the island. What if *he* can never return to Darkwood—and to me?

Two of the Similars were invited to live with their DNA families over the summer. Pippa with Prudence and her parents on the Stanwick family farm, and Ansel in Los Angeles with the de Leon family. I spot Ansel now, exiting a black SUV to join his friends. I'm flooded with questions I want to ask them. Suddenly, the Similars feel like the only people I want to be with, besides Ollie and Pru. They are my only tie to Levi.

I'm also beyond furious about this protest. I'm approaching the cluster of students carrying signs when I see another girl walking up to join them. A girl with shiny blond hair and a familiar face. It's Madison Huxley. She's proudly bearing a banner like the others. Written in large block letters are the words SAY No TO CLONES. She takes her place among the other students as the decibel of the chant rises.

I charge toward her.

"Emma…" Ollie warns, hurrying to my side. "Are you sure you wanna provoke her? I hear she bites. And she could be rabid."

But I don't stop. I'm going to tear that sign out of Madison's perfectly manicured fingers. I reach her in less than two seconds, grabbing the sign and crumpling it before she can stop me.

"What the hell are you doing?" Madison reacts, outraged.

"I could ask you the same question. You graduated. You don't even go here anymore. I've seen you all over the feeds. Stumping for your mom on the campaign trail."

"Of course I'm supporting her," Madison snaps. "My mother's a presidential candidate. If she wins, I'll be the first person *in history* to have both their parents elected to the White House." Her eyes narrow as she considers me with disdain. "Are you sure you want to continue this little tirade? Because the powerful people in my circle could made your life extremely miserable if I wanted them to."

"Emma, let's go." Ollie nudges me. "She's not worth it."

Madison's eyeing Ollie now, giving him the once-over. "Welcome back, Oliver," she purrs. "I wondered at the end of last year if you'd be too behind to come back as a senior. Maybe you'll have to repeat eleventh grade?"

I feel myself growing hot. How dare she? "He completed almost all his missed coursework over the summer—"

But Madison doesn't let me finish. "I see Emma's loyalty to you hasn't wavered. Or yours to her. Though I wouldn't blame you if you felt differently about things. You know—since Levi."

Her words sting, and I avoid meeting Ollie's eyes. Madison

can be cruel; I know this. But this is almost too painful to bear. I'm grasping for an appropriate comeback, but before I can respond, a gravelly voice interrupts us.

"Students, continue on to your dorms!" I see Principal Fleischer standing in the distance, speaking into a megaphone, trying to wrestle control of the situation. "Make a path. Let the cars through. I repeat, continue on to your dorms!"

Kids reluctantly turn their attention from the protestors and wheel their luggage across the lawn. Ollie and I walk away from Madison as the crowd begins to thin, cars start moving again, and the anti-clone cries grow weaker. Maybe they've lost some of their mojo now that Principal Fleischer and a couple of other teachers have arrived. Fleischer is engaged in a heated conversation with Madison and the silver-haired girl, who's gesturing wildly, probably defending what they're doing. I tear my eyes away and head toward my friends, eager to talk to them, to tell them in confidence about my surprise call from Gravelle. My pulse quickens as I remember what Gravelle said. That Levi doesn't want to come back. Or see me.

I don't believe him. Levi wouldn't—not after everything that happened last year. Could he have forgotten what we shared? Has he *forced* himself to forget?

Or is Gravelle telling the truth?

"I could kill every single one of those protestors," I say through gritted teeth as I approach Maude, Jago, Ansel, and Theodora. "Metaphorically, anyway."

"Ignore them," Maude warns, her voice stern. "The angrier you get, the more ammunition you give them."

We hug and exchange hellos. The others tell me Pippa and Pru are arriving later, before assembly. They've been with Pru's dad, Jaeger, on the farm, wrapping up Pru's mom's affairs; she died in July. I flew out for the funeral, determined to offer Pru some of the lifesaving support she'd given me when Ollie—when I *thought* he'd died, last year.

"So, Madison's gone full Wicked Witch of the West," Ollie notes, waving to Maude and Theodora. Fist-bumping Ansel and Jago. Ollie doesn't know my friends that well; after all, he missed all but the last six weeks of junior year, squirreled away on Gravelle's island.

"It's awful," I say. "Why won't she stay on the campaign trail? We were supposed to be rid of her after graduation!"

"We should unpack," Jago says, dismissing the whole topic. It's a good reminder of how strong he is. How strong they *all* are.

We walk together, briskly, toward our dorms. I'm dying to tell them everything Gravelle said to me, but I can't, not with Ollie here. With a pang, I realize that in some ways, I feel closer to my new friends than I am to him.

Maybe it's because you're one of them.

No. I'm not convinced I'm a clone, not by a long shot. There are a million reasons why Gravelle would lie to me about that.

We've reached my dorm, Cypress. I give Ollie a quick hug, taking in his soapy, minty smell, reminding myself that this very act, our proximity, is nothing short of a miracle. "See you at assembly," I murmur before heading into my room and letting the door slam shut behind me.

"Dash, I'm gonna need your help. And possibly a hug," I add, hoping Dash appreciates my sarcasm. He can't hug me, obviously; he's 100 percent virtual.

"Any time, Emma," Dash responds. His jovial voice is a salve to me. I survey the familiar space, settling my gaze on the few photographs and books that Pru and I left here over the summer. I drop my suitcase by my bare-bones desk, then glance out at Dark Lake, noting how black and gleaming it looks today, in the crisp autumn sun.

"Is there an email…" I can barely say it. "From Gravelle?"

"Affirmative," Dash responds. "Would you like me to open it?"

"Yes," I whisper, though I'm terrified by what it might say.

I close my eyes, bracing myself.

"Emmaline," Dash's voice warns.

I open my eyes. "What? What is it?"

"Perhaps you should reconsider—"

I don't let him finish that thought. I look down at my plum screen. A photo fills it entirely.

It's a close-up of a face. Levi's face.

He's badly bruised, with blood caked around his nose and a puffy red eyelid, like someone punched him, hard. That eye is swollen entirely shut. The other looks glossy and distant, and his mouth is unsmiling.

"Emma, don't—"

But Dash is powerless to stop me from reading the caption underneath the picture.

I warned you when you left my island, Eden. You should have listened. Levi stays here. Any and all correspondence he receives will result in more of this. Yes, he heals quickly. But this is nothing compared to the mind control. I know you remember my virtual simulations. As I recall, you're the only one who ever broke out of them. Levi doesn't possess your incomparable mental agility. Are we clear?

Fondly,
A. Gravelle

THE NINE

AN HOUR LATER, I arrive at the chapel for assembly. I have to
work hard to calm myself. To banish that picture of Levi from
my mind long enough to act like a functioning human being. I
step onto the lawn to join my friends and notice that Madison's
standing a few feet from us, and she's not alone. Jago's original, Jake Choate, is next to her, and on her other side is Archer
de Leon. I knew Jake would be returning for a fifth year at
Darkwood, to play soccer and pad his college applications with
some extra APs. But I have no idea what Archer's doing on
campus. Given how he's risen to fame these last few months, I
would have assumed he'd be off doing celebrity stuff. He must

be here to see his Similar, Ansel, because he's waving in our direction.

"Ansel, buddy! Glad you made it," Archer's saying. Ansel gives a little smile and breaks off from our group, ambling over to return Archer's greeting with a fist bump. Ansel has become a lot more comfortable in his skin than he was a year ago, when he first came to Darkwood and was so much shier than his über-popular original.

I'm about to tell Maude, Theodora, and Jago that I need to talk to them later when Headmaster Ransom walks up, and I don't get the chance. I bristle at the sight of him, my mind replaying the image of the Similars, bound to those chairs in the abandoned science building last year, unconscious, at the mercy of Ransom and his twisted "research." It's all I can do not to threaten to expose him, right then and there, but Maude places a swift hand on my arm to silence me.

"Maude Gravelle. May I have a word?" Ransom asks, looking more weary than I remember, his face heavily lined.

Good. I hope he feels guilty as hell about what he's doing to them. I hope his research is failing. And eating him up inside—

"Of course," Maude answers, interrupting my thoughts. "But whatever you have to say, you can tell me here, in front of my friends."

"As you wish." Ransom looks downright exhausted, but I have little sympathy for the man who's pretending to be the Similars' champion. "You've been chosen as this year's leader of the prestigious Ten. As the head of Darkwood's most esteemed academic society, it will be your job to plan Ten meetings,

20

formulate the group's agenda for the school year, and serve as liaison between the Ten and the Darkwood administration. Do you have any questions?"

"I have one," I say before Maude can stop me. "Are we required to intimidate the other students? Make them feel so bad about themselves that they consider leaving school—or worse?" I don't say *jumping off Hades Point*, but I don't have to. Ransom knows what I mean.

Ransom surveys me, and I wonder if he's going to issue a reprimand, but Theodora jumps in before he can respond. "Obviously, it's up to Maude to set the tone of the Ten. An honor she won't take lightly," Theodora adds with authority. "Right?"

"Right," Maude agrees.

"If you'll excuse me, assembly is about to begin." Ransom walks off as Maude lets out a sigh of relief.

"At least *that's* over," she says.

"How do you do it? Stand there and talk to him civilly like that when he's treating you like human science experiments?"

"We *are* human science experiments," Theodora says, her voice quiet. "Remember?"

"And Ransom's exploiting you for his own gain."

"What was that about Ransom?" asks a familiar voice. We all turn to see Pru and Pippa standing there on the lawn, outside the chapel, arm in arm.

I don't think. I don't need to. I reach out to engulf Pru in my arms. I'm reminded of the start of school last year, when she hugged me and I held on for dear life. Now, the tables have turned. She has lost a loved one: her mother. And unlike Ollie, Pru's mom isn't coming back.

"Pru," I choke.

Her face is pressed up against my bare shoulder, and I feel hot, wet tears on my skin. My words feel inadequate, and it's because I know there's not a thing I can say to her right now that will make losing her mother okay.

"I'm hanging in there," Pru answers when we break apart. "Really."

The Similars are hugging Pippa, asking how she is.

"We went through my mom's things," Pru explains to the group. "Sorted a lifetime's worth of belongings. My old tests. A bunch of picture frames and macaroni jewelry I made her as a kid. I still can't believe she's really gone." Pippa squeezes Pru's arm, and the others fold in for a group hug. "I kept this," Pru adds, pulling a necklace out from beneath her hoodie. It's gold, with a little sailboat and some kind of blue stone. Pru's wearing it right next to her Darkwood key. "My mom got it as a gift to herself on my fourteenth birthday. It reminded her of me, because of my rowing. And Pippa took one of Mom's rings."

Pippa holds up her hand, displaying a delicate gold band. A single, tiny diamond glints in the light. "Jaeger wanted me to have it," Pippa says, her voice contemplative, even more so than usual.

I'd wondered how Pru would feel about Pippa being there with her over the summer while Pru's mom was in hospice. Whether she'd want this girl who had only recently joined their family to share in that heartbreakingly special and sad time. When I flew to Jaeger's farm for the funeral, Pru told me that

Pippa was keeping a respectable distance. Not acting like she had any claims to Pru's mom. She's been more of a support system to Jaeger and Pru than anything else.

We're going to be late if we don't head inside, so we wordlessly file into the chapel for the first assembly of the year.

I grab Pru's hand as we filter in. "If you need anything. Any time, any place. I'm your girl," I tell her.

"You came all the way to Castor Island last year to find me," Pru reminds me with a wry smile. "I'm pretty sure you've got my back."

Maude walks up beside me. "We'll deal with Ransom," she says in my ear, low so the others can't hear. "But, Emma, think about it." We hold out our arms so Principal Fleischer can scan our plums—rendering them useless except for buzzing our families and checking school-approved feeds—and then walk inside the chapel to claim seats. "If we refuse to participate in his experiments, he'll have no reason to want us here anymore. He'll send us back to Castor Island. And then what? We may never be able to come back to the States. You said it yourself—we aren't citizens. We can't come and go as we please."

We cram next to each other in a pew, amid the buzzing student body.

"Couldn't you apply for a visa?" I ask. But I know that's a naive suggestion. Gravelle would have to sign off on that. And what if he refused?

"We aren't eighteen. Gravelle is still our legal guardian," Maude reminds me. "Once we set foot on the island, all bets are off. Emma, try to understand what it's been like for us. Why it's not as simple as you want it to be. It's why we can't prosecute him for keeping Levi there, even if we wanted to. Gravelle is his legal guardian."

"He isn't Ollie's guardian. Or Pru's," I remind her. "And he kept both of *them* prisoner last year too."

"I know. And Jane Ward has chosen not to pursue this with the authorities," she says, her eyes gazing forward, at the podium. "She thinks it would only make Gravelle more vindictive. And you know Jaeger. He's going to make things right via the Quarry. His underground activist group can take care of things far better than the legal system, anyway."

She's right. This is a lot more complicated than I'd like to admit. Gravelle is practically untouchable when it comes to the law. Especially now, since he likely hasn't stepped off his micronation in years. As long as he's there, he's immune to the laws of other countries and can create his own. My mind spins, making it hard to concentrate on the assembly. It's the same old generic speech Ransom gave last year, minus the fanfare around the Similars' arrival and the sixty seconds of silence in honor of Oliver. Speaking of Ollie, he's found me and has slid into the seat next to me. His presence warms me up by proximity.

"Hey," Ollie says quietly, in that way he has of making me feel like the only person on the planet, even in a room filled with hundreds of our peers.

"You're late," I whisper back. "You just missed the tediously boring part where Ransom drones on and on about excellence and identity, blah blah blah."

"No, I think that's now," Ollie quips.

Oh, how I've longed for this. Our rapport. Our "usness." With a jolt in my stomach I think of everything I'm keeping from him. The last thing I want to do is lie to Ollie. But I can't tell him any of it. Not now. Maybe not ever.

At dinner, we all sit together: me, Pru, the Similars, and Ollie. A few tables over, Jake, Madison, and Archer compare plums. Archer laughs at something Madison's showing him. I wonder why Madison and Archer are still here, hanging around... Probably to keep Jake company. Jake's other friends have all left Darkwood to start college, and I bet he's lonely. Not that I care.

Tessa isn't here. Although she did manage to graduate last year, she hasn't started college yet. A judge deemed her violent act against Pru, in the school boathouse, to have been brought on by post-traumatic stress disorder. He ordered her to live in a treatment center for six months.

Ansel's telling us animatedly about his summer at the de Leons'. While Archer spent most of July and August on set in Thailand shooting a movie, Ansel got to know Archer's dads, interning for them at their production company. I'm only half listening. All I can think about is Gravelle's holo-call. His sickening message to me. The fact that my email to Levi is what caused Gravelle to lash out...

"You okay?" Ollie asks, digging into his casserole.

I could kick myself for being such an open book. I force myself to hide how *not* okay I really am. "Of course. Just enjoying this delicious gourmet fare. I forgot how much I missed it," I add, grimacing for effect.

"Look, I know they aren't my family. Not really," Ansel's saying between bites of in vitro chicken.

"Who says they aren't?" Pippa pipes up. "People look for their birth parents all the time, don't they? Isn't it kind of like that for us?"

"The Huxleys are *not* my parents, birth or otherwise," Maude responds.

"No," Pippa agrees quietly. "They aren't."

"And I suppose I should start visiting Damian Leroy in prison?" Theodora snaps.

"I didn't mean…"

"Sorry," Theodora sighs. "I'm happy for you, Pippa. You too, Ansel. It's just that Maude, Levi, and I aren't exactly eager to be adopted by our DNA parents. No offense," she adds for Oliver's benefit.

"And it makes us want to vomit even calling them that. I prefer 'unwilling DNA donors,'" Maude adds, spearing a carrot with her fork.

The conversation is cut short when Principal Fleischer strides to the front of the room to announce this year's stratum rankings. She informs the student body that Maude Gravelle will be this year's Ten leader, which is met with light applause. A lot of kids twist in their seats, and some even stand up in place, to get a better look at Maude. She's the exact DNA copy of last year's Ten leader, which makes her uniquely interesting to many of our classmates, though not to me. I don't even see Madison's face when I look at Maude anymore. I only see my friend.

"Moving on to the rankings," Fleischer continues. "Please wait for your name to be called. Then retrieve your envelope." The members of the junior class straighten in their chairs, but us seniors, already ranked last year, listen with mild curiosity. I'm too preoccupied to care who'll be joining us in the Ten. It's not until the faces of the new junior members are projected on the eight-foot view screen that I snap to attention. I don't personally know most of these new Ten members or recognize them from my classes, but one face stands out to me. It takes me a second to place her.

"She was leading the protest this morning," Ollie whispers in my ear, getting there faster than me.

He's right. It's the girl with the silver hair. According to the stratum announcement, her name is Harlowe Shaw. My heart sinks. We'll be in the Ten together. And worse, so will Pippa, Theodora, and Maude.

I snag Maude and Pru at the end of dinner. "The junior with the number-two stratum? She was one of the protestors this morning."

Maude doesn't look fazed. "I'm aware."

"Ransom's still letting kids get away with that?" Pru asks, visibly agitated.

That's right; I'd almost forgotten that Pru missed that hateful display this morning. I'm glad she didn't see it. She doesn't need that right now.

"What do we do?" I moan. "Induct this girl into our group like everything's normal?"

"What choice do we have?" Maude asks. "We don't pick who's in the Ten. Madison didn't want a single one of *us* in it last year. But even she couldn't do anything about it."

"Except torment us."

"Except that," Maude agrees.

This is a disaster. Tradition dictates that we should be holding the first midnight session tonight. We're going to have to welcome Harlowe Shaw into Darkwood's most esteemed group. I don't know if I can be in the same room with her without throwing a punch.

"Excuse me." Maude clangs a spoon on a glass, getting the attention of the student body. It takes a few moments, but finally everyone quiets, curious to hear what the new Ten leader has to say. "I'd like to make an announcement, if I may, Principal Fleischer?"

Fleischer nods begrudgingly. I notice Madison bristling at her table. I feel rage course through me, thinking of this morning, those signs she was brandishing.

"As leader of the Ten," Maude addresses the dining hall, "I'd like to officially welcome our five new members into this prestigious group. I'll also remind you that it's a great honor to be a part of the Ten, one you should take seriously. Congratulations. And now for a bit of business. There are two changes happening to the Ten this year. First, the group's name," Maude goes on in her confident way. "Unfortunately, we are missing one of our senior members. Levi Gravelle did not return at the end of the last school year, and he is regrettably not here now. Since senior members of the Ten cannot be replaced, our group will, for the duration of the school year, be called the Nine."

My heart drops to my feet.

"As for the second change, I am, as leader of the Nine, hereby suspending all initiation activities. There will be no hazing—school-authorized or otherwise. There will be no rit-uals to determine whether you deserve your spot in the group. This announcement is your initiation. So, Sophie Ortiz, Ivy Li, Willa Stone, Graham Rosen, and Harlowe Shaw: welcome."

The dining hall buzzes as kids take in this news. Hazing has never been sanctioned by the school, but everyone knows it takes place under the administration's nose. All around me, students discuss this new wrinkle.

"I'll see the eight of you in the Tower Room of Cypress. Midnight, tonight," Maude declares before leaving the dining hall with the rest of us.

"Satisfied?" she asks me, all business. I nod, and Ollie looks impressed as we walk down the dimly lit path.

"I missed a lot last year, didn't I?" he says, gazing out over Dark Lake. There's humor in his voice, but behind his eyes, he's sad. I can tell.

That night, hours later, I can't sleep. It's eleven o'clock, and I have an hour before I need to be in the Tower Room, meeting the Nine for our first midnight session. I lie on top of my covers in my jeans and hoodie, my mind churning over the events of the day. Especially that photo Gravelle sent, the one of Levi's battered face. It's all I can see when I close my eyes. I'm yanked out of my thoughts by Dash, alerting me that I have a new notification on my plum. I look down at the screen to read the message there.

no hazing? that can be remedied

I check the sender. It's Harlowe Shaw.

HARLOWE

I SIT UP in bed, sneaking a look over at Pru. She's fast asleep. Good. I glance down at my plum and send a reply to Harlowe, using a voice command via my bot.

> *Not taking the bait. You heard what Maude said. Hazing canceled. Get w/ the program.*

The response from Harlowe appears almost instantly.

> *if u don't want your friends to suffer too much, meet me @ the driveway outside the main house. 5 min.*

I snap to attention. Would Harlowe really do something to hurt the other members of the Nine? The *Similar* members of the Nine?

I shove my feet into my sneakers. I won't wake Pru, not when this is probably a prank. It's got to be a trick to get me out of bed and scare me into thinking that my friends are in trouble.

I leave my key around my neck. I feel more trackable with it on my body. Traceable.

Slipping out the back door of Cypress, I note that except for the beams from a few lights dotting the campus walkways, it's pitch-dark out. And cold. And so silent, all I hear are my footsteps on the asphalt and the distant hum of crickets.

"Dash," I whisper. "Send a buzz to Maude, Theodora, and Pippa. Ask them if they're okay. Tell them to pin their location."

"Will do, Emmaline," Dash replies.

When I arrive at the circular drive in front of the main house, I'm totally alone, save for a single car waiting there. It's an older model red Volvo, probably vintage; that's how ancient it looks. I wonder briefly what it's doing there. But mostly I'm looking for Harlowe. There's no sign of her.

"Dash," I say more urgently this time. "Any response from my friends?"

"I'm sorry, Emma," he replies. "All three of their devices are off-line."

My chest tightens. Off-line? If it weren't for the midnight session, it'd be perfectly reasonable for my friends to turn off their plums. It's way past curfew. But the Nine meeting starts in under an hour. I doubt they've gone to sleep. *Why aren't they answering?*

I scan the grounds for Harlowe. Not seeing her anywhere, I start to turn back, annoyed with myself for falling for this, when someone leans out the driver's-side window of the red Volvo.

"Like my ride?" says the girl. I squint to get a better look. It's Harlowe. Of course it is. Wary, I start walking toward her. Students aren't allowed to have cars on campus, and even if we could, none of us can get a license until we're twenty-one. The car is clearly contraband. Up close to her now, I can make out her features in the moonlight. Her piercing black eyes and cropped, silver-dyed hair. The car is running, and it's not the electric hum I'm used to. This car runs on gas.

"So, you feel like targeting the Similars?" I ask, making my voice sound breezy. "Great idea. That's going to end really well for you. But go ahead. Try it."

"We did," she answers, her eyes dancing like she's holding on to a delicious secret. "It actually went swimmingly. Oh, I guess you don't know. First, we injected them with pharmas, then we transported them to a remote location, and, finally, we left them there without their plums. Or their clothes." She laughs.

I feel heat rising through my body. Anger. Rage. "You're lying."

Harlowe shrugs. "Go back to Cypress and wait for the midnight session to start. I promise you, they won't show up."

I stare at Harlowe, trying to suss out whether she's messing with me. It's impossible to know. She seems so flippant about the whole thing. Is she really that brazen? That shameless?

"Tell me where they are," I choke out, my frustration turning to mild panic.

"No problem," Harlowe says. "Just get in the car, and I'll take you straight to them."

Get in the car? Has she lost her mind? The last thing I'd ever want to do is get in an illegal vehicle and drive off campus with this girl.

"Look, it's not really a hard decision, is it?" Harlowe examines her reflection in the rearview mirror, acting like this whole conversation is no big deal. That only makes me more furious. "You get in the car. I bring you to your friends. Or if you'd rather head to your dorm and go to bed…" She shrugs.

My head spins, and I feel sick with anger. Harlowe might be totally lying to me. But if she isn't, and my friends are in trouble… I can't tolerate that.

"Why should I believe anything you say?" I press, trying to keep my voice from wavering and showing weakness.

"Oh, I get it. It's not like we know each other. You probably want some kind of proof, right? I would, if I were you." Harlowe presses a button on her plum screen, and a photo pops up. She flicks her wrist lazily in my direction, showing me a picture of Maude, Theodora, and Pippa. They're bound and gagged.

I feel bile rising in my throat, nausea swimming in my stomach. "What did you do to them?" I whisper.

Harlowe laughs, warming her hands in front of the heating vent, rubbing them together. "It's only an initiation, Emma. We don't plan to hurt them."

"Who's 'we'?" I ask through gritted teeth.

"Me, Ivy, and Graham." She scowls. "Willa and Sophie didn't want to play along."

I consider walking away. Running back to my dorm room, waking up Pru and Ollie, and scouring the campus for my friends. But if Harlowe's telling the truth, and she really has transported them off campus, we'll have wasted precious time. For all I know, she'll leave them there—wherever they are—all night. I can't head back to Cypress knowing that they could be bound and gagged somewhere, for hours on end. And with their plums off-line, I have no way of contacting them. I make a split-second decision, grabbing the handle to the back door of the car and flinging it open, then climbing in. My heart's racing with fear and increasing dread. I'll buzz Pru and Ollie. Jago and Ansel too. They can search the campus while I go with Harlowe…wherever she plans on taking me.

"Let's go." I slam the door shut. Then I glance up at the front seat, skeptical. "Do you even know how to drive this thing?" I examine the interior of the car. It's seriously old, with cracked leather seats and none of the high-tech devices you'd find in any modern car. No view screen. No digital control panel. Just a bunch of old dials and knobs. Harlowe is busy revving the engine, her foot on the accelerator. An alarm bell goes off in my head, but I ignore it. This is blatantly and egregiously against Darkwood rules. Bringing this car here, driving it in the middle of the night. Where'd she even get it? And how is she flaunting it so brazenly, when the discovery of its existence here at school could get her expelled?

"It's my dad's," she offers in explanation. She presses the gas pedal, and the car lurches forward. Within seconds, we're leaving campus, heading down the hill into the brush. "We road-tripped to school. He's going to drive it home next week. He collects vintage cars," she adds. "Don't worry, he taught me how to drive when I was twelve. I used to practice all the time back home in Wyoming. You know, lots of wide, open spaces." We're gliding smoothly through the woods of the school. I can't remember ever having ridden in an old-school, gas-powered car like this one, but I'd assumed that the ride would be jerky. It isn't. And Harlowe is right. She isn't a *bad* driver...

I type out a buzz to Pru, Ollie, and the others, hoping Harlowe's too busy driving to notice.

Maude, Thea, and Pippa missing. Harlowe did this.
LOOK FOR THEM.

We've cleared campus now. Enough humoring her. I want to know what the hell's going on. "Okay, Harlowe. I've played your little game. Now tell me where my friends are."

"Not yet," she says as she easily steers us along a curve onto the highway. "I need time for them to stew a little. Besides, I never said I'd tell you where we're going. You'll find out when we get there. That was the deal."

"Why are you even doing this?" I press, catching Harlowe's eyes in the rearview mirror. They look determined. Cold.

"Isn't it obvious?" she answers. "Ivy, Graham, and I have been waiting to be in the Ten—sorry, the *Nine*—since the day we first got to Darkwood. You weren't going to initiate us and seemed to want to rob us of that critical milestone, so we decided to take matters into our own hands. With a twist,

35

of course. One that emphasizes our core values." She's talking about clones. About how she doesn't accept or want them here. Ivy and Graham must agree.

Burning inside, I glance out the window, taking in our surroundings. We're on a fairly deserted section of road. There isn't much to see besides trees. A couple of barns. A lone diner.

"They never did anything to you," I seethe. "They don't even know you. This is all Madison's doing, isn't it? She got to you. Convinced you to take on her family's cause."

"Now I'm offended, Emmaline." Harlowe narrows her eyes in the mirror. "You don't think I can form my own opinions? Think for myself?"

I don't answer. There's no point in getting deeper into this argument with her. I need to focus on my friends. A buzz comes in from Pru, saying she's on it, but no luck yet. Maude, Thea, and Pippa aren't in their rooms...or anywhere else in Cypress.

Harlowe flicks on the radio. A popular song starts playing as she takes an exit onto a second highway, and I feel myself start to sweat. How far away is this place, anyway?

"I hope you peed before you got in," Harlowe remarks, seeming to settle in as she switches the station. "We've got a long drive ahead of us. I gassed up first," she adds with a smirk. "We can go four, maybe five hours before we'll have to stop. Sorry I didn't bring snacks. No time."

What? I feel the hair on the back of my neck prickling.

"Four or five *hours*?" My mind races, processing this new information. There's no way she drove my friends four hours out of town. There wasn't enough time between dinner and now.

It's impossible. "You played me," I say, the realization hitting me hard. "You aren't taking me to my friends at all, are you, *Harlowe*?" I spit out her name. "Let me guess. We're just driving aimlessly, while my friends are locked up somewhere at school. Somewhere right under our noses."

Harlowe laughs. "Smart. Now I see how you got that number-five stratum."

I'm stuck in this car with her until she decides to stop or turn around. For all I know, she really does plan to drive all night while I stew in the back seat, worried sick about my friends. I don't know what she has in store for them, but I get it now. This little road trip is *my* initiation. I can't believe I fell for it.

I scramble to make this all okay. To prove to Harlowe that she hasn't won. Not yet. "They'll wait," I say, feeling increasingly desperate and trapped. "Maude, Theodora, and Pippa will wait until someone finds them. Or they'll bust their way out." I don't mention their capabilities or the fact that they're stronger than she could ever imagine.

"Doesn't matter to me if they've escaped," she responds. "The damage has already been done."

"You can't traumatize them or scare them into leaving Darkwood," I answer angrily. "They've seen worse. Much, much worse!"

"Maybe we're not trying to get them to leave." Harlowe shrugs, gunning the accelerator. "Maybe we want to teach them a lesson."

I have to get out of this car. I can't stand the thought of Harlowe torturing my friends. Hurting them, even emotionally.

And there's no way I'm sitting here, her captive for who knows how long, while she leads me farther and farther away from school.

Screw her, I think, watching the highway speed past us and thinking of my dad, praying that he won't ground me for life for what I'm about to do. It's the one thing Harlowe won't expect. But she doesn't know what I went through last year. She doesn't know what I faced on that island. And how much I care about my friends.

And besides. It's also the only way out.

I open the door.

The asphalt of the highway greets me in a rush. We must be going at least fifty miles an hour. But it's too late. I'm doing this.

"Thanks for the ride, Harlowe," I say, my voice biting, and then I leap from the moving car.

The ground meets me all at once, and I try to remember to roll, like I've seen people do in videos. I think I do it—I manage to protect my head and neck, anyway—but hitting the pavement feels like it takes minutes, not seconds, and on impact, I feel broken and singed. I'm sure some skin has been ripped off of me in chunks.

I hear Harlowe's Volvo speed off. Panting, my cheek resting on the rough asphalt, my heart beating a million miles a minute, I take stock of my body. The pain is crippling, roiling through me in waves. Gingerly, I inspect the damage. My jeans are torn at both knees, and my wrists feel sprained when I move them, likely from bracing myself with my hands when I first hit the road. There are a few deep scrapes visible through the tears in my jeans, but they don't look nearly as bad as I thought they would. My hands are intact. Nothing feels particularly broken. And the pain that, moments ago, was all-consuming is already starting to dissipate, perhaps from shock or adrenaline. I might need pharmas once my body realizes what happened to it. But I'll deal with that later, back on campus. I can get my cuts mended by the school nurse. One on my right knee looks particularly gnarly. I hope I don't need stitches.

I hear the sound of screeching. Curious, I sit up. I'm able to do that, at least, which strikes me as a good sign—I can't be *that* hurt if I can move my body to a sitting position. And then I see it: Harlowe's Volvo. Making a U-turn in the middle of the road and racing back toward me.

I brace myself, then press my tender palms to the ground, giving myself leverage so I can straighten my legs and stand up.

Harlowe's stopped the Volvo inches from me, on the shoulder of the road. The driver's-side door opens, and she gets out, not even bothering to shut her car door.

"What the hell is *wrong* with you?" she demands, and for the first time tonight, she actually looks shaken.

"I think I'm hurt," I say, furrowing my brow. "My leg, it feels broken." I take a halting step toward Harlowe and the car, almost keeling over. Harlowe reaches out a hand to steady me, and that's when I push her out of my way.

Harlowe falls backward, and in that moment I'm able to slip through the open car door, slam it closed behind me, and start the ignition. I see the look of shock on her face and remember, in the nick of time, to hit the lock button on the door—before she can follow me in.

I click in my seat belt before reaching for a lever to my right and putting the car into what I hope is drive. Then I look down at the pedals, take in a giant breath, and press my foot to the accelerator. At least, I think it's the gas and not the brake...

I'm zooming forward. At the last second, I remember to put my hands on the wheel, and I grip it like a vise as the car lurches forward at top speed. Panicking, I lift my foot off the accelerator, and the car slows and comes to a near stop.

"Dash!" I yell at my wrist. "Help! Please tell me you know how to drive a car..."

I spot Harlowe in my rearview mirror, racing toward me on foot. I press my foot to the accelerator again, jerkily. The car begins lurching forward.

"Emmaline, pull over at once."

"Not happening." I grimace. "I have to get back to campus. Harlowe's done something to Maude and the others and I have to find them."

I see Harlowe far behind me, a speck in the distance. She's stopped running and stands there in the road.

"Dash! Some help here?" I groan.

"According to Google, you must keep a car length of distance between you and the next vehicle at all times."

"Dash, that's not even remotely helpful! What do I do, right now?"

"All right. Stay calm—"

"I said, something helpful!"

"You know how to brake, I assume? It's the pedal to the left of the accelerator."

I try pressing on it and feel the car immediately slow down, eventually coming to a stop...right in the middle of the road. A car is approaching behind me, its headlights bright yellow in my rearview mirror. The car comes to a stop and honks.

"Give me a second." I grit my teeth, removing my foot from the brake and placing it gingerly on the accelerator—too fast and too hard. Now we're gunning forward again...

"Tell me how to get back to campus. *Now!*" I screech as I hurtle toward the next light. It's green. "I'm going way too fast. Dammit, Dash, I can't tell how hard to press—"

"Turn left! Turn left!" Dash barks at me.

"Left?" I squeal, sucking in a breath as I spin the wheel that way.

But I've turned it way too hard, and too far, and now the car's careening far too quickly, out of my control. It's fish-tailing, and for a split second I think I'm toast. But I manage to jerk the wheel and steer myself back the other way. And just in time too—as soon as I clear the intersection, another car races past me, inches from where I had been only seconds earlier. I hear a long, protracted honk and know I narrowly missed crashing.

"Jesus, Dash, I need more help from you." But then I notice something unsettling. The car that first honked at me earlier? It's behind me. *Close* behind me. "Dash? Is Harlowe in the car behind me?"

"I'm sorry, Emmaline, I don't have that information."

I'm sure of it, though. From my rearview mirror, I think I can see her silver hair gleaming from the back seat. She must have called a cab as soon as I stranded her, and she's been following me ever since.

"Turn right at this stop sign. Stop first!" Dash barks.

"Nope," I say through gritted teeth as I speed through several stop signs, following Dash's directions and trying to lose Harlowe's car. But no luck; she's still there, right on my tail. I'm getting the hang of the pedals, even if I have no idea what any of the rest of the knobs and buttons do. I'm about to fly through a crosswalk when I spot a woman in all black, stepping right into my path across the wide white lines. I swing the wheel violently to the left, managing to avoid hitting her…

Then I hear a voice. Not Dash's. A different voice. One that sounds far off. Distant. And yet, I can make it out clearly, every word. Like someone's talking softly nearby.

What the hell does she think she's doing?

"Dash?" I whisper, feeling like I've lost my mind. My eyes are glued to the road, and I'm relieved to see that I'm at the outskirts of the Darkwood campus. But I must be imagining things. Because that sounded like a *female* voice.

"Emmaline, this entire escapade has been highly inadvisable."

"Spare me the lectures, Dash! It's not like you're responsible for me." My eyes flit to my rearview mirror. Harlowe's still following me!

She's clearly never driven in her life. What's wrong with her? Why's she so worried about those friends of hers? What made her love clones so much, anyway?

My stomach drops as I steer the car up the brush and through the woods, the last mile until main campus. That sounds like… like *Harlowe's* voice. But how…how am I *hearing* it?

"Dash, I'm not… Are my vitals… Are they normal?" I ask in a strained voice.

"You're experiencing a spike in adrenaline," he offers. "That's obvious. Why?"

Because I'm hearing voices?! I want to shout.

At least she'll never guess the pump house. That creepy old building is the last place anyone in their right mind would look…

The pump house? It would make sense. It's this dilapidated old building near Hades Point that used to house the school's water system, before Darkwood was outfitted with modern plumbing. It's full of creaky old machinery, and students never go there. But am I going completely off the deep end? Did I really hear Harlowe's thoughts? What had Gravelle said to me in his email? That I have "incomparable mental agility"?

Is that what this is? Some way in which I can hear the thoughts happening in another person's mind?

"So you're not, um, hearing anything, any*one*, besides us. Are you, Dash?"

"No, Emmaline, we're the only ones here." He sounds concerned. If only he knew.

She'll go right back to her dorm and try to call the clones. Then she'll search for her friends all night, and I won't tip her off to look in the pump house till the morning.

My palms are sweaty, and I take them off the wheel to rub them on my jeans. I can barely handle what's happening to me right now. But I don't feel dizzy or sick. My head feels *clear*. Like

I've woken up for the day after a blissful night of uninterrupted sleep. Must be all that adrenaline…

In my peripheral vision, I catch a glimpse of the rip at my right knee, and I take my eyes off the wheel to glance down. For a second, I think I'm seeing things. The cut I saw earlier, visible through the jagged hole in my jeans—it's become scabbed. The way it should look days after it first appeared. Not thirty minutes later.

Reeling, I tear my eyes away from my knee and look back at the road, focusing on the fact that we're almost there, and I need to get to the pump house. Now. But I can't let Harlowe know I'm onto her.

"Dash, does the dirt road up there lead to the pump house? The old abandoned building by Hades Point?"

"Yes, but why?"

"No reason," I mutter as I yank the wheel unpredictably to the right. We veer off the paved path and onto a rocky, uneven dirt lane that probably hasn't seen a car on it in years. Especially not a vintage clunker without four-wheel drive. But it's worked. I've lost Harlowe. In the rearview mirror, I see her car whooshing past, continuing on the paved path. She's taking the long route.

"Almost there!" I shriek as we hit a particularly large bump. This path, for all its rockiness, is going to get us there a lot faster. All we need to do is get past this next—"Dash!" I shriek as I lose control of the wheel and the car skids down a slope with the pump house as its final destination. I spot the old building in front of us, looming like a sore thumb in the distance. We're going so much faster than I intended. We're going to crash—

I slam on the brakes seconds before we plow right into the building, stopping short of it by only a few feet.

Pulse in my throat, I take a moment behind the wheel to process what just happened. All is quiet, except for the pounding in my ears. I let out a breath. We did it. *I* did it. My hands are shaking, and I'm sure if Dash had a body, he'd be sweating right now.

There's no time to waste. I tear out of the car and race toward the door. Harlowe doesn't know I read her thoughts—or whatever the hell that was—so this extra time, before she arrives, is critical. Even if she did guess where I'm headed, it'll take her at least a few more minutes to get here. Reaching the front double doors, I wrench them open.

Inside the dilapidated building are my friends—Maude, Theodora, and Pippa. They are seated in three metal chairs, and each one of them is handcuffed to a chair leg by the wrist. They look groggy, like they've woken up from a disorienting nap.

Standing in front of them are Ivy and Graham.

"We weren't expecting *you* yet," Graham says, sizing me up. "But whatever. You're just in time for the show."

THE HAZING

I TAKE A step toward my friends. "Are you okay?" I ask.

Maude shifts in her chair, trying to move her arm, but she meets with resistance. It's the handcuff, shackling her wrist to her chair leg. Frustrated, she tries yanking it, but nothing happens.

"Where *are* we?" Pippa asks, surveying our whereabouts skeptically.

I don't blame her for being freaked. This place is ancient and intimidating.

"The pump house," I answer her, about to move to help her with the cuffs when Graham steps right in my path. Something glints in his hand. It's a large kitchen knife, the kind you use to chop vegetables.

"What are you planning on doing with *that*?" I ask, contempt in my voice.

"I'm not sure you want to know," Graham says.

The double doors clang open, and in rushes Harlowe. Panting, she looks murderous.

"How'd you do it? Figure out we were here? You!" She spins on Ivy and Graham. "You told her where we were meeting," she accuses her friends. She snatches the knife out of Graham's hand. I shiver involuntarily. Is she for real? First the car, now a knife? She's even bolder than Madison was last year. Or maybe she's more unhinged.

"Of course we didn't tell her," Ivy pipes up. She's petite, with jet-black hair and white, straight teeth. "We would never."

"Then how'd you know to come here?" Harlowe turns to look at me. "And if you say you guessed it, I won't believe you."

I don't answer her. There's no way I'm telling her that I *read her mind*. Instead, I shrug. "What's it matter how I figured it out? I'm here now. And I'm not playing your little game anymore."

"Emma," Maude warns. She's gradually becoming alert but still looks groggy.

I hear the sound of wheels rolling over the hard-packed dirt floor. I turn to see Ivy pushing a fourth chair over toward my friends and settling it beside Pippa. In the dim light, I can't make out who it is at first. Then I hear Pippa gasp.

"Levi?" she asks, still sounding dazed.

My heart leaps to my throat.

Is it? For one millisecond, I let myself believe, even though I know it can't be. Levi's back on Castor Island. Not here. Still, the idea that he could be here, in this room, and I might have some slim chance of seeing him again, so soon…now, even…

I rush to the chair and see that it's not Levi—of course it isn't. It's Ollie. And he's passed out like the others were. Only he's still unconscious.

"What did you do to him?" I demand, placing a hand at his wrist, feeling that he has a pulse. I note the up-and-down motion of his chest and feel a flood of relief that he's alive, just not awake.

I spin to face Harlowe, not caring about the knife she wields, or anything else. I'm enraged.

"You dragged Ollie here too? He's not even in the Nine—"

"Someone had to stand in for Levi, since he's currently… indisposed." Harlowe shrugs. "Ollie seemed like the obvious choice of a replacement. Right, guys?"

Ivy nods. Graham shrugs.

I feel a burning sensation in my throat and swallow it back. Her words hurt, but I can't let them get to me. That's exactly what she wants. She's been playing me all night, luring me out to her car, threatening to take me miles away from Darkwood's campus. I can't figure out why she didn't just drug me too, along with my friends—except that she knew that long car ride would be worse torture for me than being locked up here, with Maude, Thea, and Pippa.

And Ollie. She set him up as an extra-special treat for me. She probably couldn't wait for me to get here and see him in that chair, couldn't wait to witness the blind hope in my eyes when I thought, for a split second, he might be Levi…

"You weren't supposed to be here for hours, after we drove

around half the night," Harlowe notes as she paces in a circle, running a finger absentmindedly down the sharp edge of the knife. "I suppose we'll have to speed up the evening's agenda. Graham?"

He takes the cue, scuttling off to follow orders while Ivy walks over and slaps Ollie humorlessly on the cheek, more than once.

"Get your hands off him—" I make a move to shove Ivy away from Ollie, feeling more protective of him than ever. Then he opens his eyes and groggily looks around.

"Emma?" he asks, confusion in his voice. "What's going on? Where are we?"

Before I can answer, the dim light in the room is unplugged, or turned off, and we're all plunged into absolute darkness.

"Now," Harlowe commands. Before I know what's happening, a holographic slideshow begins playing on the opposite wall, which is bare except for a few pipes and wires, serving as a giant, flat screen.

"What—"

"Sh," Harlowe hushes me. "Watch first. Ask later. Actually, ask never. This should be completely self-explanatory."

The first photo in the sequence is one of Pru's family, and I instantly feel myself tensing up at the sight of the image. It's Pru, as an eight- or nine-year-old, blowing out the candles on a unicorn birthday cake. Her mother stands behind her, looking young, her skin glowing and healthy, and I know this picture was taken before the cancer ravaged her body. That photo fades, and a new image takes its place: a picture of a beaming Madison standing up on a stage while her father is sworn in as vice president. Madison's about ten and wears a white dress and a pink coat. Her mother, Bianca Huxley, stands stiffly behind her, resting a hand on Madison's shoulder.

The next photos come quickly: A happy Pru graduating from middle school, her parents smiling beside her. A photo of young Madison hunting for Easter eggs on the White House lawn. And then, in quick succession, the salacious headlines about Damian Leroy's arrest and subsequent prison sentence. News stories about his family, including one article that features a close-up of Tessa's stricken face as a reporter accosts her with questions about her dad. She holds her hand up, like she's trying to shield her face from the paparazzi.

I know what Harlowe's doing, and I'm so furious at her I could scream. I don't turn to look at my friends' faces, but I'm sure if I did, I'd see the hurt written there. Harlowe's rubbing their DNA families in their faces—Pru's happy family life, including the mother Pippa lost months after meeting her. She wants Maude to hurt for never being a part of one of the most influential families in the country. And, worst of all, she wants to remind Theodora of the role she played in sending Damian Leroy to prison.

It's emotional hazing, and it's cruel.

I'm about to waltz over to Harlowe and demand that she turn the damn slideshow off, when a final image is projected in front of us, eight feet tall and impossible not to stare at.

It's me and Levi. I know it's him instantly. I know that too-long, scraggly hair, and his lean biceps, and the white T-shirt he insisted on wearing even in freezing temperatures. That's not Ollie. It's his clone, and this is last year. And we're kissing.

I feel my chest tightening, my whole body tensing. Where did Harlowe get this? Where did she get *any* of these photos? How long has she been planning this? This is the handiwork of someone who researched and gathered information all summer long. This wasn't thrown together. It was planned.

I don't turn back to look at Ollie. I can't. I feel mortified and ashamed. For him to find out about Levi like this…

Or could he have already known? *Does* he already know? I've wondered all summer if he could tell, somehow, that something was different between us. Now I don't have to wonder anymore. He's seen the evidence that Levi and I were an *us*.

The lights come back on. When they do, it's a harsh reintroduction to the room. To the creaky machinery, and to Ollie, still handcuffed to that chair. I force myself to look at my friends—especially Ollie. I can't read the expression on his face. Is it surprise? Disappointment? Betrayal? I only catch a glimpse of my other friends' faces—stoic, but clearly emotional in spite of their inherent strength—before I charge at Harlowe, wanting to wipe the smug look off her face.

"We're done being manipulated by you," I say. "So tell us what the hell you want."

Harlowe backs up, just out of my reach. "I want what I've always wanted. For this group to be run by people who actually deserve it. Me, and my friends. Legacies of this school, like the families in those photographs. Not some *copies*," she spits. "So go ahead. Give me what's rightfully mine."

"And what is *that*?" Maude counters.

"Hand over leadership of the Nine and walk away."

"Never," Maude answers calmly. "And for the record, those images can't hurt us. Do you think we don't already know how we've been shunned by our DNA families? Do you think we ever go a day without a reminder that they'll never love us, not the same way they love *them*?" She means the originals. Tessa, Madison, and Pru.

Pru. I nearly forgot about my emergency buzz to her, Jago, and Ansel. I glance down at my plum and see all the notifications from her that I've missed. There's no time to update her now. I'll have to fill her in later.

"Just admit that you don't belong here," Harlowe murmurs. "Admit that you have no business being leader of the Nine—"

I make a move to lunge at Harlowe... Before I reach her, I hear the Similars counting down from three. I turn to see my friends clench their fingers into fists, flex their arms, and strain against the handcuffs, ripping the chain of each cuff with a pop, so that each one separates from the chair it's attached to, leaving a set of cuffs dangling from each of their arms. But they're no longer bound. Their shackles hang like useless appendages from their wrists. They're free.

I stop in my tracks, stunned. They've broken out of their handcuffs through sheer brute strength.

Even though I know about the Similars' capabilities, even though I've seen them climb those trees, balancing precariously without a fear of falling, and hold their breath underwater, and I've witnessed Levi's cut healing at warp speed... I'm still shocked. I'm not the only one. I hear Ivy take in a gasp of air. The look on her face is one of surprise and terror. Harlowe appears to be similarly rattled. And Graham is shaken, though he's obviously trying not to show it, crossing his arms over his chest and assuming a casual stance.

Maude stands up, a swing in her step as she rubs her wrists together. Theodora and Pippa do the same. Then Pippa leans over and, in one swift motion, breaks Ollie's cuffs for him. He thanks her, standing up—wobbly, but seemingly okay.

"What... How..." Ivy sputters.

"Oh, that?" Maude answers. "It's something we can do. You know, after all that practice back on our island."

"But that's not *possible*," Harlowe whispers. "Those chains were *metal*."

Now I notice Sophie and Willa, the other two junior members of the Nine, standing in the doorway. They saw it too.

"You might as well give us the keys to the cuffs." Maude looks Harlowe directly in the eye, holding her gaze steady. "It's not like you can use these again, anyway." Harlowe mumbles something unintelligible, reaches in her pocket, and thrusts a key chain at Maude, who swiftly undoes her own cuffs, then the others'.

Harlowe has lowered the knife and holds it defensively at her side, obviously thinking better of threatening us with it. Her hand shakes, though I'm sure she hopes I don't notice.

I realize it then. With that display of their strength, Maude, Theodora, and Pippa revealed how strong they really are. How strong *all* the Similars are. No one knew about their abilities—not the student body, anyway. *And now they will.* If they want to, Ivy, Harlowe, and Graham can easily take this new information and use it against the Similars. My stomach roils thinking of all the ways how. Making them seem inhuman. Stirring up panic and fear…

"You okay, Em?" asks a voice next to me. It's Ollie, rubbing his wrists, looking for the most part like himself. Thank God.

"I'm the one who should be asking *you* that question, you big dope," I answer, feeling tears pooling in my eyes. I can't believe they drugged him too, and brought him into this. *Because of me.* Ollie's not even in the Nine, and he still got hazed… I try not to let myself think about the eight-foot picture he just saw, of me and Levi. If I do, I'll lose it.

"Since we're all here…" Maude's voice interrupts my thoughts. "We might as well hold the first midnight session of the school year."

"That's my cue," Ollie whispers, giving me a quick hug.

"You're going?" I feel my heart racing. I don't want him to leave.

"I don't think I should stay. Not in the group."

"But you're okay?"

"Yeah, I mean this whole night was pretty messed up, wasn't it?"

"Understatement of the year, but yes," I whisper back to him. "You're sure you're all right? Nothing feels weird, or off, or—"

"Besides being thoroughly freaked, I'm fine," he assures me. "You?"

I nod. "I might take that knife and skewer someone with it.

And by someone, I mean Harlowe. But yeah, I'm okay." Ollie starts to leave, but I stop him. "Wait. Pru," I say quickly, remembering. "She's probably waiting up for us. Worried. Can you…"

"I'll fill her in," Ollie promises before slipping out the door. I can't help but wonder if his quick exit is a cover for how hurt he must feel right now, after seeing that photo of me and Levi tangled together like that. So clearly giving in to our feelings for each other. Feelings Ollie didn't even know about until five minutes ago. Which, it occurs to me, was Harlowe's whole agenda. She wanted to target each of us with emotional land mines. That was mine.

Maude waits for Ollie to leave, then addresses the group again. "I'll make this brief." She casts her eyes over all of us, finally settling on me. "Welcome to the Nine. This group has historically been Darkwood's apparatus for lighting a fire under students, for motivating them to be their best selves. It's our job to act as role models for the rest of the student body. This year, we'll have a singular focus. Not only inspiring the students here to challenge themselves academically—motivation that I don't think they actually need, since no one makes it here unless they're exceptionally smart and talented. This year our focus will be on tolerance. On choosing to be kind. Tonight's display was the exact opposite of that goal. I thought I'd made myself clear, but I guess not. There will be no more reverse hazing of any kind. No more humiliation or emotional torture. No more initiation rituals," she says, boring her eyes into Harlowe's. "Or—well, you saw what we're capable of. And that's only the start."

Harlowe shrinks into herself. Ivy casts her eyes downward at her shoes. And Graham, who's trying not to look fazed by any of this, is obviously doing his best to act tough—but I wonder what he's really thinking. It's the first time I've ever heard any of the Similars threaten anyone. I don't blame Maude; rather, I'm angry that she felt she had to. Still, I wish tonight had never happened. The thought of the whole school knowing what they're capable of... *What you might be capable of too...*

The meeting is brief. Maude dismisses us, but not before reminding us of the burden we carry as members of the Nine—to embrace other students, not sabotage them. With a sinking feeling in my heart, I wonder if that's a realistic goal. Especially now that Maude's given these juniors ammunition against the Similars.

"Let's go," Maude tells me, Pippa, and Theodora, linking her arm through mine. Then she stops short and turns back to Harlowe. "If I were you, I'd hide that car before Ransom gets wind of it." I don't wait to see the look on Harlowe's face before we slip out the double doors, leaving the pump house behind us.

On the walk back to Cypress, I tell my friends about my night, glossing over my jump from the car so that it sounds like a minor incident. We all agree that Harlowe, Ivy, and Graham must have had help injecting them and transporting them to the pump house. But who? I can't help but wonder if somehow Madison had a hand in this... Though Maude reminds me that her original is no longer on campus. She left this evening for the campaign trail.

I don't bring up what's really worrying me. Their safety. When they broke out of those chains tonight, they showed those juniors their preternatural strength. I feel momentary relief, though, when I think about it. Certainly *I* would never be capable of something like that, would I? I'm not that strong. Which means maybe Gravelle *has* been lying to me all this time. Maybe I'm not a Similar at all.

But when I climb into the shower at one-thirty in the morning, peeling off my jeans and T-shirt and letting the warm, soapy water rush over me, I realize that I'm not in any pain. My wrists feel completely fine. And every single one of my cuts and scrapes are a faint pink, already beginning to fade.

MASQUERADE

THE NEXT MORNING, I drag my leaden body out of bed. I get dressed, noticing as I slide on fresh jeans that I feel exhausted from lack of sleep, but otherwise fine, physically. That deeply unsettles me. After soaping myself off last night and examining every inch of my body, I have only a few faint scratches to show for my tangle with the road.

I don't want to believe it, but now I have evidence staring me in the face. My cuts healing remarkably fast. All my aches and pains gone. How is this even possible? As a middle schooler, I got plenty of cuts and scrapes, even some burns. They didn't heal like this. Still, I never had any serious accidents. Is that because of who I am and my genetic makeup? Or was I not enough of a daredevil to ever test it? Or maybe the properties grow stronger the older you get. I'll have to ask the Similars to tell me everything they know, but without letting on why.

Then there's the other thing I can barely admit to myself— that something *very* unusual and disturbing happened last night when I heard Harlowe's thoughts. I'd be tempted to write it off as just one of those weird things, except that those thoughts led me right to the pump house and my friends. Which means I couldn't have imagined the whole thing, or hallucinated it. As much as I want to deny it, it happened. I heard Harlowe's thoughts like she was talking directly to me.

With no time to sit and eat breakfast and no stomach for it anyway, I grab a bagel and rush to my first class. I can barely concentrate in calculus, and English and world history fly by as I think about the message Gravelle sent me. I still haven't found the right moment to tell my friends about it.

Ollie snags me on my way to lunch and falls in step with me on the path to the dining hall. I instantly tense, thinking of last night. Are we going to talk about that photo of me and Levi, or are we going to pretend the whole incident didn't happen?

But Ollie's on another topic altogether. "When were you going to tell me you leaped from a moving vehicle? Or is that a new hobby you picked up last year while I was gone?"

I pause midstep and look into his gray eyes—relieved to see he's not angry. He looks like he always does. Warm. Generous. Open. Not mad, thank God. "Let me guess. Maude told you about that?"

We start walking again, more slowly now. I keep pace with Ollie.

"I knew something was up, Emma. Come on. That car? The huge rip in your jeans? Think you might want to reconsider the next time you contemplate breaking every bone in your body?" I sense worry behind Ollie's eyes. Worry for me. "Pippa said you *drove* that Volvo. Was she messing with me, Emma?"

"Nope," I answer. "I had to. Harlowe had the Similars locked up, and I had to find them. And you! You would've done the same thing. And if I was okay enough to drive… That's proof that the car wasn't going very fast when I jumped. Really, it wasn't a big deal." I'm angry at myself for how easily I can lie to him. *That car was going fifty miles an hour. At least.*

"I don't believe you, but okay." He laughs. Then he stops, staring off at the horizon. I do the same, wondering if he's going to bring up the slideshow now. My stomach starts to churn with anxiety. That photo is proof that Levi and I weren't just friends.

"He's staying on Castor Island," I blurt. It's too late to take it back, though I instantly regret it. I don't want to talk about this with Ollie. I can't.

"Levi?" he asks, brow furrowed.

"Yes," I breathe. "Levi. Ollie, that photo—"

"We don't have to talk about it."

"No. I mean, yes, we do. Levi and I. Last year…"

"Was the worst year of your life," he finishes my sentence for me. He isn't smiling, not now. He looks pensive. Pained.

"Of course it was," I whisper, his words throwing me back to the misery of junior year, without him. "I almost didn't survive it. You know that."

I stop walking and grab Ollie's hand. He automatically laces his fingers through my own. It's what we do, who we are. We've done it a million times. His face is so close to mine, I can see, and hear, him breathing. "If Levi helped," Ollie says softly, "if he made you less sad…"

I nod, unable to answer. "Less sad" barely even covers it. What Levi and I were… What we might never be again… I feel sick with the unfairness of it. Losing my best friend to gain Levi. Then losing Levi to gain back that best friend.

"I'm sorry, Emma. I've been meaning to say that to you for months, I just never…" He takes in a breath. "It's all my fault. All your suffering. I wish I could go back in time and prevent it. You don't even know—"

"*What's* your fault?" I interrupt. I don't understand. Nothing that happened to us in the last year was his fault.

Ollie drops my hand, shoving his own into his jeans pockets. He looks out at Dark Lake, squinting, his forehead creased with concern, and probably something more than that. "I was the one who broke into the science building in our second year," Ollie goes on. "I was the one who insisted on digging, and asking questions, and visiting Albert Seymour. I was the one who traveled to Castor Island. If I'd never done that—" He breaks off, his voice catching.

"It is *not* your fault," I say, my own voice sounding hard and tasting metallic on my tongue. "The only person to blame for all of this is Gravelle."

"My biological father."

"Your biological father," I repeat, because I know this fact means something to Oliver, and I shouldn't dismiss it, even though he couldn't be anything less like the man who gave him half of his DNA. "The father who used all of us as pawns."

"It was a trap, and I walked right into it." Ollie shrugs.

"We all did! Me, you, your parents, Maude and Theodora and Pippa, Ansel and Jago. He messed with all of our heads. Manipulated us long before you ever set foot on that island," I point out. "Ollie?"

"Yeah?"

"I need you to know something," I say, my voice trembling. I need to get this out. I *have* to get this out. "Whatever Levi and I were last year, it doesn't, it *couldn't* ever take away our friendship. It could never change you and me. I know that's the cheesiest thing I've ever uttered, but I need you to know that. Okay?"

"Okay." He shrugs and smiles, in that Ollie way of his, and I feel instant relief. The world didn't end because Ollie saw that kiss. We're okay. I think.

"Lunch?" I ask, threading my fingers through his again. Feeling his hand in mine, my breathing starts to slow. I relax, if only for a moment. *Ollie is back*, I remind myself. *Nothing can be that bad if Ollie is back.*

On our way to the dining hall, as we walk in a comfortable silence, we pass a bunch of kiosks in front of the main house, all part of the Fall Fair advertising tryouts for plays and clubs. Oliver stops in front of a booth. A printed sign reads MASQUERADE BALL in loopy letters. Two students behind the booth are selling tickets. They wear old-school masks and long capes, like they just came from a Renaissance fair.

Ollie grabs a flyer from one of them and scans it. "This looks fun. Wanna go?" he asks, a smile playing over his lips. He turns to face me. "With me, I mean."

I stop short.

"*You* want to go with *me* to a masquerade ball." I'm practically speechless. Ollie and I never do stuff like that. Never did. We were the ones making fun of organized social events, not attending them.

"Could be a trip, right?" Ollie shrugs. "I know this wasn't usually our thing, this kind of supervised, generic fun-in-a-box…"

"Um, no, it isn't. It *wasn't*. When's the last time you saw me wear a *costume*?"

"Never. You hate Halloween."

"Exactly. Why would I want to…" I skim the flyer, reading about the event. "Take part in the first annual Darkwood costume ball, a chance to shed my old identity and start a new year, fresh?" I make a face. "Sounds excruciating."

"Two tickets, then?" one of the costumed teens behind the booth asks. "It's going to be the dance of the century."

"The century, huh," I mutter. Ollie kicks me in the shin. He wants me to play nice.

"The dance is totally student organized and run," the kid continues, oblivious to my sarcasm. "Teachers will be there, but only because it's required," she adds as a disclaimer.

"No, thanks," I say quickly, pulling Ollie away from the booth so we can have a moment in private. "Seriously, Ollie?

63

Are you sure those pharmas didn't permanently alter your pre-frontal cortex?"

"Definitely not." He laughs. "But I was on that island a really long time. Alone. All I thought about when I was there, all I dreamed about, was us. Having one normal day with you. One normal hour."

"Normal for us is staying up all night on a Kubrick bender. Watching *Full Metal Jacket* and *Dr. Strangelove* and sprinkling M&M's on our popcorn... Sneaking shots of vodka from your flask."

"We can bring the flask with us to the ball." Ollie shrugs. "The M&M's too."

I shoot him a dubious look.

"Fine, this dance is cheesy and so not our style. There. I said it."

"Thank you."

"It might not be normal for us," he goes on. "But it's normal for *high school*, isn't it? When I had all that time on Castor Island to think about my life, about all the things I would miss if I never made it back home... This was one of them."

"The masquerade ball was specifically on your list of things you would miss? Why do I find that hard to believe?"

Ollie rolls his eyes, exasperated. "Not this specific dance, Emma. But dances in general. School events. Doing the regular, mundane stuff that high schoolers do. Don't say it's dumb—"

"It's dumb."

"Fine." He throws up his hands. "It's dumb. I want us to do *all* the cheesy, dumb stuff. Just in case."

Just in case. Those words rip through me like a freight truck.

"You're back," I say to him fiercely. "And I'm not going anywhere. Ever. And neither are you. But since you insist on tugging at my heartstrings and making me feel like the worst best friend on the planet for not humoring your ridiculous bucket-list item—"

"Sorry."

"I will go with you to this cheesy, dumb masquerade ball. On one condition."

"Which is?" Ollie asks, his eyes dancing.

"No costume. I would rather die."

"I will agree to those terms," Ollie says, holding out his hand. I shake it firmly.

"Fine, then, Mr. Ward. We have a deal."

That evening at dinner, I slide into a spot at the table between Ollie and Pru. With everything that's happened these last few days, I feel like a rubber band that could snap at any moment.

"Look, Jake's made some new friends," Jago points out, interrupting my thoughts. We all turn to where he's looking. Indeed, Jake has found a new clique to sit with since Madison has left campus, and presumably, Archer has too. I'm annoyed, but not surprised, to see that the group includes Harlowe, Ivy, and Graham. They're talking conspiratorially among themselves.

After scarfing down my burrito, I excuse myself, complaining of a headache. It's not far from the truth. My head might not be hurting, but it's definitely spinning.

"Walk you back to Cypress?" Ollie asks, standing up as soon as I start to bolt from the table. "We could skip homework." He grins wickedly. "Load up on sugar, watch every campy horror flick ever made?"

"I would love to scare myself silly right now," I answer, bussing my tray. "But I'm in desperate need of a good night's sleep after my daring escape from Harlowe's car. Plus, you really can't skip your homework. You're still catching up from last year! Rain check?"

Ollie mutters something about me being as annoying as his mom, and I take the opportunity to rush out of there. I feel so guilty about avoiding him. But what can I do? It's true, I *do* need to sleep. But I also need time alone with my thoughts. Time to process everything that's happened since school started. Time to figure out how to be normal around Ollie. Because I worry we may never really be normal together again.

◆—◦—◆

The next two weeks pass by in a blur. I still can't get Harlowe's voice out of my head and feel a nauseating flip in my stomach every time I think about what happened—how I *read her thoughts*—but I can't dwell on what that means right now. Not a minute goes by when I'm not thinking about Levi, but I have classwork to dive into, and prepping for the Nine with Maude. We've all been inundated with information about college applications, which are the furthest thing from my mind, though I make a mental note to start narrowing down my list. I know what a privilege college is. I won't squander it—I'd rather take time off than waste the opportunity. I don't know if I'm in the right headspace for it. But I'll try. I have to; my father would kill me if I didn't.

"Maude," I tell her one afternoon while we're finishing our essays on *Jane Eyre* in the library. "Levi…"

"Levi what?" She puts down her tablet, looking concerned.

"I got a phone call. From Gravelle," I say, suddenly feeling like I desperately need to share this with *someone*. It can't be Ollie. He won't understand.

"When?" she asks sharply.

"The day we came back to school," I admit.

"And you're only telling me this *now*?"

"Gravelle said Levi doesn't want to come back here. That Darkwood was never a good fit for him." I don't let on how loaded this is for me, how fraught with emotion. Surely Levi hasn't really forgotten me. Surely he doesn't think that *we* weren't a good fit. I know it doesn't make logical sense; what we had last year was real, and he has to feel that too—right? But my heart isn't so convinced.

"Sorry, but I don't believe that for a second," Maude says matter-of-factly.

I feel myself exhaling. "Me either. I mean, I don't *want* to believe it, but…"

"Gravelle's obviously keeping him there. Maybe indefinitely," Maude adds. "I just hope he'll let him out in time for Oxford."

"Oxford?" I repeat. "As in, England? As in, all the way across the water? I mean, the pond?"

"Yes, I believe that's where Great Britain is, last time I

checked." Maude sighs. "We think we could fit in there. Or at least, not stand out atrociously everywhere we go."

"Your accents."

She nods. "At least our voices won't sound out of place. It's a small thing, but it would help. Plus, England hasn't been so focused on us, not the way they have in America."

Maude's referring to the daily tabloids written about her and her friends, the news shows, and the feeds that constantly speculate about the Similars' interests, failings, and love lives. Most of it's made up, completely fabricated by the media, and I can't blame them for wanting to distance themselves from it. But Oxford? It's so *far*.

"Cloning is legal there," she adds. "They actually support clones and welcome them across their border. Another reason to leave."

But I'm not focused on that. All I can think about is how far away Levi's going to be…from me. Any shred of hope I've been holding on to that we'll be together after senior year, now that's gone too. "So Levi will apply from Castor Island. Meet you there. In England." A lump forms in the back of my throat.

"If Gravelle will let him." Maude sighs. "Yes. That's the plan. He'll be eighteen by then. If he can get off the island, he won't ever have to go back. None of us will. Of course, that's what worries me. Will Gravelle ever let him go, knowing that he may never see him again if he does?"

The thought guts me. What if Gravelle *won't* ever let Levi leave? It's too awful to consider.

Maude goes back to her studying. I know I'm not fooling her, acting like I'm okay with this. Still, she doesn't press me on it. I make a mental note to add the University of Oxford to my list of potential colleges. The thought of it makes me feel closer to Levi, even though I know that's silly. He might not even be going. And though I'd never follow a boy to college... even Levi...Oxford's one of the top universities in the world. If I could get in... It could never be a bad choice. *Especially if you're a Similar, looking for anonymity...* I shake off the thought. I'm not ready to think about that. About how my cuts healed so quickly. About hearing Harlowe's thoughts. Not now. Maybe not ever.

In the days leading up to the masquerade ball, it's the talk of the school: who's going with whom, who's wearing which costumes, and who's planning on spiking the punch with "happy pharmas." I'm surprised when, the evening before the dance, the Similars announce they plan on going too. Maude with Jago, and the others as a group. Pru has majorly mixed feelings about it, reminding me why we're friends in the first place, but she relents to go after I beg her to come with me and Ollie, in solidarity. The more of us who are there ironically, to laugh at the whole thing, the better.

The Friday morning of the dance, as excitement for the evening builds, our teachers have a hard time getting anyone to concentrate in class. I pass Ollie a note during chemistry that says, "It's not too late to change your mind." He shoots me a grin and shakes his head. *Damn.* I'm not off the hook.

Still, I'm sticking to my word and refusing to wear a costume, even as Ollie relentlessly teases me about how I'll be the only one to ever attend a "ball" in jeans and a T-shirt. He wanted normal, though, didn't he? That *is* normal, for me.

At dinner that night, the masquerade planning committee rushes us through the food line. They complain about the unreasonably tight schedule, moaning that an hour isn't enough time to transform the hall from drab to fab. I have to hold back a laugh as one of the girls I recognize from the Fall Fair lashes out at a first year for moving too slowly. He's so flustered and intimidated by her, he spills his pasta all over the floor, which causes her to flip out, becoming totally incensed. I remind Ollie this is why I hate balls, and school functions, in general. They make everyone forget how to behave.

Back in our room, Pru models two different costume choices—a sequined jumpsuit and a pleather unitard.

"I walked to town yesterday with Pippa to that thrift store, Common Threads," she explains, striking an awkward pose that makes me laugh. These outfits are the antithesis of Pru, who lives, breathes, and sleeps in athletic clothes. "Which one says, 'I'm wearing this costume against my will?'"

I vote for the jumpsuit but, admittedly, I'm not really paying attention.

There's a knock at the door, and I answer it. It's Ollie, dressed up in a cape and a bow tie, and he holds one of those masks in his hands that's on a stick and looks vintage, but is probably a cheap reproduction. He smiles from behind it, charmingly, and I'm so happy to see *him* so happy that I almost forget about how annoying this dance is going to be.

"Oh, look." I smirk as I survey his costume. "Someone time traveled here from the year Darkwood was founded."

"At least I dressed up."

"We had a deal," I remind him.

"One you clearly have no intention of breaking," he answers, looking me up and down. "*You* look lovely tonight, Pru." Then, to me: "No offense."

"Every offense taken. Let's go." I'm ready to fulfill this best-friend requirement so I can go back to being the nonconforming, masquerade-ball hater I was before, and still am.

Ollie laughs, holding out both of his arms. "Ladies? May I escort you to the ball, perchance?"

Pru snickers. I scowl.

"If thou must," I relent. Ollie grins.

She has no idea how cute she is. Even in those jeans she insists on wearing all the time... Does she have to dress in a T-shirt and sneakers every day like it's her job?

I stop in my tracks. *What* did Ollie say?

I turn and look at him. "You don't like my jeans?"

Ollie studies me, confused. "No, I—What are you talking about? I didn't say anything."

He didn't? But I heard—

That's when it hits me. That *thing* that happened with Harlowe, when I was driving the car. It's happening again. Now. With Ollie.

She's acting really *weird. Great. Tonight everything has to be perfect, or else I'll totally chicken out.*

We're walking down the hall, but I barely register my feet

moving. I feel oddly clearheaded. And Ollie's voice, it's like it's whispering right in my ear. The same way I heard Harlowe's voice—distant-sounding, and yet, strangely close.

You have to do it. Like you planned. Tonight, at the dance. Tell her you've been in love with her for ages. You promised yourself when you were on that island that you would. Who cares if she kissed Levi? He isn't here. I don't want him to be stuck there, that's not it. But I've known Emma longer and I've loved her forever. I just never realized it until last year, and then I almost missed my chance—

I press my hands to my ears, trying to drown out Ollie's inner monologue. As though that would ever work. Whatever's happening to me, I can't stop it. Unless I get the hell out of here.

"Emma?" Pru looks at me, her face etched with worry. I probably look like I'm losing it, standing here with my hands on either side of my head.

I have to go. There's no way I can stand here and listen to this, to Ollie thinking all about his *feelings* for me, without him knowing I'm reading his every thought.

I start to go, not bothering to give an excuse. The only thing I manage to say before I dash out of there is that I'll see them both later at the ball.

All I can think as I race out the door of Cypress into the crisp Darkwood night is that Ollie's in love with me. And he plans to tell me, tonight.

THE ORIGINALS

I TEAR OUT of there so fast, I don't even hear what Ollie and Pru yell back to me.

I think I'm going to be sick.

I run down a well-lit path, past kids fully embracing the cosplay spirit of the evening. Some are dressed in superhero costumes, some like their favorite book and TV characters. Every single person has a mask. When I hurry past the Similars, I give them a half-hearted wave, promising to see them tonight. I only vaguely register that they're all dressed in some kind of thematic costume, but I don't get the reference.

I'm gunning it out of there, feeling an adrenaline rush—or is it fear overtaking me? The simple act of hearing Ollie's thoughts like that made me feel like I was on a high. Like the world was crisp and clearer than it ever had been before. And yet…it was terrifying.

What the hell *was* that? Gravelle playing a game with me? But how? Harlowe's words were spot-on. My friends *were* at the pump house, like she said. And Ollie's voice sounded so authentic, like it was really him talking… But what he said, about being in love with me, about telling me, tonight…

It's not the first time I've heard this from him. It's why we stopped talking in our second year, why he never confided in me about wanting to visit Seymour and find out about his father. Because he'd told me how he felt about me. And I'd shut him down. And for a couple of weeks before he traveled to Boston to see his uncle, we were barely speaking to each other.

I haven't thought about that in ages. Haven't let myself. Because I feel the same way now as I did then. Ollie *can't* be in love with me, because it would ruin everything. Even if he thinks he is… We're "us." Emma and Oliver. Best friends, not more. And now, with Levi in the picture… It was probably seeing that photo that got Ollie thinking that way again. After all, he never said anything all summer, never acted like anything but a friend. I guess a part of me hoped he'd realized we would never be like that. That he'd come to his senses. He can't *love me* love me. That would never work. And I don't feel that way about him. How could I possibly, after what Levi and I shared last year?

But it doesn't really matter what his reasons are, does it? Or if he's lying to himself. Or if I'm the one in denial. Either way—if he tells me tonight about these feelings, what am I going to do?

I'm so lost in my thoughts, I only now realize that I've ventured far past the main house and the chapel, all the way to the ornate gate with the Darkwood crest on it that signals the start of campus. I unlock the gate and let the embellished metal door swing closed behind me with a clang. Out of breath, I pause under a knot of trees, my hands on my thighs, breathing in the crisp Vermont air. When I stand up, ready to continue outrunning the tangled web of my thoughts, someone blocks me on the path. It's Tessa Leroy. Next to her is Ansel's original: the famous, and famously handsome, Archer de Leon.

I stare at Tessa like I'm seeing a ghost. This is definitely not Theodora. I saw Theodora ten minutes ago, back with the other Similars in their costumes. This girl is wearing something trendy, something I doubt Theodora would ever put on. She's paired a sweater that looks like it's made of gold chain mail with distressed, wide-legged denim jeans. On her feet are the chunkiest, and tallest, woven platform sandals I've ever seen. Her face glows from some kind of shimmery makeup, and her hair looks like it's been highlighted with streaks of copper.

"Hi," she says emotionlessly, staring right at me.

"Hi?" I answer back. No one's seen Tessa since she checked into that facility. "What's up, Archer?" I say, feeling annoyed they're in my way, though I'm admittedly a teeny bit curious as to what they're doing here. Why is Archer back on campus again so soon?

"Hey," Archer says, flashing a huge smile that reveals his unnaturally white teeth.

I shift my weight, antsy. Then I make a move to walk around

them, but they both edge that same way, subtly blocking me. I decide to address Archer, because it's easier; I have no desire to talk to Tessa, and no clue what to say to her. *Are you less prone to violent attacks now?* doesn't seem appropriate.

"What are you doing back at Darkwood, Archer? Didn't I hear you were filming an outrageously popular show somewhere?"

"Thailand. Shooting wrapped. I'm starting NYU next week." Archer shrugs. "You know. At their drama program."

"So you decided to come here? Why come back to high school when you don't absolutely have to? Wouldn't you rather be at a movie premiere or something?"

"Totally, but I'm visiting my buddy Ansel. He said there's some kind of…party this weekend?" Archer pries, grinning at me rakishly. I'm not amused.

I sigh. "The masquerade ball. Let me guess. You want to crash it?"

"It's not crashing if you used to *go* here," Tessa says in that characteristic deadpan voice of hers.

"'Used to' being the operative words," I snap back. "How'd you get out of the treatment center, anyway? I thought the judge said you had to go for at least six months."

"I do, but I checked out for the weekend," Tessa says airily. "It's completely allowed."

"The dance starts in ten minutes in the dining hall," I tell them, eager to end this interaction as quickly as possible. "You'll need costumes. Masks or capes." I'm hoping this is enough information to get them to leave me alone.

"Awesome," says Archer, smiling at me again.

"What'd I miss?" asks Jake Choate, bounding up behind them. He's wearing a shimmery silver shirt and a slick blazer. "I was peeing in the bushes back there," he says to me, like I care *one iota*. "When you gotta go, you gotta go."

I don't even respond. But I do notice the time on my plum. It's almost eight o'clock. I sigh, turning back up the path, and use my Darkwood key to unlock the gate again. I hold the door open for Tessa, Jake, and Archer, who don't bother to thank me.

I leave them behind, racing back to the dance. I have no idea what I'm going to do when I see Ollie there. *Act like you never heard his thoughts, of course.* If that thing happens again… I don't know how I'll react or what I'll say. But for the sake of my best friend on the planet, I'm going to have to risk it.

◇━┝━◇

The dance is already in full swing by the time I arrive. The dining hall has been transformed: twinkling lights are strung across the ceiling in an intricate web, and there are lush plants and flowers everywhere. With all the costumes and masks, some gold and glittering, others dark velvet, the place gives off an eerie, unfamiliar vibe. I can't see anyone's eyes. As I wind through the crowd, looking for Ollie and Pru, I lift my hood up over my head, suddenly feeling the urge to be anonymous, like everyone else.

A hand lands on my shoulder, and I bristle, startled. When I spin around, it's Ollie, his gray eyes sparkling through the eyeholes of his mask, which he's holding up to his face. I feel instantly warmer from his touch, but chilly at the same time.

"Found you," he says. I relax at the sound of his voice, so familiar to me, like my favorite, worn-in jeans. The ones he was teasing me about earlier—only I wasn't supposed to hear. "What happened before?" He lowers his mask so I can see his face. "You ran out of there like you'd seen a ghost."

I wait for it to happen again. For me to hear his thoughts.

But there's nothing. Just me, and Ollie, and the crowd around us. I breathe out a sigh of relief.

"Bathroom emergency." I shrug. "Do you really want to know?"

"Definitely not."

I laugh, snagging his mask from his hand and holding it up to my own face, covering it. "I'll take that, thank you very much."

"Get your own disguise!" Ollie chuckles.

I have to keep us busy, I realize. So busy he won't have a chance to get me alone and say those things to me out loud. Because my answer to him will always be that we're best friends, nothing more. And I don't want to hurt Ollie. It makes me nauseous even thinking about it.

"Where's Pru?" I blurt. "Did you walk over with her?"

"She went to find Pippa," Ollie shouts. The music has picked up, and we have to talk loudly to hear each other. Good.

"Let's look for her," I say, grabbing Ollie's hand and guiding him through the crowd. The costumes are so intricate and colorful, the space so full, it's almost dizzying. We move past a student in an elaborate Wonder Woman costume; two girls and a boy dressed as the Schuyler sisters from *Hamilton*; a couple of fairies with smoky eyes and dazzling headdresses; multiple Severus

Snapes, Hermiones, and Harrys; and more capes, cloaks, and masks than I can count.

"Pru!" I shout, spotting her across the way and making a bee-line toward her. I tap her on the shoulder, only realizing in that moment that this isn't Pru at all—it's Pippa. She's dressed in the cloak and hood I saw her in earlier. Next to her are Theodora and Maude, and I spot Ansel and Jago nearby, similarly garbed. "Pippa," I correct myself. "Sorry, I never do that."

Pippa smiles, not offended. "Pru's here somewhere…"

I scan the room for her, but it's so hard to pick anyone out of the dense crowd. My eyes land on a knot of kids I'd much rather not run into: Harlowe, with Ivy and Graham at her side. I don't even register their costumes. I'm too busy feeling my blood starting to boil at the sight of them.

"Emma," Ollie warns, sensing that I'm about to walk up to them. "Ignore them. Let's go to the lake. Get some air."

But I can't go to the lake with Ollie, because I can't be alone with him.

Before I can respond, a thumping beat blasts through the speakers, and a makeshift dance floor emerges in the center of the room, with kids letting loose and pulling out their best moves. Ollie starts leading me by the hand, in the direction of the dance floor.

"When's the last time you saw me dance on *purpose*?" I shout. Ollie laughs, and I feel my heartbeat increasing as I wonder what he's thinking. Maybe the dance floor's the safest place to be. The Similars join us, and Pru finds us too. Soon everyone's get-ting lost in rhythm, feeling the infectious beat, surrounded by

Darkwood kids on all sides, everyone masked and sweaty and embellished. Enchanted, almost, or otherworldly. But I'm still standing solidly on the ground, and all I can think about is Levi. Whether he's safe. Whether he's thinking about me, at all. How much I ache for him to be here. How unfair it is that he never gets to enjoy these simple moments, like a regular high school student. Ollie does a little spin, flashing me his biggest smile, and that's when I hear it.

"That's Oliver Ward," a girl near me in a bedazzled costume notes to her girlfriends.

"Suuuper cute. Right?" says another girl.

A guy next to her raises an eyebrow. "We talked about this, Summer. He's mine."

"We so did *not*—"

I feel my cheeks flushing and distance myself from those kids. It's weird hearing other students talk about Ollie like that.

So when he grabs my hand, pulling me toward him so that our bodies are, all of a sudden, extremely close, my chest pressed against his, the velvet of his cape brushing up against my thin T-shirt, I feel my heartbeat start to work double time.

No, no, no. Not now. Please don't say it. I don't want to hurt you.

His mask gone now, Ollie stares down at me with those gray, familiar eyes of his. "Em," he breathes, leaning down to whisper in my ear. "There's something I gotta tell you."

"Is this thing on?" says a voice over the microphone. The music cuts out, and the room is plunged into silence. Every single person on the dance floor, including Ollie and me, turns to look at the person behind the mic.

"Sorry, everyone. Didn't mean to interrupt the par-tay," the voice goes on, laughing. Squinting through the darkened crowd, I can see who's talking—it's Archer, dressed in a sweeping cape, with his semi-long hair moussed back attractively. I get why this guy's become an overnight star. He's conventionally gorgeous, with his dark complexion, deep brown eyes, and hundred-watt smile. Plus, everyone loves his chill attitude and the way he seems to perpetually be in on some private joke. Still, I'd choose the quiet, thoughtful Ansel in a toss-up, any day. I'm happy Archer's welcomed Ansel into his family, but that's about as far as my love for Archer goes. Right now, though? I'm relieved Archer's taken the mic, giving me an out. I take a teeny step away from Ollie.

"Turn the music back on!" someone yells. There are laughs and snickers from the crowd.

"Don't you know who that is?" a girl's voice shouts. "Archer de Leon. The star of *Space Wars*! Let him talk!" There are rumblings and more talking among the crowd. It seems some kids didn't realize they were in the presence of Hollywood royalty.

Archer quiets everyone down. "This'll only take a second. Okay, Headmaster? You mind if I make a little toast?" Archer's eyes seek out Headmaster Ransom's in the crowd. I follow them till I see Ransom myself. He gestures for Archer to go ahead. That's the thing about Archer. Even as an alum who doesn't go to this school anymore, he commands everyone's attention. Archer raises the cup he holds in his hand. "To all the kids at Darkwood I used to love," he laughs, tripping a little over his feet. "Especially Ansel Gravelle. My boy." Now he looks for his Similar in the crowd, and when he finds him, his face spreads into a giant grin. It's obvious now: Archer's *drunk*. Why am I not surprised? "Come on up here, Ansel, buddy!"

Ansel, who's standing with Maude and Pippa, not far from me and Ollie, gives a half-hearted wave. "That's okay! I'm good here," he calls out.

"Come on! Dude! You're like my brother," Archer goes on, getting louder with every sentence. "And bros stick together!"

"What *happened* to Archer while I was gone last year?" Ollie whispers in my ear. I shrug, my eyes still glued to the makeshift stage.

"I don't know. Fame happened? Apparently *Space Wars* was streamed more times than any other show this summer, so…" I shrug.

The crowd's starting to egg Archer on, calling out for Ansel to join his original up at the mic. Flustered, Ansel relents, making his way through the clusters of Darkwood students to the front. Ansel hops up next to his DNA twin, and Archer throws his arm around his Similar's shoulders. The crowd starts cheering wildly.

"Lemme tell you about something that happened to me on the set of my show last week," Archer says. He's starting to slur his words. If it wasn't obvious to everyone before, it is now. Archer's wasted. And maybe even high. Who knows? "It's been hard to get used to how famous I am," Archer continues, "so when this group of teenagers practically mowed me down trying to take a selfie with me, the producers actually had to call security on 'em!"

There's a reaction from the student body. Most cheer and

holler, though a few others start talking among themselves. They're restless and wish he'd wrap up his speech. Plus, I can tell that Ansel wishes he were anywhere but up on that stage.

"I knew Archie was kind of conceited," a girl next to me says to her friend. "He posts like four selfies a day. But wow. Fame's really gone to his head."

"Anyone want to take a selfie with me right now?" Archer asks the crowd, and the girl next to me shoots her friend a look that says *See what I mean?* "You could get right in between me and Ansel. De Leon sandwich!" At that point, Ansel extricates himself from Archer's grasp and slips down off the stage, walking back toward us. He looks mortified, but relieved to have escaped.

"That's enough," barks Headmaster Ransom, who has stepped up to take the mic out of Archer's hands. "Mr. de Leon, I'm going to have to ask you to leave."

"Hey, no problem, sir. If anyone wants a photo op with me, I'll be right outside. No biggie if you want to sell it to the media! And I'm not opposed to taking my shirt off. Or my pants—" The sound of Archer's voice cuts out. Someone's pulled the plug on the AV system. Headmaster Ransom once again tells Archer to get down off the stage, but Archer's not listening. He's still trying to entertain the crowd. I crane my neck to get a better look at what's happening, and I see Tessa and Jake step up and practically drag Archer off the stage. From the looks of things, they're promising Ransom they'll handle this. Once Ransom seems convinced Archer is leaving the dance and isn't coming back, he starts toward the exit.

"Yikes," Ollie says, gently taking me by the arm and spinning me around to face him. "That was quite the show Archer put on. Wanna take a walk?"

In that moment, I panic.

"I can't, I—" I spot Headmaster Ransom making his way to the back of the room, to the dining hall entrance. My eyes follow him to the door.

—no reason to keep studying the Similars. I have their blood plasma, which is all I need now—

It's happening again. I'm hearing things. *Thoughts.* Headmaster Ransom's voice is whispering softly in my ear. Like Harlowe's and Ollie's.

—going to inject it in my office—

I'm seeing right into Ransom's mind.

"I have to go," I blurt. "It's Ransom. He's going to inject himself with the Similars' plasma."

"How do you know that?" Oliver asks, perplexed.

"I can't explain it. I just do."

"Can't you worry about this tomorrow? We haven't dissected all the ludicrous aspects of this dance yet." Ollie's eyebrows knit with tension. "I know it's important to you, this Ransom thing. I don't really get why, but—"

"It's important to me because they're my friends," I say, frustrated that he can't see why this matters so much. He was barely here last year. He isn't friends with Maude and the others the way I am. He never saw them in those chairs, hooked up to IVs. What Ollie witnessed at Harlowe's reverse hazing was only the tip of the iceberg. My friends have been through so much. "I'll explain it all tomorrow. One more dance before I go?" It's the last thing I want to do right now, but I don't want to hurt Ollie's feelings. So I stay for one more song. When it ends, I stretch up on tiptoe to give Ollie a peck on the cheek. To his credit, Ollie doesn't say anything or show his disappointment. Still, I sense it there, and I hate myself for leaving now. For not letting him tell me about his feelings. For dodging him at every turn. "Fill me in on everything at breakfast tomorrow. Make a spreadsheet!" I call out as I start to leave. "We can ridicule the dance by category. Decorations. Costumes. Awkward impromptu speeches by teen heartthrobs!"

I go, escaping the same way Ransom left, through the wide double doors.

I run all the way across the darkened campus to his office, leaving behind the merriment of the dining hall, the twinkling lights, the costumes, the festivities. Leaving Ollie behind too, his unsaid words still lingering in the air between us.

I'm not even out of breath when I arrive at Ransom's office. I've got that adrenaline-rush feeling again, like I did after I heard Harlowe's and Ollie's thoughts. I'm starting to think there's some connection. But I don't dwell on that now. I reach for the knob of the unlocked door and push it open. Ransom is behind his desk, sitting in his imposing leather chair, when I slip inside.

PLASMA

"YOU CAN'T DO this!" My voice sounds breathless, and I'm shaking. I was a lot more confident about this on my jog over here. Now I feel like someone who's about to accuse the head of her boarding school of something unthinkable. And criminal.

Ransom looks up from his desk, which is littered with vials and tubing. Next to him is an IV pole with a bag hanging from it. My stomach turns at the sight of it. What kind of illicit medical procedure is going on here?

"Emmaline? May I help you?" He doesn't make any moves to hide the medical equipment or try to mask what he's doing. For some reason, that makes me feel even sicker.

I hate this man and his hypocrisy. I stare at him, bracing

myself to hear his thoughts again. But nothing comes. I'm starting to think that this thing—this disturbing ability—is entirely out of my control.

"I know what you're about to do," I say before I lose my nerve. I feel my cheeks flushing, and I don't take my hand off the doorknob. Gripping it is the only thing keeping me from running straight out of here. "I bet Principal Fleischer told you last year, didn't she? About how I discovered the Similars in the abandoned science building? Hooked up to all those machines? I know the Huxleys have been funding your research, if you can even call it that. Personally, I'd call it exploitation."

"Emmaline," Ransom warns. "It would really be in your best interests to return to the masquerade ball. I don't remember inviting you into my office. Do you?"

"That's it, isn't it?" I indicate the IV pole and bag. "The product of your 'research'?"

"That is the cocktail, yes," Headmaster Ransom says, almost reverently.

"I'll expose you," I say, my cheeks burning. "I'll tell the whole world that you only invited the Similars to Darkwood so you could exploit them. To use their blood and cells for your own gain, because you're ill."

Ransom picks up an IV cannula, tying a blue band tight around his arm so his vein will be properly positioned. "You're too late. This infusion contains the platelets and plasma that will provide me with the longevity I'm seeking." He pricks his arm with the cannula and inserts the IV. I watch, intrigued but disgusted. I want to take in every detail, in case this information may be useful later on. "Once it's in my system, you can't do anything about it, Emmaline."

"Yes, I can. I'll go to the authorities. The FBI. I'll tell them that you stole that cocktail, that you have no right to it! You'll be prosecuted!"

"How?" The IV starts to flow through the tubing and straight into his veins. "Your friends gave their permission to be a part of this scientific study. In writing."

"But they're minors!" I point out. "Their guardian didn't agree to it, did he?"

"Certainly he did," Ransom responds. The plasma continues to flow through the tube. Headmaster Ransom leans back in his leather chair, letting his fingers relax and breathing deeply. "We're old friends, John Underwood and I. He was a student here when I first began my teaching career."

"I know." I've seen Gravelle's—I mean, Underwood's—memories. Ransom was in charge of the disciplinary hearing that ended in Underwood's expulsion, after the prank in the science lab that went horribly wrong. Underwood was the only student asked to leave Darkwood, even though some of his friends were equally guilty. They didn't stand up for him—which is why he's been seeking revenge on their families ever since.

"I believe we're done here. Or would you prefer a detention, Emmaline? Because you're turning misbehavior at the outset of the school year into quite a pattern."

Wait, *I'm* the one doing something wrong? When he was the one who forced my friends to sit in those chairs and be subjected to weekly "treatments" at the hands of Principal Fleischer?

"Did you hear me, Emmaline?" Ransom makes a fist with his hand, then flexes his fingers, letting the contents of the IV continue to flow into his body. "You just confessed to me that you were in the abandoned science building last year without faculty clearance. I'd be happy to add on an extra week of duty for that infraction, which went unpunished. But I can let that slide—if you leave. Now."

I don't want to go and let Ransom win. But what can I do? If the Similars really did give their written consent, and Gravelle did too, would a contract like that hold up in court? Even if it wouldn't, the Similars would never want to sue Ransom. Without him and his "hospitality," they might be deported and sent back to Castor Island. The thought of that, of them leaving Darkwood and taking with them my one solid tie to Levi, makes my stomach churn.

There's not a thing I can do or say right now. Without another word, I go, simply turning and walking down the hallway, away from Ransom's office, suddenly missing Levi so acutely that tears begin to stream down my face.

◇━┤ ┆ ┝━◇

We're sitting on the bed in our hotel room in Bar Harbor, the one we shared before the final leg of our journey to Castor Island. Levi's on one side, leaning back on the pillows, his hand behind his head. I'm sitting cross-legged mere inches from him, but it feels like miles. With every breath I take, I sense Levi watching me. In my mind, all I can think is I want the gap between us to disappear. We're only on opposite sides of the bed, but I never want to be this far from him again. Ever.

"Levi?" I say, my voice breathless and unsure.

"Yes?" he answers. I cling to his voice like a lifeline.

"Did you mean what you told Gravelle? That coming to Darkwood was…a mistake? That it—that *I*—wasn't good for you?"

Levi looks at me, his brow furrowed. With his fingers, he smooths out the thigh of his dark-washed jeans. I see the lean muscles of his arms tensing, and I'm reminded of how much I love the feeling of those arms wrapped around me…

In two seconds flat, he's bridged the distance between us on the bed.

"Levi, I—"

Whatever I was going to say doesn't matter, because Levi's mouth is on my mouth, and we are kissing, and finally, *finally*, I have him back.

I wake with a start, sweating, grasping for the image of him and me, together, in each other's arms. I know before I even open my eyes that it's gone, because it was only a dream. Levi isn't here. All I want to do is buzz him. Talk to him. Write to him. But Gravelle's threat lingers in my mind. I can't put Levi in danger. *Maybe you already have.*

I trudge to a late Saturday morning breakfast. On my way to the dining hall, I pass Archer, who's looking surprisingly fresh this morning after his drunken interlude. He's standing with several first-year kids, posing for pictures with a plum on a selfie stick. They're fawning all over him.

When I make it to the cafeteria, Ollie's there, sitting with

Pru and the Similars. He surprises me with a tray of my favorite foods: a bagel, dry toast, one egg sunny-side up, and black coffee. The selection makes me smile. He knows me so well.

"No sugar, no milk. I don't know how you drink it without gagging, but there you go." Ollie smirks.

I play punch him, relieved the spell of last night seems to be broken. He's acting like normal Ollie.

"What'd I miss last night?" I ask my friends in between bites of toast.

"After Archer's over-the-top speech?" Pru answers. "Everyone danced. Masks came off. The usual. But tell us about Ransom! What happened?"

"Ransom?" Maude asks sharply. "What about him?"

"Emma followed him out of the dance," Ollie explains. "Said he was going to inject himself…"

"With the plasma from his 'experiment,'" I explain. "*Your* plasma. Let's just say, if I go missing, it's because I've been sentenced to duty for the rest of my life. Ransom didn't even deny that he's been experimenting on you. He's already injected himself with the 'cocktail.' That's what he called it. He said you have no rights because you signed a contract…"

"We did," Jago answers. "He's not wrong."

"But would it even hold up, in court?" I press.

"We've talked about this, Emma," Maude jumps in. "It's not in our best interests to fight him on this."

"Prudence?" says a voice, and we all look up to see Tessa standing there by our table, balancing a tray in one hand and a supple leather bag in the other. She wears another funky outfit—a purple bomber jacket with shredded jeans and patent leather booties. "Pru?" she repeats. "Can I sit here?"

"Um. Sure?" Pru answers, completely blindsided. Tessa wants to sit next to her? After conking her over the head last year with a rowing oar in the boathouse and leaving her for dead? What could she possibly have to *say* to Pru, anyway? Tessa's lucky that judge took pity on her and sent her to a treatment facility, not prison. How can she act like everything's normal?

Tessa sets down her tray, places her bag on an empty chair, and gingerly takes the spot next to Pru. I find myself tensing, feeling protective of Pru and everything she's gone through this last year.

"I'm not that great at this," Tessa says, looking for once like she actually cares about something other than her nail polish color. "So please hear me out. I've been practicing for weeks. I'm sorry for what I did to you last year. It wasn't fair. I screwed up badly, and I really, really hope we can be friends going forward. Okay?" Tessa pauses. What is she expecting, applause? Ollie and I share a look. Pru bristles.

"Friends. You want us to be friends," Pru repeats.

"Yes. I've been participating in these workshops at Creekside—that's my treatment facility—and all the experts say the first step toward gaining self-acceptance is to apologize to all the people you've wronged." She suddenly looks unsure of herself. She fiddles with the strap of her bag.

"I seriously can't believe you're making this about *you*," I snap.

I don't have a chance to say more, because there's a

commotion on the other side of the dining hall. We all look over to see what's going on.

"No way." Ollie laughs, looking surprised and maybe a little impressed. "Seriously?"

"What? What's going on?" I ask him. "I can't see." I stand up to get a better look.

"Is that a *goat*?" Pru says, incredulous.

It does appear to be a goat—in the Darkwood dining hall. Running between the tables and benches, streaking here and there, the animal seems to be thoroughly enjoying itself. Most of the student body is cheering, laughing, and pointing. Some kids are standing up on benches and chairs. I'd venture a guess that this is the first time in Darkwood history that livestock has been let into the cafeteria. But who did this? And why?

Then I notice Jake, wearing that same slick blazer he had on yesterday, surrounded by several other seniors. They're trying to corral the goat, rather unsuccessfully. "Here, boy!" Jake calls out. "This way! No—you can't eat eggs Benedict! Bad goat! Bad!"

Jake's cracking up, obviously having the time of his life, and he's not the least bit concerned that whoever is responsible has broken about fifty school rules by inviting this farm animal here.

"Who did this?" a voice barks. We turn to watch Headmaster Ransom stride into the dining hall, looking even angrier than he did when Archer made that ridiculous speech last night.

"It was me, sir," Jake pipes up, holding back a grin.

Ransom stares Jake down. "And why, may I ask, did you bring this ruminant animal onto campus?"

Pru and Ollie are barely stifling their laughter. Maude,

Theodora, and Ansel exchange looks. I glance over at Tessa, who's watching all this unfold without saying a word. She seems mesmerized by the sight of the frisky goat. A small smile creeps over her lips, and I swear she looks almost pleased and proud of Jake. But I can't imagine why Jake would do this. It's funny, and I'm sure he's amused to have pulled off such a great prank, one that'll likely go down in the Darkwood annals. But is it really worth all the trouble he's going to get into?

I notice that Archer has walked in, just in time to see his buddy facing off with Ransom. Archer skips to his friend's side, clapping his hands a couple of times to get the goat's attention. The goat's trying to eat the hem of a girl's skirt, and she's attempting to shoo him off.

"It wasn't only Jake's idea," Archer tells Ransom. "We both thought it would be hilarious to invite a goat to breakfast. Goats love pancakes, don't they?"

"Right now he's loving pima cotton!" The girl in the skirt scowls at him. Jake and Archer manage to pull the goat away from her. Annoyed, she flops back into her seat.

Ransom flexes his hands into fists. "Archer, you are no longer a student at this school. Lucky for you, or you'd be in quite the pickle, following up last night's display with this morning's shenanigans. Jake, I'll see you in my office, *after* you detain that animal—"

His words cut off abruptly, and not everyone notices at first, since they're all still whooping and hollering at the goat, trying out names for it and skipping out of the way as it continues to race around the cafeteria. But I see it right away: Ransom, faltering.

He grabs the back of the chair next to him to steady himself. Then he closes his eyes, like he's suddenly overcome with a wave of nausea or wooziness. Before I can fully comprehend what's happening, he has collapsed to the ground, his body splayed out on the ancient wooden floorboards.

"Ollie," I say, pointing in Ransom's direction.

"Is that Ransom?" he asks, jumping up to see.

"He collapsed. I saw him grab the back of that chair. And then..." I make a falling gesture with my hand.

Maude jumps up on her seat, craning to see. Jago and Theodora head into the crowd to get a closer look.

"Someone call the school nurse. Or 911!" a voice shouts. Word has gotten around that Ransom has fallen. That he fainted, or had a heart attack, or *something*. The whole room erupts in chaos, and that seems to only rile up the goat, which has now leaped right onto a table and is eating the food off every single plate.

Within minutes, paramedics arrive and rush to Ransom's side. I watch them load him onto a gurney and slide him out the double doors as quickly as they possibly can. The goat being long forgotten, now all anyone can talk about is Headmaster Ransom. Is he going to be all right?

"The plasma," I whisper to my friends. It's got to be the reason he collapsed. "His treatments are as experimental as you can get," I tell them. "I doubt he even has a doctor on board, advising him. For all we know, that cocktail he injected in his arm last night was lethal."

For all we know, Headmaster Ransom is dead.

JAKE

THE REST OF Saturday, all anyone can talk about is Ransom's collapse. We have next to no information about what hospital he's been taken to, what condition he's in, or if he's even alive. All anyone can do is speculate. Theories abound, but none of them come close to what I believe is the truth: that Ransom's risky experiment may have killed him.

Pru, Ollie, and I meet up with the Similars at lunch, grabbing sandwiches and bringing them to the shore of Dark Lake for a makeshift picnic. Ollie's next to me, spreading his backpack and lunch on the grass and stretching his legs. His brown hair hangs in his eyes, which are grayer than ever, and his lips turn up in a smile as he holds out his peanut-butter-and-jelly sandwich to me.

"Wanna go halfsies?" he asks.

"Always." I hand him half of my grilled cheese.

I'm hiding how nervous I feel that he's going to bring up his feelings. It's like they're a booby trap, lying in wait for me to step on them so they'll detonate.

I'm drawn out of my reverie by Jago, who's referencing this morning's antics with the goat. "Jake's getting *more* immature as he ages. Not less. Must be because he's back for a fifth year," Jago says. "He's embarrassed that he's not at college yet, so he's showing off."

"You mean acting out," Pru notes.

"But what about Archer?" Maude wonders, directing the comment to Ansel. "What happened on the set of *Space Wars* this summer that made him so cocky? Besides the paparazzi, I mean. And all those fans… And why is he spending all this time *here*?"

"He said he was bored after shooting wrapped," Ansel answers. "NYU doesn't start till next week, so he's hanging out at the old alma mater, crashing with me on the floor of my room. I really hope this is a phase. I don't feel like being 'bros' with this new, unimproved Archer."

"Dash," I address my bot, feeling suddenly curious, "pull up Archer de Leon's social media feed."

"Certainly, Emma," Dash answers, and within moments, my plum screen is filled with Archer's posts. There's a picture of Archer, last week, with his castmates on *Space Wars*. Archer, five days ago, posing for selfies with fans. And one from last night. A photo taken from a beach in Thailand. Archer's not in it; it's a landscape of a gorgeous sunset, captioned "Bangkok Nights. Can't believe I have to go home next week. *Space Wars*, it's been real."

"Guys?" I say to my friends, interrupting their conversation. "How did Archer take this photo from a beach in Thailand last night, if he was here, at the masquerade ball, acting like an ass?"

Ollie, Pru, and the others crowd around my plum to get a look at the photo.

"That's weird," says Pru.

"It's not just weird; it makes no *sense*," Maude counters. "But there's got to be an explanation. A perfectly logical one. Obviously."

"Ansel?" Jago asks. "When exactly *did* Archer finish up filming? Wasn't he here at the beginning of the school year?"

"Yeah, he was," Ansel says, perplexed as he stares at the screen. "He came back to the States on the first day of school to see me off and do some interviews in New York. The *Today* show or something. I dunno. I can't really keep up with his schedule. He's all over the place. Back and forth between New York, Cali, and the set."

"Maybe that's an old photo." Pippa shrugs. "A throwback. And he posted it last night, even though he was here. He probably even has one of those social media consultants to do it for him."

"I guess," I say, but something about it's not sitting right with me.

"Or his account was hacked," Maude says with authority. "It happens all the time." Then she completely switches gears. "Who wants to go for a swim?" Maude jumps up and tosses off her cardigan. She grabs Jago by the hand and begins pulling him to his feet. He laughs, following her to the shore of the lake. Soon Ansel, Pippa, and Theodora are joining them.

Ollie looks from me to Pru, dumbfounded. "That lake's *cold*. Are they seriously going swimming?"

"Looks like it," Pru answers, crumpling up her lunch sack and collecting her bag.

"But they're not wearing swimsuits," Ollie points out.

"It's something they kind of…do," I explain to Ollie. I don't want to get much further into it; Ollie knows the Similars have capabilities, but not much more than that. I watch as my friends dive into the lake, fully dressed, swimming in a synchronized way that reveals they've been practicing like this for years.

"I've gotta go—crew team meeting," Pru explains. I give her a quick wave goodbye, and she scampers off. Now only Ollie and I are left lying back on the grass, like we always used to do. Alone. My heart starts pounding wildly with anticipation and dread. He's going to say something to me now, about his feelings. It's the perfect opportunity.

"Emma?" Oliver asks me, his face turned up to the sun.

"Yeah?" I answer back, my pulse racing.

"The last thing I want to do right now is crack a book, but you were right," he sighs. I feel my heartbeat start to slow. Enough that I'm even capable of making a joke.

"What did you just say?" I tease. "I didn't hear you."

"You were *right*!" he laughs. Then he groans. "If I don't get up now and start doing some of my homework, I may not graduate from this place till I'm forty."

I let out a breath. "Then you'd better start. Come on, I'll walk you back to the dorms."

Out of the corner of my eye, I see the Similars on the shore of the lake, laughing as they dive back into the water. I'm sure they're making a concerted effort not to stay under the water for too long; they wouldn't want anyone else to see what they're capable of, how long they can hold their breath. The water's cold, but not so cold it would raise too many eyebrows if anyone saw them. This is their last chance to do this. Any later in the year, and they'd call too much attention to themselves.

As Ollie and I walk back up the grassy lawn, I feel a pang deep in my gut. We've all enjoyed a beautiful afternoon—picnicking, chatting, laughing. Levi should be there on that shore, swimming with the others. I feel so much guilt at the thought of any of us having fun, without him.

As we round the bend, approaching main campus, I notice there's an unusual grouping of kids at the entrance to the main house. They're standing in a line that stretches all the way around the building. Probably fifty teens or more stand in a queue, waiting—for what?

I squint to get a good look at what's happening at the front of the line, and I see that Archer is sitting behind a table, with groupies swarming around him. The kids in line are waiting to get Archer's autograph and take a photo with him.

"Okay, this has seriously gotten out of hand," I say to Ollie. Why are the teachers letting this go on? I'd give this five minutes before Principal Fleischer arrives to break it up. As we approach the line, I hear a couple of kids saying they just got off the train from New York. When they heard Archer was going to be signing autographs, they skipped school to be here.

"I don't think all these kids even go to Darkwood," Ollie says. "And some look really old." He's right; a couple of them look like they could be in their twenties.

I approach a girl at the back of the line. "Do you go here?" I ask her.

She shakes her head. "No, why?"

"Where'd you hear about this, anyway?" I press.

"The feeds. Where else?" She looks at me like I'm an idiot.

There's a commotion in the line, and Ollie and I turn to see two kids fighting each other. One is saying that the other one cut him off. The accused kid gets up in the other one's face and threatens to punch him.

"So this is what happens when the headmaster is rushed off to the ER," I muse. "But where's Principal Fleischer?" There's no way she'd allow this.

"Maybe she's at the hospital with Ransom," Ollie suggests. "From the look of things, there aren't *any* teachers around."

He's right. I don't see any of the teachers who usually sprinkle the grounds on the weekends, keeping students in line. Is that how all these kids got on campus? Is someone stationed at the gate, temporarily holding it open?

"You need to study," I tell Ollie, steering him away from the spectacle of Archer and his fans, toward the dorms. "I won't let you fall behind on my watch. NYU is waiting for you," I add. "Film school's been your dream since you were ten and you made your first documentary about the fourth-grade snack program."

"I still can't believe they switched out Oreos for Ritz Crackers. But dreams change, don't they? I don't know if my parents want me so far from home. I don't know if *I* want to be so far from home. And…you," he adds quietly. My heart skips about twelve beats. Is he going to say something now, about his feelings for me? "Have you thought about where you're gonna apply? Because I'm thinking maybe California's my best bet. You know, USC. I'd only be a one-hour plane ride from my parents…"

I breathe out, relieved he's still talking about colleges and nothing more…personal. Still, I don't know how to answer him. Up until the start of school, college was the absolute last thing on my mind. Now, I have thought about it a little, if only because it's something I simply can't avoid. Oxford is on my list, and so are a dozen schools all over the country. I know Oxford's a long shot. From what I've read online, the university doesn't accept many American students straight out of high school, since the British and U.S. curricula are so different. Of course, the Similars will have no trouble getting into any college they choose, thanks to Gravelle's rigorous academics on Castor Island.

We round a corner, heading down the narrow path that will take us back to our dorms. Someone's in our way, though—or two someones, I should say. They're so entangled in each other, hooking up under an awning of low-hanging tree branches, that they're completely oblivious to us, and the fact that we need to walk past them. It's not a wide walkway, and there are trees on either side. We have no place to go.

"Ahem," I say, feeling awkward, not only because we're interrupting their heated moment, but also because I'm all too aware of Ollie next to me, and the fact he never got a chance to tell me about his feelings. There's no way he's watching these two and not thinking about…whatever it was he was planning to say to me last night, at the dance.

The couple doesn't budge or make any sign that they've heard me. They continue kissing, getting more enmeshed in each other. I raise an eyebrow at Ollie.

"We could go around the back way?" he whispers.

Before I can answer, the girl whisks her shirt off and throws it into the bushes. The boy pushes the girl up against a tree trunk, and I catch a glimpse of her coppery hair and realize who she is: Tessa Leroy. How did I not realize it before? That's her purple bomber jacket on the ground, next to her patent leather booties.

She's in only her bra now—a lacy purple one that's a shade darker than her jacket. She and the boy are going at it, all arms and legs and touching in all the places, and I wonder where this is coming from. Maybe she's been feeling a lot of pent-up sexual frustration or something, since she's been at Creekside all this time.

"Somehow I imagined the treatment facility would make her really zen," I whisper to Ollie. "Guess I was wrong."

"Isn't that Henry Blackstone?" Ollie's nudging me in the side, indicating the boy. I hear moaning, and I cringe, turning away from them. We have got to get out of here.

"Wait." I stop in my tracks. "You mean the kid who asked Theodora out like five times last year?" I rack my brain to remember.

"I guess. I wasn't here for that. But in our second year, Henry was pretty vocal about wanting to date Tessa. She repeatedly turned him down," Ollie remarks.

That sounds right. I vaguely recall Tessa telling Madison and Jake she'd rather eat nails than go out with Henry. What changed? Why would she suddenly want to hook up with Henry, of all people? Did he get hot over the summer? It's possible…

"Let's go." I grab Ollie's hand. We'll have to take the long route.

We turn and leave, right when it seems these two are about to get even more into each other. I think I hear them collapsing on the ground in a sweaty, hormone-fueled heap. I can't get out of there fast enough.

I try to make small talk with Ollie the rest of the way to the dorms, hoping I can get his mind off of what we both just saw, but it's a struggle. Before, we would have just laughed off a scene like that. Now, it feels loaded.

It feels like eons later, but we finally make it to the door of Nightshade, Ollie's dorm. "Go be brilliant. I'll meet up with you later," I say, almost shoving him through the door. "Go, go, go!"

Ollie salutes me before heading inside. I turn in the other direction and start walking. That was a close call. I'm surprised he *didn't* say anything about his feelings. I need air. I don't know how long I can do this, waiting for the other shoe to drop.

I head the other way from the dorms, making sure to avoid that same shady path. I'm not looking where I'm going, and I've stumbled up to the soccer field, where a rowdy Saturday practice is in session. I'm not really following the players as they scurry over the grass, hunting the ball down. But as I gaze over them, vaguely noting the athletic shorts and T-shirts they wear with their cleats and soccer socks, I notice Jake. He's running around like he didn't just completely luck out, not getting into trouble for that stunt with the goat. If Ransom hadn't collapsed, Jake would be in detention right now, paying for his crimes.

Jake's got the ball now, and he's kicking it lazily between his legs while another student—it looks like Willa, from the Nine— blows on a whistle, trying to get her team to pay attention.

"Coach Young isn't here today, so you're all gonna listen to *me!*" Willa shouts at her teammates through a megaphone. I'm not surprised Willa's a soccer star; she's athletic and elegant, with an easy confidence that radiates through everything she does. Knowing what I do—that she refused to take part in Harlowe's reverse hazing ritual—makes me like her all the more.

Jake's not listening to her, though. He's goofing off with a couple of other kids, passing the ball and then tackling one of the other guys for fun.

"I said, *I'm* in charge!" Willa directs this comment pointedly to Jake, who continues to ignore her. "I'm gonna count down from five, Jake Choate. And if you're still acting like an utter child, you'll be banned from the field for twenty-four hours. Five. Four, three, two…one!" Jake's lying on the grass, cracking up at something one of the other kids has said. Willa waltzes straight up to him, grabs him by the shirt, yanks him to his feet, and starts marching him to the edge of the field.

"What the hell?" Jake protests. "It was a joke! Diaz and Cooper weren't listening, either."

Jake stops talking when he looks up to find himself face-to-face with his exact DNA copy.

It's Jago. And Jago is looking *really* pissed. Willa shoves Jake on the grass.

"Good," Willa says, nodding at Jago. "Maybe you can talk some sense into him, Jago." She turns back to the field, leaving him there with his Similar.

But wait. Wasn't Jago *just* swimming in the lake, in his clothes? *This* Jago isn't wet, not even his hair. Plus, he's wearing pajamas—flannel ones that look expensive and fancy. I doubt Jago owns pajamas like this. They're too pretentious. I'm so confused. If this isn't Jago, then who is he? Which one of these people is the real Jake? And *who* is the other one?

"I need to talk to you," the pajama-clad Jake is saying to the one in soccer gear. "Now."

"So talk," soccer Jake answers.

"Some kids saw you passing out beers to a bunch of first years last night behind the dining hall," Jake says, with intensity. If this is the Jake Choate I know, I don't think I've ever seen him so worked up about anything in his life.

"So?"

"So, you could have gotten me in major trouble if a teacher had seen you!"

"Good thing they didn't, then." Soccer Jake shrugs.

"That's totally not what I had in mind when I let you—"

"*Let* me?" soccer Jake says. "You didn't let me, man. You're not my boss."

"You can't do stuff like that," pajama Jake goes on, impassioned. "It was fine when you wanted to check out my classes. But now you're gonna get me in serious trouble. Bringing that goat into the school? Getting me banned from the soccer field? And now this thing with the beer? You could ruin my chances to play soccer at UCLA!"

Pajama Jake yanks soccer Jake by the arm so soccer Jake is forced to follow him down the path to the athletic building. My head's spinning as I watch them go. That definitely is *not* Jago… It's like it was *two* Jakes. But how can that even be?

I feel like maybe I'm losing my mind. I can *hear* people's thoughts. I just saw *two* Jake Choates. Feeling like something is seriously off, maybe with me, I race out of there. I can't deny something's really out of whack with the whole school this weekend. Maybe it's the cycle of the moon. It's not only Tessa's hookup with Henry, or Archer's autographing booth. *Who* the hell was Jake talking to? I casually bring it up to Jago later, not wanting to alarm him. Did he happen to run back to his room, dry off, and quickly change into pajamas after diving into Dark Lake? He gives me a strange look and assures me that he didn't. So I make up a lame excuse about thinking I saw him on the main quad, but it must have been Jake.

I find my friends at dinner and slide into a spot between Ansel and Maude. I'm about to launch into the story of my strange double-Jake sighting, but before I get the chance, a voice booms over the loudspeaker.

"Attention, everyone. I have an important announcement." I look to my friends, confused. Who's talking? It doesn't sound like a teacher. The voice sounds like a *student's.* "This is Tessa Leroy. You may have noticed the lack of teachers on campus today."

It's true; I don't think I've seen a single teacher today. That's probably why no one broke up Archer's autograph session. And didn't Willa say she was filling in for Coach Young? I figured Fleischer was with Ransom... But where are the others? Dinner is automated—prepared off campus and loaded onto our trays by bots—so it's not like there's any cafeteria staff to ask. The more I think about it, the stranger it seems that we haven't seen anyone over the age of eighteen all day.

"We're currently looking into it, since we're as concerned as all of you," Tessa goes on.

"Who's *we*?" I ask Maude. She shakes her head.

"Article ten, section four of the Darkwood handbook stipulates that the oldest person on campus should lead in an emergency situation," Tessa asserts. "Which means I'll be taking on an authority role until the teachers return. We're sure there's a reasonable explanation for this. Until we find out what that is, please, do not panic. Finish your dinners, return to your dorm rooms, and hopefully by morning, we'll know what happened to our beloved educators."

"Tessa forgot one action item," says a second voice that chimes in over the loudspeaker. It's Archer. "While we sit tight and wait for our teachers to return, don't forget to have as much fun as you *possibly* can."

The room erupts in laughter and cheers.

"Ansel," I say, my wheels spinning, "has anything else been posted on Archer's social media accounts? Since that picture from Bangkok?"

"No," he says quickly, checking his plum. "Why?"

"I saw something earlier," I tell my friends under my breath, and they huddle in close to hear me. "It was Jake. Only he was with…*another* Jake. Ollie, after you and I walked back to the dorms this afternoon," I go on, "and you left to study, I saw Jake talking to a Jake clone. Someone who looked *exactly* like him. Only…it wasn't Jago. Because Jago, you were swimming in the lake, right?"

"Yeah," Jago says, shooting Maude a look. She shrugs.

"He was wearing pajamas. In the middle of the day. And this guy and Jake were arguing. Jake was saying that this other Jake was going to get him into loads of trouble. And then they left. And I didn't think I could follow them without them knowing…"

"You're saying there's another Jake clone on campus right now?" Pippa asks, incredulous.

"Either that, or I'm hallucinating," I tell them.

"So where is this other Jake now?" Pru asks, looking as confused as I feel.

"I don't know," I say. "But things have been super weird since the dance last night. Archer with that over-the-top speech, and Jake with his goat… Ransom collapsing… And now, the teachers are gone? What if…"

I pause, collecting my thoughts.

"What?" Pru presses.

I lean in closer, whispering. "What if Tessa, and Archer, and Jake…aren't Tessa, Archer, and Jake? What if the guy who let that goat loose is the other Jake clone I saw. What if—Ansel, what happens if you try calling Archer?"

Ansel immediately dials on his plum. "It's ringing." He ends the call. "Voicemail."

"Beach party!" someone yells, and we all turn to see a couple of kids standing on tables, addressing the student body. "Bring sodas and anything *else* you can get your hands on. The party started ten minutes ago!" they shout.

Everyone in the dining hall starts cheering as dinner breaks up, and Pru, Ollie, the Similars, and I make our way outside into the warm night. The "party" on the shore of the lake is already in full swing. That was fast.

"Do you think the teachers are in danger?" Pru asks. "I mean, where are they? They can't all be at the hospital with Ransom, can they?"

"Shouldn't we tell someone?" Pippa asks, speaking up over the loud, electronic music that's pumping through outdoor speakers. The party's growing larger, and louder, with each passing minute. I shiver in the warm air with an eerie sense of something being wrong, but not knowing what it is. Meanwhile, the rest of Darkwood is so oblivious, they're throwing the party of the century.

We wander over to the shore of the lake. Kids are dancing, some are drinking from flasks and others straight from vodka bottles, and there's a bonfire going. A kid I recognize from Pru's crew team is keeping watch over the lake from a make-shift lifeguard tower. Smart, given that these kids might get out of control…

"Someone buzz Tessa," I tell my friends, leading them to a quieter spot, away from the lake. "Does anyone have her number?"

"I do," Theodora replies. She sends off a hasty buzz. "No response yet. But I bet they don't let you text all day at

Creekside. We could call Creekside directly. If you really think there's a chance that's not Tessa out there at the party, and the real Tessa could still be in at her treatment program…"

This all sounds so strange, and we all know it. Not the real Tessa? Then who *is* it? Another clone? From *where*?

"It's worth a shot," I say. "Dash, locate the number for Creekside Rehabilitation Center." The others start to make plans. Ansel is going to talk to Archer.

"I'll hunt down Jake. Ask him what the hell was going on earlier today. And who that other Jake is," I say, feeling more and more concerned with every passing second. "Pru and Ollie, come with me?" They agree, and we all split up, promising to keep each other apprised if we discover anything. Like any of our teachers…

Pru, Ollie, and I head to the dorms. We knock on doors, check all the common areas and the Tower Room. Nothing suspicious there, but then again, we don't know what we're looking for. Pru offers to head to Ransom's on-campus house, and Fleisher's, to see if there's anyone there. She goes, and I lead Ollie to the soccer field.

"They were right here, talking," I explain. "One of the Jakes—the one in pajamas—was accusing the other Jake of screwing with his life. He said the other one was passing out beer to first years. Not that I'd put it past Jake to do something like that, but… He does take his soccer career pretty seriously. I don't think he'd want to risk wrecking his whole future by getting caught. And the other Jake didn't deny it. Then they left." I lead Ollie in the direction the two Jakes walked, down the path and into the empty athletic building. We enter through the front door and start down the main hallway.

I hear a faint banging sound coming from the other end of the hall. My eyes flash to Ollie's.

"Did you hear that?" he asks. We sprint toward the noise. It's followed up by a feeble voice that sounds muffled, like it's coming from far away.

"Help! Get me out of here!" the voice shouts. "*This is not okay!*"

I notice the janitor's closet a few feet away. "Someone's locked in there," I tell Ollie. We run to the door, undo the dead bolt that's pulled neatly across it, and wrench the door open. There, huddled on the floor of the cramped closet, head in his hands, is Jake. Pajama Jake.

"Thank God," he says, leaping to his feet. "I've been in here for *hours*. Took you long enough to find me!" he barks, stretching out his legs and making a beeline for the door.

"Wait," I say, blocking his path. "Not so fast. Who was that Jake look-alike you were arguing with earlier?"

"Where are the teachers?" Ollie demands. "And what's up with Archer and Tessa—"

"Nothing's 'up' with us," says a dismissive voice behind us. I turn to see Tessa herself, right behind me, with Archer flanking her on her left and the other Jake—soccer Jake—on her right. Before we can demand answers, they've shoved us into the closet with pajama Jake, and locked the door.

THE DUPLICATES

TEN MINUTES LATER, we're pounding on the door of the janitor's closet, screaming for someone to let us out. I'm trying to bust the door down, but it's futile; it barely even gives. Ollie tries to pick the lock, but we know it's probably pointless. That dead bolt on the other side isn't budging. Meanwhile, my plum won't work—when I try to call up Dash, he doesn't answer. I can't connect to the school Wi-Fi at all.

"Same," says Jake, showing me his own unresponsive plum. "They must have one of those black-market signal blockers," Jake explains. "When I get out of here, those guys are toast."

"Hang on," says Ollie, trying to remain calm. "First things

first. Who *were* those kids? They aren't Tessa and Archer. And obviously, if you're really you, then who is that other guy?"

Jake sighs, leaning back against the wall and kicking off his expensive designer loafers. "I met them yesterday, right before the dance. Someone helped them breeze right onto campus. Directed them straight to the ball."

I feel a sick twisting in my stomach. That person was me. *I* mentioned the masquerade ball when they were coming up the path to Darkwood. I told them because I was sure they were who they said they were. Who they seemed to be. And then I buzzed them through the gate, let them walk in right behind me...

"When I found out there was this other Jake clone walking around—and not Jago," Jake clarifies, "but this other kid who wanted to have fun and pretend to be me for the weekend..." He shrugs. "I thought it was hilarious. And harmless. Maybe if I let him crash with me, have some fun as me for a bit, I'd be able to convince him to go to my classes on Monday. So I could sleep in. You know, goof off for a change."

"So you realized these kids were clones," I say, incredulous, "and that they were planning on impersonating you, and two of your best friends, and your first thought was to use the whole situation to be incredibly *lazy*?"

"I didn't know what they were planning to do!" Jake insists.

"So that goat was not your idea?" Ollie asks.

"Of course not. That goat was idiotic. I told him so," Jake says, defending himself. "I also told him he wasn't going to my soccer practice for me, but he didn't listen. And then he went and locked me in here!"

"Do you know where the teachers are?" Ollie presses.

"The teachers? No, why?" Jake looks genuinely perplexed.

"They're all gone," I explain. "Which is why there's a giant, raucous party happening down by the lake. And why Tessa—or whoever she is—announced that, as the oldest person on campus, she'd be taking over."

"Where did they come from?" Ollie asks, folding one leg up and leaning his elbow on it. "Did they say? What else did they tell you?"

"Not much," Jake admits.

"And you didn't ask them?" I pound on the door in frustration, then turn back to Jake. "You didn't question why they were here, or who created them?"

"Does it matter?" Jake answers.

"Of course it matters! We'd know what they want."

"Isn't it obvious? They want to mess with us. With our lives."

I kick at the door, and Ollie grabs me by the arm. "You're gonna break your foot. That door's solid steel. Pru and the others will find us. We have to sit tight."

I let him pull me back down to the floor, where we spend the next couple of hours speculating about where the clones came from. Predictably, Jake's not helpful and repeatedly expresses his annoyance that he's missing out on the one night at Darkwood with no teachers—and a rager on the shore of Dark Lake. Eventually, I fall asleep with my head on Ollie's shoulder.

◇—⊢—◇

I wake up to the sound of the dead bolt on the other side of the door being slipped off. I have no idea what time it is and am momentarily flummoxed to find that I've been asleep this whole time, leaning on Ollie. Light filters in, and I rub my eyes, seeing Pru, Maude, Theodora, and Pippa standing framed in the doorway.

"What time is it?" I ask.

"Eight o'clock. Sunday morning," Pippa explains, holding out a hand and leading me from the janitor's closet. My legs are aching, I have to pee like crazy, and all I want to do is brush my teeth.

Ollie follows quickly behind me, as does Jake, looking ready to murder someone. He doesn't even thank Pru and the others.

"Where are they?" he growls.

"We aren't sure," Pru answers honestly, shooting a look at me and Ollie. "The whole campus was up till four in the morning."

"And the teachers?" I ask, as we all briskly make our way out of the athletic building, having stopped only to use the restroom on our way. Jake's already taken off, presumably to find the clones himself.

"Still no idea," Theodora answers. "But I have news, about Tessa."

"Yes?" My heart's pounding out of my chest as we make our way outside, where the campus lawn is littered with students— some sunbathing in bikinis, others playing Frisbee and bocce ball. Music is blasting, and a couple of kids are floating on giant unicorn- and flamingo-shaped rafts in Dark Lake.

"We reached her. At Creekside," Theodora explains. "She's on her way here. She's a little…"

116

"Mad," Pippa supplies.

I feel my heart sink.

"Who *are* they?" I ask Pru and my friends, as we hurry to the dining hall to snag some breakfast. The last thing I'm thinking about is food, but my stomach reminds me with a rumble that I'm starving.

"DNA copies," Maude says, stating the obvious. "The real question is: Is this our guardian's doing? And why—"

Maude is interrupted by the sound of the fire alarm blaring. "This is not a drill," an automated voice booms out. "There is a fire on the premises. I repeat: there is a fire on the premises. Immediately move to all exits and vacate all buildings. Immediately move to all exits and vacate all buildings."

I manage to grab a bagel before we turn back to the double doors of the dining hall, which is now a bottleneck of kids yelling that we have to leave. Students are shoving each other out the door, some shouting. A first year's crying, saying she barely escaped a fire when she was ten. Another girl grabs her by the arm and pulls her bodily out the door.

Once we're outside, the alarm continues to blare. Kids stream out of the main house and every dorm, all convening on the grassy lawn by the circular drive. I'm scanning the grounds for any sign of our teachers and spot Tessa not far off—or Tessa's look-alike, I guess I should say. She's sprinting across the lawn, wearing only that purple bra from yesterday and underwear, and grasping her clothes in one hand and a fire extinguisher in the other. Why isn't she dressed? Was she hooking up with Henry Blackstone again? She's yelling something—I'm not sure what, or who it's directed at. No one notices her at first, but once they do, everyone stops their conversations to watch her run across the lawn.

"You have got to be kidding me," Ollie says, his eyes glued to this Tessa impersonator. So are mine.

That's when Jake runs past. *Our* Jake. He's wearing the pajamas he had on all night in the janitor's closet. And he is *pissed*.

"What's happening?" I yell at him, but he runs right past me, his eyes still on Tessa as he chases her across the lawn.

"My clone set fire to one of the dorms, that's what happened!" Jake shouts back. I run to catch up to him, with Ollie on my heels.

"How?" I yell over the blare of the fire alarm.

"With a lit joint," Jake practically snarls as he finally catches up to Tessa, grabbing her and pulling her to the ground. That's when Jake—impersonator Jake—shows up, jumping on top of his original. The two Jakes begin to wrestle each other on the grass, with the entire school watching, including Jago, who has surfaced and is standing next to me and the other Similars.

"Holy crap," is all Jago can utter. I scan the dorms for signs of smoke. I don't see any. The Jakes are still fighting each other on the lawn. Archer runs up to help Tessa to her feet—she's frantically throwing on her clothes—and he tries to stop the fight between the Jakes, but to no avail. They're still going at each other, with no intention of stopping.

I never thought I'd be happy to see Principal Fleischer, but when she emerges, stumbling onto the grass and looking furious,

I'm relieved. Following her are three other teachers who look dazed and zoned-out. From the other direction, five more teachers emerge, several in their pajamas and two wearing robes.

"Attention!" Fleischer yells over the blare of the fire alarm. "*Attention!*"

The fire alarm stops. The ensuing silence is almost shocking, after all that noise and commotion. Even the Jakes stop fighting each other and lie back on the grass, spent.

"I've just been alerted by the system that the fire has been extinguished. The damage to the dormitory was minimal," Fleischer says, livid. "However," she adds, "*someone* drugged every single teacher at this school. Repeatedly. Which is why we've been asleep for more than a day, oblivious to the complete and utter mayhem that has transpired in our absence. It goes without saying that this kind of behavior will not be tolerated, and that whoever was responsible for that fire, and for administering injectives to Darkwood's faculty, will be fully and uncompromisingly punished. In the meantime, return to your dorm rooms, and *do not leave them* for the next three hours, until lunch. If it were up solely to me, I'd keep you there all day. But the board feels you are entitled to meals." With those last words, Fleischer turns to the other teachers, speaking sternly with them while the student body dissects everything that just happened, from the dance on Friday up until now.

Moments later, I notice three men walking across the grassy lawn, and the crowd parts for them as they approach the Jake, Tessa, and Archer look-alikes. They wear uniforms, though I can't place what kind; they appear vaguely official, like guards.

But whoever the men are, and wherever they came from, the three clones stop what they're doing as soon as they notice the guards. All three of them stiffen. The Tessa double shoots the Archer clone a look, and he shrugs. Then Tessa's clone looks like she's considering something. Thinking about what to do. In a split-second decision, she takes off, running across the grass, still only half-dressed, until she trips in her bare feet over a rock, stumbling. One of the guards is on her tail and closes his hand around her upper arm, grabbing her. A second guard approaches the Archer look-alike, who isn't running but, rather, has shoved his hands in his pockets, resigned to the fact that he's been caught. The third guard pulls the imposter Jake up from the ground and appears, from his body language and stern expression, to be lecturing him. Or giving him a warning.

"What did I say about returning to your dorms?" Fleischer's voice booms out. Nearly everyone around me starts to gather up their backpacks and hustle, in a mass exodus, including Pru and the Similars. But I don't move. I'm enthralled by what's transpiring in front of me. These three clones are being reprimanded by guards who've only just shown up on campus. Who are these men? And how are they connected to these copies of Tessa, Archer, and Jake? Principal Fleischer must have the same questions, because I watch her charging toward the guards, confronting the one who's hustling the Jake clone across the grass. She and the guard get into a discussion that looks heated, and I assume she's questioning who he is and why he's here—and how he has the jurisdiction to handle Tessa, Jake, and Archer like this. Because she likely doesn't know they aren't themselves, does she? After all, she's been asleep, drugged in her room for the last twenty-four hours. Then the guard shows her something on his phone. I wish I could see what it is, because after reading it, her expression morphs from outrage to resignation. She makes a gesture that looks, from my vantage point, like "go ahead."

"Em?" Ollie asks me. "We should probably listen to Fleischer or risk a decade in duty."

"You go if you want," I tell him, not taking my eyes off the guards.

"I'll wait," Ollie says. "Someone needs to make sure you don't do anything reckless."

I can't even acknowledge his joke; I'm riveted to the action in front of me. The guard holding the Tessa clone by the arm marches her right past me, and before I'm even conscious of what I'm doing, I reach out and grab this Tessa girl by the hand, nearly tripping her.

"Who *are* you?" I ask her. "Where did you come from?"

The Tessa clone looks at me with wide eyes. Her stare rattles me. She's not Tessa; no, now I see she's nothing like her original, who's been through so much, and done so much, good and bad. This girl's not like Theodora, either. There's something naive about the way she looks at me. Something hollow.

"I'm Tessa," she says, her voice emotionless. "Tessa Leroy."

"Let's go," the guard says. "Car's waiting to take you back."

"Back where?" I ask, hurrying alongside them, with Ollie next to me. They start to move toward a black stretch SUV with dark, tinted windows idling in the circular drive. In all the mayhem of the fire alarm, I hadn't noticed it.

Neither the guard nor the Tessa clone answers me. Frustrated, I'm about to demand answers when I spy an article of clothing on the ground—Tessa's jacket. She was carrying it, still not fully dressed, and in all the chaos, she must have dropped it on the grass. I reach down and grab it. It's that purple bomber jacket she had on yesterday. I check the tag—H&M, size 6—and notice that a name tag has been sewn inside next to the manufacturer's. It says only one word: "Duplicate." And next to that, some numbers: 001.05.

Duplicate? What on earth does that mean? And those numbers…

"What's a Duplicate?" I ask the Tessa clone as the guard shoves her toward the SUV. She shrugs, looking me in the eyes. "How would I know?" I sense something in her look now besides emptiness. There's a kind of hopelessness there too.

I spot the other two guards bringing the Archer and Jake clones around to the waiting car. They're handling their charges roughly; the Jake clone's arms are pinned behind his back, and the Archer clone is yanked into the back seat. The guard holding the Tessa clone opens the back door of the SUV and is about to shove her inside when she bites his hand, hard. He winces, letting go of her. She starts to bolt, but he pulls a syringe from his pocket and stabs her in the arm with it. In moments, she goes limp. He catches her before she falls, carrying her to the car and resting her inside.

I'm following all this, still holding the jacket, when I notice a man in the last row of the SUV. He leans forward to help the guard settle the unconscious Tessa clone into the car.

"She'll come to. By the time you get her home," the man advises.

I get a full view of the man's face. The chunky tortoise-shell glasses resting on his nose. The unkempt hair.

He meets my eyes for a split second, and I freeze, feeling like I've seen him somewhere before.

"Ollie," I call out. He's at my side; he hasn't left it this entire time.

"Yeah?" he answers.

"Isn't that…" I point to the man in the back seat. Within moments, the door has slammed shut in my face, cutting off my view of this person, whoever he is.

I turn to look at Ollie.

"Albert Seymour," he says quietly. "That was my uncle. Gravelle's half brother. The creator of the Similars."

It's what I suspected. I only have a second to process this development before I turn back to the car, running to the rear and rapping on the window. I bang as hard as I can, hoping Seymour will open it.

He does.

"Mr. Seymour," I say, my eyes darting from the man's care-worn face to Ollie and back again. "What are you doing here? Who are these—these *copies*?" I ask him, praying that he won't brush me off.

Ollie runs up next to me to address his uncle directly. "We're not letting you leave until we get answers," Ollie says with conviction. "So go ahead. Enlighten us."

Seymour sighs like he has the weight of the world on his

shoulders. "I can't. Not now. Meet me at Fillmore Park tonight. Eight o'clock. I'll tell you everything you need to know." He puts his window back up, and the SUV takes off seconds later.

"Mr. Ward! Ms. Chance!" a voice barks at us. We turn to see Principal Fleischer standing in front of us, arms crossed over her chest, irate. "You have three seconds to hightail it to your respective dorms, or—"

"We're going!" I shout, grabbing Ollie by the arm and rushing out of there.

"Look at this label on her jacket," I say, as we follow the last of the students who are moving in a group toward the dorms. "It says 'Duplicate.' What do you think that means?"

"No clue."

"When I asked her who she was, she said, 'Tessa Leroy.' Like it was obvious. I think she believed it too." We approach Nightshade, Ollie's dorm. "We'll bring Pru with us tonight to meet Seymour. And Maude. Not everyone. I don't want to scare him off."

At lunch, I fill in my friends about Seymour and our plan, asking Pru and Maude to come with us to Fillmore Park. It'll mean sneaking out, and given the chaos caused today by the three newcomers, I'm wary of breaking curfew and angering Fleischer. But we have no choice, not if we want to know who those kids are and why they came here.

From what we can tell, most of the student body has no clue that the Tessa, Archer, and Jake copies weren't actually Tessa, Archer, and Jake. Quite a few people saw the guards, of course, and those who didn't certainly heard about them. Rumors abound about the new Darkwood security measures that include uniformed guards. I overhear a group of students in the dining hall saying they're glad they weren't on the other side of Fleischer's wrath, especially now that discipline at Darkwood is getting taken up a notch. I certainly don't try to correct them or explain that those guards had nothing to do with Darkwood at all. If the student body's in the dark about the guards—and the clones—all the better. Right now, we have one priority: getting our questions answered. And only one person can do that. Seymour.

◇—┤ ├—◇

After the thirty-minute walk to the main road, followed by fifteen minutes of trudging down a dark country lane, Pru, Ollie, Maude, and I arrive at Fillmore Park a few minutes before eight o'clock. It's dark out, and silent, and this park is deserted. Probably has been for hours.

Albert Seymour is standing still as a statue by a park bench. He looks scholarly in a camel-colored coat, corduroy slacks, and Adidas. Like an absentminded professor. I think of that memory of Gravelle's I watched when I was held captive on Castor Island, remembering how disheveled Seymour looked as a teenager at Darkwood. I guess that hasn't changed. We approach him nervously. We're all on edge.

I briefly tell Seymour what we witnessed over the weekend, starting with Archer's memorable speech at the dance and ending with the lit joint that set fire to one of the dorms. "I assume you knew all this was happening, and that's why you sent the guards? Who *are* those clones? The Tessa clone's jacket was labeled Duplicate. What does that mean? *Why* were they here? *Where* did they come from?" I spit out the questions like bullets, barely taking time for a breath.

"Please. Give me a moment. I'll tell you everything," Seymour says, pushing his glasses up the bridge of his nose. He's awkward and uncomfortable in his own skin. I shoot a look at Ollie. Seymour fits the description Ollie gave of how he acted in Cambridge, when Ollie spent a few weeks with him the summer before last.

"We're listening," Maude says, her voice steely.

Seymour takes off his glasses, rubs them clean with a cloth kept in his shirt pocket, then slides them back on. "Those three were never supposed to be here. Not like this," he explains. "In fact, I'm planning to have a word with my brother as soon as we're done here."

"You mean Gravelle," Pru cuts in. "Did he create them? Those…Duplicates?"

"He and I did, together," Seymour says. "They were created last year using my most advanced technology. Before that, I had only tested this technique with primates, never with human subjects."

"Advanced technology?" Maude asks. "You mean the same method used to clone us?"

"Not exactly," Seymour explains. "I have since iterated on the technology used to create you and the other Similars. The new technology creates fast-growing clones, who mature from infancy to adulthood in a matter of months. Because they have so few lived experiences, I downloaded thoughts, and even memories, into their brains."

"Memories?" I press. "Whose memories?"

"Some borrowed from their originals. Others created specifically for them."

"Are there *more* of them?" Ollie asks.

"No," Seymour answers quickly and definitively. "Only the three you met. Clones of Tessa Leroy, Jake Choate, and Archer de Leon. Actually, that's not entirely true. There was a fourth." Seymour fiddles with his glasses again. "The clone who died in your place, Oliver," he says, turning to address Ollie. "He was also a Duplicate. The very first one we created."

We take this in. It suddenly makes so much sense that I don't know how I didn't think about it before, or wonder who that boy *was*. I feel a deep pang of anguish for him as I consider how he was created—as a literal science experiment—and how little regard Gravelle had for his life, taking it just like that.

"That boy's death was unconscionable," Seymour adds, clasping his hands together. "A cautionary tale, of how science can be so drastically, and dramatically, misused, in the name of progress. I will regret his death for the rest of my days." Seymour is looking down at his shoes, and I wonder if it's because he's close to tears. "The only consolation of that entire debacle is the fact that he felt no pain when he died. And he had very few—if any—life experiences or memories."

"So that makes his life expendable?" Ollie speaks up. He's agitated, I can tell. And angry. This is, after all, his biological uncle. The boy who died was Oliver's clone. I reach out to grab his hand.

"Absolutely not," Seymour says, finally meeting his nephew's eyes. "If anything, that tragedy taught us something we should have known already. That the technology is far too risky to use in any large-scale way. The Duplicates are like children. Inexperienced. Reckless. As you saw, the three who came here never should have been left unsupervised."

"Then why *were* they?" Pru asks.

"I honestly don't know." Seymour sighs. "But I can assure you, it must have been by mistake. My brother and I—"

"Your brother, our guardian, has a warped view of the world," Maude interjects. "Don't tell me you agree with his methods. Or his madness."

"I absolutely do not," Seymour says sternly. "But he is still my brother, and as you well know, blood is thicker than, well, almost anything. I remain in his life for one very important reason. I keep him from taking his schemes to the wild places they would go, if they were left unchecked. I remind him constantly of how tenuous this kind of scientific experimentation can be. The last thing I'd ever want is to put the students at Darkwood at risk. Or the Duplicates themselves."

"Except for Oliver's Duplicate," Pru reminds him.

Seymour lets out a weary breath. "Except for Oliver's Duplicate." I'm happy he doesn't try to deny it, that what happened to that boy—what Gravelle *made* happen—was unethical, and twisted, and wrong. It was murder. He goes on. "The only reasonable explanation is that the three Duplicates who came to Darkwood this weekend escaped their home on Pollux Island. Which is where they're being returned, immediately."

"Pollux?" Maude asks. "What's that?"

"The twin island to Castor, where you grew up."

"Like the Gemini constellation. The twin brothers immortalized in the sky," I say.

"I know the myth," Maude answers. "But I've never heard of this island, or seen it. And I lived on Castor for sixteen years. Where *is* this island? How could none of us know about it?"

"Pollux is positioned in such a way that it's not visible to the naked eye from Castor," Seymour explains.

Maude looks like she doesn't fully believe that, but she doesn't push it. I know she won't drop this, though.

"As I was saying," Seymour continues. "The Duplicates need far more training on Pollux—more nurturing and education—before they'll be ready to assimilate into mainstream society. That's clear now more than ever."

"What will happen to them?" Ollie asks, his voice coming out in a near whisper.

"Sounds like they'll have the same happy childhood *we* had," Maude mutters.

"We'll do our best to raise them with as much care as we gave you," Seymour says thoughtfully, addressing Maude. "I know it wasn't the perfect upbringing. But you can't deny that we supplied you with everything you could want."

"Except parents," Maude cuts in.

"Fair enough," Seymour says. "Now, if you'll excuse me, I have a lot to do to make sure these three clones are settled comfortably back in their home. I'll be informing Principal Fleischer of what happened, so there's no need to worry. The originals won't be accused of any reprehensible behavior. One more thing, before we part ways," Seymour adds. He looks over at Ollie. "I am sorry for what happened the summer before last, Oliver. You came to me for answers, and I stood in the way of helping you get them. Indeed, I regret that now. I had no idea you'd go seeking those answers on your own."

"And travel to see my maniacal father on his micronation island?" Ollie snaps. I take in a breath, feeling so much for Ollie right now that my heart's racing in my chest.

"You must understand," Seymour says, his voice betraying his emotion. "I believed I was protecting you. Your father is who he is. It was my wish for you to never personally know him, or anything about him. It was far, far better for the world when Johnny Underwood was dead."

"His death was a lie," Ollie counters. "You can't protect someone with lies. I would have thought someone as brilliant as you would know that."

I grab Ollie by the arm, suddenly feeling like all I want to do is get out of this eerie park, and not subject Oliver to these painful truths any more than we have to.

"Let's go," I say quickly, gently shoving Ollie behind me. The others follow my lead, turning to go.

"Thank you," Maude says to Seymour. We aren't his biggest fans—not after how he treated Ollie, and what he allowed to happen to that Oliver Duplicate—but at least he's told us the truth.

"I hope we don't see you again," Pru tells him as we leave the park.

We walk quickly, hoping we can return to campus before anyone realizes we've been gone. "I still can't believe I'm related to him," Ollie says as we make our way back up the country lane. "Seymour I've made my peace with. The guy's a kook," Ollie tells us. "He loves science so much, it blinds him to everything else. It's Gravelle who makes me ashamed to be me sometimes." Pru, Maude, and I don't have a good response to that, so we don't say anything at all. I reach out and squeeze Ollie's hand, though. It's all I can think to do.

"I feel sad for them." Pru's voice rings out in the silence, wavering a little. "The Duplicates, not having a life. Wanting one so badly they came here to try and live someone else's."

"I know the feeling," Maude says quietly, as we begin the uphill walk back to campus, and our home.

JANE WARD

THE REST OF September passes by in a whirlwind of senior year syllabi, mountains of homework, and college application prep. I've downloaded the common application for the U.S. colleges and a separate one for Oxford, but my cursor blinks on my blank screen every time I sit down to work on the personal statement for the schools. What can I say about my life? That I miss Levi? That I'm worried he's being held against his will? Or, almost as bad, that he just doesn't want to see me? It's not exactly appropriate college essay material.

The one light in my Levi-deficient existence is Ollie, who luckily hasn't brought up his feelings for me. I hope he's changed his mind, or realized that what he thought was "love" was simply affection for his oldest, and dearest, friend. Maybe he somehow sensed at the dance that I was trying to avoid being too close to him. Whatever the reason, I'm grateful. The only thing keeping me afloat these days is his consistent, unwavering optimism. He's so relieved to be back where he belongs, it radiates off him.

I still can't wrap my head around what happened to me—how I "heard" his thoughts, and the others'—all three times unwillingly, and at random. I know what it all means. Of course I do. It's proof that Gravelle wasn't lying to me. That I'm a Similar. But I simply can't face it yet. If I do, I'll break apart. One day after world history, I snag Maude and ask her to meet me in the circular drive that afternoon, to talk.

When we both arrive, I hand her a coffee from the dining hall.

"I miss him," I tell her. "Levi. I don't, I *can't* believe that this is it for us. I'm so worried about him," I confess. "Every night, I—" I stop, not able to tell her how much he occupies my every waking and sleeping thought. Maude's so tough. I don't know if she'll understand.

"If it were Jago, I'd be crushed," she explains simply. Maybe she *does* get it.

"I need to know everything about him," I say. "It's the only thing that will make me feel like he's not gone. Can you tell me more about what it was like when you discovered your capabilities?" I don't tell her the real reason I'm asking, of course. I can't. "We never talked about it, he and I."

"We trained on the island all the time," Maude notes, taking a sip from her cup. "But you already know that. How Gravelle made us hold our breath and swim laps... We were strong and athletic, and we had unusual endurance, but that all stemmed from practice. It wasn't until we were fifteen that we started noticing things. Our bruises healing quickly. Our scrapes scabbing over within a day, rather than several. It was gradual, though. I think puberty may have had something to do with it," she remarks, blowing on her coffee. "The year before I came to Darkwood, when I was barely sixteen, my abilities exploded. I could suddenly lift enormously heavy weights and leap from trees easily, without worry that I'd sprain an ankle or even break a bone. Because if I did injure myself, I instantly healed."

"So it didn't happen until you were a teenager," I say, processing. "Was it like that for all of you? For Levi?"

"Yes. We all developed our abilities around that same time. But each in our own, unique way. We discussed them endlessly. Compared and contrasted."

"Are anyone's abilities...mental?" I ask. Maude looks at me, her face taut.

"Not that I know of," she explains. "But Gravelle was always hoping one of us would display that kind of talent. Why?"

"No reason," I tell her, dismissing the whole idea.

The rest of the day, all I can think about is the fact that the Similars' properties are relatively *new*. Which means it could all be true.

I've been putting it off for so long, confronting this truth that Gravelle insists is my past. I consider my options. I could ask my father. It's not foolproof; he could easily lie to me, and then I'd be right back where I started. I could ask Gravelle to send proof—the birth certificate he mentioned in his original note—but again, I'd have no way of verifying if he forged it. I can't think of a single option that would give me the irrefutable evidence I'm looking for, that I'm a clone. A DNA test won't work, obviously, and I doubt I'd have much luck finding the original Emma's death records—if she did, indeed, die. It's beyond infuriating to think that this critical piece of my history, of my identity, is so far out of my grasp. And that Gravelle is probably enjoying making me squirm like this. Keeping me in the dark, indefinitely.

I do some research on telepathy. I'm scared of what I'll learn and how it may apply to me. When I do find some relevant reading material, I go deep into a rabbit hole about evolution, and how the tweaking of genetic code that Gravelle and Seymour must have done when they created the Similars—and me, if I'm one of them—could be extended to this kind of mental manipulation. According to a bunch of journals, people hooked up to sensors are already moving objects with their minds. I can't do that—at least, I don't think I can—but I'm able to *access* other's thoughts. It's not the same thing, but is it possibly related? Late one night, after hours of googling and reading, I instruct Dash to erase my search history. No one can know about this.

I long to tell Ollie everything. At breakfast one early October morning, a Saturday, he slides into the bench next to me. Pru is on my other side, and Maude and Ansel are across from us.

"Uh-oh," Pru says, nudging me in the side.

"What? Do I even want to know?" I ask, my mouth full of egg whites.

"Probably not." She points to the side wall of the dining hall, where Harlowe and her friends are hanging up flyers. DAAM flyers, soliciting new members for the Darkwood Academy Anti-Cloning Movement. I feel a sickening lurch in my stomach. Of course, I'm not surprised; Harlowe was protesting with Madison on the first day of school. She made it clear how she feels about the Similars, and clones in general, that night she pulled that renegade hazing stunt. I'd hoped the Similars' warning would scare her off. Apparently, it didn't.

"Attention, Darkwoodians," Principal Fleischer's voice rings out over the dining hall. Ollie and I look over to see her standing in front of the wide double doors. Pru and the Similars follow our gaze. "I have some unfortunate news to relay. Headmaster Ransom is still unwell. He will not be returning to Darkwood this academic year." Students start whispering and reacting, but before they can get too many words in, Fleischer barrels on. "Do not despair. You will not lack for proper leadership. In his absence, an interim head will be taking over."

An interim head? I feel instantly nervous, hoping it won't be someone who will make life miserable for the Similars.

"Please give a warm welcome to our temporary headmistress," Fleischer continues. Her voice sounds anything but warm, but then again, she's probably bitter she wasn't promoted to the post herself. "Jane Ward."

I turn to Ollie, sure my surprise is written across my face. His *mom* is the interim head of Darkwood?

I strain to catch a glimpse of Jane, who has entered the far side of the cafeteria. I notice the contrast between this year and last, how her thin frame looks noticeably healthier than it did last year when she was grieving the loss of her son, and she's smiling as she takes the mic from Principal Fleischer. I can't imagine two more dissimilar people. Jane, who has been like a surrogate mother to me all these years, and Fleischer, who has been helping Ransom with his abhorrent experiment.

"Thank you, Principal Fleischer," Jane says into the mic.

"Did you know about this?" I ask Ollie under my breath.

"Yes, but she swore me to secrecy."

I almost call him out for not telling me, before I realize how hypocritical that would be.

"Wait, I thought your mom got a business degree," Pru whispers.

"She did," Ollie answers. "She was a teacher before that."

"I'll keep this short," Jane says. "I'm saddened by the news of Headmaster Ransom's illness, but I'm pleased I can be of service to the school. I attended Darkwood as a young woman, and some of the best memories of my life were made here. I also managed to get into quite a bit of trouble that ended in my fair share of duty," she adds. "I'm looking forward to shepherding all of you through this year, bearing in mind Darkwood's founding tenets: loyalty, excellence, identity, and inclusion." Her eyes settle on the bulletin board boasting the DAAM flyers.

"I'll admit I have an ulterior motive," Jane continues, and I think I hear a tremor in her voice. "As you may know, I had the scare of my life last year. I am immeasurably grateful that my son has been returned in full health to me, and to his life here at school. I'm sure you can't blame me for wanting to keep a close eye on him." Students smile, and a few clap. "Oliver, forgive me, but I couldn't bear to be so far away from you, not when I just got you back." There are cheers now from students all around us. Ollie smiles and gives a little wave.

"Will we have to call her Headmistress Ward?" I joke to him and Pru.

"I think I'll stick to 'Mom,'" Ollie mutters.

Jane ends her speech with some final words. "I'll leave you to finish your breakfast. Don't hesitate to stop by my office at any time, with questions, concerns, or constructive feedback. Not on the food, though; I have no control over the in vitro meat," she adds lightly, garnering another round of laughs from the student body. Principal Fleischer plasters on a tight smile.

I'm not sure what reactions I'm expecting from our table. Pru's happy about the arrival of Ollie's mom as interim head. Indeed, it feels like a small victory that Ransom has been replaced by someone I respect so highly. Ransom's opposite, really. The Similars, however, seem intently focused on their food. Maude's looking down at her plate. Ansel's staring at his plum. It's obvious why—because of how things were left between Jane and Levi, the last time Jane was at Darkwood and learned Levi had played a pivotal role in duping her and Booker out of their stock in Ward, Inc. As far as I know, Levi and Jane haven't spoken since. I feel a longing to explain to her why Levi did what he did, why he was so conflicted about the task that Gravelle, his only family, had given him. But since Ollie's return near the end of the school year, I haven't mentioned Levi to Jane once. Not when Ollie, Jane, and I returned home to California, and not at all over the summer. It feels wrong to, like it would hurt her. It also feels like a betrayal of Levi, because he wouldn't want me speaking on his behalf. So I haven't.

The next thing I know, Harlowe has taken the mic from Principal Fleischer. "I have an announcement, y'all," she says, her eyes flitting over the dining hall. "The Darkwood Academy Anti-Cloning Movement will be holding a new-members meeting tonight at eight o'clock. I assure you, you won't want to miss it. See you tonight in the main house common room. Later," she says, handing the mic back to Fleischer.

I shoot Maude a look. We both know Ransom granted DAAM a charter last year. But with him gone—can Jane revoke it? As interim head, will she have that kind of power? Maude stands up abruptly. "Excuse me," she calls out. "I also have an announcement. Sorry to interrupt your meals once again, folks," Maude says evenly. "But there's one more meeting that members of the Nine need to know about. Midnight session, tonight. In the Tower Room of Cypress." Maude scans the room, and I see her eyes land on Harlowe. "Oh, I almost forgot. The time." Maude pauses for dramatic effect. "Eight o'clock."

Harlowe stops talking. She whips her head around, staring daggers at Maude. I can barely hold back my smile.

"Harlowe will have to go to the midnight session instead of the DAAM meeting, right?" Pru asks, ripping off a piece of bagel. "Or she'll forfeit her spot in the Nine?"

"Yup," I answer, feeling vindicated. I'm not even thinking about the fact that Maude's thrown down the gauntlet. Or that the girl across the room who hates clones has just been shown up by one, in front of the entire school. I'm not thinking about that—but I should be.

Ollie snags his mom after breakfast. She hugs both of us, and when I'm in her arms, I notice how much stronger she's grown, even since the summer.

"Hi, kids." She smiles, resting a hand on Ollie's shoulder. "This is going to be fun, isn't it?"

"Way to cramp your son's style during his senior year of high school," Ollie mutters. "You realize I'm the only kid at boarding school, probably *ever*, to have his mommy there with him?" Ollie crosses his arms over his chest like a petulant child, but I know, deep down, that he doesn't mind. And after the year he's had— she'll be a built-in support system for him.

"Sorry." She shrugs, but her eyes are shining, and she looks so happy, it's hard for me not to smile too. "Couldn't help myself. When word got around that a temporary head was needed, I jumped on the chance."

"And Chloe and Lucy?" Ollie asks.

"Your sisters and I are going to try our hand at Vermont living," Jane says as she starts to walk toward the exit. Ollie and I follow her steps outside to a wooded path. "I've enrolled the twins in a local school, and we've rented a cottage a few miles from here. It'll be an adventure, won't it?"

"But what about—"

"Booker will fly in when he can. He doesn't mind, honey. Coming here will be a nice break from everything he's dealing with." I know she means Ward, Inc. and the disaster that is Gravelle's influence over their family's company. "After you graduate, we'll go home. It'll be easier this way. Over fall break, I'm taking you on an East Coast college tour. NYU. Vassar. Cornell. Emerson. BU. Emma—you're welcome to come along, if you'd like?" We've stopped walking and are standing by the shore of Dark Lake, staring out at its opaque waters. Ollie looks thoughtful. Pensive, I guess.

"Thanks," I answer quickly. "But I need to use the time off to work on my college apps." I leave mother and son to catch up, sprinting back down the path to my dorm room. I feel a lightness in my chest that's been missing since I returned to school. I know it's because of Jane's unexpected arrival. Before Ollie died—before we *thought* he died, anyway—Jane had always filled some small portion of the hole left in my heart by my mother's absence. That hole feels a little less gaping now.

Suddenly, I feel an intense wave of remorse. Here I am, allowing myself to feel safe and happy when Levi is there, with that man. Hot tears threaten to fall as I change my course, heading not toward Cypress after all, but down the secluded path to the boathouse. I'm not thinking, only moving.

Ten minutes later, I burst through the brush and trees to stand in the exact spot where Levi and I spent our duty, exactly one year ago. As I stare at the boathouse doors, at the peeling paint we never did rectify, I remember the scream. Pru's scream. And how, with Pru's attack, everything changed. I saw glimpses of Levi's kindness as he carried Pru to campus. I think I fell in love with him a little bit that day, and every day after, even if I only admitted it to myself much later.

I've run here faster than I meant to, and my heart is pounding wildly in my chest. Still, I keep going. I pull open the stiff wooden doors of the boathouse and clatter inside, past the row of canoes and the racing shells lined against the walls. I'm on a mission—to do what, I'm not sure. All I know is I don't want to stop, to rest and feel the weight of it, of my sadness for Levi, of my acute longing to kiss and touch him and feel the electrifying rush of his skin on mine. My eyes race over the room as I spot what I'm looking for: stairs at the far end. They lead up to a loft. I've never been up them and have no idea what's stored up there. I begin to climb the rickety stairs. A window waits for me at the top. I wrench it open, brushing cobwebs away, and peer out.

Below me is the ground, ahead of me is the pearly Dark Lake, and beyond is the edge of the boathouse roof. Perfect.

I duck under the windowsill, crouching low to force my body through the small opening. Once my feet are firmly on the roof, I stand, feeling all of a sudden reckless and oddly brave. My heart's battering wildly against my rib cage, and I'm a whole story up from the ground, feeling dangerously free and untethered. Somehow I'm closer to Levi in this moment than I have been since I left him. Like there's some kind of inexplicable connection between us. Me, here, alone on the roof. Him, there, alone on the island. Maybe he's doing, and thinking, the exact same thing I am. In this moment, I feel so desperate to see him, to feel him, to be near him. I don't think I realized it until now, but I long to see Levi again the same way I long to know who I am—if I'm a Similar, just like him. If we have in common this one, gigantic piece of our pasts. I feel like I owe it to him to find out.

I jump.

TENSIONS

I'M FALLING THROUGH the air. I know I won't die; the boat-house roof isn't *that* high up. Only a story. But still. The like-lihood is that I'll break a bone, maybe two. And yet, there's something so freeing about jumping from this roof. Like I'm leaping, unavoidably, toward my fate, my future, and—wrapped up in that like a big, tangled mess of twine—my past.

I'm halfway to the ground when I accept that I've made a massive mistake. My hands fly up to protect my head, and my stomach feels like it's being ripped out of my body as I land with a sickening crunch on my right side. I hear something twist and snap, and the wind's been knocked out of me. Adrenaline must be kicking in, because I only vaguely hurt, and I remember this is how I felt when I leaped from Harlowe's car. I know I've done something incredibly stupid. At least I'm alive.

I'm able to sit up. There's no blood, which is something. After taking stock of my limbs, I pull up my pant leg to assess the damage to my throbbing right leg. There's an enormous bruise spreading over my ankle, which is swollen and red. It's probably sprained, but judging by how tender it feels, there could be a hairline fracture as well. I grimace as I try to put weight on it. I can stand, and so I do, gingerly testing my weight to see if I can walk back to campus.

I hear something. A rustling in the trees by the shoreline. My eyes dart in the direction of the noise, and I spot the outline of a figure there. Someone who's been watching me. Someone who probably saw me jump.

"Hello?" I call out. I don't get an answer back. By the time I've hobbled over to where the noise came from, there's no one there.

Wincing as I begin the walk back up to campus, I chide myself for acting so recklessly. What was I thinking, throwing myself off a roof like that?

You were thinking you wanted to see if you'd be hurt. If your injuries would heal quickly. You were thinking you'd test, once and for all, your capabilities. To see if you have the same regenerative properties as the Similars.

By the time I make it back up to main campus, a good ten minutes later, my ankle doesn't hurt anymore. When I pull up my pant leg, the bruise and swelling have almost entirely healed. It's as if I never jumped off that roof at all.

I stay in my room until the midnight session at eight o'clock, only briefly stopping by the dining hall to grab dinner. I avoid my friends by waiting until the last second to slip in and fix a plate. I've done nothing but study my ankle, which is now completely fine.

I splash water over my face before the midnight session, in hopes that no one will be able to tell I've been crying. When I arrive, I slip into a seat between Maude and Theodora and wait for the other members of the Nine to filter in. They do, but it's clear Harlowe's pissed, and her friends, Ivy and Graham, take seats without making eye contact. I'm barely able to concentrate on the meeting, not with my mind spinning over confirmation of what I've suspected. I'm a clone.

The evidence is staring me in the face, and yet it's too big to grasp. I was born on Castor Island. I lived there, raised by British nannies, till I was three. I lived there with my friends, and with Levi. Which means Levi and I weren't strangers when we met last year. We'd known each other as kids.

And my father has lied to me for fourteen years.

I debate pulling the Similars aside after the meeting, telling them everything.

Why not? They would understand. They would welcome it—you. Wouldn't they?

But I don't want to tell them. Not yet. Not before I've figured out what this means for me. Besides, there's only one person I want to tell, and he isn't here. Levi.

Maude takes her time with the meeting, plotting out a strategy for the school year that includes mentoring new students and setting up fund-raisers for charitable causes. She's dragging this out for as long as possible; Pippa and Theodora are in on the joke too, raising their hands to ask tangential questions. With each one, Harlowe grows angrier, finally standing up to declare that she has somewhere else to be.

"I haven't dismissed you yet, Harlowe," Maude says coolly.

Harlowe flounces back down in her seat but doesn't get up again until Maude officially ends the meeting at ten o'clock. I don't know if the DAAM meeting happened without Harlowe there, or if she'll simply reschedule it. Still, Maude made her point already in the dining hall, in front of the whole school. She won't tolerate Harlowe's bigotry. *She's* the leader of this group. Not Harlowe.

The next morning, Pru wakes me up after a fitful night of tossing and turning. "Emma," she says, tapping me on the shoulder. "Emma! Wake up!"

I turn over and see her peering down at me. She's still in her pajamas, and when I glance at the clock, it says it's 7:00 a.m. It's Sunday morning, so I can't imagine why she'd wake me up so early.

"Pru, I love you tremendously, so I say this with all due respect," I mumble. "WTF?"

"Look at this." She shoves her tablet at me. It's opened to the school blog, *The Daily Darkwood*, a site where students can post essays and articles and opinion pieces. I take the tablet in hand and scan the headline she's pointing to.

CLONES AT DARKWOOD, DUBBED "SIMILARS," MAY NOT BE HUMAN

I pause on those inflammatory words, large and in all caps.

"Read it." Pru sighs, directing me to the article below it. I look to see who the author is. The byline reads *Harlowe Shaw*. My eyes narrow. I begin to read.

Fellow Darkwoodians, it is with shock and despair that I write this blog post, a public service announcement of sorts, to inform you of something troubling I've discovered in the past few weeks at our beloved school.

First, some context. At the beginning of last year, we welcomed the Similars into our school and into our lives. Since then, we've gone above and beyond to be tolerant. We've given them the benefit of the doubt and every consideration. We've allowed them to join our clubs. We even accepted one of them as leader of this year's prestigious Ten—sorry, Nine. We've broken bread with them and trusted them in our sacred spaces—our classrooms, our sports teams. But perhaps that trust was misguided.

All this time, the Similars have lobbied to be treated exactly like the rest of us. They've made the case for themselves as regular teenagers. Only, they aren't. A few weeks ago, I witnessed some disturbing evidence that the clones at Darkwood possess a kind of super strength that, IMHO, makes them dangerous, to us and our community at large. I'll spare you the specifics, but I will tell you this: they were able to break metal as if it were as flimsy as thread. They are preternaturally strong, and it's clear to me that they were born this way, although when challenged, they dismissed their strength as something they trained for on their island. But I can assure you—no normal teenager could do what I saw, no matter how much they trained.

Regardless, this otherworldly strength is frightening, and there's no denying that the Similars are an inherent threat to everyone at our school. What's most concerning, however, is the fact that, when pressed, the clones denied everything. What's more, for the last year, they've felt no obligation to divulge to anyone here at Darkwood the truth about what they're capable of. And who they really are. Which begs the question: Are they even human?

I throw the tablet down on my bed, sitting up and sliding my feet into my flip-flops. The patronizing tone of Harlowe's essay makes me want to scream. She's twisting the truth, or at the very least, spinning it in favor of her bigoted agenda. I know, in an instant, why she's done this: because of what Maude did yesterday, one-upping her with the midnight session.

Pru and I don't change out of our pj's. We head directly to Pippa's room. A crowd has formed in front of her door.

"What's going on?" I murmur to Pru as we hurry toward the little knot of kids, probably ten or twelve students, who are all trying to get a look at something.

"No idea," she answers. We push our way through the group of our classmates to get to the front. There, on Pippa's door, spray-painted in messy red letters, are the words, GO HOME, CLONE.

I don't have to look at Pru to know how upset she is. She raps on the door, which is slightly ajar. When no one answers, she pushes the door all the way open. The kids around us whisper and watch, wide-eyed, as we tread lightly into Pippa's room. When we reach her bed, we see rumpled blankets but no Pippa. She's not here.

I send a buzz to my friends, asking them to meet us outside the library. I don't know if they've seen the blog post yet, or if they know about the hate speech scrawled across Pippa's door.

When we arrive at the library's front steps, Maude and Pippa are already there, talking quietly to each other. Ansel moves up with Jago, followed by Theodora. Ollie's right on their heels.

"We saw it," Maude says brusquely, before I can even ask. "It's payback, of course, for what I did to Harlowe yesterday. Embarrassing her in public."

"It was bound to come out," Ansel says softly. "I'm surprised no one found out sooner. You did," he addresses me. "That day at the lake last year. But—"

"But I didn't tell a soul," I remind him. "I would never."

"We know," Pippa says, brushing away a tear. "And yes, I saw my door. It wasn't only me. There were messages for all of us."

"I've already told my mom," Ollie jumps in. "She took pictures, and she's informed the administration. She won't tolerate this."

"But can she stop it?" I ask. "Harlowe's not the only one who thinks this way. She's getting all this ammunition and encouragement from her parents, probably. And lawmakers who want clones to leave the country, permanently."

"So we'll fight back," Theodora says.

"Or we'll ignore it," Maude says sternly.

"Look at this," Jago says, pulling a scrap of paper from his pocket. "It was in my bag when I woke up."

He shows us a message, written in messy scrawl.

Like it here? Great. Enjoy it while u can

That's all it says, but I instantly get the subtext.

"It's a deportation threat." Jago sighs.

"An empty one," I remind him. "As long as you're here at Darkwood, you belong in the States."

"But we graduate in seven months," Pippa interjects. "And what happens after that? *If* we even make it that long."

It's a quiet, chilly walk to the dining hall to grab breakfast. We ignore the stares and comments from kids all around us, who've obviously all read the blog post. I'm not surprised; that kind of propaganda would have gone viral in minutes. Some kids give us a wide berth. Others can't stop looking at us. It's like the Similars have arrived at Darkwood all over again. Only this time, I feel like one of them. *Because you are.*

We visit Jane in her office. She's been here twenty-four hours and already looks the worse for wear. I hope she can handle the toll this job will take on her.

"The dorm room doors are being scrubbed clean," she assures us. "I'm sorry you had to wake up to something so despicable."

I'm alone in my room later that day. Pru's off at crew practice.

When Ollie knocks on my door, I've been curled up for so long that I'm not surprised it's already four o'clock in the afternoon.

"I brought sustenance," he says, holding up a bag of M&M's in one hand and Slushees in the other. The minute I see him, tears spring to my eyes, and I go into his arms, into that space in his chest that feels sturdier than it used to. Ollie wraps his arms around me, and for a second, I can almost believe it's two years ago. Before everything changed so irrevocably.

"Walk?" I ask him. He nods, following me out of Cypress to the grassy patch behind the dorms where we used to study, or pretend to, lying on our backs looking up at the cloud formations. That's what we do now, only there's no pretense of studying. He's lying inches from me, like he always used to, and the grass is still green beneath us. It will stay that way for another month before the cold Vermont winter lays its gloved hand over our campus, rendering everything gray and withered.

"Em. I need to tell you something."

My throat tightens, and I keep my eyes squarely on the sky. *Don't say it, Ollie. Please. Because I don't know what I'll do…*

"I know I've been putting on a happy face," he says quickly. "But the truth is—I'm struggling. To make sense of everything that happened last year."

That gets my attention. It's not what I was expecting, and I turn on my side, resting my head on my hand, my arm propped up on my elbow.

"The thing is," Ollie says, squinting up at the cloud cover and shading his eyes with his hand, "I can't deal with the fact that my father is a murderer. Before you say anything. He is. He killed that boy, that Duplicate who had my DNA. Gravelle treated him like he was expendable. Not even human. Half of my genes come from him. From that *monster* who is my *dad*—"

"Wrong," I say emphatically. "That man is not your father. How many times do I have to say it?"

"But he is!" Ollie says, sitting up and flexing his hands into fists. "I know he didn't raise me. I didn't get my values from him. Or my beliefs about right and wrong. The Similars got all that," he mutters, and in that moment his face looks shaded and hardened, like he's not a boy anymore, not really. "I was lucky," Ollie goes on. "I had my mom and Booker. I don't know what's worse, honestly. Being Gravelle's biological son, or being the kids he raised from birth. All I know is that the Similars can choose to distance themselves from him. They can eventually walk away. I can never walk away from his DNA—"

"And neither can Levi," I say, my heart lurching in my chest as I sit up too.

"That's the other thing," Ollie presses on. "Levi's there, on that island. I know what that's like. How painful and lonely it is. And there's not a damn thing I can do to help him, because I'm afraid. Of going there, and having to see my father again. So I'm here at school acting like everything's peachy, when the truth is, I've abandoned him. I'm letting the guy who's practically my brother *rot* in that place!" Ollie stands, wrapping his arms around himself. I feel a pulsing in my chest and in my veins, like all I want to do is close the distance between us and make him not have to feel this, any of it.

But I don't do that. I simply watch him, my heart breaking for him.

"And everything that's happening with the Similars," he goes on, pacing the grass. I'm instantly reminded of how Levi used to do that. He was always so pensive, never letting me in. "That's all because of my father too. This is only the beginning, Emma. Do you see that? How Harlowe and those other kids are out for blood? My mom won't be able to stop it. You can't stop a freight train once it's left the station, can you?"

"We have to," I say. "We can't let them be deported. Ejected from the only home they have—"

"I wake up every day thinking about my role in all this," Ollie says, and beneath that shaggy hair and his lovely gray eyes is a face so somber, it's painful to gaze at it. "Gravelle created the Similars in the first place to get revenge on my mom."

"On all the parents," I remind him, wishing there was something I could do to take away his pain for good.

"It all started with my mom, didn't it?" he says. "They were married, and then they grew apart. He got angry, and that started scaring my mother, so gradually she let him see less and less of me. She used Gravelle's angry outbursts against him in court, to get full custody. And that's when Booker replaced him as my dad."

"None of that was anything you could *help*! You don't even remember it! You were a little kid!"

"But if I'd stayed in his life. If he hadn't felt abandoned by all the people he loved," Ollie says. "If I had found out who he was, and reached out to him…"

"He faked his death, Ollie! You couldn't have known that he was really alive."

"But before that. If I had figured out a way to let him know I still cared. Maybe he never would have cloned me, or the others. And everyone would have been spared all this pain."

Ollie is silent for a moment. I take in what he's said. He's not wrong; his logic isn't faulty. But blaming himself—that's so unfair.

"I guess if you have monster DNA…" Ollie says, and I can't be sure, but I think he's fighting off tears. "You're little more than a monster yourself."

I have no words. I have no idea what to say, so I do the only thing I can think of. I stand up and bridge the gap between us, wrapping my arms around him. I feel the softness of his gray sweater on my cheek, and his body underneath. I feel his breath mingling with my own as we both stand there, holding on for dear life.

Then I feel his lips on mine. I'm so taken aback at first, I don't react.

Ollie's hands are on my body, and every one of my nerve endings is standing at attention. He's kissing me, and his hands are cradling my face. It's the gentlest kiss I've ever experienced—not that I have much to compare it to, anyway—but all I keep thinking is that it's so *tender*. He tilts his head slightly to the side, deepening the kiss, and the entire world becomes background noise as we stand there, our bodies closer than they've ever been in the nine years since we've been inseparable. But never like this. Definitely not like this. And he's not Levi, and I *know* that, because Levi doesn't feel like this... Familiar and knowable and constant, warm like the cookies Jane used to pull from her oven...

I push away from him, flustered, confused, and utterly stunned—but it's too late. I don't know how many seconds passed while we were kissing, but enough that it happened. Enough to make that kiss *real*.

I gasp for breath, the reality of this sinking in—*you kissed Ollie you kissed Ollie you kissed Ollie*.

Is it possible to go into shock...from a kiss?

"Levi?" I say, feeling like I'm seeing a ghost.

"No, not Levi," Ollie replies, his voice rough and low and, in a way I never noticed before, actually *sexy*. "*Oliver*."

"No," I gasp. "I don't mean that you're... Look." Ollie turns now to follow my gaze, and he sees for himself what I'm talking about.

There, across the grass, standing in the late-afternoon light, is Levi.

THE LEGACY PROJECT

LEVI IS HERE.

Is my mind playing tricks on me? Levi can't be *here*, at Darkwood. Not when Gravelle told me he wouldn't be coming back here. Not when… I can't even let myself think about it. *Not when he saw you and Oliver kissing, seconds ago.*

Levi won't know that Ollie kissed *me*, and not the other way around. It's too mortifying to consider.

So I come up with the only explanation that makes any sense: it's not him. This must be another Duplicate, like the ones who came to campus to impersonate Tessa, Archer, and Jake. But I know in my heart that's not the case, because the look on his face, on *Levi's* face—it's the look of a boy who saw me kissing someone else.

I force words to form in my throat. "Levi," I say quietly. "You're—are you back?"

"It would appear that way, wouldn't it?" he finally answers. Now I'm even more sure that it's him. Only one person sounds like that, like Levi, and he's here, on the grass, standing right in front of me. Looking like the Levi I've longed for since I left him last April. Looking every bit like himself—but wearier. Battle-scarred. My mind flashes with all that he must have suffered there, at the hands of Gravelle, and an ache begins to fill my chest that nearly bowls me over. Levi's standing there with his hands deep in his pockets, a slouchy sweater draped over his torso. He looks so...uncertain. The only thing I know for sure is that his eyes are focused on mine like some kind of direct link, and the rest of the world has vanished, and it's just him and me.

"You're safe." I breathe out, never feeling more relieved in my life to see him standing here, his face and body unscathed. "But Gravelle," I choke out. "He called me. He said—"

"Things change." He shrugs. There's a double meaning to his words, and I know he's referring to Ollie. To what he witnessed between us. *That kiss. Oh my god, that kiss.*

"You're here, man. Welcome back," says a voice that's outside of the two of us, infiltrating this moment we're having. It's Ollie. He's striding over to Levi, fist-bumping and then pulling him into a stiff, but brotherly, hug.

"Thanks," Levi says, hugging back and offering Ollie a smile. It doesn't reach his eyes, and I know why. He's as confused and torn and conflicted as I am.

For a minute, the three of us stand there, awkwardly. I'm

sure Ollie doesn't know what to say, and I certainly don't. No way are any of us going to talk about what just happened. I can barely process it myself. The last thing I ever imagined was Levi, returning here, *now*.

I'm brimming with questions, but I don't ask them. I don't know where to begin. All I know is that I can't run into Levi's arms, even though it's what I've been dreaming about, and hoping for, all these months. Because of what just happened with Ollie, and because I have no idea where Levi and I stand. I've heard nothing from him in months. For all I know, Gravelle was telling the truth, and Levi doesn't want me. Not in the way I want him.

"Levi?" says a voice behind me. I turn, startled out of my thoughts, to see Maude standing there. Next to her are Pippa and Pru. And the others—Jago, Ansel, and Theodora—are a few paces behind.

Levi makes eye contact with Maude, standing there like he is with his hands still firmly in his pockets. He looks like he always does. Stoic. Maybe I'm the only one who can see that under the surface, there's more than meets the eye. He doesn't breathe a word to Maude. But then, after a moment, a smile breaks over his face, and she runs to him, throwing her arms around him and holding him like a lifeline. The other Similars follow, one by one at first, and then in a group, shouting, angling to get in a hug with him. Pippa's outwardly crying, and Levi's laughing, teasing her for missing him so much.

"After all this time, Pip," he says, his face looking considerably lighter than it did five minutes ago, "I didn't know you cared." I realize with a pang in my gut that this was the first time any of them had been separated from one another, for their entire lives. No wonder this reunion is so joyous and full of life, if bittersweet. I hug my arms to my chest, trying to harness some of that happiness myself. But my eyes can't help but flutter to Ollie's face. If he's feeling anything besides happy to see Levi, he doesn't show it. But I wonder: *How does he feel, really, about Levi's return?*

Everyone has questions for Levi. Everyone but me. Sure, I want to know it all too. How he got here. Why. If Gravelle let him go. But there's only one question I really want to ask, and it's the one question I can't: *Did you come back for me?*

As I watch the Similars pepper Levi with questions about whether Gravelle hurt him, and when he left the island, and how he got here, I feel like an onlooker to a private moment, one I'm witnessing but not central to. Some of the Similars even ask questions in Portuguese. Levi answers in English, though, so I get the gist of what they're talking about, even though I don't catch every detail. All the while, there's that pull to Levi—that thread—that feels like it's only ours. He doesn't look at me now, or direct any of his conversation to me, but I feel like we're both hyperaware of each other, and of the fact we haven't hugged, or touched, or said anything to each other besides a few cursory words. I'm waiting until we have a chance to be alone. I wonder if he is too.

"You look exactly the same," Theodora's saying, her hand squeezing Levi's shoulder through his white T-shirt. Is it weird I feel instantly jealous of her, standing so close to him? Touching him?

"You look good to me, man, but I guess I'm biased," Ollie interjects, making us all laugh with that icebreaker.

"What did he make you do?" Pippa finally asks, and the group quiets down as we find seats on the grass. We're all hungry for information. We want to know what went down on Castor Island.

"Nothing any worse than usual." Levi shrugs. "There was training. And brainwashing. You know, normal senior year kind of stuff." He doesn't mention the injuries to his face. The black eye I saw in that photo. I don't bring it up, either.

"Why did he want to keep you there?" Jago asks. "Besides the obvious."

"You mean to torture him?" Maude cuts in. "And us?"

"I'm not really sure," Levi answers, his face a mask as he runs a hand through his brown hair, his gray eyes catching the light. "He's lonely. He's miserable. I think a part of him wanted me to share in that. Since he has no one else."

"Don't take this the wrong way, because we're beyond happy to see you," Theodora says, still not taking her eyes off Levi. "But why are you *here*? And why now? Emma said—" She stops abruptly, looking over at me as if to ask permission to keep talking. I nod, not letting myself look in Ollie's direction. "Emma said Gravelle called her. Told her that you wouldn't be coming back this year," Theodora continues. "That you were going to wait it out on Castor Island until after graduation."

Levi looks over at me. Our eyes meet for half a second, and in that moment, I feel every nerve ending in my body tingle and stand at attention. If I could make everyone around us vanish, so it could be only the two of us… It's all I want right now, all I can think about. Then he tears his eyes away from me to stare out at Dark Lake, and I feel an instant loss, a hollowing out of my chest, when he breaks our connection. "Gravelle wouldn't let me leave. Of course I wanted to. I'd never want to stay there with that man of my own free will. But then he changed his mind. Decided to send me back here."

I notice Maude shoot a look at Jago, who shrugs. Theodora squeezes Levi's hand, and Ollie and Pru hang back to the side, observing but not wanting to interfere. I'm sure they feel like I do—bystanders who don't really belong.

"What do you mean?" Pippa finally speaks up. "Gravelle *sent* you back here, to Darkwood? Or he let you go?"

Levi sighs. "Both, I guess. I'd been petitioning to leave the island for months. Entreating him every minute I saw him to let me go. I wanted out. Being there, in that desolate place—it didn't feel like my home anymore. It felt like a prison, in spite of all the memories I have of us there. I guess in retrospect, it was a pretty grim childhood, wasn't it?"

I feel my throat catching at these words, not only because it pains me to hear Levi talk about the Similars' upbringing this way, but also because now I know it's a childhood I only barely dodged. *You could have been there for sixteen years too.* For the first time, I consider that my own formative years after age three, spent with the father I always thought of as cool and distant, were not half bad.

"He put me through things," Levi says. "Mind control in the portal with those damn virtual reality simulations we all

161

hate. Daily exercises that were grueling, mentally and physically. On one particularly awful day, he tested how long I could stay underwater, to the point of me passing out."

"Levi," Theodora says, looking pained, but Levi shakes his head.

"All that stuff wasn't as bad as the loneliness. Being there without all of you," he adds. "That's what made it unbearable. Because before, we had each other."

I wonder if, in some small way, he's including me in that statement. Or only the Similars.

"One day, I woke up, went to breakfast, and Gravelle told me I could leave," Levi continues. "On one condition, of course."

Maude seems to know where this is going before Levi has to explain. "Why do I have a really bad feeling right now?" she asks.

Levi sighs. "Because you know what I'm about to say. Our guardian's nothing if not predictable, right?"

"Sorry, but I'm not following," says Pru.

"Our tasks," Ansel says, in his quiet, reserved way. "I bet we each have one."

"Twenty points to Ansel," Levi jokes, but his voice sounds far off and devoid of emotion. "He's not calling them tasks anymore. It's our 'Legacy Project.' And we all have the same one. Getting close—closer—to our DNA families."

I notice Theodora physically cringe at the news. The others don't look much better.

"I knew this was coming," Ansel says. "I tried to tell myself maybe he'd given up, but..."

"Gravelle, give up?" Levi answers, raising his voice for the first time since he got back here. "Gravelle, let go of his plan to ruin our DNA families once and for all?"

"So that's what he wants?" I ask. "To ruin them."

"He doesn't phrase it that way," Levi explains. "No, he says he's standing up for us. He claims that the Legacy Project is a way for us to demand our birthrights. Because *we* are the true legacies who should be walking these halls, not our originals. And we must ensure that our DNA families pay us the attention we were robbed of all those years—"

"That *he* robbed you of," Ollie interjects.

"Yes," Levi agrees. "He wants to make the families stand up and take notice. He says we did a decent job last year, putting Damian Leroy behind bars and transferring all that Ward, Inc. stock to me…"

"You mean, to *him*," I say.

Levi sighs. "Right."

"Sending Tessa's dad to prison was the worst thing I've ever done," Theodora says, her eyes growing wet with tears. "Maybe what I did was technically the right thing, but…"

"It was more than that, Thea," Pippa says, walking over to sit next to her. "You had an obligation, didn't you? Damian Leroy was committing fraud."

"Then why couldn't Gravelle have exposed him? I'm a teenager. It's not my job to turn in criminals."

"He couldn't do it because he's a coward." Levi shrugs. "I know he's hurt, and messed up, and a part of his soul is missing, and maybe that's not entirely his fault. But that doesn't change the fact that he's done unconscionable things. Or that he's using us to do his dirty work. He spins this as us claiming what's right-fully ours, but let's face it. He wants us to screw over our DNA families, once and for all."

We sit in silence. Maude looks like she's about to say some-thing, then thinks better of it. She stands and kicks at a rock, let-ting out a guttural scream of frustration. Jago jumps up, grabbing her arm and speaking softly to her. I can't hear what he says. All I know is that what Gravelle is asking my friends to do is despica-ble, and they must feel so trapped, and angry, and sickened by the idea of manipulating their DNA families once again.

"So what is it?" Ansel finally asks. "This 'Legacy Project'?" he asks with disdain. "What is it that our guardian wants us to do?"

"I don't have a lot of details," Levi answers. "He said to continue to forge relationships with our DNA families and our originals."

Pippa's brow furrows. "I'm already doing that, but not because I want to ruin your family, Pru!"

"Of course not," Pru answers her.

"What if we refuse?" Theodora says. We turn to look at her. "What if we simply won't do it?" She stares back at all of us, challenging her friends to come up with a good reason why they shouldn't simply say no and walk away from the Legacy Project before it's even begun. "When we first came here, and we had our tasks...we had nothing," she reminds us. "We were alone, and scared, and Gravelle was our only parent. Our only family. We trusted him implicitly because we had to. But now... Now, everything's changed, hasn't it? Pippa, you have Jaeger in your life. Ansel, you have the de Leons...your *dads*. And Levi..." She meets his gray eyes. "I know you'd rather die than hurt Jane and Booker again. We have seven more months till graduation. Then we'll all be eighteen. We don't have to do what our guardian wants anymore."

I consider Theodora's words. I watch the Similars; they, too, are letting her words marinate. Considering whether what she says makes sense. If there's some way out of this.

"Don't you think I've thought of that?" Levi asks. "Don't you think that was the first thing I said to him, when he told me about the Legacy Project? I explained that you'd never do it. That we all played his game last year because we knew nothing else; we *had* nothing and no one else!"

Levi clenches his hands into fists, and all I want to do is go to him and reach for him. The longing in my chest is so intense it's almost unbearable.

"I don't understand," says Maude. "What did Gravelle say when you told him that?"

"He said we have no choice, naturally," Levi answers, letting his fingers relax as he returns to his characteristically controlled demeanor. "He's right, of course. We *have* to complete our tasks. Because otherwise, he'll kill us."

"Hold on," says Maude, who walks right up to Levi and forces him to look at her. "Did he threaten that? Say he'd come after us? Send someone to gun us down, right here on campus? Does he even think that would *work*—"

"Have you forgotten who you're dealing with? Gravelle would never do something as plebeian as shooting us." Levi looks beyond emotion now. Aloof and hard as stone.

165

"Then *what*?" Oliver asks, his voice tinged with pain.

"He made sure he would always have a fail-safe way of killing us off," Levi explains. "Even from afar. He programmed our genes eighteen years ago, before we were born, with Seymour's help, of course. Added certain characteristics, took others away. Tweaked us to perfection, I suppose you could say."

"And?" Pippa implores him.

"And one of those tweaks was to insert a stealth virus into our DNA. It's been lying dormant in our genes for our entire lives. At any moment, Gravelle can choose to activate it. Which means that whenever he feels like it—if we haven't performed to his liking—he can terminate us. Instantly."

STEALTH VIRUS

"DON'T YOU SEE?" Levi keeps talking. It's clear that Levi's been living with this information for a while now, and we're all scrambling to catch up. "Gravelle wasn't stupid enough to create us without some kind of an *out*. The stealth virus allows him to exert control over us, even when we're not with him. Wherever we live, wherever we go, we can't escape it. That's the beauty of it, after all," Levi quips. "All this time we thought moving to England would be some kind of escape for us. An opportunity to start over, fresh, and leave our bleak childhood behind. What idiots we were, thinking we'd outsmart Gravelle. He's been one step ahead of us since before we were even born."

"Would he really do it?" Pippa asks. "He's been reminding us for years that he's our only family. That he'll always love us more than our DNA families do. That he knew we'd always return to him because, eventually, we'd see how cruel the real world is."

"Joke's on us, I guess." Levi shrugs. "I think he'd do it, sure. I don't think he wants to. He was hoping we'd come here last year and find a world so hardened and bitter toward us that we'd run straight back to Castor Island begging for our old lives back."

"But that's not what happened," I say.

"No." Levi finally meets my eyes again, this time lingering on them long enough for my stomach to flutter. "So now he's falling back on plan B. The back-up plan he probably doesn't want to have to use."

"So maybe he won't," Maude says, inserting some cool logic into the conversation. "He could be bluffing. He's got the upper hand, of course, because we have no way of proving that this stealth virus isn't real."

"But he also has no way of proving that it *is*, does he?" I ask. "Why should we even believe him?"

"Because," answers Levi. "You've already seen the stealth virus at work. And though I wasn't here for it, I'm quite sure it wasn't pretty."

"What are you talking about?" Jago asks.

It hits me with the force of a truck. "Ransom," I say softly. "It was the stealth virus that nearly killed him. Wasn't it?"

Levi meets my eyes again, and this time, as I notice the rush I get from his gaze, I also think I see approval written there. "Exactly."

Maude stops her pacing to stare at Levi. "You're saying

that when Headmaster Ransom injected our plasma into his system…"

"Plasma containing DNA that was tweaked by Gravelle eighteen years ago," Pru adds.

"He was also injecting the dormant virus?" Maude pauses, looking at Levi for confirmation.

"More or less, yes," Levi says. "When Ransom injected our plasma, the stealth virus went into his system too. Gravelle was expecting this to happen. Obviously he knew about Ransom's plan; after all, he signed off on the 'research' and signed the waiver himself. He must have had someone on the ground to confirm that Ransom had gone through with it, because then he activated the code to trigger the virus."

"But if the virus was built specifically to react in *our* bodies…" Maude says, trying to work it out.

"How did it also take out Ransom?" Levi finishes her thought. "The quick answer is that the reaction Ransom had wouldn't manifest itself in the same way for us, not exactly. Still, you had a front-row seat to all the evidence you need that Gravelle is not playing around. The stealth virus exists. Ransom's collapse proved it."

"So this is why Gravelle didn't interfere with Ransom's experiments," I conclude. It's all making sense now.

"I couldn't get him to admit it outright," Levi answers me. "But yes, I believe he *wanted* Ransom to exploit us for that plasma cocktail, so that eventually Ransom would inject it into himself and show us all how big a threat the virus really is. How deadly," he adds.

There's silence as that sinks in. If the Similars refuse to act on their new task, they risk their own lives. But if they do what Gravelle wants, who knows what they'll end up doing to hurt their DNA families?

"How did you find out about this?" Pru asks Levi. "The stealth virus…and what happened to Ransom?"

"I had a lot of time on the island to do my own research," Levi explains. "Including convincing the guards to give me Wi-Fi access. It wasn't easy, but little by little, I gained enough information to put the pieces together. When I saw on the Darkwood feeds that Ransom had collapsed, I began to construct my own theory as to why. Gravelle all but confirmed it, when I finally confronted him."

"Why'd he let you come back?" Theodora asks.

Levi shrugs, stuffing his hands deep in his pockets. "To drop the hammer. And deliver a warning that if you try to interfere with his plan…" He pauses for a beat. "We're all, for lack of a better word, toast."

"If he needs us, really truly *needs* us," Pippa says, "he wouldn't dare kill us. Maybe it's an empty threat."

"I don't know, Pip," Levi says thoughtfully. "He might kill us out of spite. I think he's more twisted than ever. He's angry at us. Deeply disappointed that we've turned on him. He'd convinced himself that we'd come running back to Castor Island at the end of last year. He thinks we don't appreciate all he's done for us."

"You mean creating us for his own sick agenda, keeping us isolated on a remote island for sixteen years, and then sticking us in a boarding school with our originals, knowing most of them would despise us?" Maude snaps. "Yeah, he's been stellar."

"I still don't understand what he wants us to do," Ansel pipes up. "Get even closer to our DNA families? I'm already as close to Archer as I'll probably ever be. I interned with my DNA dads over the summer. What more does Gravelle want from us?"

"May I make a suggestion?" Levi responds.

"Yes?" Maude answers, her voice sounding edgy, like she's ready for a fight.

"Can we get dinner?" Levi asks, the trace of a smile playing on his lips. "I haven't eaten since I left that godforsaken place."

Maude stares at him for a moment, then lightly punches his arm. The others laugh; we're glad Levi's broken the tension and relieved to have some sense of normalcy injected into what is most definitely *not* a normal conversation.

We stand up and brush off the grass clinging to our clothes.

My heart's hammering so loudly, I can barely focus on anything. All I know is that Ollie and I kissed—whether it was my idea or not—and Levi saw it, and the thought of facing *either* of them right now is terrifying. As long as we were all together on the grassy lawn, I was safe. Safe from having to confront the fact that Levi saw me and Ollie kissing. Safe from having to face Ollie, when I have no clue why I didn't immediately push him away. Why it took seconds, maybe minutes, for me to realize what I was doing. In spite of all this, I'm so relieved Levi's back safe and sound that it's torture for me not moving right up to him and going into his arms.

As we make our way up the hill in the fading light, Pru comes up next to me and grabs my elbow. There's no way she knows what has just transpired. But maybe she senses how fraught with emotion I am, because she's gripping my arm like a vise.

"You okay?" she whispers.

"Absolutely not," I answer without meeting her eyes.

"Deep, calming breaths. Imagine you are a flower, opening and closing in the sunlight." I can't help but crack up. Pru knows good and well the meditation exercises my father's psychiatrist gave me two summers ago never worked for me.

"Thanks. I'll work on my inner daisy." But my smile fades when I see Levi trekking up the hill with Ollie at his side. I stop walking, and Pru stops with me. She must instantly know what's bothering me, because she urges me forward.

"It was weird seeing me and Pippa together too," she reminds me. "But you got used to it."

I don't tell her that, for reasons I can't explain, I will never, ever get used to this.

I still haven't spoken to Levi alone. And Ollie must have noticed I haven't made eye contact with him, but maybe he's too busy catching up with his DNA replica to care. Ollie, for his part, looks really relieved Levi's okay.

Jane finds us at dinner. She informs us that the graffiti has been scoured off the Similars' doors. "I'm writing a response to that unacceptable blog post," she reassures us. "Which will be required reading for the entire sch—"

She doesn't finish her sentence, because her eyes have landed on her son. Who is sitting right next to Levi. She hasn't seen Levi since the dedication ceremony last year, when he betrayed her and walked away with that Ward, Inc. stock. I feel an ache on Levi's behalf, hoping she can find it in herself to forgive him, once and for all, for what transpired.

"Levi," she says quietly. "I didn't realize you'd returned to school."

Levi meets her eyes, his own gray ones steady, and nods. "I got back today. Gravelle, I mean, my guardian, was hoping I'd be able to enroll midterm."

"I'm sure that won't be a problem," Jane answers distractedly. I can tell she doesn't know what to make of this. "I don't know if your friends told you, but—"

"Mom's the interim headmistress," Ollie pipes up. "Which is the best thing that's ever happened to me. Because every guy wants his mom trailing him for three-quarters of his senior year." He pops a tater tot in his mouth, giving Jane a little salute. I know what he's doing, trying to lighten this tense moment. It works—sort of.

"I'm afraid I have a million things to do," Jane says briskly. "But I'll loop back in with you tomorrow, Levi... Oh, dear. We don't have a room ready for you."

"He'll stay with me," Jago offers. "Would have been my roommate, anyway. Can't he take his old bed back?"

"Er, yes. Great idea," Jane says, staring at Jago like she still can't put all this together. "Goodnight, all," she adds before tightening her sweater around her and slipping out.

"That went surprisingly well," Levi mutters. The others don't respond; heavy on all of our minds is this latest development about the tasks, and, of course, the stealth virus.

I'm relieved when Pru gives me time alone in our room, to think. To try and process what happened today.

What was I doing kissing Ollie like that? I've never thought of him that way; for weeks, I've been panicking that he'd confess his feelings and I'd have to turn him down.

But today, when we were standing there in the late-afternoon chill, and he was telling me how much he blames himself for everything that's happened... And his lips collided with my own...

I felt something. Something *different* and new and, frankly, terrifying. It was like Ollie wasn't exactly the boy I've loved as a friend all these years, but something, *someone*, else. Someone kind and generous, who feels everything. Someone who takes all the burdens of the world and makes them his own.

And yes. Someone *hot*.

I'd never seen him that way before. He was always just Ollie. But in that moment...

I cringe, thinking of Levi, and how he watched us, and how mortified I am. How I might never be able to talk to him again, because I have no idea what I'd say for myself. *I've missed you for months, with an ache like a gaping wound? But then when Ollie kissed me, I changed my tune so fast, I probably gave myself whiplash?*

I don't even know what to think. I've likely ruined everything. What Levi and I had...and my friendship with Ollie... Because things can't stay the way they are. Inevitably, what I've done is going to hurt people. Myself included.

We convene in the Tower Room later that night to discuss the Legacy Project, and what Gravelle could possibly want from all of them. I'm a ball of nerves when I settle into a chair between

Pru and Maude, deliberately avoiding Ollie and Levi. When my eyes land involuntarily on Levi across the room, I feel that flip in my stomach again and strike up a conversation with Pru to distract myself. It doesn't work; I still feel him there, and I wonder with every passing second whether or not he notices *me*.

My friends throw out theories—what Gravelle could be setting up this year to destroy their DNA families. They're sure that whatever it is, he's using the Similars, once again, to do his dirty work. We talk for hours, but without reaching much of a conclusion. We're as confused as we were earlier. But one thing's clear. We all feel a sense of dread we can't overcome. Whatever Gravelle is going to make the Similars do, it's sure to be something awful.

I take my time leaving the Tower Room in hopes I can walk back to my dorm room alone. I still haven't processed what happened with Ollie. And Levi's return... It's too much for me to handle in the span of a few hours. I linger behind, the last one to leave the room—but when I step into the dimly lit spiral stairway, Levi's standing there, hands in his pockets. The shadowy light emphasizes his strong, broad shoulders. His face is a mask, like always.

I nearly keel over from the intensity of what I feel for him in that moment. Longing, because I've missed him more than I would have thought possible. Elation, because he's safe, and he's here. Anguish, because now, after everything that's transpired, I have no idea if he feels the same way about me.

"Levi, I... Earlier today. Me and Ollie—"

"Don't," he says softly. "You thought I wasn't coming back."

"I prayed you would. I hoped, I begged the universe."

"And then you moved on."

He says it so emotionlessly, so point-blank, I gasp for breath. *I didn't move on. That's not what happened!* I want to shout. But I don't, because even I don't understand it.

"I didn't come back here for you," Levi says. "I came back because I had a job to do. To issue Gravelle's warning. And because I would have done anything to get off that island. That's all."

I feel my eyes swimming with tears, and I clutch the banister of the staircase. How can I possibly explain to him how messed up things got, when I don't understand it myself?

He didn't come back here for me. There's no mistaking those words he said. And maybe he means them. Because maybe, just maybe, what we had wasn't what I thought it was. Or maybe the kiss with Ollie hurt him so much, he's saving face.

I mutter good night and hurry down the stairs, leaving him standing there in the half-light. It's one o'clock in the morning when I make it to my dorm room and collapse on my bed. Pru's already passed out on top of her covers, but I'm not even considering sleep. How could I?

Levi didn't come back here for me. He doesn't want to be with me. Does he mean it? *Could* he mean it?

I cry myself to sleep, getting only two fitful hours before I have to wake up for my classes in the morning. My agitated dreams are tangled landscapes featuring Ollie, Levi, my past, and the unknown of my future, all melting into one frightening Daliesque topography. When I wake the next morning and see the harsh light filtering in through the window, I can barely face myself in the mirror while brushing my teeth. What have I done?

I spend all my time on homework and helping Maude try to hack into Gravelle's server, so she can learn everything she can about the stealth virus. If there's a way to deactivate it, she's determined to find it. Alone in my room, where I'm hiding out these days, afraid to confront Ollie and afraid that facing Levi will feel like another blow to the chest, I gobble up articles on telepathy, wondering if that's the name of what I did, or what happened to me, when I read the thoughts of Harlowe, Ollie, and Ransom.

October passes into November. The air grows colder, and students drag their heaviest coats out of suitcases. I'm dismayed to see that anti-clone sentiments have only increased on campus since Harlowe's blog post was published. Students have petitioned Darkwood to investigate the Similars' extraordinary strength, and several parents have threatened to withdraw their kids if the school doesn't address and disprove the claims. Every time I see Jane, she's talking with a teacher or administrator, a deep furrow in her brow. I overhear her tell a parent that an investigation would be unfair and unlawful. The Similars are minors, and any salacious claims about their strength are pure conjecture. It's also none of the school's business.

Ollie and I have reverted back to our pre-kiss rapport, which is a giant relief to me for the most part. Not only because I don't know how I feel about what happened between us, but also because I'm afraid that any discussion about it would lead to one, or both, of us getting hurt. How can I possibly tell him that at least half of my heart belongs to Levi—even if Levi doesn't want it? Ollie seems happier these days, and I don't know if it's his mother's presence on campus, Levi's safe return, or the fact we did what we did. I try to be grateful for his change in mood without reading too much into it. *He's alive, and he's okay,* I remind myself. *That's what matters.* I know things are fine between us—for now, anyway—when he asks me to try out for the spring musical with him, and I give him a death stare. He laughs, assuring me that's one bucket-list item he never expected me to agree to.

I'm avoiding Levi. Since our brief meeting in the stairwell, we've only spoken in group settings, with the Similars and Pru as a buffer.

One early November day at lunch, we end up right next to each other at the long, rough-hewn dining table.

"Hi," I say quietly to him.

"Emma…"

"Yes?" I answer, heart in my throat.

"Can you pass the salt?" Levi asks, no expression on his face.

I hand the shaker to him, feeling like I'm dying inside. Is this how we're going to be from now on? Destined to only speak in the most perfunctory way?

It's Thanksgiving break, and Ollie and Jane get ready to leave for their college tour. Jane invites me, again, to accompany them, but I turn her down. Spending that much time alone with Ollie, even with his mom there, sounds like the worst idea possible. A small part of me longs to go with them and experience the kind of unconditional love that's absent from my own splintered relationship with my father. But what if we finally talked about that kiss? With all that time together, it would inevitably come up.

Or it might even happen again. I never would have thought that possible, but now, I can't even trust myself to know what I want. I love Levi—that isn't changing—but if he doesn't want to be with me, is there some part of my heart that could open up for Ollie?

No. You'll only end up hurting him, and yourself.

I can't risk that. Because even I don't understand my own fragile feelings. How Ollie suddenly seems like someone I could *fall for*...someone I could have loved...if we hadn't been best friends since forever...if it weren't for Levi.

Pru and Pippa head to Jaeger's farm to spend the holiday with him. It'll be their first Thanksgiving without Pru's mom, and before Pru leaves for her train, I hug her tighter than I have in a long time, reminding her to be kind to herself. I'm nothing if not well trained in the stages of grief. Losing Ollie was not the same as losing a parent, but it taught me some things about survival, so I think I understand a small fraction of what Pru's experiencing. Meanwhile, Ansel makes a quick trip back to Los Angeles to meet up with the de Leons, and Jago takes the train to stay with the Choates, but the rest of the Similars—Maude, Levi, and Theodora—remain on campus, without homes to return to, or invitations to Thanksgiving dinner.

With Pru gone, I'm alone in my room after dinner when I get a holo-call on my plum from an unknown number.

I tense up, fearing it's who I think it is.

"Hello?" I brace myself.

A hologram pops up across from my bed, a strange hybrid between two- and three-dimensional.

It's exactly who I expected, and dreaded. Augustus Gravelle.

EDEN

I HAVEN'T SEEN his face since the start of school, when he called me to warn me against contacting Levi. He's the *last* person I want to see, ever again.

"Hello, Eden." I'm not afraid in the immediate sense; this floating image of Gravelle is an eerie likeness of the real man, but it appears hollow, and I'm sure if I tried, I could swipe my hand right through him. Still, I fear whatever it is he's called me about.

"What do you want?" I refuse to give Gravelle the courtesy of a proper greeting. He doesn't deserve one.

"Your manners seem to have deteriorated since you visited me last April," Gravelle tuts. "But no matter. They weren't all that impressive to begin with."

I scowl. This is the man who led me to believe Ollie was dead for nearly a year. Who is forcing the Similars to go along with his Legacy Project. Who killed that clone of Oliver two summers ago. I consider hanging up on him, but he stops me before I can.

"Let's get down to brass tacks, Eden. You, my dear, are a Similar."

"Your point?" I snarl.

"You *have* accepted it, haven't you? That you were raised, until the age of three, on my island? And your mental agility…" The smile slips from his face, and even though it's made entirely of light, something about the way his expression changes feels entirely real—and troubling. "I suspected last year," he goes on. "When you were able to exit my virtual reality portal so quickly. I'd never seen anything like it. Tell me, Eden. How have your capabilities progressed? Have you mastered the brain-to-brain communication skills that were programmed into your genes before you were even born?"

So he knows. I stand up abruptly, positioning myself in front of my closed door. I know he's only a hologram and he can't hurt me, and yet, my instinct is to prepare myself to flee.

"Perhaps it all still seems a little surreal?" Gravelle prods. "I thought you might feel that way. I suppose a little context might help you, Eden. Your father may never have felt the need to tell you the truth, but I do. He endured great pain at Emma's death. But you—you were always meant to be his salvation. Another chance at being a parent. This news shouldn't distress you, Eden. It should bring you joy, to know how wanted you were. How needed. *I* provided that, for my oldest friend. It was the least I could do for the roommate who was kind to me from the first day I ever set foot on Darkwood's campus."

I've had enough of this emotional manipulation. "What do you want?" I snap. "To torture me, like you're doing to the others? To remind me you can terminate me with your stealth virus, at any moment? I already know all that."

"It's important to me that you fully accept who you are," Gravelle purrs.

"Do I have a choice?"

"We all have choices, Eden. We make them every single day of our lives. I hope you choose to appreciate all I've done for you. Sending you Levi. Returning *both* my sons to your life—"

I can't take this any longer. This man is so sick. So twisted.

I end the call. I don't care if that means I've angered him. He may control my fate from afar with that virus, but I won't let him get the last word.

I collapse onto my bed, shaking in spite of myself. I bundle my covers around me, trying to tame my wildly beating heart.

You hung up on Gravelle.

What if he takes it out on me? Or worse—on my friends?

All I want to do is talk to Levi. He would understand. He would make this okay.

And yet, he all but said he didn't want to be with me.

Still, he's the one person I want to confide in, more than anyone else on the planet. Ever since that night I leaped from Harlowe's car, it was Levi who I wanted to tell that I'm a Similar. It's not that I don't think Oliver would understand; after all, his own discovery that Gravelle is his biological father has rocked him to his core. In a way, he might relate more than anyone. But I worry it would forge an insidious gap between us. That somehow it might cast our childhood—the shared history we based our whole friendship on—in a different light. After all, it changes everything between me and my father. He lied to me for years. Plus, I hate to bring Ollie any more pain when it comes to Gravelle. He already feels so tortured about the fact he's related to that man.

Before I can think rationally about what I'm doing, I'm running out of my room, down the darkened path to Dark Lake. It's freezing out, and I haven't bothered to grab my coat. I pull my sweater tight around my body, welcoming the harsh Vermont chill in my bones. At least the cold makes me feel alive, and not like a ghost of a person—Eden Gravelle—who doesn't even know who she is.

I stop in my tracks when I reach the shore of Dark Lake. There, in the moonlight, is Levi, flying through the air in one of his martial arts moves. I don't stop to worry that he might see me here, watching him. I stare, entranced, as he flings himself into the ether with an acrobatic somersault-like movement that takes my breath away. I haven't seen him manipulate his body like that in so long. I've missed it—his skill, his agility, his raw strength.

When the move reaches its conclusion, and he lands on the grass, it's as if what he did was nothing. He shoves his hands in his pockets and turns to walk back up to the school. He sees me then, and I instantly regret my decision not to turn around and leave when I first saw him here. Because now, the thing I want with every fiber of my being, but also don't want at all, because it's too hard and complicated, is happening. It's me and Levi, here, alone.

Levi surveys me for a beat, not moving, his hands still nonchalantly buried in his pockets. I don't say a word, or breathe, or even move. Like a deer in headlights, I can't make my brain force my feet to walk even an inch. I feel rooted to the spot, like an old oak tree. Anchored.

"Hey," he says quietly, not sounding angry. I let out a breath of air. I'm relieved he's not mad at me for sneaking up on him.

"I wasn't—"

"It's okay," he says, his words overlapping mine. The air is fraught between us, and this feels awkward and wrong. Like we're two people who barely know each other. Or two people who know each other so well, they both silently acknowledge how much they want to say to each other, but can't.

But *why* can't we? Because of my kiss with Ollie? I feel hot tears springing up in my eyes, and I brush them away. But I'm not embarrassed or ashamed.

"Looks like you kept it up, on the island," I say, referring to his martial arts.

"Practiced every day." Levi shrugs. "It's not like I had much else to do, besides study."

I take a step toward him, bridging the distance between us by a few inches. He's close enough now that I could reach out my hand and touch his cheek if I wanted to. It's all I can do not to close the gap between his body and mine, pulling him into my orbit. It would only take a second.

"I know you said you didn't come back here for me," I breathe.

"Emma—"

"Actually, it's Eden," I say so quietly, I don't know if he can hear me. "Not Emma."

His gray eyes glow in the moonlight. "What do you mean, you're not Emma?"

"Gravelle called me today. An hour ago."

Levi stares at me, and something like comprehension dawns on his face, but I can't be sure if he's following what I'm saying or not. I forge ahead. I have to do this, have to say this *now*. I've waited so long. Too long.

"He called me to explain who I really am. Which I already knew, but—" I stop myself. Those details don't matter right now, the *how* and the *why*. I have to get this out before I crack. "My real name isn't Emmaline Chance. It's Eden Gravelle. Levi, I'm a clone. A *Similar*. I'm one of you."

PAST AND FUTURE

"THERE WAS A letter," I explain. "When I left Castor Island last April. When I left *you* there," I add, reliving that moment of misery as I stare into Levi's warm, piercing eyes and again feel the ache of that boat ride back to the mainland, without *him*. "It was from him. Gravelle. It said that the original Emma died when she was three, and that Gravelle, with Seymour's help, had created me as a replacement for her. So that once she was gone, my father would not be childless. He would have a new 'Emma' to replace the one he lost. I knew I was sick," I barrel on. "As a very young child—a baby, even—I had leukemia. It's why my mother—" I stop, for some reason having a hard time saying this next part. "It's why she killed herself." I force myself to say the words. They're true, aren't they? There's no denying them.

"For my whole life, my father told me that experimental treatments in Sweden saved my life. That he flew me there against the doctors' orders and found a miracle. But now I know that was all a lie. The original Emma *did* die. I took her place," I add, in case there's any confusion. I barely notice that my cheeks are wet from the tears that stream down them, unabated. "I never thought of it until now. What that little girl—what I—went through. Being taken from her home—with you—and delivered to some crazy upside-down world where she was supposed to stand in for a dead girl." I realize, now, that I'm shaking. Full-on trembling, but not because of the freezing cold air. It's because I haven't processed it. I knew I was a Similar already. But I never considered what it meant for *her*. That little girl. All I could think about was how this affected me *now*. But that girl, back then…

It was so unfair, what Gravelle did to her. Snatching her from the only life she knew, with the other Similars on Castor Island, to become someone else's stand-in. And even though growing up with my father was the normal childhood I was lucky enough to get…

"It was wrong," I gasp. "And it's the reason my father's never loved me. Probably because I could never love him, not knowing… Not knowing he loved this other girl, this first girl, more. I was only three, but I knew even then, didn't I?"

Before I know what's happening, I'm in Levi's arms. The warmth of his lean, muscled body is enveloping me, pulling me toward him, and even though I am distraught and so deeply,

deeply sad for that little girl...for me...for *all* the Similars...the comfort of Levi's touch is like a jolt of electricity to my system.

His lips mash into mine. We kiss, in the rough, intense, and raw way I remember. Not sweet and gentle like my kiss with Ollie, but hard, the kiss of two people who know they belong together, but maybe for all the wrong reasons. This doesn't feel like some kind of pity on his part. It feels like we've never done or said anything before this that was even a fraction as real as what we're doing now. His hands roam my body with a force and ferocity that lifts me out of everything I've just confessed and fills me with only one thing: need. All I can think as I sink deeper into him, my body outlining his, is that this is what I was waiting for. This is right.

The kiss breaks, and Levi's eyes stay on mine. He brushes the tangle of hair off my forehead.

"He told me my name is Eden," I say, not letting go of Levi's torso as I dig one hand into the hem of his shirt and twist it, wanting to anchor myself to him. To make myself a permanent Levi fixture, so that this moment never has to end. "I didn't believe him, not at first. I thought it was all another lie. A trick. But then..."

"Then what?" Levi asks me, tracing his finger down my cheek in a gesture so tender it makes goose bumps stand up on my arms.

"Then I jumped out of a moving car. And...off of the boat-house roof," I mumble, not wanting him to reprimand me the way Ollie did. Ollie... *Ollie*. "Levi, what you saw. Between me and Ollie. I have to explain."

"No, you don't," he says, his hands framing my face. "I was gone. Gravelle told you I was never coming back. I wanted you to be with him; it's what I would have said if I could've gotten a single message to you."

"But that wasn't... I could never..." I stammer. "You have to understand. Ollie and I, we've always loved each other. Since the third grade, he's been my person."

"Your chlorophyll," Levi supplies, but with no edge to his voice. I can't believe he remembered that.

"Yes," I breathe, still not letting go of his shirt. I twist my fingers deeper into the fabric, fearing this closeness between us will disappear into the void like it never happened. "I never, ever thought I'd get him back."

"But you did," Levi answers, his eyes suddenly looking distant and aloof. *No*, I want to cry out. *Don't do that. Don't shut me out.*

"I did, and having him back in my life has been, well, it's a freaking miracle, isn't it?" But now there's a bitterness to my voice. Because if Gravelle had never taken Ollie in the first place, I never would have had to get him back. "But leaving you tore me up inside. And Ollie, he's broken now too. Maybe not as broken as you and me. But in his own way. Gravelle is his father, his biological one. He thinks that makes him a monster." I turn and wipe my tears away as I sink into Levi's embrace, resting the back of my head on his chest as his arms encircle me. He traces his fingers up and down my arm. All I want to do is sink into this moment, but I have to finish this. I have to say it.

"But I don't love him, not like I... Not like *this*," I say, my voice catching. "Every night you were gone, my body missed you. And now…" I turn to look at him, because I need to say this to his face. "Now I'm *one* of you, don't you see? I can't go back, not now that I know what I am. Who I am… Levi?" I ask, searching his eyes, willing him to say something.

"Emma, I… I know you're a Similar," he says, that distant look still in his eyes.

"A-plus for your listening skills?" I snap. I've just told him the biggest secret of my life, and his reaction is no reaction at all?

"Look, Emma, you don't understand." He lets go of me, pulling away to pace the grass. "I know you're a Similar because Gravelle told me before I came to school," he says softly, his hands back in his pockets, his shoulders slumped. "Before our *junior* year," he clarifies. "I've always known."

I can't comprehend what he's saying to me. What does he mean, *he's always known?*

"It's why I tried to stay away from you for much of last year," Levi explains. "Not the only reason. I really did worry that if we were ever close, if we were ever an 'us,' you wouldn't be able to love me for me. Or separate me from Ollie's memory. But I also wanted more for you. A normal life. One where you could be secure in your father's love, and not plagued by everything my friends and I live with, every day. I hoped that you'd be the one Similar to get away. To have a chance at all the things we'll never have."

"I don't…" I trail off, not even able to form words. "You knew I was a clone and you never told me?" I feel divorced from the words as they come out of my mouth, like they've been spoken by an entirely different person altogether. Maybe they have; after all, they are Eden's words, not Emma's.

Levi nods, still slumping like the weight of the planet is pressing down on him. "It's another reason I fell for you, you know. Besides the fact that you're irreverent and brilliant and a total pain in my arse. Emma, if one minute element of your life had been different, if our guardian *hadn't* sent you to replace the original Emma, we would have grown up together. Been on the exact same path. We would have understood each other the way the other Similars and I do." He pauses for a beat to squint at the horizon, and I wonder what he's looking for, but really, I'm too stunned to care. Finally, Levi turns to face me again. "Knowing that potential was inside you, but that you had *lived*, beyond the limited childhood we experienced. That you had the kind of life we never would… It made you the single most intriguing person on the planet to me."

I hear what he's saying, and in some corner of my mind, I'm processing it. Why he was so reluctant to be close to me last year, and yet, why he seemed to gravitate toward me, in his own way. It's another wrinkle, another piece of the complex puzzle that I wasn't privy to, but that makes complete sense. *Levi knew you were one of them. It's why he fell in love with you—and why he tried to push you away.*

"The others didn't know? Maude, Thea, Ansel, Jago? Pippa?" I whisper. I can't bear the idea that they all kept this from me. "Why would Gravelle tell you and not them?"

"We all had training on the island," he explains. "We studied our DNA families. Our originals," he says, bitterness in his voice. "In my one-on-one sessions with my guardian, he told me about your history. He said it was important that I know, so I could understand Ollie, since the two of you were so close. At the time, I couldn't fathom why I was learning this—any of it— but so little made sense to me then, I accepted it, like I accepted most everything he told me. Now I see that this was all part of Gravelle's plan to torture us. To drive rifts between us and our originals, so that we'd eventually come back to him, convinced our DNA families would never love us. I think, somehow, Gravelle knew how I'd end up feeling about you."

I take this in, processing the facts, but not what they mean. I can't; it's too monumental. "Is this why you didn't communicate with me all summer? Because you were afraid to have this conversation? Afraid to confront the secret you'd been keeping from me all this time?" I whisper, my voice nearly void of emotion. "Or did you try to reach me, and Gravelle stopped you?"

The air between us is thick with anticipation. I can feel it, a living, breathing thing.

When Levi finally answers, his voice is strained. "I wanted to spare you. I wanted you to have this year with Ollie. The way you should have all along."

"But that's not your decision!" I erupt. "You *lied* to me. For the entire time we've known each other." I'm shaking, and the reality of what he's done is finally settling in my bones. "Just like my father did. I bet he did it to 'protect' me too!" I wheel on him, and I can't remember a time when I felt so red hot, like I might explode. I feel betrayed, by the one person I trusted the most.

"I knew you'd be angry," Levi says. "I'll understand if you…

If you and Ollie…" He shrugs, not finishing the sentence, but I know what he means. *If you and Ollie want to be together.*

"You're the only person who knows," I say, resignation flooding over me. "The person I chose to tell. I confided in you. Not Ollie. He can't know."

Levi nods. "Of course—"

But he doesn't get to finish his thought, because I'm already gone. Gunning it back to campus, tripping through my tears, leaving Levi standing there alone on the desolate shore.

THE CASE FOR CLONES

I HAVE NEVER felt more relieved to have a mountain of college applications to finish. It's December 1 already. I only have a month to narrow down my list of schools and complete my personal statements. I need to throw my energy into something productive. Something besides Levi.

He lied to me. He *has* lied to me, the whole time I've known him. I don't know how, or if, I'll ever trust him again.

I've submitted my Oxford application—it was due earlier than the rest, in October—and I'm still attracted to the idea of leaving the United States entirely and getting as far from California, and my dad, as I can. But I know, now, how naive I was to fantasize about Levi and myself being at Oxford together. He and I aren't anything to each other, not anymore.

I feel the loss of him acutely. Knowing he lied to me all last year, even by omission, makes me feel like I never really knew him. Logically, I understand why he made the choice he did. He felt like it wasn't his place to tell me what he knew. Maybe he questioned whether it was even the truth. But still. We were *close*. So close it's hard to imagine how he wasn't tempted to tell me everything.

At least I haven't lost Ollie. He doesn't ask what we mean to each other, or bring up that kiss, and I'm grateful. He remains steadfast, in spite of everything that's happened this year. Thank God. Because if I lost him too—again—I don't know what I'd do.

The threats against the Similars haven't stopped. More nasty notes are left in their bags. Someone scrawls a hateful message on the whiteboard before English class, and another "op-ed" appears in *The Daily Darkwood*, on the day everyone returns from Thanksgiving break. It asserts that the Similars are dangerous and that Darkwood should strongly consider whether they belong here. I burn inside, at the hatred exhibited by my fellow students, and at the knowledge that I, too, am included in that statement.

With Ransom's return nowhere in sight, Jane's tenure as headmistress continues, and I stop by her office one Saturday after the break, hoping her familiar face can offer me some comfort. As a kid, I always loved seeing her, imagining she were my real mother. I know it's childish, but I need her right now. I knock on her office door. It's ajar, and when I don't get a response, I push it open.

"Jane?" I ask on my way in. She's at her desk, head in her hands. "Oh. I'm sorry, I'll come back—"

"No, Emmaline, please," she says, looking up from the scattered piles of papers in front of her. Dark shadows ring her eyes. "Sit." She gestures at the couch in the corner, where I curl up with a blanket. I'd never sit this way, so casually, were this still Ransom's office.

"Am I interrupting something?" I hug my knees to my chest.

"Just a woman at a loss for how to manage a single one of her headmistress duties." She smiles wanly. "But other than that, no."

"Are things that bad?"

"Oh, no. Worse." She sighs. "Emma, there is absolutely no way I can do my job here. Which is to protect the Similars," she adds. "I don't take that lightly, you know. As the head of this school, even as interim head, I must protect their privacy and their civil rights. I'm failing at both."

"The laws keep changing, don't they." I've seen enough on the feeds to know there's a new protest every day from anti-clone factions who don't believe clones should be allowed citizenship. Who believe they should all be ejected from the country. "But where are they supposed to go?" I ask, feeling desperate. "Most clones were born here, even if they weren't conceived on U.S. soil. And the Similars—they can't go back to him, Jane. They can't."

The thin smile on her face becomes a line as she sets her pen down and settles back in her chair. "I know they can't. Don't think I don't know everything that man is capable of. I was married to him."

"You know it wasn't his idea to do it, don't you?" The words tumble out of my mouth. "Levi, I mean. He didn't want to swindle you out of that stock last year. He couldn't care less about the money. Or controlling your family's company. He never would have wanted to become a part of your lives by tricking you. That's not who he is. Gravelle *made* him do it. He had no choice."

I take in a breath, unsure if I should go on.

"Gravelle put them through so much. Growing up isolated like they did," I add, when she doesn't respond. "They had nothing. Can you imagine? Him, as your only parent? And he never let them in. Never showed them the kind of unconditional love every child needs to thrive. That's why I don't blame Levi for the decisions he made last year."

Jane rubs her temples, and I can see she's considering what I'm telling her. She spreads her hands out over the desk, turning her wedding ring around on her finger. "I've tried, Emma. I thought after I got Oliver back, *especially* then…" she says. "I thought I'd easily forgive Levi. Snap my fingers and welcome him into the family. But it's not so simple," she explains.

I wish I could be a better person. That boy, he deserves a better mother figure than me. Because I'm not strong enough to forgive him, not after he—

It's happening again. I am hearing Jane's thoughts, like she's whispering them in my ear.

Oh god. Oh heavens, no…

"Jane?" I shoot up from my seat. Something's obviously wrong. "What is it?"

Jane's face falls as she looks down at an incoming buzz on her plum. "A clone was killed today. Two men attacked her on a subway platform in New York City. They chanted 'go home, clone' before stabbing her and running off. The men are still at large. I'm sorry, Emma, but—"

If anything happens to a single one of them, it will be on me...

"I'll go," I say quickly, heading to the door. As soon as I'm in the hallway, I bolt to the exit. I don't know what to be more scared of, my own ability to see into Jane's mind, or the fact a clone was killed...for being a clone.

When I find my friends in the dining hall, the feeds are already playing a news story about this brutal act. Jaeger Stanwick's been invited to speak as an expert, and he calls for legislation that would protect clones, not endanger them. The faces of my friends go rigid as they take in this news. Jago grabs Maude's hand. I want to search Levi's face, but I avoid looking in his direction. I can't right now. I'm not ready to face him.

"My dad's returning to the Quarry," Pru tells us, taking her eyes off the feeds. "He took a leave of absence, after my mom..." She looks at each one of us in turn. "The Quarry is ramping up its efforts. They say this is a full-blown crisis, and that the time is *now* to protect clones against this wave of bigotry. The hundred members and counting are dedicating themselves full time to the cause. Dad's forbidden me to join until I've graduated," she adds, scowling. "Apparently it was my mom's dying wish that I get a Darkwood diploma."

After lunch, Ollie and I walk back to our respective dorms. He's rehashing all the details of his college trip—telling me for the third or fourth time since he got back that NYU's film program is basically his whole reason for living. "You were right, Emma," he adds. "I can't go to USC just to stay close to my family. If I get into NYU...I'm going." I'm so happy to see the smile in his eyes. But my own mind's so far away. I *heard* his mother's thoughts. That's four people now: Harlowe, Ollie, Ransom, Jane. With a sense of dread, I wonder whose mind I'll see into next. The thought sends a shiver down my spine. We turn a corner and almost walk straight into Harlowe, who's handing out freshly printed DAAM flyers.

"Big rally coming up in March. There's still room for volunteers." She grins at me.

I snatch one of the flyers out of her hands, irate. I crumple the flyer in my fist, slamming my hand against the metal of the recycling bin as I try to discard it.

"Ow!" I gasp, clutching my throbbing hand. "That really hurt."

Ollie takes my hand and cups it gently between his own. "You didn't have to take it out on the poor, unsuspecting trash can, you know."

I will away the tears that spring to my eyes. Tears not just of pain, but for the Similars, and clones everywhere.

I want to tell him. Not just that I'm a Similar, but *everything*.

Am I doing the same thing to Ollie that Levi did to me? Lying by omission because I can't bring myself to tell him the information that could change everything between us?

Maybe that really is why Levi lied to you. Because he couldn't bear to upend your entire world, in one fell swoop. Maybe it wasn't his secret to tell.

Staring at Ollie now in the brilliant light of this cold December afternoon, I feel a rush of longing in my chest that's hard to ignore. It's not lost on me that this is the guy who's always been there for me. Through thick and thin, tragedy and trauma, pizza and horror flicks. *He's* the boy who would do anything for me. Who'd never lie to me. It pains me to compare him in my mind to Levi, and I know it's not fair, but I do it anyway.

You're lying to him too.

It's not like I haven't known this all year, or felt guilty about it. I'd convinced myself of the narrative that it wasn't wise to confide in him before I had any proof. But now, as I think about that crumpled DAAM flyer in the recycling bin, I feel the weight of what I'm doing, heavy like an anvil. I'm keeping the most important secret of my life from him. Telling Levi didn't give me any sense of closure or comfort, and now, in a way that's hard to admit to myself, I wish I hadn't.

You should have told Oliver.

"Ollie?" I say, as he rubs my fingers between his own. I'm not worried I've broken or even bruised my hand; the pain has completely subsided. *Because of your properties. Because you're a Similar.* The only pain I feel right now is a distinct pang of guilt.

"Yep?" he asks as I pull my hand away, flexing my fingers to show him that I'm fine.

In a flash, I realize exactly what I have to do.

"I'm in the middle of a personal statement. I don't wanna lose my train of thought," I say hastily. "It's for the common application, for most of the U.S. schools. Though…not for Oxford. I'm applying there too. Actually, I already have." I breathe out those words, forcing myself to say them. I should be able to tell him that detail, at the very least. "It's far," I add, hoping the surprised look on his face won't turn into disappointment. Or worse, hurt. "It's really hard to get into, and it's only one of a million places I'm applying, but… I thought you should know."

Ollie grins. "I love Oxford."

I frown. "You do? Since when?"

"Since forever. Haven't you heard me talk about the documentary I want to make about British crime writers?" Ollie shrugs. "I talk about it all the time!"

"No, you don't!" But I can't help laughing.

"And who isn't dying to try some authentic bangers and mash? Because me. I am."

I smile, giving him a peck on the cheek before reminding him to work on his film reel for NYU. Then I go, returning to my room. On my tablet, I pull up my college essay, the one I started that was all about Levi, and really not suitable as a personal statement at all. I begin again, this time giving it a title. A little pretentious, I know, but I have a point to make. The title helps with that.

The Case for Clones

The first time I met a clone, I was mourning the death of my best friend, Oliver. At the time, I cared about little else besides my grief. That's when I met Levi—Oliver's exact DNA copy.

I wanted to hate Levi. I wanted to blame him for having Ollie's face. It was more than that; I wanted to blame him for existing. Even though it wasn't his fault he looked just like Oliver. It certainly wasn't his doing; he was created from cells in a test tube, much like many babies are created and gestated these days, via fertility treatments and artificial wombs. No, it was not Levi's fault that he looked just like the friend I missed, on a cellular level. Still, I couldn't forgive him for doing something he had no control over—wearing my best friend's face.

Then something happened. I got to know Levi. I got to know the boy behind the face. The boy who was kind and thoughtful and cleverer than anyone I'd ever met. He wasn't perfect; far from it. He could also be aloof and frustrating and sarcastic. Contrary to popular belief, he wasn't some perfect specimen who always did or said the right thing. He was human.

He was also completely different from my friend Oliver, in every way that counted. He had hard edges where Oliver was soft. His words could bite, while Oliver's had usually comforted. Levi also knew pain that Ollie never did. He knew suffering, and he was strong because of it.

I realize now that I judged Levi—pre-judged him—and how unfair that was. Because little did I know that nearly eight months later, I would receive news that would change everything. Change the way I saw myself.

I, too, am a clone. Created in a test tube, gestated in an artificial womb. I grew up not knowing this, thinking my life was my own, when in reality, I was created to replace a little girl who was dying. The original "Emma." I still can't wrap my head around what this means, or how it will change my life. I am still me, I know that much. I still feel the same things I felt before. Fear and hurt and, yes, joy. Perhaps I have a different name now, this name "Eden" that I'm told is on my birth certificate. But what makes me *me* at my core isn't any different, just because I have the same DNA as another person, who lived and died.

What meaning lies behind the name "clone," or "Similar," if any at all? I'd argue that there is no meaning there, because, in the end, clones are humans, just like everyone else. We are individuals who are as different from their originals, on the inside, as any two people walking this earth. The clones at Darkwood—myself included—are kids. Teenagers worried about how they look and who they love and who loves them back. Nothing more, nothing less.

I know now why I hated Levi the first time I met him: it was because I was afraid. I was afraid that he'd take the place, in my heart, of Oliver. I feared him because I didn't know what I know now—that Levi and Oliver are not the same person at all. That one could never replace the other, not for me. Just like I didn't replace that little girl I was copied from. The fact that anyone ever thought I could was misguided at best, and dangerous at worst. All I shared with that other girl was some genetic coding. Some DNA. Just like Levi shares Oliver's DNA. Which, when you think about it, makes them equally capable of love. Of kindness. And of being loved back.

The first thing I do is send a copy of this essay, which I'll use as my personal statement for my college applications, directly to Ollie's plum. I don't stop to let myself think about what I'm doing—or change my mind. I add a note to the beginning of it:

Dear Ollie,

This is what I wanted to tell you earlier. I've known for a while. I guess it took me some time to come to terms with it. To accept it, and realize that I can't deny it to myself anymore. I'm sorry I'm only telling you now. I hope you can forgive me.

Love,
Emma

Then I send the essay to *The Daily Darkwood* for immediate publication.

CONFRONTATIONS

I WALK INTO the dining hall the next morning like nothing's different. Like I haven't dropped the biggest bombshell this school's seen since the Similars' arrival. I went to bed last night without talking to anyone. Not Pru, not Ollie, and certainly not Levi or the other Similars. I have no idea how my friends will react to my admission, my confession that I'm one of them. Will they welcome me with open arms? Or will this mean nothing to them, because—like I said in my essay—the name "clone" doesn't change anything about me, fundamentally? I still didn't grow up with them. To them, I'm the girl who had a vastly different chance at childhood than they did. I know Ollie won't believe it changes anything for us, even though I've worried all this time that it will. It's hard for me to know what it means, really. It's such a cosmic shift of my world. One I haven't sufficiently processed yet. It could take me years to fully digest and to fully accept.

When I walk through the double doors of the dining hall, all eyes are on me. I'm used to this; I've given the student body a lot of reasons to stare at me over the last year. Still, today feels different. I've put myself out there in the most vulnerable way. I've officially stood up to Harlowe and her group of clone haters. I'm not proud of myself as much as I am relieved. Keeping this secret was eating me up inside. Now I feel lighter. Freer. Kids whisper as I move past: "That's the girl who wrote the essay." "That's the girl who's a *Similar*." I don't look directly at Harlowe's table, but I feel her eyes on me. I know my essay is going to piss her off. She likely took it as a direct attack on her. *Good. It was.*

Pru hugs me as soon as I reach the table. I'm grateful for her, now more than ever. I scoot in next to her, making room for my tray, which I've filled with food I have no intention of eating. Not when my stomach is tied up in knots.

The other Similars are here, but not Ollie. *Good. I can't face them all at once.* I don't look at Levi, but I don't need to. I force myself to look up at my friends. At Maude, Ansel, Theodora, Jago, and Pippa.

Heart hammering so hard and fast it feels like it will break my rib cage, I do the only thing I know how. I make a joke. "What? Did something happen last night? What did I miss?"

No one speaks. They all stare at me, silently.

"For the love of God, would someone say something?" I finally explode. "Yes! I'm a Similar. Gravelle told me at the end of last year, but I didn't believe him. Not until I'd tested...certain hypotheses."

Still, no one's talking.

"Didn't my essay for *The Daily Darkwood* cover it? That's why I wrote it. And to put Harlowe and everyone else who keeps leaving you those threats in their place. Plus, it's going to make a pretty kick-ass college essay—"

Before I know what's happening, Pippa has run around the table to hug me. Maude too. Ansel smiles, and only Jago looks a little nonplussed, like he's not sure how this news affects him. Theodora grins at me across the table.

"We *knew* you were special, Emma," she says.

"Or should we say 'Eden'?" Maude cuts in.

"No," I correct her. "Don't call me that. Please. I'm still..." I lower my voice when several first years stop right in front of our table and stand there, trays in hand, obviously eavesdropping. "I'm still coming to terms with all this." Levi gets up from the table, claiming to need a utensil. I try not to let my gaze follow him. The last thing I need is to think about how angry I am at him, still, for keeping this secret from me.

"Have you talked to your dad yet?" Maude asks, lowering her voice so the first years can't hear. They reluctantly move on from our table.

"No. Also..." I look around the dining hall for Ollie. "Have any of you seen Ollie this morning?"

They shake their heads.

"Uh-oh," Jago announces to the table. He's looking down at his plum. "You have a rebuttal."

We all check *The Daily Darkwood*, where my essay has more than a thousand comments. I had no idea that after I posted it last night, a debate started raging and has been going strong all morning. Meanwhile, Harlowe has posted a rebuttal essay titled "But She's Also a Clone." She means me.

I don't read it. I stand up, grabbing my tray. I have to find Ollie. He's had time to read this, to process it, and now I need to stop being a coward. I need to talk to him in person.

On my way out, I run smack into Levi, returning with his fork.

"Sorry," I mutter as I try to step around him. He does the same, and we end up at a standstill.

"Your essay," he says quietly. "I thought you didn't want anyone to know."

"Things change," I say, my voice tight. I'm quoting what he said to me his first day back here. I don't wait to gauge his reaction. I go, on a mission to find Ollie.

He's not in his room, or the library, or any of our usual spots on campus. So I head to the only other place I can think of—Jane's office.

I knock softly and announce myself. "Jane? It's Emma. Can I come in?"

The door opens, revealing Ollie, pacing and gazing out the window at Dark Lake. Jane's behind her desk, looking a lot less like a headmistress and a lot more like the Jane I know and love.

"Hi," I say to them both. It's all I utter before Jane walks up and throws her arms around me, holding onto me like she doesn't want to let go. I'm surprised; though I've always thought of Jane like a surrogate mom, I've never quite known where I stood with her.

"That was a brave thing you did, Emma," she says, breaking the hug but still holding onto my shoulders.

"I wasn't being brave," I explain to her. "I was being honest." My eyes flick to Ollie, standing there with his hands shoved in his jeans pockets, surveying me. I can't read what's on his face, and for the first time since that thing started happening and I began reading minds, I actually *want* it to happen so I can know what he's thinking.

It doesn't.

"Either way," Jane goes on, her eyes still fixed on me. "I need you to know that I support you. As a friend—as your *best friend's mom*, I support you—and as your headmistress, I stand by you. Interim or not."

"Thank you," I breathe, appreciating every word she's saying, but still focused on Ollie. With each passing second, I grow increasingly worried about what his reaction will be. Why is he being so quiet? "Ollie," I begin, not at all sure how I'm going to say this. "I couldn't tell you last year. Not when I first got the note. Gravelle's note. You had gone through the biggest ordeal of your life. You'd come back from the *dead*. It didn't seem fair to tell you something that might have been fake. A lie. Another trick on Gravelle's part. But then— things happened this year. I jumped out of Harlowe's car. I lied to you, Ollie. That car was going fifty miles an hour. Maybe more."

Jane starts to jump in here, a look of concern on her face, but I hold up a hand.

"I wasn't hurt. I mean, I was, initially, but my scrapes healed so quickly. That was when I realized something was wrong. Or, maybe, right," I fumble. "It's taken me a long time to realize that while this changes everything—*everything*—I'm still me. Right? Ollie, please say something."

His lips quirk up in a smile. I feel myself breathing out a sigh as he crosses the room to envelop me in his strong arms, pulling me to his chest, where I burrow my face into the soft wool of his sweater and don't let go. "You're still Emma to me. Always were. Always will be."

Tears prick my eyes. "Aren't you mad?"

"At Gravelle, for continuing to manipulate you? And all of us?" Ollie asks. "Hell yeah, I am. At you? Never."

I let out a half choke, half sob of utter relief, then wipe my tears away with the back of my hand.

"I never knew the 'original' Emma," Ollie muses, holding onto my shoulders and wiping a tear away from my cheek with his thumb. "*You* are the only Emma I care about. Okay?"

I've never felt more relieved. I don't deserve a friend this loyal. But, selfishly, I know I need him. I always have, ever since we were kids.

The next few weeks pass quickly as we prepare for end-of-term exams. Ollie's initial surprise at my confession that I'm a clone has morphed into concern. If I'm a Similar, then I, too, can be terminated by Gravelle's stealth virus. Though I tell him not to dwell on that—even as it hangs over me, a constant threat—I notice he seems even more protective of me than usual. I can't go anywhere on campus without Ollie popping up.

I manage to avoid Levi until we all leave for Christmas break, except for one encounter in the library. We're both returning books we've checked out over the semester. I feel an intense pang as I see him standing there at the book return, wearing his signature crisp white T-shirt, even in the dead of winter. I remember how strong and warm his arms are. I feel so vulnerable in his presence, I could break.

I notice the book on the top of his stack: *Brave New World*. I start to tell him what I think of that novel, how it woke me up and shook me to my core. But I stop myself, afraid of what I might say instead, without meaning to.

I walk out the library door into the blustery air. It's the last time I see Levi until the new year.

◇→⊢◇

Jane invites me to spend the holiday with her, Booker, Ollie, and the twins in the Caribbean, and a small part of me longs to say yes, but I know I can't. I'm not that Emma, the one who can be casual and free and light, and who can throw herself into a beach-filled vacation with Ollie. I doubt I ever will be again. There's too much uncertainty. Too many fractures in my battered heart. I wish I *could* love Ollie in an uncomplicated way, and be like any other girl I know he'll end up loving, one day. But right now, my life's too messy. I can't put this off any longer. I have to talk to my father.

I haven't seen him since he accompanied me to school in September. I don't know for a fact he saw my essay in *The Daily Darkwood*, but if I had to guess, he's spotted it, one way or another. And if he has, he knows that I know. I'm a clone.

The morning of my flight, two days before Christmas, I walk with Ollie along the path by Dark Lake, my hands deep in my coat pockets. The air is freezing and crisp, and Ollie's hair, wet from the shower, glistens in the light.

"You're going to get icicles on your head," I warn him, teasing. "It's below freezing out."

"Yeah, yeah," he answers, smiling. But he flips his hood up over his ears.

"So you're spending the holiday here in Vermont, right?" I ask as we round a corner and the lake becomes visible through the trees. I wonder if it's completely iced over by now.

"Yup. Then Booker's flying out to meet us so we can travel together to Saint Lucia," Ollie answers, his gaze on the distant horizon. "You sure you can't come with us, Em?" Ollie asks, turning toward me. I've taken my hands out of my pockets to rub them together—even with gloves on, my fingers are chilly—and before I know it, Ollie's holding my hands in his own. I feel an instant warmth radiating from my hands to my arms. It's sudden and unexpected. And not unwelcome.

"I can't avoid my dad any longer," I answer quickly. "We haven't talked yet." I don't have to elaborate; Ollie knows what I mean. Of course, this isn't the only reason I can't come with them on their trip. But it's the most pressing, and it's the only one I can say out loud.

"Em…"

"Yes?" I breathe, my mind suddenly bombarded with the image of us kissing. I can't stop it from filling my mind, as much as I want to. It's because we're standing here, so close. And we're holding hands.

"No matter what your dad says, or what happens," Ollie says, "you are still you. I'm still me. This news only changes the facts of your birth—but not everything your life has been since. Not who you are, fundamentally, as a person."

I nod, feeling tears pricking my eyes. "Same goes for you. Gravelle being your father only changes the *facts*. Not the meaning."

"Touché." Ollie laughs, but I can tell what I've said has gotten through to him. Why didn't I tell Ollie about my suspicions from day one? Why didn't I let him in, so he could help me work through all my complicated feelings around being a Similar? That was such a mistake. Ollie's been my person since forever. The person who's loved me unconditionally and stood by me and somehow—in spite of all my flaws—never judged me, not for one second. How did I miss that? How could I *forget* that?

"Emma, I've been wanting to tell you something for ages. Ever since the night of that stupid masquerade ball I forced you to go to. Before that, even. But then I never got a chance to, and when it seemed like maybe you were pushing me away, I started to doubt myself. And I told myself not to say anything at all—"

"I know."

Ollie looks taken aback. His brow furrows under his too-long bangs. "You do?"

"You kissed me, didn't you?"

"And you kissed back."

I nod. "Why now? What's changed, Ollie?"

"Everything's changed!" he blurts, his gray eyes piercing mine in the morning light. There's something desperate behind them, and hungry. My throat catches and I'm hyperaware that my hands are still in his. "Nothing's been the same since last year. We play our roles and make our same jokes, and we hang out like nothing's different. But Emma—I never would have even known about you and Levi if I hadn't seen that photo, the night of the hazing. Sure, I knew in my gut that something was different. But you never told me. I'm your best friend. In the whole world. We lost each other, and we were somehow lucky enough to get each other *back*. Shouldn't that make us close enough to *always* tell each other the truth? No matter what?"

"He's your Similar," I gasp, feeling my eyes welling over. "How was I supposed to tell you that he and I…"

"And the fact that you're a clone," he keeps talking, clearly needing to get this out. "You kept that from me, all that time?"

"I'm sorry—"

"No, Em, you're not understanding." He's dropped my hands now and is pacing on the grassy path. "I'm not mad at you. I would never be angry at you for holding back something like that. I know you didn't do it to hurt me. On the contrary, you did it in part to *protect* me. But Emma, don't you see what all this means? We've been shutting each other out. Growing apart. Keeping things from each other. You didn't tell me everything, and I—I didn't tell you how I really feel. Which is this."

My breath quickens, every nerve ending in my body standing at attention. He's going to say it now, and there will be no going back.

"The entire time I was there, on Castor Island, you were all I could think about. I've loved you for years now, Emma. You know that, don't you? When I first told you how I felt—back in our second year—I was awkward and immature about it and my words were clunky and inadequate, and it scared you. I get that. It scared me too. We were kids—what did we know about love? We had our whole lives ahead of us. Love was this distant concept, and it always felt like we'd have time. So much of it. I guess it took me being kidnapped and separated from you for *months* for me to realize how much that love I felt, it wasn't going anywhere. It was real. And almost dying, thinking I might never see you again… It gave it all an urgency I'd never felt before. Like I'd always just taken us for granted. Because I always thought we'd just be there—an *us*—and that life would take us in all kinds of different directions, but we'd always come back to each other. And that one day, everything would just fall in place. And we'd be together."

Ollie stops pacing now and grabs my hands again. His face is inches from mine, and my body responds to his, leaning into him as he draws me closer.

"Emma, you are pretty much everything to me. And if we don't…if something were to happen again… I can't wait any longer, for you to know that. I need you to know it *now*."

The world spins, and Ollie's hand is on the small of my back, and our mouths meet in that gentle, sweet way they did the last time we kissed.

I sink into him, feeling the heat rising from my toes up my body, and for a few more seconds I'm not thinking about anything, or anyone, else.

When the kiss breaks, I am reeling.

I know how I just felt; I can't deny that.

But is this what I want?

Levi, a voice in my head reminds me. *Levi's the one you want. Even if you're angry at him. Even if the two of you can never be…*

"I can't," I whisper to Ollie, wrenching my hands from his and reacting with the force of a freight train barreling into me. "I'm sorry." I take one last look at his familiar face before turning in the grass and running, away from him, away from everything that just happened. And everything he said.

I gun it back to main campus, my mind whirling, my heart thumping against my rib cage. I remind myself I'm not that carefree girl who could see myself with him. *Loving Ollie, the way he should be loved.* I can't be that girl. I'll never be that girl.

I feel like I've cut off my own right arm. If Ollie's hurting right now, if he's angry, and if he feels betrayed…it's all my fault. I shouldn't have let him kiss me again. I should have pulled away. I should have been clear with him, that we can't be an us. That he deserves someone who isn't in love with someone else. That he deserves someone without so many secrets and fears and demons.

On the two-hour car ride to the Burlington airport, the kiss plays on a loop in my mind, driving me close to madness. Desperate to banish from my head the image of Ollie's stricken face as I left him standing there on the shore, I concentrate on what I'll say to my father when I see him. How will I react? Will I cry? Will I be numb, like I feel now?

I work on my college applications the entire flight home, trying to be productive for eight hours instead of obsessing about Ollie, and about my looming confrontation with my father. Because that's what it will be, isn't it? There's no having this conversation in a casual way.

Finally at my house, I let myself in the front door and make sure the security alarm's not on.

"Genevieve?" I prompt our household bot. "I'm home."

"In here, Emma," a voice calls out from the kitchen. I park my rolling suitcase in the foyer and steel myself for what I'm about to do. My dad's home. This is going to happen now. It has to. There will be no more putting it off.

I step inside our light-filled kitchen. Even close to twilight, the sun streams in through our floor-to-ceiling windows. My dad's at the kitchen island, typing away on a tablet. Work, I'm sure. He finally looks up.

"How was your flight?" he asks, crossing from the island to hug me. I let him, though it's stiff, and I'm trembling. Who's going to say something first? It's going to be up to me, isn't it?

"Dad. That essay. *My* essay—"

"I wish you'd consulted me first, Emmaline." I watch as my father walks to the sink, fills a glass with filtered water.

"Consulted you?" The words sound like they're coming from someone else, not me.

"Did you consider how political that essay would be? How polarizing? How, with its publication, you may have invited scores of trolls and clone-haters into our lives?" My father takes a sip of his water. I can't read his expression. All I hear are the words he's saying to me: words of disapproval. Shouldn't he be apologizing for lying to me my whole life? Not criticizing what I've done?

"It's lucky Jaeger Stanwick alerted me to your essay a few days after it was published," my father continues. "I immediately asked Jane Ward to take it down, and as a courtesy to me, as old friends, she complied. She agreed it compromised your safety," my father adds. "Thank goodness it wasn't picked up by any national news outlets."

My father took my essay down from *The Daily Darkwood*? Without my permission? Without even *telling* me? And Jane was in on it?

"Emmaline," he goes on. "Before you berate me. This is a security issue. It's not only your safety I'm concerned with, but mine as well. I'm the CEO of a highly public company. This kind of information could be used against both of us—"

"I'm sorry I've put your business dealings at risk," I snap, willing tears not to pool in my eyes.

"That's not what I meant," my father answers, looking hurt for the first time. *He's* hurt? After what he's put *me* through? "I'm a target, Emmaline. Or I would be, if anyone were to find out."

"Is that why you didn't tell me the truth all these years? Because you were afraid I'd spill the beans? Let the world know what you'd done?"

My father takes in an audible breath. "What I…"

"Sorry," I answer. "I mean what Gravelle did *for* you. You

certainly didn't refuse his generous gift, though, did you? I mean, you could have given me back. But you didn't."

Those words hang in the air, fraught. I know I really have hurt him now. I meant to.

"I can't believe you'd think that I ever could have…" my father says, his voice low. "Given you back, as you so bluntly put it. Emma, when you came into my life—"

"No," I choke out. "Don't. I came home to get an apology, and a real explanation. Not to hear lies and manipulations and half-truths."

"I wish you could see—"

"What? That you've never really loved me, because I'll never be *her*?" I don't bother to wipe away my tears. I let them flow, unabated. "Save it, Dad. I'm going to my room."

I turn and go, leaving my suitcase behind, forgotten, in the front hallway.

HOLIDAY

A FEW HOURS later, I venture downstairs. There's no sign of my father.

"He's upstairs in his office," Genevieve informs me, in that uncanny way she has of anticipating my needs before I voice them. She's far from personable, but still, even hearing her matter-of-fact voice pipe through the sound system is comforting.

"Dinner's in the fridge," she continues. "Your dad has work to catch up on but will see you later this evening."

Genevieve doesn't say it, but it's obvious my father's avoiding me after our tense conversation. I understand his urge to hide. We aren't that different, he and I. I fix myself the lasagna and salad he's set aside for me and am digging in when the doorbell rings.

"Emmaline," Genevieve's voice rings out. "There's someone at—"

"I heard," I answer, climbing down from my barstool and padding to the front door in my socks. "Thanks." It's almost seven o'clock. Who would be visiting us *now*? If it were a package, they'd leave it in the garage.

I peek through the curtain on the window and see a man and a woman, snazzily dressed, standing on the front stoop.

"Yes?" I say through the intercom.

"Delivery for Colin Chance. We're his interior design team," says the woman.

I sigh, opening the door for them. They walk in busily with bags and boxes, introducing themselves and explaining that the house is getting an update. New lamps, new throw pillows.

"Whatever." I shrug. I had no idea my dad cared about that kind of stuff. Our house is decorated just fine, albeit impersonally. "He's upstairs, in his office," I inform them before returning to my lasagna.

As they bustle about, replacing a lamp and measuring for new window shades, I wonder when my dad will emerge from his study. I wouldn't be surprised if he stayed in there all night, to avoid finishing our conversation. I curl up on the couch and try to lose myself in mindless TV, but all I can think about is what I'll say to him, when I do see him later. If I'll finally tell him how hurt I am. Because it occurs to me he might be so focused on how all this affects him—he might not even know.

❖—ı—❖

I wake up the next morning to find I'm still lying on the couch. Someone's laid a blanket over me and tucked in the edges. Confused, I sit up.

"Genevieve? What time is it?"

"Eleven o'clock in the morning. You were extraordinarily tired last night," she explains. "Your father left you a note. It's on the kitchen counter."

I pad over in my socks, rubbing sleep out of my eyes, and pick up the paper. It's my father's monogrammed letterhead. CC, for Colin Chance.

> *Dear Emma,*
>
> *I had to leave abruptly this morning for a last-minute trip to Tokyo. Unfortunately, business goes on even with the holiday tomorrow. I hope you can understand.*
>
> *There's nothing I can say in this note that will instantly make everything okay between us, but please know that I love you, and we'll talk in the new year.*
>
> *Your Christmas gift is in the living room under the tree.*
>
> *Love,*
> *Dad*

I set down the note, feeling spent. This isn't the apology I was looking for, and it definitely isn't the explanation. So that's how it's going to be. My dad's going to continue to skirt the issues of who I really am, of what he's done.

If only he would sit down and talk to me like an adult. If only he would show me he respects me enough to answer all my questions. To hear me out.

I pad into the living room and retrieve the lone envelope that sits under the tree, a forest-green fir wrapped exclusively in tiny silver bells. The envelope has my name on it, but I don't open it. I slip it into a side pocket of my suitcase.

"Dash? Any buzzes from Ollie?"

"No, Emmaline," Dash responds. "I'm sorry."

Ollie and I haven't exchanged as much as an emoji since I left him standing there by Dark Lake. I feel miserable without my best friend to talk to, and even more so knowing it's my own fault. Ollie's right; there has been a chasm growing between us. Now I've made it even wider.

I spend the next two days alone, watching old films and eating the worst junk food I can find in our pantry. Alone in my empty house, feeling so isolated I'm this close to asking Dash and Genevieve to watch a movie *with* me, I'm beyond relieved when I get a buzz from Ansel, reporting that he's been hanging out with Archer and his dads over the holiday. Trimming the tree, going for a hike up to the Hollywood Hills. He shares a snapshot of him and Archer in sneakers, taking in the fresh air. Archer's arm is draped lazily around Ansel's shoulders, and they both look pretty content. I'm happy for Ansel. He deserves a family, even if it's complicated.

Theodora buzzes that she's spent a five-star holiday with Frederica Leroy and Tessa in Manhattan, but I can sense the sarcasm even in her written words. Maude also buzzes with a chipper "Merry Christmas to us" that makes me miss my friends so much, I almost can't stand it.

Staring down the twinkly tree in our vast living room, lacking any wrapped presents nestled beneath it, it occurs to me that right now, I understand my friends' lonely existence more than I ever realized.

⟡━┤ ├━⟡

When I return to Darkwood after the break, I've submitted all fourteen of my college applications, and I've completed video holo-calls with several of the schools that require interviews for admission. I've received a couple of buzzes from Ollie, mostly photos with funny captions that don't really tell me much about what's actually on his mind.

I miss him, and I feel so anxious about what things will be like when we both return to school. I also miss Levi. I want to ask him what he did over the break, and whether he missed me. I know I can't, though, and won't.

I arrive at the circular drive on the Thursday after New Year's Day. We'll have the long weekend to get settled before classes resume. I'm alone in my room, unpacking, when I see the envelope from my father sticking out of the side pocket of my suitcase. I'd forgotten it was there. I yank it out, ripping it open along the edge.

Inside is a printout for two plane tickets. A summer graduation trip to Europe. My dad has scrawled a handwritten note.

Just us. No work, no plums. Are you in? Love, Dad

I feel my pulse catching in my throat. It's an olive branch, I'm sure of it. Last year, I would have been cautiously optimistic a trip like that would be a fresh start for us. But now, I wonder if it can make up for everything that's transpired between us? I don't know.

"You aren't seriously considering heading to Italy for the first time in your life without *me*?" a voice behind me demands.

I whirl and see Ollie standing there, holding his rolling bag by the handle.

Relief floods my body. He's here, making a joke. He's not mad. At least, he's not acting like it.

"Snoop much?" I tease, running up and hugging him, careful to pull away quickly. "How was your trip—"

"How was home—"

We both laugh.

"Jinx," I say, wheeling his bag inside and praying we can have some semblance of normal. At least for a little while. I need my best friend right now. I can't bear the idea of us not talking, not hanging out like always. "*Harry Potter* movie marathon?" I suggest.

"Do you really have to ask?" he teases.

Pru's out training with her crew team, so Ollie and I settle on my bed with a tablet and *Sorcerer's Stone*. This is normal. This is nice. Like old times. We can easily get through *Prisoner of Azkaban* by dinnertime.

It's easy, sitting here with Ollie, leaning on the wall that forms one side of my twin bed. I've got the tablet on my knees, and his own are crunched up between his elbows. I notice in that moment how small the bed seems, and how tall Ollie is. Things could not be more loaded and complicated between us. But this is how it should be. Us, as friends.

Only friends.

Then why do you feel a zing up and down your spine, sitting here so close to him?

I swat that thought away and try to focus on Harry and Hermione and Hogwarts.

But I'm distracted when I notice Ollie checking his plum. "You expecting a super-urgent message?"

"Nope, just seeing what time it is."

"It's 3:52 p.m., last time I checked," I quip. He looks guiltily away from his wrist.

A minute passes, and now he's pressing pause on the movie.

"That was fun." He stretches his legs. "More tomorrow?" he asks, slipping on his sweater.

"More tomorrow?" I look at him like he's lost it. "Are you kidding me? They've literally *just* gotten past Fluffy."

"And then they'll play wizard's chess, and Ron will get knocked out, and don't pretend you haven't seen this forty-seven hundred times." He laughs.

"I thought we were going to watch *all* of them," I protest feebly. I know I'm trying to hold on to some normalcy. I cling to it because right now, it's the only thing that feels stable and safe. "That's what movie marathon *means*. It's not a marathon if it's two-thirds of a film!"

But Ollie's already slipping on his sneakers. "Em, chill. It's not a big deal."

"I just don't understand what's so important you can't watch the end with me," I say, feeling myself getting riled.

"Stuff, Emma," Ollie says, all of a sudden sounding testy and cryptic. I stare at him, surprised. I'd been teasing him before, giving him a hard time. But now he's being downright standoffish.

He moves to the door. "Wait," I say, leaping from the bed and nearly tripping in my socks. "I'm sorry. I was just messing with you."

"Emma," he says sternly. "I have. To go." He yanks open the door and leaves.

I sigh, pressing play on the movie. At least I can lose myself in Hogwarts for thirty more minutes. But deep down, I'm worried. Have I ruined everything between us? Dug a chasm between us that's so wide, we'll never bridge it again?

A few hours later, I'm heading toward the dining hall with Pru, Maude, and the others, but not Ollie. And Levi's not with us, either. I don't know where he is, but I'm equal parts relieved and disappointed that he's not here. Theodora's filling us in on her awkward holiday with the Leroys, including their fancy Christmas meal at Gramercy Tavern. I'm only half listening.

But when I reach the entrance, something grabs my attention. Hanging from the double doors of the dining hall is a blown-up photo of me. Scrawled across my torso, in a messy blood-red script, is one giant word: CLONE.

RETALIATION

WE ALL KNOW who did it. It was Harlowe and her crew. I study the picture for two seconds before stoically moving right past it and snagging a table with my friends. There are the usual snickers and comments all around us—Darkwood students can't resist an opportunity for gossip—but we stay in our tight-knit group, only leaving the security of our table to grab trays of food.

"I'm calling a midnight session," Maude says, interrupting our silent chewing. She stands up, abruptly, rapping a knife on her glass. "Attention, everyone. I have a short announcement. Members of the Nine—I mean, Ten. Our tenth member has returned, I almost forgot—please convene in the Tower Room tonight for the first midnight session of the New Year." She sits back down and digs into her tacos.

I hear a commotion by the double doors. Someone has ripped down the poster of me. I squint and see that person crumpling it up and walking toward the recycling bin with it.

It's Levi. I hear whispers about how he's my boyfriend. That of course he had to defend Emma's honor. They're a *couple*.

I bristle at the words, and heat rises through my chest, moving to my outer extremities. When he walks over to our table with a tray, joining us, I'm angry. I don't need him to be my champion. I was diplomatically ignoring that sign and showing this whole damn school I'm above all this.

Levi's chosen a spot at the table directly across from me.

"I couldn't stand it," he explains. "I was worried if I didn't take it out on the sign…" He shrugs. "I would do something a lot worse."

We don't talk after that. I pick at my dinner, wondering where Ollie is, suddenly nauseous about how we left things earlier today. Is it my imagination, or was Ollie being particularly quiet? Avoiding serious topics, trying to get the whole movie marathon over with? And then leaving so abruptly like he did? Am I completely overreacting? Or is there some chance he's so hurt by what I did, by how I reacted to that kiss, he can't even stand to be around me?

I'm so relieved when Ollie slides into a seat next to me—until I remember Levi's right across from us.

"I would love to walk up to that girl right now and give her a piece of my mind," Ollie grumbles. He means Harlowe. He must have seen the poster before Levi ripped it down.

"What is wrong with you two?" I set my water glass down with a thud. "Both of you. Yes, you, Levi. And you, Ollie. Do you think I can't take care of myself?"

They both stare at me like I've lost my mind—then both of them smile, exchanging an eye roll. That only makes me angrier.

"I will deal with Harlowe, thank you very much." I grab my tray and leave the table, bussing it and exiting into the blustery night air.

Late that night, waiting in the Tower Room with Pippa, Theodora, Maude, and Levi for the junior Ten members to arrive, I refuse to meet Levi's eyes. I can't believe he and Ollie shared that look, like they were in cahoots. Like they think I can't fight my own battles.

I'm tired after my long day traveling cross-country, despite being on California time. But I'm hit with a jolt of energy the moment Harlowe and the other juniors walk in the room, with Harlowe leading the charge. I notice Sophie and Willa; they trail the other three, hesitant. I can only hope they haven't gone over to the dark side.

"Things are really coming along in our planning for the rally," Harlowe announces to the group gleefully as she plops in a chair. "Too bad none of you are DAAM members." She shrugs. "You're really missing out." Her eyes scan the circle, finally landing on mine. "Oh, hey. Good thing your boyfriend rode in like a knight in shining armor this evening," Harlowe says to me coolly. She has no idea how much that comment rankles me. But I don't let on.

"I don't know what you're talking about. All I saw was that poster," I answer her, emotion absent from my voice. "And it spoke for itself."

"Did it?" Harlowe asks, shooting Ivy a look. "Because there's a lot more it *could* have said, besides 'clone.'" She pretends to pick a piece of lint from her jeans. "Maybe the next poster will be more explicit. Like detailing how you leaped from that boathouse roof like someone possessed."

I stare at her, my wheels turning.

It *was* her. The person standing behind the trees watching me that day. I *knew* it.

"I already let the colleges know, so you can thank me later," Harlowe adds.

"Let the colleges know *what*?" I feel my entire body tensing, like a rubber band about to snap.

"About your suicidal tendencies." She shrugs. "No one attempts a daredevil stunt like that unless they *want* to die—"

"That is so horribly offensive, I could slap you," I snap at her. "Suicide isn't a joke. When we thought Ollie…" I stop myself, feeling my throat clog up like cotton has been stuffed there. I am not discussing that most personal and hellish time of my life, and Ollie's, with this spiteful girl.

"The only other possibility is that you knew you wouldn't hurt yourself, because you're so freakishly *inhuman* that you can leap from a building without a scratch," Harlowe goes on, her eyes boring into mine. "I'm sure Oxford really wants a half-human cyborg *freak* walking its campus."

I stand up, about to walk right up to Harlowe and punch

her in the face. If there were ever a time to read her thoughts again—to hear exactly what's in that twisted mind of hers so I could use it against her—that time would be now.

Before I know what's happening, I feel tingly all over. I barely register that my friends are defending me, because I'm inside Harlowe's head.

Freak. They're all freaks. Which is why the colleges they've applied to are going to love all that footage I sent them of Tessa running around half naked on Darkwood's campus. I bet Theodora won't get in any-where *since I told them it's her. And Maude's prospects are going to be pretty bad once the schools find out how many time she's broken Darkwood rules. Hacking into every system out there—*

"You bitch," I hiss at Harlowe. There. I've said it. I am done being nice; I am done being civil. "All you've wanted, this entire year, has been to run us out of school. Or to drive us to total humiliation. Or to get my friends *deported.*"

"But not you, Eden?" Harlowe asks innocently. "You've admitted you were born on Castor Island. Which makes you… oh, right. Not a citizen of this lovely country at all."

"You won't get away with it," I say, ignoring that last comment. "That video, that was Tessa, not Theodora." I don't tell her it was a Duplicate. I'm not getting into that right now. "Using it to derail Theodora's college applications is a totally evil thing to do." As soon as I've said it, I realize it's too late. I've given myself away.

Harlowe stares at me, and for the first time ever, she's rendered speechless.

How does she know about that? I never said anything. It's like she could read my mind. But that's insane—no one can do that.

I don't flinch. I don't let on for a second that I'm continuing to hear everything that's in her head. It's a standoff of sorts, until Levi steps up next to me, and I can feel the outrage radiating off his every cell. It's sexy as hell, but I don't need him defending me.

"Don't," I say to him. "She's not worth it."

"Sorry to interrupt," says a voice, and we all turn, surprised, to see a figure standing in the doorway. It's Jane. My mind is spinning. This is the first time I've ever seen a teacher, or any adult at all, stop by a midnight session. "Harlowe Shaw, Ivy Li, and Graham Rosen? Please come with me," Jane says with authority.

Harlowe's eyes flit to Graham's and then Ivy's. They seem as surprised as she is.

"What for?" Harlowe asks.

"A student videoed the three of you hanging that sign on the cafeteria door," Jane explains, crossing her arms over her chest. "As you know, that kind of display of intolerance is not to be abided at Darkwood. Not while I'm in charge. Maude? Is this meeting dismissed?"

Maude can barely contain her smile. "It is now."

Harlowe and her cohorts grumble as they file out of the Tower Room, following Jane.

"Should we go now?" Sophie asks. Willa twists her hair awkwardly. These two may have a moral compass, but they could use some confidence.

"You're dismissed too," Maude answers. Sophie and Willa leave.

The rest of us try to process what just happened.

"Who recorded the video from the cafeteria?" Pippa asks.

I shrug. "Someone who really wanted to see those kids put in their place. Nice work, whoever you are."

"Emma—what did you mean by footage of Tessa?" Theodora asks. "And my college apps?"

I twist my hands in the fabric of my shirt. It's now or never, I guess.

"I read Harlowe's thoughts," I say briskly, wanting to say this before I chicken out. "It's happened before," I explain quickly, "but never on purpose. The first time was the night she locked you up in the pump house. That's how I knew you were there. Tonight, I was so, I don't know, *angry*, I willed myself to hear what she was thinking. And it wasn't good," I add. I explain more about how she's planning to derail Theodora and Maude's college apps with "evidence" that they aren't the shining students they purport to be. Mine too.

"This is what Gravelle always talked about," Pippa speaks up.

"What is?" I press.

Levi deflates, and I remember he's standing there next to me. Not that I ever could forget. I only force myself to ignore the electricity that thrums through me any time we're in a room together, in spite of everything. "He was obsessed, Emma," he says, turning to face me. "With this idea of us conquering all human physical limitations…"

"And all mental ones," Pippa supplies. "None of us ever got to that point, of being successful at brain-to-brain communication. I think Gravelle was always angry about that, and disappointed. He'd let you go, to live with your dad, and I think he always knew you were the one who got away."

"The special one," Levi adds. "The one with this unique ability to control your mind. And see into others'."

"I hate it," I confess to them. "For the most part, it makes me find out stuff I absolutely do *not* want to know. Ever," I add. "If this keeps up, I'll be sitting on thousands of secrets by the time I die. Maybe more—"

"Not if you learn to control it, like you just did," Maude cuts in. "If you think of it that way—like a skill you can hone and practice and control—then you can use it only when you really want to. When you have a good reason to. Like just now."

"What good did it do us?" I complain. "So now we know Harlowe's planning to screw you over so you can't get into college."

"We can try to stop her," Pippa says softly.

"And at the very least, write to those colleges to explain that there's been a mix-up. A mistake," Maude adds.

"You did good, Emma," Theodora tells me with a wry smile. I don't return it.

"She knows," I tell them. "She knows she didn't say anything out loud about that college admissions stuff."

"So what?" Maude scoffs. "Let her have a field day with this. We're stronger than she is. Smarter. And you have the most useful skill of all."

I don't share in their enthusiasm. As I make my way down the spiral stairs of the Tower Room, Levi catches up to me, grabbing my hand in the darkened hallway and pulling me close. It's torture being mere inches from him and not acting on it. But I can't. He lied to me. That hasn't changed.

"Have you ever…you know," he says, his voice husky. "Read my thoughts?"

"No," I say quietly. For a second, we're so focused on each other—our breathing, our silent acknowledgment of how much we want this, whatever *this* is…

"If you did," Levi says, "you'd know how truly sorry I am. For everything."

He drops my hand and moves off down the hallway, stuffing his fists in his jeans pockets. I watch him go, wishing I'd stopped him.

That night, I dream about this skill of mine, this ability to see into others' minds, now on command. I imagine why Gravelle spoke of it over the years, even expressed his fury that I'd gotten away. What would he have forced me to do, had I grown up on Castor Island with the other Similars and not left at the age of three? In the dream, I'm still a young child, maybe five or six. I'm reading the thoughts of everyone I encounter. Famous people. World leaders. In a cold, white room, not unlike the one where I was imprisoned on his island, I am questioned by Gravelle. I'm hooked up to a polygraph machine that shoots out page after page of red squiggles. Suddenly, Gravelle's face clouds over in rage, and he shoots to his feet, interpreting one of the printouts and accusing me of lying.

I wake up in a sweat, terror seizing me. It only subsides when I realize I'm in my bed, in my room at Darkwood. Pru is asleep in the bed next to mine, her dark form rising and falling minutely, but enough for me to see her breathing. I unclench my fingers, considering for the millionth time how differently my life would have played out had I stayed on the compound with the others. Gravelle plucked me from the only home I knew before I was old enough to form strong bonds with the place—and with the Similars. Though I wonder, now, if subconsciously, I always knew we were connected, even last year when they first arrived at Darkwood. Is that why I felt so pulled to them? So curious to learn everything about them? Because somewhere, deep down, I knew they had once been my family?

Maude and I spend the morning together in the library, going over everything she learned about the stealth virus over the holiday break. She's managed to reverse engineer it—a feat in itself—and she's done it by remotely logging into Gravelle's server on Castor Island.

"The good news is, I know how the virus works," Maude tells me. "The bad news is, Gravelle is not bluffing. The virus is real, and it took out Ransom."

"Could you turn it off?" I ask. "Is that a dumb question?"

"No. Not dumb. Yes, it can be shut down. But not remotely." Maude sighs.

"I'll never stop being impressed by you," I tell her.

"I'm not the one who can read thoughts," she quips.

I blanch. That's definitely not something I'm proud of, and I tell her as much.

"Emma, you need to stop viewing this as a burden and see it the way I do. It's a gift." Her tone is probably harsher than she means it to sound. Or maybe it's intentional. Maude isn't one to mince words. "I meant what I said yesterday. If you can harness it, use it for good... Emma, I don't want to scare you," she says, her tone changing. She sounds less certain now. More hesitant.

"Maybe don't, then?" I crack a smile.

"I've been going over and over this Legacy Project of Gravelle's, trying to get one step ahead of him and figure out what his endgame is. I can't," she says. "What does it mean that he wants us getting closer to our DNA families? I refuse to take Gravelle's words at face value, that our tasks are simply part of our birthright. There has *got* to be something we're missing. I'm sure of it."

"And you're afraid we're not going to figure it out until it's too late," I conclude.

She nods. "Please, practice that mind reading. If you can learn to do it on command… We may need it, Emma. And you."

Maude's words haunt me till lunchtime, when I walk into the dining hall. She's right. I've been acting like a brat about this talent of mine, when, in truth, it could prove so useful. What was I thinking? Wouldn't most people kill to be able to see inside others' heads?

That thought sends a shiver up and down my spine, and I wish I hadn't gone there. Considering what a government might do to get its hands on this ability…on *me*… I feel sick at the thought of Harlowe having this intimate knowledge of what I'm capable of. How she might try to use it against me. To hurt me or my friends—or worse.

I'll simply have to stay one step ahead of her.

As I thread my way through the dining hall tables, I try to open my mind to the thoughts around me. I focus on a first-year girl in chunky glasses, willing myself to hear what's in her head.

—going to fail out of trig and my dad's going to kill me—

I turn away from her, staring at a boy at the next table.

—can never tell him that I love him, can I? I mean he has no idea, no clue at all—

And finally, I walk over to a crowded table of second years and laser in on a heavily tattooed student in suspenders.

—is it weird that I kind of want new friends? Is it too late for me to get new friends—

I shake off that last thought and walk away, willing myself to forget any personal details I've picked up about my classmates. That's not the point; I'd never look inside someone's head to learn gossip about them. It was purely a practice session. And I aced it.

I don't know whether to be happy I've begun honing my skill, to use Maude's words, or terrified of what it means.

All I want right now is to curl up next to Ollie and not think—about anything. I buzz him, asking him to meet me for part two of our movie marathon.

He's standing outside my door when I return to my room, and he's wielding a cafeteria tray loaded with our favorite snacks. I don't ask him where he got all that junk food—clearly not the dining hall. Wordlessly, I open my door, pull out my tablet, and start the movie.

We relax on my twin bed, and I think back to yesterday, and how this felt so safe and normal. And yet—something feels wrong. Off. *It's the kiss*, I remind myself. *You hurt him, Emma. It's going to take time for him to heal. You rejected him. Didn't you?*

"Ollie?" I nudge his foot with my own.

"Yep?" he asks, chewing on a Snickers bar.

I hit pause on the movie, then pull my knees up to my chest. "We promised no more secrets between us, right?"

He turns to look at me, his face earnest, and in that moment, I feel so much love for him, as my best friend on the planet, it hurts, like an ache in my chest.

"I can read people's thoughts. Or hear them, I guess. It's a mental agility thing. Something that was programmed into my DNA before I was born. It's been happening since the beginning of the school year. The night of the hazing was the first time. It's like the person's talking directly in my ear. At first it would happen without me being able to control it. Without me even *wanting* it. I heard your thoughts, the night of the dance," I add, my heart pounding. "That's how I knew about your feelings for me. And you're right, I tried to stop you from telling me. I'm sorry. I shouldn't have kept that from you. I shouldn't have kept *so many things* from you. But that stops now. I swear."

Ollie sets down his candy-bar wrapper, looking like he's trying to process what I just told him.

"Em—who knows about this? Who else, I mean?"

"The Similars. And…" I hesitate, not sure if I should tell him the rest. But I *just* promised him no more secrets, didn't I? "And Harlowe," I whisper. "Or, she suspects, anyway. I don't know if she's put it all together, but knowing her, she will. It happened by accident. I never would have wanted her to find out."

"We should tell my mom," Ollie says. "If this could put you in danger…"

"It won't," I insist, even though I'm not convinced of that, not at all.

"You might need heightened security. My mom could arrange that—"

"Aren't we getting ahead of ourselves? I've barely figured out how this skill of mine works. What it all means…"

Ollie combs his hands through the hair at his temples, looking frayed. "I'm worried, Emma. Things are happening so quickly."

"It will all be okay. As long as *we're* okay. Right?"

But Ollie doesn't answer me. He's jumped up from the bed and is stuffing his feet in his sneakers.

"I almost forgot. There's something I have to take care of. I'll see you at dinner. Okay?"

"But Ollie, *wait*." I feel flustered, and anxiety creeps up in my chest. He's running off again, so abruptly? "We *are* okay, aren't we? I mean, I know you're probably hurt and maybe even mad at me, and rightly so, but we should—" I don't even get to say "talk." He's already out the door.

It only takes me a moment to decide I'm not letting him leave here again so quickly. Not when there's been so much left unsaid between us. I slip on my boots and race out of my room. Ollie's at the end of the hall, hurrying toward the exit. I follow him.

"Ollie!" I shout, racing in his direction. "That's the second time in a row you've left my room like you had somewhere a *lot* better to be! Stop! We need to talk. You're the one who said it, before break. And maybe you've changed your mind, but you were right. I'm not letting you brush me off. Not again!"

But Ollie's not turning around. He's quickening his pace,

and I chase after him, my mind churning. Why isn't he stopping? Why is he *running away from me*?

I've followed him all the way to Nightshade now. Ollie stops in front of the double doors, taking his key from around his neck and scanning it in front of the door. It buzzes, opening for him. But another kid in his dorm—a kid I recognize but don't personally know—stops him.

"Ollie! I was looking for you," the kid says brightly. "I had this calculus question—"

"Can we talk later? I'm kind of busy right now," Ollie answers, exasperated but trying not to be rude. The delay gives me my opportunity. I lunge up the steps to where Ollie stands and plant myself in the doorway, so he can't get past me.

"Ollie! What the *hell* is going on?" I demand. "Why are you running from me? I know you're angry, but *talk to me*, for God's sake!"

Focus. Ignore her. Send the buzz. You have to.

I blink, unsure at first what's happening. Then I know. I'm hearing Ollie's voice in my head. Talking to me in that familiar, quiet way that sounds far off, but also like he's speaking right in my ear.

It's all right. Even if she reads your thoughts, she won't know. Just do it, now, before you lose your window. You only have five minutes.

Window? What window? And what does Ollie mean, five minutes? I look down at my plum. It's 4:00 p.m. I can't make all this compute. I have no idea what these thoughts of his mean. They're just empty words. A jumble.

Give the report. Everything's fine. No one suspects… Make your mind a blank. Even if she reads it, there's nothing there. Nothing she'll understand.

I'm so confused I can't even speak. All I'm trying to do is make sense of these thoughts in Ollie's head, coming at me in a stream of consciousness. The weirdest part is, they don't sound like him. They don't sound like him at all.

Ollie's typing, rapid-fire, on his plum. I'm simply watching, confused and mildly terrified.

"Ollie?" I whisper, my voice sounding as hollow as I feel. "What's going on?"

But he's still ignoring me. Typing faster and faster.

Eden has no idea. None of them do. Everything you've planned is prepped. Airtight.

Everything *who's* planned? What's he talking about? *What's* airtight?

Installation went off without a hitch. She'll never check the time stamp on my wrist with an infrared light. She'd never even know what that means. I'm safe. She won't understand.

I still don't know what's happening, but a distinct feeling of dread is filling me. What is Ollie talking about? Infrared light?

This is 002.04, sending this message to Pollux. Signing off now. Goodbye.

Ollie stops typing and pockets his plum. He turns and looks at me, recognition dawning on his face. It's like he finally sees me. *Me*, Emma, for the first time since I chased him down.

"Hey!" he grins at me. "Ready to finish our movie marathon?"

I have never been so frightened of Ollie's smile in my life. I don't answer—I don't breathe a word—I simply turn and run.

I'm racing from Nightshade as fast as I can, my mind churning and fear creeping its tendrils up my limbs. I look down at my plum, like somehow the time is going to ground me, or make me understand the gibberish I just heard. It's 4:06 p.m.

What were all those strange, jumbled thoughts in Ollie's head? What is it that we don't *suspect*? What did he mean by "time stamp" and "installation" and "airtight"? Those are all meaningless words.

Only something about them is sending chills up and down my spine, causing me to take in gulps of the freezing air like I might hyperventilate. Because when it comes down to it, *none* of what I just heard makes any sense. And not only that—for those few minutes when I was standing there, watching Ollie type away on his plum, and hearing his nonsensical thoughts... *It didn't sound like him.*

I stop at a bench, gasping for air as everything I witnessed roils through me. The way Ollie seemed to finally notice that I was there—five minutes after I arrived—and then turned on a dime just like that, smiling and referencing our movie marathon... It was terrifying.

Because for the five minutes before that, he didn't seem like Ollie at *all.*

And if he didn't seem like Ollie, is that because he's been brainwashed? Did Gravelle get to him again? Do something to him?

The time—4:00 p.m. I remember now. It was 3:52 p.m. when Ollie left my room yesterday. And today, when I was reading his thoughts, he said something about a window. A five-minute window between 4:00 and 4:05 p.m. By 4:06, he was back to normal again.

Are there five minutes a day when Gravelle has some kind of hold over him? Is *that* what's happening?

Then I hear it again, in my mind, suddenly remembering it so clearly.

This is 002.04, sending this message to Pollux.

002.04.

Pollux, the twin island to Castor. The one Seymour told us about.

I grab on to the back of the bench, feeling stabbing pains in my gut as the revelation hits me. How did I not see this right away?

Ollie wasn't brainwashed.

He called me Eden. No one calls me that, except Gravelle.

002.04. It's like the number that was written on the tag of the Tessa clone's purple bomber jacket, 001.05.

That didn't sound like Ollie back there because it *wasn't* Ollie.

It was a Duplicate.

THE PRETENDER

OLLIE HAS BEEN replaced by a Duplicate.

But how? How can this be? I try to find some semblance of order in my scrambled thoughts.

There was another Duplicate of Ollie. The first one. The one Gravelle murdered in Ollie's place.

Ollie's been cloned before, twice. First when Levi was created. And then, years later, when that Duplicate was introduced as a stand-in, a lifeless placeholder.

Now, there's another one. A third, and I was just talking to him. Sitting next to him, on my bed, thinking everything was normal. I was trying to have a heart-to-heart with him, for God's sake. Only it wasn't my best friend. It was his copy.

But he's so clever, I remind myself. *He seemed so real. So exactly like Ollie.* Those Duplicates who came to campus at the beginning of the school year—the Tessa, Jake, and Archer copies—they were reckless and immature. Barely able to stand in for their originals convincingly at all.

This Ollie, except for his strange behavior around 4:00 p.m., didn't act like those others. He was smart. Thoughtful. He had Ollie's mannerisms, knew his sense of humor, was able to reference our shared history. If he hadn't run out of my room twice in two days, and if I hadn't been able to read his thoughts, I never would have known.

It was only during those five minutes today when he didn't seem like himself. When he was turned off, or on, or whatever it was that allowed him to communicate with Gravelle. That's what he was doing, isn't it? He said he was "sending this message to Pollux." Which can only mean one thing. He was contacting the Similars' guardian.

I feel light-headed, like the world is tilting sideways. That isn't Ollie back there. That isn't my best friend. It's a fake, an imposter. Someone pretending to be Ollie.

But was he pretending? Those other Duplicates, immature as they were, really believed they were Tessa, Archer, and Jake.

This Ollie did too. In his mind, he *was* Oliver Ward. Still is.

The thought sends a wave of nausea through my body.

How long has this Duplicate been standing in for my best friend?

I can't stay here a minute longer. I have to do something. I have to tell someone.

I begin running, letting the cold January wind ravage my

face as I race back to Cypress, my mind whirling with questions. With fears.

He said the word "installation." He said it "went off without a hitch." That must mean it happened recently. I rack my brain, thinking. How did Gravelle do this? When did Gravelle do this?

I'm hit with a jolt of electricity as one question looms in my mind above all others: Was that the real Oliver I kissed on the shore of the lake before the holidays—or this imposter? It seemed like Ollie. It *felt* like Ollie. But this Duplicate, he seemed like Ollie too. If I hadn't been so in tune to his every movement... If I hadn't been so insistent on knowing what he was up to... If I hadn't been able to *read his mind*, I never would have known anything was wrong. I would have been annoyed by his abruptness, but he could have easily brushed it off, made excuses.

I only discovered the truth because of my unique abilities. And because I'm so goddamned stubborn.

I don't know why that rattles me deep in my bones.

Because you weren't supposed to find out. Because Gravelle meant to install this Duplicate Oliver without you ever knowing.

But how? And when?

It hits me then, like a light bulb turning on. The holiday break. I stop in my tracks, my hands on my thighs, bending over to catch my halting breath. I don't have any proof, but it would make sense. Gravelle must have made the switch over the break. He sent this Duplicate back to Darkwood in Ollie's place, after New Year's.

And now I know why I'm so afraid, in every cell of my body. Because if a switch was made—if this Duplicate Ollie was "installed" over Christmas break—that means the real Ollie, *my* Ollie, isn't here.

It means he's been taken. It means he's *gone*.

◇—ı—◇

"Dash, buzz my friends. *Not* Ollie. The Similars and Pru. Tell them it's an emergency," I whisper into my plum when I make it back to my empty dorm room. "I need to talk to them. Ask them to meet me at the circular drive. *Now*."

Fear and adrenaline are coursing through me. Ollie has been kidnapped again by Gravelle. I'm *sure* of it.

And we all let it happen.

Of course, it's not my fault, or that of any of my friends— how could it be? I never could have imagined this, never would have suspected that Gravelle would do this.

But with increasing dread, I remind myself that Gravelle is unpredictable, and sick, and that his agendas are so twisted no normal person would ever anticipate them.

I grab my coat from the back of my desk chair and slip it on, then run to the circular drive in a haze, finding my gloves in my pockets and shoving my fingers into them. Tears encroach on my eyes as the gravity of what I've discovered hits me.

Ollie isn't here. Ollie is *missing*.

For all I know, he could be dead.

No. I won't let myself think that. I can't. This is one of

Gravelle's plots. To pull the wool over our eyes yet again, for some messed-up reason I can't even begin to guess at. But he wouldn't kill Ollie—his biological son. Would he?

My friends arrive and crowd around me.

"Emma?" Pru exhorts. I must look the way I feel on the inside: utterly bereft. "What's going on? What's wrong?"

I tell them everything. About leaving my room at 4:00 p.m. the past two days. About how I read his thoughts and heard him communicating with Gravelle about the installation. How he mentioned Pollux.

"Four p.m.," I tell them in a rush, my words tumbling out in no order, with no organization. "That was the time when Ollie's Duplicate... It was like he turned off, or on, or something," I say, trying to explain it. "He was there physically, but mentally, he wasn't. I heard these strange thoughts, not the thoughts of Ollie or someone resembling Ollie, but more like instructions. I bet they aren't even in his head the majority of the day, when he believes he's Ollie. Because they do believe, don't they? Even the first Duplicates who came here believed they were Tessa, Archer, and Jake. When Ollie deactivated—or whatever it was that happened from 4:00 to 4:05 p.m.—he communicated with Gravelle via his plum. He mentioned a time stamp on his wrist," I add, recalling that detail now. "I don't think he consciously wanted me to hear him think that. Maybe he knew it might give him away? But you know what it's like when you try *not* to think about something. It only makes you think about it more."

I stop, getting my bearings, then remember I haven't told

them everything. "He said something about an infrared light. That must be how you can see the time stamp," I explain.

I watch as my friends process this, going through the same line of thinking I did. Wondering how, and when, and why?

Maude's pacing, trying to work this out in her mind. "The first Duplicates who came to campus were Duplicates of original kids. Of Tessa. Of Archer. And of Jake…"

"And now Ollie," I supply. "It's the kids who were originally cloned…"

"Resulting in us," Ansel says.

"Who does that leave?" I jump in. "Just Madison."

"And Pru," Pippa says, her voice sounding deflated.

We all turn, on reflex, to stare at Pru, who shakes her head.

"But I'm not—I'm *me*," she says, squaring her shoulders. "This time stamp. What is it exactly?"

"My guess is that the Duplicates were all given date and time codes, kind of like birth-certificate records from when they were 'born,'" Jago says. "And Gravelle put that information on their wrists so he could track them. Like produce or a carton of milk."

"Or cattle," I add, disgusted.

"He'd have to, wouldn't he?" Theodora asks. "Otherwise, things could go totally sideways, if he had no way of differentiating original from Duplicate. He had to build in some kind of marker to be able to quickly check on his creations, keep them in line."

Pru's pacing, thinking this over. "Where do we get this infrared light the Ollie Duplicate mentioned?"

"The science lab," Maude answers with authority. "I'm sure I saw one there last year when Emma and I were snooping around. I bet I still have access from Ransom's experiment. I'll meet you back here. Twenty minutes," she shouts, already taking off and disappearing into the thick woods.

"If this Ollie seemed so similar to the real Oliver," Pippa wonders out loud. "Then where did his memories come from? How would he have access to every thought and feeling Ollie ever experienced? How would he know all of Ollie's history?"

"My guess is that it's a combination of downloaded thoughts and incredibly meticulous training," Ansel says, thoughtful. "We already know Gravelle's been manipulating minds with his portal. And he showed you those memories last year, didn't he, Emma? Of his time at Darkwood?"

It's true. Those memories transported me to the time when Gravelle was Johnny Underwood, when he was expelled from Darkwood in his junior year.

"The first Duplicates didn't seem to have all those memories," I say. "They didn't possess all the nuances and life experience that this Ollie clone has. Why?"

"Gravelle kept Ollie on the island for nearly a year," Ansel reminds me. "Who knows what he did to him, what he put him through? The tests and studies and 'research'? He could have downloaded every single memory of Ollie's, every single thought, and transferred it to this Duplicate."

I lean against the stone wall by the circular driveway and pull my arms around myself, suddenly shivering in the frigid air.

"Where is Ollie?" I whisper, looking from one friend to the next. "Back on the island? What's he done to my best friend now? What if—"

But I don't allow myself to say the thought out loud. *What if he's dead. What if I never see him again.* It's incomprehensible.

"I can't lose Ollie again," I cry out. My chest feels like someone's tightening it in a corset, pulling it so taut I soon won't be able to breathe.

I don't say out loud what I'm thinking about, which is the way we left things, before Ollie was taken... How I pulled away from that kiss and told him I couldn't love him that way. If that's the last thing I ever said to him...

No, no, no. It can't be. It won't be.

"We'll find him," Pru says gently, moving up to wrap her arms around me. When I look over her shoulder, too numb to even let myself cry, my eyes land on Levi's. He's standing there in the cold air, hands in his pockets, watching me with such an expression of pain on his face, I have to look away.

◇━┤ ├━◇

We're all still standing by the wall in silence as twilight falls, when Maude returns from the science lab in record speed, a pen-size device in her hand. It must be the infrared light.

"Give me your wrists," Maude instructs Pru, who's already holding her arms out for inspection. Maude scans them thoroughly with the light. We're all on edge; what will we do if—I can't think about it. Not Pru too...

"Nothing," Maude declares, slipping the light in her pocket. "You're clear."

"The rest of us should check too," Pippa says. "Me, Ansel, Thea… Just to be sure."

"But Ollie's an original, not a Similar," I say, working through this in my head. "Gravelle's replacing originals, right?"

But Maude's already shining the light on her own wrists. Nothing. She quickly scans Pippa and Jago's wrists. Same.

"He's not making Duplicates of you!" I say, unable to keep the emotion out of my voice.

"Well, technically, the Ollie Duplicate could be a Duplicate of me as much as Ollie," Levi says quietly.

"Except he isn't a copy of you," I remind him. "He has Ollie's memories, not yours. He believes he's Oliver Ward." I try not to let myself cry, but it's all I feel like doing. "What are we going to *do* with him?" I mean the Duplicate Ollie. And another thought occurs to me. I don't want to confront this one either. "Do we tell Jane?"

That thought guts me. Because I don't know if Jane will survive this again. When she thought Ollie died last year, it nearly killed her too.

"What options do we have?" Levi asks, finally speaking up. My eyes fly to his. For the moment, I can't even remember why I've been so angry at him. All I know is that Ollie is gone, and nothing else matters.

"I could confide in my father. He could alert the Quarry. Get their backing," Pru says.

"No," Maude answers quickly. "Not yet. What if—"

"It's a mistake?" Pru cuts her off. "I had the same thought. If we show our hand—if we let Gravelle know that we've discovered this Duplicate…"

"We'll have no cards left to play," I finish her thought. "I say we wait. If we can figure out what Gravelle wants, what his ultimate goal is…"

"We can get two steps ahead of him," Theodora says, her voice resolute.

I don't know if I believe we can. Or if that seems even remotely possible. Gravelle has spent nearly two decades scheming, making plans. We have no idea what he *wants*, except to screw with everyone we know and love.

"If we tell Jane," Ansel speaks up, interrupting my thoughts, "she'll immediately leave Darkwood, won't she? And try to look for Ollie?"

"If she suspects he's back on Castor Island…" I think out loud.

"Then that's where she'd go, welcome or not."

"Isn't that what Gravelle wants?" Pru asks. "To lure her there? He still loves her, in his warped way. What if this is all a ploy to get her on his turf?"

"Then we can't let that happen," I say quietly. "Jane won't be able to do anyone any good if she's locked up there. Which means we have to keep this a secret from her."

"But is that fair to her?" Levi asks. "What if we knew about Ollie, that he was gone, that he'd been replaced by a clone—and we didn't tell *you*?"

"I'd kill you," I answer wryly.

"Exactly," he says. But his voice is soft and lacking any edge. He's trying to help. They all are.

Levi's right. I have to tell Jane. Still, we can't let her go off on a suicide mission to Castor Island. As much as I want to find Ollie, we have to be smart about it. We have to figure out what Gravelle wants and find a way to stop him, to outsmart him.

I wish I had even the slightest idea how.

Later that night, when I finally collapse in bed, the tears come. I am racked with sobs as the reality of what I've discovered hits me hard, like a speeding truck. I cry myself to sleep at two in the morning.

THE PARENTS

THE NEXT MORNING, I head straight to Jane's office. I've barely slept at all. Telling her that her son has been replaced is going to be the hardest thing I've ever had to do. Harder, even, than telling her last year about Levi's existence. Losing her son the first time broke her in two. I don't know if she'll survive the blow this time.

When I get to her office and knock softly on the door, a gravelly voice answers.

"Yes?"

I'm confused. That doesn't sound like Jane. It sounds like…

I push open the door. Principal Fleischer. She's sitting behind Jane's desk, acting like she owns the place.

"I don't remember inviting you in." Fleischer surveys me with disdain.

"Oh," I say, flummoxed. "Where's Ja—I mean, Headmistress Ward?"

"Interim headmistress," Fleischer responds curtly. "And she's gone to California on urgent business. Won't be back for quite some time."

"What kind of business?" I demand.

"That is none of your concern, young lady," Fleischer answers coldly. "You may go."

She turns back to her papers—probably detention slips she's filling out—leaving me with no choice but to turn around and leave, my head spinning.

Jane's not *here*? She's gone back to California. Why do I get the sense that this is Gravelle's doing, because he somehow *knows* that we know about Ollie? Could this be a coincidence? Possibly. If what he truly wants is to lure Jane to Castor Island, then this wrinkle won't help him.

As I walk away from Jane's office, blindsided, I consider my options. I could call her. But I can't tell Jane about Ollie over the phone. She'd panic. And whatever has brought her back to California, whether it's urgent Ward, Inc. business or something with Booker, I can't spring this Ollie news on her. It could send her into a tailspin.

"We'll wait," I tell my friends, resolutely, at lunch.

"Are you sure?" Maude asks, barely touching the sandwich on her plate.

"No," I answer honestly. "But I don't see how freaking her out so she rushes back here will help. Do you?"

None of my friends answer, because the truth is, we simply don't know.

I'm a wreck for the next week. I can barely concentrate on my classes and only manage to go through the motions of extra-curriculars and homework and meals. There's only one thing on my mind: Ollie.

I worry that he's suffering. I worry that Gravelle is putting him through more mind control on Castor Island. I worry that he's being forced to relive the worst moments of his life, over and over again. I don't let myself indulge in my worst fear of all—that Ollie's not with Gravelle, but lying dead somewhere, lifeless.

Compounding my heartbreak over Ollie's absence is the unwelcome presence of his Duplicate. He's so like Ollie, in every way—yet I know it's not him. It isn't this boy's fault. He's a pawn like the rest of us. And I do my best not to let on that something's wrong, because I don't want him reporting back to Gravelle that we're on to him. Until we figure out what we're going to do, we have to play the game. That means I have to act like everything's normal when Duplicate Ollie's around. We all do.

It takes every effort I have left to continue our easy banter. To answer his sweet and sarcastic comments with our usual relaxed rapport. My heart's not in it. In fact, it's tangled and battered and more bruised than ever. Pretending this Duplicate

Ollie is my best friend is one of the hardest things I've ever had to do.

I wake up one late January morning after a fitful night of sleep. I can't hide the dark circles under my eyes anymore, not even with concealer. What's the point of trying? I know I'm depressed—deeply so. I have no pharmas this time around to alleviate my pain. I could see the school therapist, but what would I possibly say to her? My best friend's been taken, *again*? And this time he's been replaced by a clone? But, oh yeah, don't tell a soul?

Every day, I think of how I left things with Ollie—my Ollie—and I'm filled with regret.

Of course I love him. Of course there's a part of me that could see myself with him. Loving him. I wish I'd said *that*, instead of pulling away, running away, like I did.

Pru's already gone to crew practice when I roll out of bed at seven. I slip on jeans and my warmest coat, rooting around in my closet for my gloves. I'm on my way out when Dash interrupts me.

"You have an incoming email, Emmaline," he tells me in his comforting voice. "From the University of Oxford. It looks quite official."

I stop what I'm doing and pull up the email on my plum. I'm momentarily confused—why would they be contacting me now?—until I remember that Oxford sends out its admissions decisions early. In January.

My heart sinks when I see what they've written. In spite of my "strong academic record," I've been wait-listed until the university has a chance to review recent materials submitted to the school. I know instantly that those "materials" must be the video Harlowe sent them of me leaping from the boathouse roof. Surely Oxford isn't taking this footage seriously, is it? Furious at Harlowe, I swipe off my plum screen and head to the dining hall.

Duplicate Oliver is in line there when I arrive. I'm exhausted and shaken, and my heart almost breaks its steady rhythm at the sight of him.

"Em," he says, brightening at the sight of me. "Why do I feel like I haven't seen you in days?"

It hasn't been days. But I've been distant with him, and he must sense that. Coexisting with him, here at school, is almost harder than it was to accept Levi last year. Tears prick my eyes, and I feel Ollie's absence like an open wound. But what can I expect this Duplicate to do? It's not like I'd want to send him back to that island; his life there couldn't have been meaningful, and it was probably filled with suffering.

"Homework," I say. "Been swamped." I'm not going to be able to brush him off. But that doesn't mean we'll be having any deep conversations. I couldn't. Pretending like that—it would break me. When we make it to our regular table, the Similars are already there. Maude raises an eyebrow when she sees Duplicate Ollie plop down next to me, and I shrug.

"Ollie," I say, hating every second of this but knowing it's necessary. "Has your mom buzzed you at all? Told you why she left Darkwood?"

Theodora shoots me a look, but I ignore her. As far as Jane knows, Ollie is himself. I'm sure that's Ollie's actual plum he has on his wrist. His clothes, his books. It's sickening to think about how Gravelle's men must have made the switch, installing this clone into Ollie's real life, so I don't let myself. All I know is that if Jane contacted Ollie, then *this* Ollie would be the recipient of that buzz.

"I got a quick note yesterday. She said it was something to do with the family business," Ollie says between bites of oatmeal. "My mom had to deal with it in person."

A shiver goes up and down my spine. I'm more sure than ever, now, that Gravelle had something to do with this. He's a majority shareholder in Ward, Inc. and has been ever since he manipulated Levi into taking that stock. Maybe Gravelle *doesn't* want us to tell Jane what we know and, realizing somehow that we'd found out about Ollie, he lured her away.

Maybe I'm just losing my grip on reality. I set my spoon down, unable to eat another bite.

Instead, I pull up the email from Oxford on my tablet to show my friends. I need the distraction right now, unwelcome as their letter is. Maude pulls up one of her own, explaining she was also wait-listed until further notice. So was Theodora. Duplicate Ollie grabs my tablet from my hand and scans it, confused and ticked off. I tell him what Harlowe's done.

"You have to call them and explain," he responds. "Tell them I was already planning on spending the summer with you there! This is unacceptable. What about my bangers and mash?"

My heart flips. This isn't Ollie. This is a stand-in who thinks he's my best friend. And I'm going to have to spend the foreseeable future pretending he's not an imposter. Pippa, Ansel, Jago, and Levi rescue me from having to respond. They jump in to say they were accepted, though they make it clear they haven't committed to going. Ansel's exploring NYU, where Archer goes. Levi sounds like the whole idea of college doesn't appeal to him, though I can't pinpoint why. I don't look at him, but I secretly agree; without Ollie, what's the point of thinking about the future at all? But this isn't about me. It's about Harlowe, and her vindictive scheme against us.

"She keeps trying to one-up us," I mutter. "But we can make sure her rally's dead in the water, can't we? Jane will cancel it when she returns to campus. She's already said she's dismantling DAAM. Revoking their charter."

"Why do I feel like Harlowe will find a way to throw the rally anyway?" Pippa says.

"Let's make sure she doesn't," Maude responds neatly as she digs into her breakfast. "But just in case, I have something else in the works. Something Harlowe is really not going to like."

We all stare at Maude as she chews. "What?" Theodora finally yells, then lowers her voice. "That's all you're going to tell us?"

"For now? Yes," Maude answers.

⟡—⊣⊢—⟡

The next few weeks pass uneventfully—in the worst way. With each new day, I'm increasingly disturbed that Jane hasn't returned to campus yet. Why? What's happening in California that's pressing enough for her to abandon her post at Darkwood? And worse—what if I've made a huge mistake by not telling her about Ollie?

On top of that, we all feel awful that we're attending classes and choir concerts and school assemblies while Ollie is likely trapped on Castor Island. But we know that trying to rescue him there, without a plan, without knowing what Gravelle *wants*, could prove deadly for all of us. I have to admit, I feel very alone, more so than ever. I know my friends care that Ollie's missing. But apart from Pru, who loves Ollie nearly as much as I do, I can't help but feel resentful that Maude, Theodora, and the others don't really understand my loss. They *want* to. They know intellectually how terrifying this is for me. But Ollie isn't one of their own. They simply can't know how devastated I am over this—with the exception of Levi, who, in his own way, may understand me more than I'm willing to admit.

The only problem is, he and I still aren't speaking. Not about anything real.

I move in a fog from class to meals to Ten meetings, barely aware of the day or time, following Dash's gentle reminders that it's time to eat or get out of bed. The only silver lining is learning that Harlowe, Ivy, and Graham were sentenced to a month of duty for hanging that poster of me. Jane ordered it before she abruptly left for California. They shoot us dirty looks from across the dining hall, but we mostly avoid interacting. Maude holds off on the midnight sessions. We're not eager to spend any extra time with Harlowe.

In a school-wide announcement, Principal Fleischer reminds us that Dark Weekend is only a week away. I feel dread at the thought of having to see my dad again. It's hard enough being around Duplicate Ollie. But facing my dad now, after he never made any attempt to say he was sorry—it's too much. I don't know if I can handle all the pent-up emotion roiling inside of me. I might break.

I pray my dad will be too busy with his work to make the trip, but no such luck this time. He buzzes me that he'll be there, and he's hoping we can talk. Unless he can find Ollie, talking is the last thing I want to do.

The Friday of Dark Weekend dawns bright and crisp. It's a frigid February morning, but at least the sun is out. Still, that offers me little consolation as I stand in the circular drive in front of the main house, shivering, and not just from the cold, but because my whole world is off-kilter.

I watch as Jaeger Stanwick ambles up the hill and greets Pippa and Pru. Frederica Leroy exits a limo, clad in a dramatic cape and heels, and she approaches Theodora, who waves half-heartedly from the brick path. Following Frederica out of the limo like a loyal puppy dog is a harried-looking Tessa. I assume she must be officially out of Creekside. It's been more than six months since her court-ordered tenure began. I'm a little surprised to see her here, at Dark Weekend, but I guess she had nothing else to do.

Then I hear Frederica loudly insisting that Tessa talk to Principal Fleischer about internship opportunities.

"Dartmouth wants you to have some real-life work experience before you matriculate in the fall," Frederica hisses at Tessa. "Go on. Talk to Principal Fleischer. *Now!*" She practically pushes Tessa in Fleischer's direction.

I feel for Tessa in that moment. As much as I take issue with the girl and what she put Pru through last year, I wouldn't wish that awkward conversation with Fleischer on anyone. Still, she's lucky Dartmouth is taking her at all after what she did, even if it wasn't entirely her fault. I see Tessa shuffle her feet in her platform wedges before hobbling over to Fleischer.

"Emma," says a voice, commanding my attention. I lift my gaze from Tessa over to where my father stands, buttoned up as usual in a suit, his rolling suitcase at his side. I tense up but try not to show it. We exchange a cursory hug before walking down with the rest of the school to the chapel, where assembly will start in a few minutes.

"Did you open your Christmas gift?" my father asks as we stroll down the path, the wind whipping us and snow flurries starting to fall. I catch a few on my mitten, doing whatever I can to hold it together.

"Yes," I answer. "I opened it."

"Good," he says. "I meant what I wrote. This trip will be for us. No work, no distractions. I want the chance to get to know you again, sweetie. To make up for lost time."

Is this my father's half-hearted attempt at an apology? Though a part of me welcomes it like fresh oxygen, another part of me wants to shut down this conversation entirely.

"Can we not do this now?" I plead with him. He can't know how much I have on my mind right now. If he did, he'd understand why this isn't the time to pick up our curtailed discussion from Christmas break. I might crack from the intensity of it all.

We reach the chapel and follow the growing crowd through the double doors. Sliding into a pew, my father at my side, I spot Bianca Huxley across the way. She and Maude aren't sitting together, but she's here. Fresh off the campaign trail, she's dressed in a smart Chanel suit and pearls. I recoil thinking of her latest stump speeches and her stance on cloning.

I catch sight of Levi across the aisle, noting with a pang that he's sitting alone. Booker and Jane aren't here to support him for the weekend. And even if Jane *were* here, she wouldn't be here for Levi. Only Ollie. Levi and Jane never were given a second chance to reconcile, and I don't know that they ever will. That thought makes me infinitely sad.

I'm drawn out of my thoughts when Principal Fleischer steps up to the podium. She welcomes everyone to Dark Weekend and begins a bland speech about excellence that captures none of my attention. Ollie slides in next to me, and for my father's sake, I have to act like everything's normal. Like this isn't a copy of my best friend.

The only part of Fleischer's speech I catch is the end, when she informs us that the Ten dinner is canceled this year. Jane isn't back yet from California, and Fleischer believes the dinner is a frivolous, unnecessary affair. Even though I can't stand Fleischer's brand of education—devoid of any fun or humor— I'm secretly relieved. That dinner would have been another event I'd have to sit through, pretending I'm okay.

My father insists on taking me to out to a restaurant on Saturday night, before he leaves early Sunday morning on the first flight back to San Francisco. I reluctantly agree, because I can't think of an excuse to get me out of it. But when he asks Ollie to join us, I inwardly cringe. It's not my father's fault; he has no idea that Ollie isn't himself. I hope I can rush us through the meal as quickly as possible.

I'm still considering telling my dad everything. It's all I've been able to think about since he got here. I've run scenario after scenario in my head. How he might be able to help us, if I told him the truth about Ollie's Duplicate. How he might just as easily insist on going to the authorities or the FBI, putting Ollie in grave danger without meaning to. How he might try to protect me, and his company, instead of putting Ollie first.

We're at a cramped Italian restaurant downtown, near my father's hotel, silently eating spaghetti while Duplicate Ollie shares details with us about the new documentary film he's working on. Ollie's copy is oblivious to all my woes, of course, though a part of me wonders if he can tell something's been off with me for weeks.

"Stress," I tell him when he asks me if I'm okay. "Waiting to hear from colleges. I promise, that's all it is."

My father's quiet, but that's no surprise; he's a man of few words as it is, and he never was good at father-daughter outings like this one.

I'm about to suggest we skip dessert—desperate as I am to end this whole affair and send my father back to his hotel, and California—when I get a buzz on my plum.

Eager for any excuse to flee this dinner, even momentarily, I gaze down at the message, even though I know it's rude. How many times has my father left a dinner midway through to attend to business? I know he won't dare say anything.

I'm surprised when I see who the message is from: Jane.

Emma, I only have a second. I'm writing because I think you'll know what to do. There's no time, they're outside my study door, two men, I think they want to take—

The buzz stops there, midsentence. I read it again, to be sure I'm not imagining things.

Take what? Take *her*? Two men? Outside her study?

My stomach drops to my feet, and I think I'm going to be sick if I don't get out of this cramped, hot restaurant.

"Air," I tell Ollie and my dad. "I just—need. Air."

I bolt. When I make it outside onto the sidewalk, I suck in the cold air in gulps. It burns my chest, and I double over, panting, feeling like I can't breathe. The Vermont chill is choking me. Suffocating me.

Two men, trying to take Jane? But who? And why? How did she write me this buzz? They must have been in her house, and she momentarily got away from them. She was in her study, she said.

But who would take her? *Why* would they take her?

My insides turn to icicles as it dawns on me *exactly* why they'd take her.

Why Gravelle would lure her back home, to California, with a made-up work emergency involving Ward, Inc.

Why he would send two men to kidnap her like he kidnapped Ollie.

There's only one possible reason. To replace her with a Duplicate.

THE REPLACEMENTS

MY MIND RACES as I process this. Jane is being kidnapped as we speak. Replaced with a copy. I'm sure of it.

A voice in my head playing devil's advocate tells me I must be wrong. Duplicates have all been copies of original *kids*. Like Tessa, Archer, and Jake. And Ollie.

Not adults. Not *parents*.

But this is Gravelle's master plan, isn't it? I don't know how I didn't realize it before. This is what he meant by the Legacy Project. Gravelle would never just replace Ollie—his plans are never that small, that simple.

No, I'm sure now that his plan, this entire year, has been to replace *all* the DNA parents with clones.

My heart races as I remember where I am. Standing in front of the restaurant, with my father inside. *My father.* It hits me all at once that if I'm right, that might not really be my father in there. It's likely his copy.

The realization slams into me like a body blow.

"Dash," I ask, my voice breathless. "I need your help. Ask Genevieve if my father hired interior designers to come to our house over Christmas break."

"Certainly, Emma. Your heart rate is elevated."

"I know!"

Seconds later, Dash reports back. "There are no such employees on record, Emmaline. Why?"

I can't answer. My voice feels stuck in my throat. Those weren't designers. They came to my house to *replace* my father. To install his Duplicate. I'm sure of it.

I buzz Maude and ask her to meet me here, with the infrared light.

There's only one way to know for sure if my father's an imposter or not. I'll have to check for the time stamp on his wrist.

But first, I call Jane. I get her voicemail, of course, but I don't leave a message. What if she's not the one who would receive it? I can't take that risk.

Before I can figure out what to do next, Duplicate Ollie's at my side. "Em? Don't tell me again that you're okay. Because I know you aren't. What's wrong?"

I rack my brain for an excuse but can't think of anything to say except that I'm sick, which isn't far from the truth. I do feel sick, totally off-kilter, like my world is spinning. "I think I'm coming down with something," I tell him, hoping I sound convincing. "But let's go back inside. I want to finish dinner before my dad has to leave."

I need to kill time now, until Maude gets here. It's torture, but I know how important it is I get a chance to scan my father's wrists. If my theory is right, and he's a Duplicate, I'll know for sure why those men were trying to take Jane.

For the first time ever, I'm grateful to Ollie's Duplicate for launching into another long-winded story about his latest documentary subject. Heart pounding wildly in my chest, I keep glancing at my plum, barely holding it together as I fear for Jane. I feel so helpless to act, to do anything that could save her.

Maude arrives right as my father's paying the bill. I slip out to talk to her privately, hoping Ollie will continue to keep my father occupied while I confess my suspicions. That my dad's a Duplicate. That Jane's being replaced as we speak.

Maude's shocked by my news but rallies quickly. I sometimes forget how strong she is. How capable. "How do you want to do it?" she asks, indicating the infrared light.

"There is no good way, is there?" I say. "I'll distract Ollie. He can't see this."

She nods, and we both head inside the restaurant. I pull Ollie aside, asking him privately to please skip dessert because I don't feel well but don't want to worry my dad. I make sure Ollie's back is turned to our table, but I have a direct line of sight to Maude sitting down next to my dad, grabbing his right wrist, and shining the light on it.

I don't know why I'm so stunned to see it there: the time stamp, plain as day.

003.68.

"Emma? What's going on?" my father asks, looking confused. I'm too shocked to speak. At least he doesn't seem to understand what we've just uncovered. Gravelle must have programmed him that way—all of them—not to know anything about the time stamps except during the five minutes a day when they communicate with him.

"I have to go. I love you, Dad," I say quickly before taking Maude by the arm and fleeing. Duplicate Ollie says a quick goodbye to my dad and follows after us. I explain to him hastily I might throw up and just need a good night's sleep.

I feel a pang of distress over leaving my dad so abruptly, but I have to remind myself that that man is not really my father. My father is somewhere else, probably Castor Island, locked up, hopefully not tortured. *Or dead.*

Back on campus, a protective Maude promises Ollie she'll get me back to my room and will stay with me to make sure I'm not feverish. Duplicate Ollie looks skeptical but agrees, promising to check on me in the morning. Once Ollie's gone, Maude and I double back to the circular drive, where our friends are waiting for us when we get there.

I show my friends the buzz from Jane. Maude tells them, her voice flat, about the time stamp on my dad's wrist.

As she's talking, I'm struck by a memory, from yesterday. Tessa in those platform wedges. Those were the wedges her *Duplicate* wore, during that September weekend when the first three Duplicates crashed the masquerade ball. It hits me like a ton of bricks. That wasn't Tessa getting out of that limo. *It was her Duplicate.*

With increasing dread closing in on me, I wonder: How many have been "installed"? How many replaced?

Ollie... My father. Jane. Tessa.

"I think it's everyone," I whisper.

"What are you saying, Emma?" Pru asks, tears encroaching in her eyes.

"I'm saying that I think Gravelle's plan was, *is*, to replace all our DNA parents. The de Leons, the Choates, Booker, Frederica and Tessa Leroy, my dad, and now Jane." I feel utterly bereft. This was all happening right under our noses.

"But how would that even work?" Jago asks, pacing the snow-covered ground. "Did your dad seem like himself?"

"Very much so," I answer, breathless.

"How would Gravelle have downloaded your father's memories and thoughts and personality into this Duplicate? It doesn't make sense. Ollie was on Castor Island long enough for Gravelle to obtain all his thoughts, but—"

"An implant," Maude cuts in. "A tiny device, inserted near the base of the brain. One that can send memories to a host body remotely. It could be implanted while a person is sleeping. They'd never know."

I'm reeling as I try to sort this out in my mind.

I'm also despairing. "Jane's being kidnapped right this minute, and there's nothing we can do about it?" I feel myself start to crumble under the weight of what we've discovered.

Levi must sense me faltering, because he reaches out a hand to steady me.

"I should have realized. I should have known," I tell him, meeting his eyes. "He replaced Ollie over Christmas break. Probably a lot of the others too. Not just my dad but Booker, Archer's dads…"

"What about Bianca?" Pru asks quietly. "And my dad? They're here on campus for Dark Weekend. I'm going to tell my father, tonight," she says, interrupting my downward spiral. "He has to know. If he gets the Quarry on board, they can protect him. And her."

"Bianca's a presidential candidate," I say, stating the obvious. "If she's replaced…"

None of us want to consider that possibility. It's too huge, too terrible, to consider the kind of power and influence her Duplicate could wield.

"You can't tell Jaeger until you've checked his wrist. Bianca's too," I say. "We may already be too late."

Gone are my concerns about telling Jane about Ollie. This is so much bigger than just Ollie now. This is massive, and the potential consequences are horrifying.

"We'll do it together," Maude tells Pru.

"And if we find a time stamp?" Pru asks, near tears.

No one answers. We all know what that would mean. And none of us want to face it.

Late that night, we convene in the Tower Room. Maude and Pru aren't here yet, and we're a silent crew, waiting to hear about the time stamps. Waiting to find out if Gravelle's plan has gone off without a hitch.

Pru is breathless when she reaches us and opens the door. I leap to my feet, my heart pounding in my chest.

"No time stamps," she says. "On Bianca or my dad. Gravelle hasn't been able to replace them, not yet."

I feel my breathing slow, and I'm utterly thankful. And yet, my father is still gone. Ollie too. And Jane. Even as I'm filled with relief over Bianca and Jaeger, I'm still reeling, walking on shaky ground.

"I told my dad everything," Pru explains as Maude arrives at the doorway. "He's already alerting the Quarry and will put safeguards in place, including extra security to ensure he and Bianca aren't taken. Bianca has super high-level bodyguards, but Gravelle obviously thinks he can infiltrate them. My dad will make sure he doesn't. The Quarry's tailing her car all the way to the airport, standing by to intercept any kidnappers."

I don't even remember falling into bed, but I must have at some point, because when I wake up Sunday morning, bright light is streaming in through the windows, and everything comes crashing back to me.

The Duplicates. My father and Jane, replaced.

I feel a new sense of dread now that the adrenaline of yesterday has worn off. The thought of both Ollie and my father, held prisoner on Castor Island. Or worse…

We're a solemn bunch the rest of the day. I feel like there's been a death. Multiple losses. The absence of the real Jane, and Ollie, and my dad—it's too much.

At dinner that night, Pru tries to offer me some comfort. "I know you're worried, Emma."

"Worried? I'm not *worried*. I'm terrified. My best friend's being held or tortured or *worse*. So's my *dad*. If Gravelle kills them, I'll have…" I'm about to say *no one*, but I don't, because it's not entirely true. I'll still have Levi. At least, I think I will. I'll still have Pru and the other Similars. But the prospect of losing my dad and Ollie and Jane in one fell swoop, it's unthinkable. "Look, I don't expect you to understand," I say to my friends. "I know you care about your DNA dads, Ansel. And Jago, you never wanted your DNA parents to be replaced. But this is Ollie we're talking about. And my dad. I know your childhood was lonely, but you had each other. I only had them. And Jane, she's the closest thing to a mother I'll ever get. So if something happens to her—"

I can't help it; I start crying. "I'm sorry," I tell Pru. "You lost your mom. And she's not coming back." I don't say that to be cruel, but to let her know that I acknowledge her loss—and that it's cavernous.

"It was devastating," she admits. "And it sucks worse than anything. But that's why I won't let you lose your family, Em. Not your dad. Or Ollie. We'll find them."

But I'm not comforted.

THE RALLY

FEBRUARY PASSES INTO March, and although Jaeger keeps assuring us that the Quarry is keeping him and Bianca safe, I worry. With every day that passes, I dread that I'll never see Ollie or my dad or Jane again.

Duplicate Jane has arrived to assume her headmistress role. Of course, no one at Darkwood is even remotely aware she's a stand-in clone. But *we* know, and now there's no chance that I'll confide in her about what's happened to Ollie. I pray that wherever they've taken Jane, whether it's Castor Island or some other remote location, she's *with* her son now. I feel guilty; if I'd told her about Ollie, maybe she could have saved herself. But I know it's not fair to blame myself. How could I have known that Jane was Gravelle's next target?

It was bad enough coexisting with Ollie's Duplicate, but now the sight of Jane's copy striding around the school, wearing Jane's clothes and mingling with students, guts me with equal measure. We wonder who we could reasonably go to for help. The Darkwood board? But what if they didn't believe us? Or worse, what if they're in Gravelle's pocket? It's not lost on any of us that, except for Jaeger, the adults we can usually count on, like my dad and Jane, are the very people we can no longer trust, because they aren't themselves.

In my head, I make desperate plans to leave school and look for them myself. I know it's a reckless, stupid idea, one that could get me killed. But I'll crack if I consider the reality that my hands really are tied. That I have no out, no way to help my loved ones. So I let myself imagine a heroic rescue. It's the only thing that allows me to close my eyes at night and get any rest.

The only consolation in any of this is that Bianca and Jaeger haven't been replaced yet, and we discovered Gravelle's master plan in time to keep them safe. Still, we know Gravelle is nothing if not persistent. I believe in my gut he has not given up on his plans to kidnap them. I wish I knew how, and when.

One early March morning, I arrive in the dining hall to new flyers being passed around to the student body. They advertise the Darkwood Academy Human Rights Club, and I'm fooled, at first, into thinking someone's actually started a civil rights organization on campus. Then I see Harlowe, flanked by a couple of first years, Ivy, and Graham. Harlowe stands there watching as the others hand out leaflets. I get my hands on one.

Darkwood Academy Human Rights Club
Help Us Defend Humanity
<u>Our</u> **Rights**
<u>Our</u> **Safety**
<u>Our</u> **Identities**
<u>Our</u> **Freedoms**
First meeting: March 22, the gym, 7:00 p.m.
Spread the word...

It's vague enough that you could miss it if you didn't know what you were looking for. But it's clearly DAAM, restructured and given a new name.

"Who approved this?" I ask the Similars, slamming the paper onto the table.

I get my answer when I notice Principal Fleischer walking over to where Harlowe and her friends are answering questions and recruiting members. Fleischer doesn't seem angry at Harlowe. If anything, she looks pleased.

"Fleischer is their faculty sponsor," I blurt, almost spitting out my soup. "I bet she signed off on this. After Jane dismantled DAAM, Harlowe must have bypassed her and gone straight to Fleischer for a sign-off. Probably when Jane was back in California."

"So the 'first meeting' is basically another anti-clone rally," Pru says in disgust. "Disguised as a pro-human rally. As if you're not *human*." She almost can't say the word.

"Is that how they're going to spin this? With rhetoric around us not being fully human because of our 'super strength'?" Theodora asks. We shrug. It's likely. But we won't know unless we go to the rally and see for ourselves.

It's a freezing Saturday when March 22 rolls around. We head to the gym, furious that this rally's going unchecked but not daring to miss it. This rally goes against everything Darkwood stands for. I burn inside at the thought of Fleischer approving this.

When we arrive and take our seats in folding chairs, it looks like the entire student body is here. I guess everyone realized this wasn't a club meeting, but something a lot more sensational. Kids chatter all around us. Some whisper that this new club is DAAM reinvented. Others seem clueless about what's about to unfold.

"Welcome, students," says a voice over the chitchat. It's Harlowe, talking into a microphone. She addresses the crowd. "Thanks for joining us today for the first official meeting of the Darkwood Academy Human Rights Club, otherwise known as DAHRC." She pronounces it like "Dark." "Fitting name, don't you think? Because of Darkwood... Never mind." She laughs. "You all get it." Kids laugh and lean in to listen, and I can't help but feel sick. Harlowe hates the Similars. She hates *us*. I know how much she's relishing this moment.

"First order of business: explaining the club's mission statement and how it came to be. Some of you know that another group I was involved in, one I'll refrain from naming, had its charter revoked, because of some unseemly politics on the part of the administration. DAHRC is a new club that focuses not on the folks who are trying to take *away* our freedoms, but on *us*, and preserving the liberties we hold dear. That's why we're here today. To champion *our* rights. Our freedoms. Our individuality. Our humanity."

I scan the gym for Jane. I know it will be her Duplicate, not her. Still, if she possesses all of Jane's thoughts and memories, she'd be equally disapproving of this rally. I don't see her. Only Fleischer, who stands in the corner, arms crossed over her chest.

"Let's just call this what it is," a voice speaks up from the crowd. It's Willa, from the Ten, standing up in the audience, her face scrawled with fury. "A hate group." I'm impressed. Willa seems to have found her confidence, and her voice.

There is muttering in the audience, a stir of reactions. Some agreeing. Others not.

Harlowe stares Willa down for a moment, then laughs. "I'd appreciate if you'd wait for the question and answer portion of the event to make unsolicited comments. But sure, I'll respond. This organization is the opposite of a 'hate group.' Like I said. We're here to celebrate human freedoms. Like free speech. And the right to our own individuality."

"At what cost?" Willa speaks up again, not backing down. "At whose expense? The Similars'? They graduate in two months. Let them finish their senior year in peace."

There's a rumbling in the audience. Apparently, a lot of kids agree.

Harlowe holds up a hand to silence the crowd. "I would love to do just that, Willa. But how can I, when they pose a threat to the very freedoms I just outlined?"

"How?" another student calls out, as someone else yells, "Lies! All lies!"

"I didn't want to bring this up today…" Harlowe sighs, regaining everyone's attention. "But you've left me no choice. I'm sure you all read my essay detailing the Similars' super strength. What I didn't know then, but I do now, is that the Similars' abilities are more far-reaching than that. More *inhuman*, some might say." Harlowe scans the crowd until her eyes land on me.

I feel my stomach churn. Is she going to call me out? Tell everyone about my mental abilities? What would they all think? I wouldn't blame them for finding it strange—even *fearing* me—but they'd have to know, I'd never use it to hurt anyone.

I feel Pru grabbing my hand. I'm not sure if it's a gesture of support, or a warning that I shouldn't storm up there and give Harlowe a piece of my mind.

"You talk about the Similars like they aren't human," another kid says. I crane my neck to see that it's a first year whose name I don't know. "But they were created from the cells of a couple of *humans*, weren't they? Or are you telling me that your good friend Madison Huxley isn't human, either?"

The crowd erupts, either at the mention of Madison's name or the fact that this kid has made a solid point. I see Jane slip into the back of the auditorium. I know it's her Duplicate, and not really her, but still, her presence calms me.

Harlowe raises a hand, trying to silence the crowd. "If you let me speak, you'll understand why I'm afraid the Similars' abilities are so dangerous—and criminal. Some of them can do things no human should be able to. Like read the thoughts of another person." Harlowe pauses for dramatic effect, letting that bombshell sink in for the crowd.

I hear a few laughs from the audience, and several gasps. Obviously, most of my classmates don't know what to think of what Harlowe's just said. I wouldn't if I were them.

"That's right," Harlowe continues, milking every second of this. "I have reason to suspect that one of the Similars has a unique ability to tap into others' thoughts."

"That's impossible!" a kid shouts from the crowd. Others react, agreeing with him.

"I assure you it's not, though I wish it were," Harlowe goes on. "This Similar was likely programmed from birth to be able to do this. And, as you know, that kind of genetic programming is illegal. It's against the law to choose your baby's hair and eye color. That's called eugenics, and it's dangerous. Just like it's dangerous for people to possess the ability to invade our privacy. Think of the power she could wield—"

"Enough!" Willa shouts over the crowd. Kids seem to be rallying behind her, nodding and standing around her in an ever-growing clump of solidarity. "We don't care what you have to say!"

"But—but this is my group," Harlowe answers, finally looking flustered. "I'm the president!"

A second later, someone grabs the mic out of Harlowe's hands. It's Ivy, and she's crying. In a rush, stringing all her words together almost incoherently, she blurts out into the microphone, "I want to say one thing, I'm so sorry, I never meant to hurt anyone or cause anyone pain. I just wanted to fit in."

"What are you *saying*?" Harlowe hisses at her.

"You're a bully, and I quit," Ivy whispers. She drops the mic and flees.

Without warning, Jane's Duplicate approaches Harlowe and picks up the dropped mic. I hear her say something to Harlowe, who looks increasingly pissed—and maybe even on the verge of tears.

Duplicate Jane taps on the microphone. "Attention, students. I have an announcement to make, and I'm afraid it's an unpleasant one." She addresses the crowd solemnly. "Not ten minutes ago, I received concrete evidence that three of our junior members of the Ten—Harlowe Shaw, Graham Rosen, and Ivy Li— hacked into the stratum system at the beginning of the school year in order to fix their scores. As of this moment, they are officially no longer part of the Ten."

A deafening silence fills the room. You could hear a pin drop. I look from Harlowe, who appears totally stricken, over to Ivy, who is openly bawling. In fact, it's the only sound anyone's making at all. I hear her hiccupped words between sobs, something to the effect of how she deserves this.

It only takes a moment for Harlowe's shock to morph into outrage.

"Evidence?" Harlowe protests. "I demand to know what this evidence is!"

"I can assure you, it's irrefutable," Duplicate Jane answers her, her voice emotionless.

Harlowe's eyes find me and the Similars in the crowd. "You did this," she hisses at us. We just stare like she's gone off the deep end, like we have no idea what she's talking about. It's the truth; we don't. "Don't you all see?" Harlowe addresses the crowd now, wildly grasping at straws. "The Similars set us up! They've been out to get us from day one! They hated us being in the Ten, and they've been planning something like this for months!"

The gym remains eerily quiet. Not a single person is stepping up to defend Harlowe.

"Harlowe, Ivy, Graham," Jane says. "I would urge you to consider yourself lucky you aren't being expelled from this school. Immediate removal from the Ten is nothing compared to what could have happened to you. Sophie and Willa, you were not involved in this incident and will retain your Ten status. But let this be a warning to you, to *all* of you. Being in the Ten is a privilege, not an inherent right."

That's it; the rally is officially over. Kids get up from their chairs, some looking stunned, others shaking their heads. I catch Maude's eyes as we filter out the door. Something glinting there makes me realize—*she* did this. She must have hacked the system and somehow pinned it on Harlowe and the others.

"Well done," I tell her.

"I couldn't let them antagonize us anymore," she admits. "It was necessary, but I didn't enjoy it."

"You did a little," I whisper back. Maude doesn't answer, but I know I'm right.

I file out of the gym with my friends, feeling victorious—but it's a hollow victory. Maybe Harlowe really will leave us alone from here on out. But what does that matter, when Gravelle is wreaking havoc on our lives? Who cares what Harlowe or anyone at this school thinks when Ollie and my dad and Jane are still gone?

"Guys?" Pru says, snagging me as we exit the gym. We all crowd around her, worried she has bad news.

"What's wrong?" I press, feeling my heart sink. What now?

"It's a buzz from my dad. He says Bianca's going to be appearing at a large-scale, public political rally in April. In New York City," Pru explains, checking her plum to get the details right. "It's her first big appearance, where she'll be officially declaring her candidacy for president."

I'm sure everyone else realizes it too, but I'm the only one to say it out loud.

"It's where she's going to be replaced," I whisper. "Isn't it?"

⟡—┤—⟡

We conclude that we have to go to the political rally. If we don't, if we stay here and allow Bianca to be replaced…Jaeger too… we'll never forgive ourselves. Luckily, the event falls over spring break. At least we can leave campus without raising too much suspicion. Of course, we have little idea what we're getting ourselves into. But we have to try.

Pru tells Jaeger about our plans. He doesn't even try to talk us out of going, which scares me. If he's willing to let us help, he must be as desperate—and worried—as we are. We ask him if Bianca would consider canceling the rally, but he knows she won't; without this high-profile public event, she'll lose her chance of making it to the primaries. Jaeger sets up a place for us to stay—an apartment in the East Village that's part of the Quarry's safe network—and we plan to leave the first Saturday of spring break, the day after midterm exams wrap up. The rally will be held on Monday, which gives us a day in New York to prepare.

On the last day of March, I finish my tests, turn in my papers, and return to my room, where Dash alerts me to a bunch of incoming emails. Official emails—my responses from the colleges. Admission, or rejection, letters. I don't open the messages. I leave them unread in my inbox, telling myself I'll open them once I've found Ollie and my dad. Without them, I'm not going to college. Either I find them, or I keep looking. Those are my two options. The third one—that they are dead—is not an idea I can entertain. But first: saving Bianca and Jaeger. Nothing else can happen if we don't do that.

I'm only bringing my backpack with me to New York City. I toss in a change of clothes, my wallet, my tablet, a water bottle, and a selfie of me and Ollie that's been taped to the corner of my mirror since I started at Darkwood as a first year. The morning of April 1, I wake up at five o'clock. I stay in bed for a good thirty minutes, and for half a second I let myself believe that Ollie is as safe and sound as I am here, under my covers. I've sent Duplicate Ollie a hasty buzz—a lie telling him I'm flying to meet my dad on a business trip in Chicago, since I know he and Duplicate Jane are heading home to California over the break. I'll be gone before he even reads my note.

"Pru," I finally whisper when the numerals on my plum hit 5:30. "Wake up. It's time."

She stirs and opens her eyes. "Are you ready?" she asks me,

her dark eyes meeting mine. I feel such strong affection for her in this moment, it's almost too much to bear. We've been through hell and back, Pru and I. I can read all of it on her face, in her expression.

My heart hammers in my chest as Pru and I exit our dorm room and meet our friends at the edge of campus. It's barely six thirty when everyone arrives—the rest of Darkwood is still asleep. That's our plan, of course. To leave before anyone has a chance to question our whereabouts or contact my father or the other DNA parents who've been replaced. The rest of the Similars have told Duplicate Jane an airtight story about which kids they're going to spend the break with.

I've called a car to take us into town. It's a stretch SUV, and we're silent as we all pile in. Each of us carries no more than a small bag or backpack, and we're all as tense as we could possibly be. It's one thing to plan to show up at Bianca's rally and potentially have to face Gravelle's guards; it's quite another to actually be on the cusp of *doing* it. After all, if we don't save Bianca and Jaeger, we'll have failed completely. And Bianca's clone could become the next U.S. president. It's too awful to consider. Who knows what Gravelle might program or brainwash her to do then, to further his twisted agendas? Sure, there's the possibility that, over time, she would become less and less anti-clone—eventually even reversing her stance on cloning, under Gravelle's influence. It's tempting to think of having a clone supporter in the White House, and Gravelle is, in his own way, the most pro-clone of anyone.

But we've talked about it at length. It would set a dangerous precedent if Gravelle got away with so directly influencing a major world leader. The potential dangers far outweigh any theoretical benefits. As much as we hate what Bianca stands for—the real Bianca—we can't let Gravelle get away with this.

After the SUV drops us off in Derby, we wait for the self-driving bus that will take us to Manhattan. We're tense and silent, and it's been so long since Levi and I talked directly that I feel the chasm between us acutely.

"It's here," I call to my friends, waving at the others—and briefly catching Levi's eyes. He's wearing a soft blue sweater under a camel-colored coat. He squints in the sun, shielding his eyes with the flat of his palm. His hair is long again around the edges. Something about his stance makes me ache inside—for our bodies to touch again, head to toe, like they haven't in ages.

It's time to board. I yank my eyes from Levi and focus on the tasks in front of me: sliding my bag into an overhead compartment, finding a seat next to Maude. Before I can do anything about it, Levi takes the seat across the aisle from me. Which means we'll be a mere foot apart for the entire nine-hour trip. That is a hell of a long time to avoid him. But I can't change seats, because he'd know why, and I don't want him to think I'm obsessing about our proximity. Even though I am.

We alternate between planning, strategizing about the rally, and gazing out the window at the budding New England landscape as we pass small towns and fields just starting to turn green. At some point, I doze off, and in my dream, Levi is right next to me, his fingers threaded through mine.

I wake up and feel an instant loss, knowing he's across the

aisle from me. It wasn't real. And Ollie is still missing. I don't know which ache is sharper—for Levi or for Oliver. When an automated voice announces we've officially arrived at our destination, we disembark at the Port Authority Bus Terminal and enter the frenetic streets of New York.

"It's as crowded as everyone said it would be," Pippa remarks.

I turn to stare at her, confused. "You've never been to New York City before?"

Pippa, Maude, and Levi shake their heads. "The Leroys live here," Theodora reminds me. "Before I first came to Darkwood, I lived with them for two weeks. On Central Park West. That was my first time setting foot in New York."

"The Choates are in Manhattan too," Jago adds. "And Ansel's visited Archer at NYU."

"People *live* here?" Pippa asks, incredulous, as she gets jostled by a man in leather pants and a couple of boisterous tourists.

"Not exactly here, near Times Square," I explain. "There are a lot of quieter neighborhoods. This one's mostly for visitors," I add as Pippa stares up at a couple of flashing billboards. "Hot dogs," I say, switching gears and leading them toward a food truck with a sign boasting in vitro dogs. "Come on, we have to eat something."

I'm taking on the parent role of the group, which feels ironic and strange considering I've been practically parentless for so long. Or maybe that's exactly why I'm good at this. I remind the others to keep their backpacks close and not to lose sight of each other as we make our way through the thick, pulsing crowds. As smart as the Similars are, and well trained as fighters and thinkers, when it comes down to it, they lack some of the basic life experience and street smarts I learned at an early age. As a kid, I had no choice but to teach myself to read a Muni map—that's San Francisco's public transit. I often cooked up my own mac and cheese, with Genevieve's help. I've never thought about it much before, but now I'm acutely aware of how well my father prepared me for adulthood. *An adulthood without him.*

After we've eaten two hot dogs each, I direct everyone to the subway, where we catch an N train to the East Village. I've mapped the address of the apartment and lead our group toward that spot. When we finally find a ramshackle building on Avenue A, it's so unassuming I almost wonder if I have the right address.

But then again, a safe house *would* be discreet, wouldn't it?

I type the encrypted key code into the lock and am relieved when it works. If it hadn't, I don't know where we would have gone. I'm pretty sure minors can't rent hotel rooms, even with my dad's credit card. We'd be wandering the streets all night.

The apartment is small—a cramped three-bedroom with a tiny living area, kitchen, and bathroom. We bolt the door, since it makes us feel a tiny bit safer. We work late into the night learning everything we can about the rally, which is being held on the lower western edge of Central Park. Someone orders pizza, and eventually we all find spots to fall asleep, in our clothes. Levi and I haven't talked since we got here, but there hasn't been a minute when I haven't felt connected to him. Maybe it's because of our close quarters; maybe it's because I've missed him for so long now, in spite of our breathing the same air space.

We spend Sunday visiting the rally site, where volunteers for Bianca's campaign are already setting up seating, a temporary stage, lighting, and kiosks.

"I bet he'll do it right before she goes on stage," Maude says, assessing the situation. "When she could be whisked off for hair and makeup, or to prep for her speech..."

"And whoever Gravelle has planted to infiltrate her team will drug her and send Duplicate Bianca on stage instead," Levi cuts in, grim.

"We could still tell her," I suggest, my fear mounting as I realize how complex this scheme of Gravelle's really is. Are we any match for him?

"That could be a disaster for us," Theodora reminds me. "Even Jaeger agrees."

"Jaeger," I say, remembering. "Is he being careful? Where's he staying?"

"Another Quarry-sanctioned apartment. Don't have the address. No one does," Pru answers.

I nod, feeling only mildly confident that this will work out. *But it has to. Otherwise...* The idea of a presidential candidate being a stand-in clone is unimaginable.

We regroup at our apartment for more pizza and agree we should go to bed early. The rally starts at noon, which means we need to show up at ten in the morning, giving us enough time to ensure we're at the front, by the stage, where we'll meet Jaeger.

It's only eight o'clock now, but I'm so tired I can barely keep my eyes open, so I sneak off to one of the bedrooms to rest. I shut the door, kick off my shoes, and lie down on top of the bed, not even bothering to climb underneath the covers.

"Hey," a voice says quietly.

I tense.

Levi's here, in this room. I hadn't even realized it.

And now, we're finally alone.

LEVI

"HEY," I SAY back, sitting up on the bed and staring at Levi's form in the darkened room. He's sitting in the corner, propped up with his back against the wall, reading one of his paperback books. I squint to see it, but I can't make out what it is in the low light.

"*The Great Gatsby*," Levi says, supplying me with the title.

"A little escapism?" I ask him.

Levi nods. "That's what reading's best for, isn't it? Being anywhere but in your own life?"

I nod, not sure what he's trying to say—something deep and profound about us? Or am I reading too much into a simple phrase?

"Emma."

Hearing my name in his voice, like I'm someone to him, like he knows me... I want to sink into the feeling of right now and never let go.

"I'm..." He pauses, running a hand through his long bangs.

I nod, worried I can't trust my voice.

"You're..." I finally say, dipping my toe in the water.

"What—" we both say at the same time. A beat of silence.

I feel blood rushing to my extremities. *Stop beating like a marching band, heart!*

"What if this is all a mistake, and we shouldn't have come?" My words rush out in a torrent. "What if Gravelle's on to us, and it's a trap—"

"Stop," Levi says, standing up from his spot on the floor and sitting gingerly on the other end of the twin bed. I wipe the damp from my eyes and look at him. We're less than an arm's length away from each other, and every nerve in my body is standing at attention. This is the boy I've missed for months like a kind of homesickness. This is the boy I chose to be a keeper of my secret.

In a flash of realization, I discover I'm not angry at him anymore. The frustration and betrayal I've felt toward him has somehow evaporated, vanished like Ollie and my father, and it's an intense relief to know that, and to acknowledge that. I just miss him, plain and simple. But I'm also saddened when I think of us, the "us" we were. Because we'll never be that again. Too much has happened, and his lie still hangs between us like a thick fog. I don't know if I'll ever feel as safe with him as I did that night we spent together in the seafront hotel, eating chocolate bars for dinner before traveling to Castor Island...

I start to lose myself in the memory, but I force myself to shake it off. It feels like the worst kind of betrayal of Oliver to even think about my feelings when he's still missing, and we're here, stuck, unable to help him.

"What if we never find them?" I voice my fears out loud.

"Emma. I said stop," Levi repeats. He sounds almost angry, which I guess we are. We *all* are. Gravelle has messed with all of our lives to an untenable degree. "Maybe it is a trap. So what? Would you really rather sit at home and not try?"

"Of course not." I stand up, making it clear with my body language that sitting so close to him, on this bed, isn't a good idea. If he views that as some kind of rejection... I can't think about it. Not now.

"It was *your* idea to go to Castor Island last year, even when it meant risking everything. You're the girl who did that. You," Levi says. He frowns, and in spite of myself I gaze in his eyes, those eyes that reflect the depth of his suffering.

Emma! Focus. On Ollie. On your dad. On Jane.

"Last year we barely made it back alive," I remind him. "You almost didn't! I can't face that again. I can't."

All of a sudden, my knees are shaking so violently, from exhaustion and fear, I can't hold my legs up, and my body sinks down on the bed, where I finally rest, grabbing my legs and hugging them to my chest.

Levi moves closer to me, gingerly, on the bed. Not too close; there's a handbreadth space between us. "I don't know what's going to happen, Emma. I can't make you any promises, because I've never lived in fantasies," he says, raw and low and under his breath. "All the time I was growing up on Castor Island, all throughout my childhood, I knew there was this other life. This other *way*. And then, a few years ago, I found out about *you*. I hardly remembered anything about the three years we spent on the island as toddlers, growing up together. Gravelle showed me plenty of video footage, though. And I knew you were the one to escape our limited life on the island. Still, I didn't dream that my life could be *your* life. It was impossible. I knew the life you were experiencing, with a real dad, and real friends, in the real world, would never be anything but a painful nightmare for me, since, as dreams go, it was wholly unattainable. It's much harder to lose yourself in a dream and then be disappointed when it's wrenched from you, than to never let yourself dream at all, isn't it? That's why it became my rule. No dreaming. Ever."

I stare at Levi's face, taking in every last familiar section of it. The pain there. The soul, and wisdom, in someone so young, who only ever wanted a childhood. Who was denied that from birth.

"What if he kills them?" I say, finally letting myself speak out loud the thought that's haunted me every night since I realized Ollie was a Duplicate. "Or already has? What if he kills us too? Would he? Would he really do it?"

Levi sighs. "I believe that Augustus Gravelle feels so alone and isolated and abandoned that he would not hesitate to terminate every single one of us. Once he's gotten everything he needs from us."

He folds his arms over his chest, and I watch as he shifts his position, crossing one leg over the other. His strong, broad shoulders lean lightly against the headboard.

Now. All you'd have to do is scoot closer. Just an inch. Or less...

An ache starts in my chest that quickly travels to every extremity.

"Gravelle is unpredictable. The fact is, we just don't know what he'll do." Levi furrows his brow, thinking hard, and I make a mental note how sexy he is when he's contemplating something deeply. Then I mentally smack myself: *Stop it! This is definitely not the time. It's never going to be the time.*

"Do you think they even know they've been replaced?" I wonder out loud.

"Hard to say. Who knows what lies Gravelle has told them."

"Or what pharmas he's given them," I add. "They could be so brainwashed and lethargic they don't even realize they should be trying to escape!" The thought hits me so violently, I slam my hand into the wall in anger. I instantly regret it.

"Dammit," I say, folding over myself and cupping my smashed right hand with my left. The tears that prick my eyes sting, and there's no stopping them. Even once the pain subsides, which it does, quickly—thanks to my fast-healing Similar body—the tears come hot and fast, rushing out of me in a torrent, and in seconds I'm sobbing. I'm bowled over, releasing all the anger and frustration and fear that's been welling inside me these past few months, ever since Ollie went missing. I'm ugly crying, and I know it. I'm beyond caring what I look like, or who's watching. All I want right now is to curl up in a ball and cease to exist. Because staying alive without the people I love is too unbearable to endure.

I feel his presence beside me, his soft breathing, before I feel his hands gently rest on my back. Then his preternaturally strong arms are folding around me, and I'm sinking into them just like I imagined. Into Levi's warm and comforting frame, into the chest I've longed to sink into all these months. Every night, when I've been awake, unable to fall back asleep. Even those nights when I was so angry at him, I wanted to scream at the universe. Even then, I dreamed of his smell. His touch. The taste of him.

"Like I said," Levi breathes into my ear as he holds me and rocks me, with such a gentle touch, I almost can't believe this is the same boy who possesses all that raw strength. "Better to never let yourself dream at all. Because last year, that's what I did. I broke my rule. I let myself dream."

I look up at him, feeling lost and childlike and also like I'm home. With his thumbs, he wipes away the tears staining my cheeks. I react to him touching my face like that; it's so intimate somehow, and electrifying, setting every nerve of my body alight.

"What do you mean, you broke your rule?"

"Believing that you, that you and I—" He stops short, clearing his throat. "Believing that *we* could ever last."

"But we could have," I say, suddenly feeling defensive of us, of what we had. "It's not our fault the universe got in our way. That *Gravelle* kept you on his stupid island."

"But it is my fault that I lied to you," he answers simply. I see regret written in the creases of his forehead, and I long to wipe it away. "If I could go back in time…"

"But would you?" I ask him, running a finger over his hand, tracing the lines in his palm. "Would you do anything differently? Because…" I pause for a second, gathering my thoughts.

"Because I understand," I finally say. "I understand why you did it. And I think if I'd been in your shoes, I might have done the exact same thing. If I had been the Similar to grow up on Castor Island, and I had met you, knowing you'd had this whole life beyond the micronation, I might have stayed silent to protect you. Just like you did for me."

"There's still Oliver," Levi says, and I'm caught off guard by the mention of Ollie's name. "He's still missing. And you still kissed him."

"I know."

Ollie. My heart pangs at the mention of him. The boy I also love. The boy I miss to an unbearable degree.

"I would completely support you being with Ollie if that's what you wanted," Levi says, his voice holding steady. "But..." He stares into my eyes again, then pulls me closer. So close we're not even a hairbreadth apart. I gasp at our proximity. I'd almost forgotten how it felt to touch him. For our planets to orbit each other like this.

"But we could die tomorrow. Or the next day, or the day after that," I answer him.

"We could."

Then our lips are meeting. They find each other like magnets, completely unable to resist the force. I'm sliding so I'm practically sitting in his lap, with his back propped up against the wall. He's warm to the touch, and that warmth feels transferable, like if I press every part of myself to him, it'll spread over me. So I keep kissing him hungrily, and for as long as we keep kissing, this room disappears, and the fact that Ollie and my dad might be dead is the furthest thing from my mind. And we're just me and Levi. Two people laying everything bare. Needing the comfort of this, the certainty of this, the finality of this.

"Do you—"

"Yes," I breathe, not needing him to finish that question. I'm sure. This is what I want. I grab the hem of Levi's white T-shirt and start to pull it over his head. I feel no doubt, none at all. This isn't some boy; it's Levi. Levi, who carried Pru to safety from the boathouse. Levi, who loves classic novels as much as I do. Levi, who sees me for all that I am and accepts the good along with the bad. Who's never known me as anything but complicated and broken. And who's loved me anyway. I tug at his shirt, and he raises his arms above his head. My heart works overtime once his shirt is off and I can take in the contours of his chest. His body is next to mine, and his bareness makes me bold. I kiss him again, utterly wrapped up in Levi's force field, and nothing short of Gravelle himself could tear us apart.

"This is—" I gasp.

"I know." His words are breathy and full of longing, and something else. "Emma," he says, tracing one hand down my arm. His bangs hang loose in his eyes, and the look on his face is something I don't recognize. Reverence, maybe.

"Yes?"

"I don't care about anything but you right now."

Then he kisses me with a ferocity that's both startling and welcome. Our limbs are tangled, our breathing synced, and the next thing I know, my shirt's coming off, and I'm vaguely aware of the fact I've never done this before, and it should feel momentous, but instead, it just feels uncomplicated and right.

"I—I haven't," I stammer. Then I find my voice. "But I want to."

"Me either," Levi murmurs. "And me too."

Levi seems to find some kind of confidence deep within himself. He presses me back onto the bed with a quiet strength I know is only a fraction of what's contained there. As his muscled body covers my own, I have only one thought: I never should have doubted him, or us.

The rest is as it should be, unfolding moment by moment. Not rushed. We may have so much uncertainty looming over us, but we take our time, because right now, tonight, time is all we have.

Afterward, I lie the crook of Levi's arm, his fingertips glancing my hip. He's fast asleep, but it takes hours before I can calm my erratically thudding heart.

BIANCA

"IS IT MORNING?" I ask when I open my eyes.

I'm hoping it isn't. Not yet. If I could stay here with Levi indefinitely... But I can't. I know that.

It takes me a moment to readjust to my surroundings. I'm in the tiny bedroom of the apartment, and now that it's daylight, I can appreciate its details: a simple bed, a bare-bones desk, a lamp, and a floor-to-ceiling shelf filled with books. Those details fade in comparison to the one that really matters: I'm still in Levi's arms. His body is gently draped over mine, our legs still entwined. Every inch of my skin tingles at the memory of last night. How we memorized the landscapes of each other's bodies, connecting in an intimate way that was so many things at once. Epic. Tender.

Simple, and full of laughter, the kind you only share with someone who appreciates and knows every inch of you. Snuggling in closer to him, I allow myself one more minute of bliss in his arms before I wake him. There's something so peaceful about Levi's expression right now, I can't stand the idea of wrecking that. But today is the rally. The whole reason we're here.

Levi opens his eyes slowly, yawning as he does. He kisses my shoulder lightly, like this is something we do, waking up like this, together, and I involuntarily shiver.

"Cold?" he asks, his voice low.

"How could I be? You're like a furnace," I tease.

Levi smiles. I've missed that smile, the creases around his eyes. I ache for it, even though it's right in front of me. I ache because beneath that smile is an undercurrent of fear we're both refusing to acknowledge. "You know I run hot. Another one of my fun attributes." He shrugs, then kisses my cheek, pulling me in closer to him. I want to lose myself in the warmth of his chest, to think of nothing but the night we spent together, learning each other's geometry, memorizing each other's angles and curves.

"No matter what happens," I say to him, echoing something I told him last year, on our trip to Castor Island. "I'll never regret this. Our night," I say simply. "No one can take it away from us, okay?"

"Who would?"

"I don't know. The universe. Anyone. Just please, promise me—"

"I promise."

"You don't even know what you're promising yet!"

"Sorry." He grins impishly, and I would swat him playfully if I had a free hand.

"Promise me it'll *stay* ours, no matter what else happens. To us. Or to the people we love. Promise me this will stay transcribed in our memories forever, even if…even if…"

"I promise," he says, his voice full of a familiar longing I recognize because I feel it myself, all the time.

I disentangle myself from Levi's arms—not an easy feat, as he's reluctant to let me go. I pull on my jeans and hoodie and carefully open the door, relieved to see a couple of my friends still asleep on the couch. Pru's in the kitchen, brewing coffee that looks stale but better than nothing. Maude waltzes out of the bathroom, fresh from the shower. Neither of them lets on they know where I was last night, even though I'm sure they noticed. This is why we're friends, because when I need them to, they let me be, and vice versa.

"Are we ready?" I ask my friends, getting straight to business. The clock on the microwave says it's eight thirty. We need to hustle.

"Everyone up!" Maude shouts, rousing her friends and kicking Jago lightly with her bare foot when he covers his head with a pillow.

"Five more minutes," he moans.

"Not a chance," Maude mutters, drawing the shades on the windows and pointing to a bag on the counter. "Bagels. Eat and get dressed. I brought us these," she continues, pulling a couple of signs out of her backpack. They say slogans like HUXLEY FOR PRESIDENT, WE'RE WITH BIANCA, and SHE'S THE ONE.

We all stare at her. *Really?* We have to hold these?

"What? We have to blend in," she explains, then gathers them up and shoves them in her bag.

Everyone's scurrying around, finding clothes, locating extra socks, stuffing themselves with bagels, and getting ready to leave. When Levi emerges from the room we shared last night, I can't help but reflexively meet his eyes. He smiles, a little, in a bashful way that feels so different from our strained rapport of the last few months. His expression right now is anything but aloof. He's almost *shy*. Which sends tingles up and down my spine. What we shared last night was special, almost sacred. He feels it too.

We're hurrying out the door now to catch the subway. Jaeger buzzes Pru that he'll meet us there, up front. When we arrive at Central Park, at least fifty people are already milling about, finding spots and holding signs like the ones Maude brought us. She was right; at least with the signs, we fit in. We snake our way to the makeshift stage, craning to see if Bianca's here yet.

"Where's your dad?" I ask Pru.

"He's here," she tells me, checking her plum. "He says we should sit tight. He'll find us."

It's hard waiting, with nothing to do but observe all these people who are here to support Bianca—and her anti-clone agenda. It's ironic, thinking that we're here to *save* her, when in reality, her politics defy our very existence. But we can't let her be replaced. That would give Gravelle a level of control and power that's untenable.

Jago and Theodora leave to canvas the area and check out the red tent behind the stage that's obviously where Bianca and her team are prepping for the event. They return ten minutes later, reporting back that three guards are stationed in front of the tent. A minute later, Jaeger pushes through the crowd and approaches us, looking worse for wear. I can't imagine what a toll this is taking on him.

"Quarry members are surrounding this place," he explains. "My people haven't let Bianca out of their sight."

Still, fear courses through me. "He's going to do it when she's most vulnerable. When your Quarry members take a break." Someone grabs my hand and squeezes it. It's Levi, and I feel his immediate warmth. I squeeze back.

"I think we should talk to Bianca," Maude says, making a decision. "Warn her even, if we have to."

"I'm afraid I have bad news on that front," Jaeger cuts in. "I did warn Bianca this morning. I got so concerned about her safety, it felt wrong not to tell her everything."

"And?" I press as I'm jostled by a couple of rowdy folks dressed in Huxley for President hoodies.

"And she didn't believe me," Jaeger says, looking somber. "She thought it was a ploy to derail her campaign. To make sure she didn't get up on this stage today."

"She believes you'd lie to her like that?" I ask. "About something so important?" Bianca and Jaeger go way back. I've heard they were even an item once, before they married other people.

It's hard to believe Bianca wouldn't listen to Jaeger about something life and death.

"What exactly did she say?" Pru presses.

"She said that even if there *were* a threat, she's hired top-notch security. And with the Quarry as an extra layer of protection, she has nothing to worry about." Jaeger explains. "She's right. My people won't let anything happen to her."

But as I'm elbowed once again by the crowd—so thick now, it's hard to even see through it to the stage—I get a very bad feeling. I can't explain it or put my finger on it.

"Maude," I say quietly. "Check his wrists." I don't know why, but a sickening feeling is spreading over me. My gut is telling me something's wrong. *Very* wrong.

She looks at me. "Okay, but—"

"I think we should be sure. Don't you?"

She nods in agreement, then pulls out the infrared light, grabs one of Jaeger's wrists, and shines the light on it.

I don't know why I'm so shocked that my instincts were right. There it is, crystal clear, in the bright morning light. The time stamp.

We don't stop to think about what this means. We already know.

We rally.

"The red tent," I bark at my friends. "That's where she's being prepped?" I address Jago and Theodora.

"I'm certain of it," Jago responds.

Jago, Theodora, and Ansel take the lead while the rest of us squeeze through the increasingly dense crowd. I have to punch a sign out of my way and end up stepping on more than one foot to burrow through the crowd. Sweat's settling on my brow. As Levi makes an opening for me to pass through, I hear him tell me not to panic. Maybe we aren't too late.

But Jaeger. We're too late to save him. He's already been replaced.

In minutes we make it to the red tent. Maude has switched on her best version of a Texas accent and is acting offended that the guards don't know who she is—Madison Huxley.

"You'd better let me in to see my mom," she lilts. "It's an emergency. I don't want to have to tell her you got in the way of official campaign business."

"Sorry, kid. No ID, no entry," the guard answers.

Maude knees him in the groin. Theodora, Pippa, Ansel, and Jago surprise elbow the other two guards, knocking them sideways so they can enter the tent. Levi, Pru, and I follow.

When we get inside, several more guards instantly grab us, holding us by our wrists, even as we struggle to get away.

But that's not the worst of it. There, across the room, shackled to a chair, is Jaeger—our Jaeger. The real one. His mouth is bound with duct tape. His eyes reach mine, pleading.

Next to him is Bianca, also bound to a chair, her mouth muzzled.

A second Bianca—Duplicate Bianca—sits on a high stool as a hair and makeup crew put the finishing touches on her look. She studies the note cards she'll refer to in her speech.

I shout to one of the stylists. "You've got it all wrong. She's not Bianca!"

"Of course she is," the stylist answers, running a flat iron through Duplicate Bianca's hair. "That other one's the imposter," she tuts.

I bite the hand of the guard holding me by the neck, wondering if that stylist's been paid off by Gravelle. The guard yelps but doesn't let go.

"I'm ready," Duplicate Bianca tells her prep team. She hands them the note cards. "You can take these. I don't need them. My message to the world is simple, really. I am the best candidate to run this country. A vote for Bianca is a vote for humanity. For decency. For America's core values." She checks herself in the mirror, smiles at her reflection, and steps down from the stool she'd been sitting on.

It's a frenzied scene. I'm wriggling to get out of the guard's grasp. He's even angrier now that I put teeth marks in his skin. Levi has wrenched his guard's arm backward in its socket, causing him to squeal in pain. He involuntarily releases Levi, who runs up to Jaeger and rips the tape off his mouth. My other friends are similarly trying to fight off the guards. Theodora manages to swiftly kick one in the mouth and grab his Taser. She holds it out in front of him, threatening to use it. Out of the corner of my eye, I see a guard who has Pru in his grasp. He holds a gun to her head and warns us that he won't hesitate to shoot, if we don't fall in line. Jaeger's eyes widen in fear.

"Put it down," I tell Theodora under my breath. "The Taser. They've got Pru."

Theodora lowers it—we have to play this carefully. The Similars have super strength, but Pru, Jaeger, and Bianca don't.

And the guards have guns, making us well matched. I don't know who would win if we charged the guards now. Or who we might lose in the process.

Meanwhile, Levi rips the bindings off Jaeger's wrists. I notice tears in the real Bianca's eyes. A guard grabs Levi by the armpits and drags him across the room, as we hear Duplicate Bianca take the stage outside, to the deafening roar of the crowd.

Maude has nabbed a gun from a guard's belt and trains it on a different guard across the room, the one fighting Levi, but another guard knocks it from her hand, and it fires…shooting Jaeger in the leg.

I feel myself scream but don't know if any sound comes out.

Jaeger crumples in his chair, howling in pain, as Pru elbows her captor and tries to get to her father across the room. "Dad!" she screams out. That's when a couple of people I don't recognize rush into the tent, guns trained on the guards.

"Let them go," one of the men says. I assume he's a Quarry member. "Let Bianca and Jaeger and the kids go, and we won't have to use these."

A scuffle ensues, shots are fired, and the next thing I know, I'm being dragged from the tent and shoved into a black SUV. I hear the crowd cheering Duplicate Bianca on the stage. She's speaking so eloquently and with such conviction, there's no way anyone would ever suspect she's not who she claims to be.

The car door slams, and a guard slaps duct tape over my mouth and thrusts the barrel of a gun in my face. The message is clear—cooperate or die.

312

I hear some of my friends behind me in the car, and when I crane my neck, I see Maude and Jago. Then someone else is shoved next to me on the seat. It's Levi. I'm shaking on the cool leather, fear coursing through me. But Levi subtly moves his hand next to mine, so that our fingers are touching. It's the only thing that keeps me from totally losing it.

◇━┤ ├━◇

The car ride is short and no words are exchanged. One guard drives the SUV; the other rides shotgun and points a weapon at us. I can tell my friends have done a similar calculation to my own. We may be strong, but the guards are armed. Super strength won't save us if they're willing to shoot. So for now, we don't try to fight them. Not until we have to.

When we pull up to a towering office building in Midtown Manhattan, we're ordered out of the car and told to walk single file into the building, where we ride an elevator to the top of the tower.

I feel my body shaking with every step. What's their plan—to throw us off the roof of this fifty-story building? Is that really what Gravelle would want, to kill us all so brutally in one fell swoop? Surely he didn't raise and train the Similars just to kill us off so unceremoniously, did he? Then again, we know about the Legacy Project and that Bianca has been replaced, along with all the others. We're a liability, thanks to our snooping—*my* snooping and discovering that Ollie was a Duplicate.

Tears prick my eyes as I meet Levi's. I hear him breathing next to me in the elevator, and I long to tell him the one thing I didn't last night—that I love him. But it's too late. We're on our way to our deaths, and I wasted my chance. And Ollie. I'd been so worried he might be dead, and I'd never see him again. What if I never see him again because *I'm* the one who's killed?

No. If you give in, Gravelle wins. We won't let them do this to us. We'll fight them tooth and nail.

Ding! The elevator doors open. A guard prods me in the back with his gun, jolting me forward. The wind hits us hard up here because we're so high up.

But wait. That's not the wind blowing us. It's man-made wind from a helicopter.

We're poised on a helipad. We're not alone. Pru, Theodora, Ansel, and Pippa are already here. And next to them are Jaeger and Bianca. Jaeger's leg is bandaged, but blood seeps through it, and it looks like standing on that foot is pure agony. Several guards are directing them into the mouth of the copter, and I see now that we're next.

I feel an immediate rush of relief. They're not pushing us off this roof. But I also feel a sinking dread, because I know where we're going: Castor Island. It's obvious, isn't it?

Still, if that's the case, I'll soon be reunited with Ollie and my dad and Jane.

And that's what matters. Making sure Ollie knows how much he means to me. My dad too. Doing whatever's in our power to rescue them.

I follow in a line behind Maude and board the helicopter. I locate a seat belt that's like backpack straps, and I wordlessly strap it on. I notice the floor I'm sitting on is made entirely of glass. With a lurch in my chest, I realize how disorienting it's going to be to watch the world below me shrink as we take off into the air.

Levi is beside me, and I feel his constant reassurance. I try to give him the same vibes but, admittedly, I'm scared out of my mind.

There's a deafening roar as the helicopter's turbine engines whine, and my heart flips as we head up into the sky, leaving the helipad far below us until it's a mere speck. I look up; there's no way I'll make it through this ride without throwing up unless I refuse to look down. Pru and Theodora are across from me, and Maude's kitty-corner from where I sit. We try to communicate with our eyes, but what can we really say right now? We all know where we're headed, for better or worse.

What feels like hours later, the duct tape's being ripped from my mouth, painfully, leaving my face stinging.

"We talk. You listen," a guard instructs us. I keep my mouth shut, happy to have it free, even if I can't use it.

"Help him," Bianca moans as soon as the tape's been ripped from her mouth. She means Jaeger. He's passed out, from pain or loss of blood. "Please. You must have painkillers. *Something*."

"What did we just say?" a guard bellows, striking Bianca in the head with his gun. She winces in pain. I take stock of who else is in this helicopter with us: two of the Quarry members who rushed the tent at the rally. At least they're alive.

"Emma," Levi whispers to me. "Look."

Even though I'd vowed not to look down, I do, for a split second. I see it now, below us. Castor Island, jutting up out of the water like a small cityscape. It's all glass and steel and impossible geometric angles, just like I remember it. It's breathtaking. For a minute, I forget to be nauseous.

And I forget all the suffering Gravelle has caused there.

Then it all comes crashing back to me, and I bristle. This is where he's keeping Ollie and my dad. Which means we aren't merely Gravelle's captives; we're his enemies. We will have to fight to get our loved ones back and restore them to their lives, or die trying.

This is what I'm thinking as Castor Island looms larger beneath us in the glass-bottomed copter: that we may not leave this place alive.

THE LEGACIES

THE COPTER DELIVERS us to the island's helipad, where we disembark. I'm relieved to be on solid ground again, but I feel a growing sense of dread as we follow the guards into the bowels of Gravelle's compound. Jaeger is whisked off, too weak to walk, and I pray this isn't the last time we ever see him. I shoot Pru a pained glance, and I can tell she's doing everything she can not to scream in fear and frustration.

The guards lead us into a room I recognize from the last time I was here, a year ago. The long, cavernous chamber is as vast as a school gym, with high, narrow windows at the top. Out of those, I see hills and blue sky. Gravelle's disturbing lab is here too, tucked away behind a set of doors. Being back here is painful, and I'm sure Levi feels this even more acutely than I do. After all, he just escaped this place. It's both his prison and his home.

We're standing in the center of the room, eager to organize, to come up with a plan. *Find Ollie and the others. Get the hell out of here.* But no one feels bold enough to launch into that, not with guards stationed all around us.

I start to ask Pru about her dad but don't get a chance. She's looking down the length of the room to where a video screen is set up. It's got to be ten by ten feet, at least. The screen comes to life, turning on, and we can see it's divided into six squares. A grid.

"Like surveillance footage," Maude murmurs. It does look like the footage from a surveillance camera, divided into different zones. We all step closer to the screen to get a look at what's on it. When we do—we can't look away.

In the left-hand square at the top of the grid, Ansel's dads are working away at their production company. Only I know it isn't really the de Leons; one or both of them have been replaced. The Duplicates—or maybe the guards who replaced their originals—probably set up this camera on Gravelle's orders, so that Gravelle's master plan could be rubbed right in our faces. I look over at Ansel, who audibly gasps when Archer enters the screen, laughing about a social media post and showing his phone to his dads, who laugh too. There's no sound, but we get the gist of what's happening. My stomach drops at the realization that this is Gravelle showing us *proof* that he successfully replaced Archer and his dads. He's bragging about it, using this footage as a way to boast about what he's done.

Suddenly nauseous, I gaze at the next live feed. It's video footage of the Frederica and Tessa Duplicates trying on dresses and coats from a giant pile on the bed. All the clothes still have the tags on them. I don't even know what to make of those two—it's not like I was fond of their originals—but still, it's sickening to think of their lives being snatched from them like that, and with no one the wiser.

The rest of the squares in the grid are equally disturbing. A live feed of Zeke and Mira Choate and their son Jake, and one of Bianca answering questions from eager supporters at her rally. Next, there's a feed of Jane at home in California for spring break with Oliver, Chloe, Lucy, and Booker, and I have to hold back the bile in my throat when I see that one. The thought of Jane and Booker Duplicates infiltrating that house, and Ollie's sisters having no idea that their parents aren't really their parents... And that their older brother isn't really their brother... We're watching Jane bake cookies with them in the kitchen. The girls are making a mess of rainbow sprinkles and chocolate chips, grabbing fistfuls of them and popping them in their mouths when Jane isn't looking.

Finally, my eyes rest on the last square in the grid. It's footage of my father in his office. I'm prepared for the tears that will inevitably come, watching this clone impersonate my dad, but surprisingly, or maybe not, they don't surface. At least I *know* he's not really my dad. Unlike Chloe and Lucy, who are so little and innocent, and who would never suspect their parents are imposters.

"Popcorn, anyone?" a familiar voice reverberates through the chamber, and I instantly know who it is. I spin to see Gravelle standing across the space from us, leaning on his cane, looking exactly as he did in his holo-call. "It's nice to see you're all enjoying the entertainment. I regret not setting up chairs. Guards! Grab our guests some seating. And sustenance. I'm sure you're all starving."

"Let's not pretend we're here for a friendly visit," Levi addresses his guardian. "You've replaced every single DNA parent and original. Congratulations. Now where are they?"

"You never were patient, Levi. Even as a little boy," Gravelle muses.

I stare at Gravelle, never feeling more furious in my life. He's going to draw this out as long as possible. Torture us.

The guards set up chairs for us to sit on in front of that giant screen, and my stomach churns as I imagine what he has in store for us for the rest of the day. Maybe even the rest of our lives. Watching this reprehensible footage, indefinitely. We don't sit. It's the last thing we want to do.

"It's fascinating to see so many Darkwood legacies out in the world, enjoying all the benefits of a top-notch education," Gravelle continues. "Most of these folks were my classmates, and I couldn't be happier for them. Experiencing the kind of success some people only dream about."

"You sick bastard!" I shout. "These are *clones*. Not your classmates!"

"Can you prove it?" Gravelle asks, a smile creeping over his scarred face.

"Of course I can," I snap. "That's not my father up there on that screen, and you know it. He has a time stamp on his wrist."

Gravelle laughs. "Ah, but no one knows about that, do they?"

Maude reaches out and grabs my arm, presumably to keep me from doing something I'll regret. I take a deep breath, reminding myself to save my strength—and anger—for later. This is Gravelle's warm-up act. I have to pace myself. Still, there *is* something I can do, and Gravelle won't even know about it. I can try to read his mind. Find out where Ollie and my dad and the others are.

I focus as hard as I can on Gravelle, sending all my fury and desperation at him, tuning out everyone and everything else around me.

But even though I'm concentrating as hard as I possibly can, I get nothing. I hear nothing. It doesn't work.

"Of course you'd try to read my mind, Eden. I would expect nothing less from you."

I'm startled out of my thoughts to see Gravelle staring me down. He looks almost...amused.

"Don't you think I'd prepare myself for that? I've had years to practice shielding my mind from yours. Which means, I'm afraid, you won't be getting anything from me. Don't take it to heart—your talent's still remarkable."

I don't answer him. I just silently fume as Levi steps up next to me.

"What now?" Levi asks, his voice sounding dead. "You've won, old man. You got us here. The others are presumably locked up here too. What more could you possibly want from us?"

"You are critical to the next phase of my plan," Gravelle says, almost reverently.

"And if we don't cooperate?" Maude cuts in. "Then what? You'll terminate us all, just like that?"

Gravelle paces, clunking his cane down on the concrete floor, the sound reverberating in the cavernous room. "I'd hate for you to go the way of Headmaster Ransom, that sad old fool. Of course, for you it will be worse. The stealth virus wasn't designed to completely wipe Ransom out. He's on the mend, actually. Still comatose, but alive. The virus was designed to specifically target your red blood cells and gray matter. It's stored in your plasma and can be remotely activated via a trigger mechanism built into its cellular structure. I haven't had the opportunity to study its effects outside of the lab, but, by my estimation, it would, once activated, only be a matter of minutes—an hour or two at the most—before every organ in your body begins to fail."

"You say that like there's no choice in the matter!" Pippa speaks up, indignant. "It's entirely in your power to make sure that virus is *never* activated!"

"No, my dear Pippa, it's entirely in *your* control. Do as I ask—and I'll be more than happy to never bring up the stealth virus again."

"But...you *raised* us," Theodora finally speaks up. "All those years, you told us we were special. You said there was no one like us in the world, and that's why we'd never be understood by anyone but you. All those days in our lessons, you proselytized about how the world would never accept us, but that *you* would. Was that all a lie?" Theodora chokes. "Did you mean a single word of it?"

Gravelle considers Theodora. If I believed this man truly had any empathy left in him, I'd say that he looks, for perhaps the first time ever, like maybe her words have gotten through to him. "Of course I meant it, Thea," he says. "I meant all of it. You *are* special. More special than anyone else on this planet. But being special requires responsibility. You have an obligation to the world, and as your guardian, it's my job to ensure that you fulfill it. Caring for someone, raising a child requires tough love. In your case, it requires a steady hand, to show you where you've faltered. You are all soft. Too soft. You see the world a certain way because you're still full of childish hope. I can tell you with certainty that hope is a losing proposition. No, no. You must not hope, ever again. You must do. You must fulfill your true destinies, the very ones you were created for. You must step into your roles as my legacies and never look back."

Theodora moves to stand in front of her chair. Her eyes are glassy from the tears that have pooled there. I take in a breath, unsure of what she'll do; what she'll say.

"Go ahead, activate that virus, if you must," she says coolly. "From this point onward, I won't do anything else you ask of me. Ever again."

THE ISLAND

"THEA!" I CRY out. I hear my friends echoing the same concern.

"No." Theodora holds up a hand. "I meant what I said. Sending Damian Leroy to prison was the worst thing I've ever done. And after everything you put us through, everything we already lost... A chance at a real childhood. A chance at a real life, and a shot at connecting with our DNA families... Why did *we* have to be the ones to ruin it all, for the families we only wanted to be a part of?"

"Sounds like revisionist history to me," Gravelle answers, looking like a tightly coiled spring about to snap. "I cost you a real childhood? *I* gave you everything you could have ever wanted! The best tutors. A facility where you could train to become the best of the best. The brightest and most knowledgeable people this world has ever seen."

"And love? And compassion?" Theodora says quietly. "And self-esteem and resourcefulness?"

"He gave us plenty of *that*," Levi quips. "We're nothing if not resourceful, because we've had to be. But the rest. Theodora's right. You raised us via your twisted template, to be your warriors. Your soldiers—not your children."

"An opportunity most people would kill for. You have every possible future at your fingertips. Top colleges. The best careers. *You* are the true legacies at Darkwood. *You* are the better versions of your originals. If only you'd see it the way I do."

"But we don't!" Maude argues. "Don't you understand, old man? We don't care about accomplishments and fame and money, and we certainly don't approve of your sick scheme to replace all these families, to get the ultimate revenge. Because that's what this is, isn't it? Revenge, plain and simple."

Gravelle begins pulling a holographic keyboard out of thin air, and within seconds, he's typing commands into it.

"Pru almost died because Tessa felt the need to take revenge on her," Theodora says, all the while watching Gravelle. My pulse pounds, reacting to his cold silence. I can only imagine what he's doing with those commands. It can't be good. "I've done your bidding my entire life. You can torture me or terminate me, I don't care. This is where it ends. I won't do it anymore."

Gravelle keys in a final command, then turns to Theodora, surveying her. "This rebellion of yours causes me a lot of suffering, Thea. You may not acknowledge it, but I have loved you for the past seventeen years as though you were my own. And now, you've given me no choice. That was the activation command I keyed in, for the stealth virus. It will momentarily begin invading your cells, and I'm afraid there's no antidote. I'm distraught that things had to come to this, but if I were to let you get away with this reckless display, I'd be sending a dangerous message to the others. I'm sorry, Theodora."

"I don't believe you," Theodora says. "I bet you wanted to build this virus into our DNA, but you never found out how. You would have needed your brother's help. And from what I can tell, Albert Seymour was never on board with any of this. He's a scientist with a moral compass. Which is a lot more than I can say about you."

"Believe what you want." Gravelle shrugs.

"I will. And I'm calling your bluff," Theodora continues. "Look at me. I'm completely fine." Theodora addresses all of us, and she has a point; she *does* look fine. She hasn't fallen to the ground like Ransom did that day in the dining hall, seizing. Still, I worry she's taken this too far. Gravelle meant what he said. I have no doubt he would do it; he doesn't love us. He doesn't know the meaning of the word.

"Enjoy the feeds, and the snacks," Gravelle barks. "I'll return shortly." He walks out, conferring with his guards, who have brought out plates of food. We don't even touch the snacks. Eventually, we'll get hungry enough, and we'll have no choice. But for now, we huddle around Theodora. Is she feeling okay? Is she too hot? Too cold? Feverish?

"I'm fine," she insists. But none of us are convinced. We

have no idea what we're dealing with. The virus could hit her immediately or in several hours. And either way, it's a grim thought. We're all too aware of the guards at the door, watching us. Maude, Jago, and the others begin a rapid-fire conversation in Portuguese, the language they speak to each other when they don't want anyone else to understand them. It's a smart move now, since the guards likely don't speak it.

"We have to find them," I tell Levi and Pru, hearing the desperation in my own voice. "Ollie, my dad, and the others. Then get to the boats and leave." It's simple, really. And also more complex than anything we've undertaken. Where are they? How will we release them when we're captives ourselves?

Everyone starts talking over each other, but I let their voices wash over me, not listening to any one of their conversations. It all becomes noise, and I get lost in my thoughts of Ollie. *Where is he?* That's when I'm hit with an idea.

It's a tiny shred of hope in what feels like a hopeless situation. I turn and go, walking to the wall with wide windows at the top and staring out at the hint of blue I can see from where I stand.

I couldn't read Gravelle's mind, but he is the exception, isn't he? And I've read Ollie's thoughts before, back at Darkwood. More than once. I know it's a long shot because he could be anywhere on this compound. I'll have to concentrate as hard as I can on reaching his mind, without having him near me. There's no guarantee it will work, but I pray that it might.

Ollie, I think. *If you're here, somewhere on this island. It's me. Emma. I miss you like peanut butter misses banana, on that sandwich you shared with me back in third grade, when you took a chance and sat next to the new girl at lunch.*

Nothing. I let out a breath, trying to get into that meditative state my father's psychologist used to lecture me about. *Come on, Ollie! If you're alive...* I suck in a breath that nearly chokes me but force myself to push through the pain. *Let me in. I need to help you. This is your only shot, unless you've discovered time travel and have sent yourself back to third grade. Then maybe you're on to something.*

I pause.

Another simulation. When is this gonna end? I don't wanna see that twisted version of my childhood again.

I gasp. What was that? A thought. It was definitely a thought. Another one comes. And then another, flooding my brain in a stream of consciousness, fading in and out, but definitely there. And definitely real.

So much worse than it was last year. If we ever get out of here...

It's Ollie's thoughts I'm hearing. I'm sure of it. These thoughts *sound* like Ollie. Which means he must be alive, and that in itself is a miracle.

If Emma ever finds us...

It's him. I'm one hundred percent sure of it now. He's alive. Thank God.

Okay, Ollie. I hear you. Come on. Tell me where you are.

I close my eyes, willing him to say more, to think more.

Ninety-one freaking days and counting—

Oh, God. I'd suspected he was replaced over Christmas break, but hearing it spelled out like that...

Colin, dude, you've gotta try harder. I know you're worried about Emma—

Colin. I almost gasp again. My dad. He's with Ollie. I feel myself tensing, concentrating harder than I ever have in my life. *Please, Ollie, give me a clue. Something.*

This cage is sick. Trapped here, no windows. One meal a day… We're all freaking losing it… Everyone's so skinny… I'm gonna get this all on film and send that bastard straight to prison.

A cage? What cage? Where is there a cage on this island? It's somewhere without windows…

I spin around to face my friends. I don't run. The last thing I want to do is catch the attention of the guards. I approach Levi deliberately. Of all of us, he knows this island the best.

"A cage," I whisper to him. "A place on this compound without windows. It's where Ollie and the others are. Where could that be?"

I watch Levi's expression morph from confusion to recognition. "There's a lab on the second floor. Strictly off-limits. There might be a cage there—I'm not sure."

It's the best lead we have. The only lead.

"Ollie and the parents," I exhort my friends under my breath. "They might be in the lab on the second floor. It's a windowless cage. Get everyone to the boats. *Go.*"

Before I've even processed what's happening, Ansel and Pippa have kicked two of the guards to the ground in a surprise attack. One guard's gun goes flying, shooting into the air. Jago grabs it and points it at the third guard's head. Which gives Maude and Theodora an opening to pound open the door to the room. "Go," Theodora orders me and Levi. "We'll find you. Just go!"

I'm torn; I don't want to leave my friends. What if more guards show up with more guns? They'd be outnumbered. But Theodora's right. Levi and I need to find Ollie and the others as fast as we can. Conflicted, we run. Tears streaking down my face, adrenaline pumping, I blindly follow Levi down the first hall, and as he rounds corner after corner. Then he stops for a beat, abruptly, trying to work something out in his mind.

"What's wrong?" I take in a breath. Levi concentrates, then starts moving again, this time walking rather than running. I match his footsteps. We don't hear any guards. I pray that they aren't on our tails.

"I was confused at first, but now..." Levi reaches for my hand, and I accept it, a thrill going up my spine that's a mix of fear, adrenaline, and yes, longing. We jog together, measured at first, then increasing our pace. "Emma, I don't think we're on Castor Island."

"Um, did you get knocked in the head when I wasn't looking?"

"The layout of the halls. It took me a bit to figure it out." We reach a stairwell and start tackling the steps, going up two at a time.

"Figure *what* out?"

That's when an alarm sounds. It's jarring and earsplittingly loud. I tense, assuming it's an alert to the guards that we've gotten away.

Levi sucks in a breath. "All of the rooms here look exactly

like the ones on Castor Island," he explains. "But now that we're in the halls, it's clear—the layout is reversed."

"Reversed? How? Like a mirror image of Castor Island's floor plan?"

"Exactly," Levi says as I follow him to the metal door at the end of the stairwell. "Look. The training quarters should be that way, but based on what I've seen in the last five minutes, they're likely *that* way." He points to the right, and that's the way we run. "It's so obvious to me now, I can't believe I'm only just realizing it. We're not on Castor Island. We're on its *twin*. Pollux."

RESCUE

WE'RE NEARING THE hallway that will lead us to this window-less section of the compound, the one Levi believes is the "cage" Ollie was referring to. I'm still reeling from Levi's revelation about Pollux.

"We never knew about this other island, the entire time we were growing up," Levi explains.

"But when we were on the helicopter," I protest, still disbelieving. "Wouldn't we have seen two islands?"

"Not necessarily. It would depend on the approach the copter took." We stop in front of a stark metal door boasting a steering-wheel type mechanism. It's essentially a glorified doorknob, but a lot more complex-looking. This is one knob our Darkwood keys won't open. "I guess once Gravelle was done raising us on Castor, he moved his operations here, to Pollux, to create and train the Duplicates."

"Do you think Castor's empty, then?"

"Maybe." Levi shrugs, trying to make the wheel turn, but with no luck. We hear voices and footsteps behind us. Panicked, we dart toward some nearby equipment and are about to duck behind it when I realize who's here. Pippa, Maude, Ansel, Theodora, and Pru. They all look uninjured, even Theodora. With a rush of relief, I run straight to them.

"You got past the guards," I say. "Where's Jago?"

I have to yell over the alarm to be heard. It's a deafening sound.

"Two more guards showed up, and he took one for the team," Maude shouts back. She gets to work trying to pry open the door. "This must use a combination... Dammit!" she cries out, more rattled than usual. But of course she is; Jago didn't make it out of that room.

"He's..." I'm afraid to ask.

"Injected," Maude informs me.

I let out a breath. Not dead, but indisposed. Stuck in Gravelle's portal. I've been there before; I *was* there last year. I know how terrifying those simulations can be. And now Jago's suffering through them.

Theodora explains that Jago took a hit, but the rest of them managed to escape the room. With one Similar fighting two guards each, they made it out, grabbing a gun and shooting one of the guards in the leg.

"Where's the gun now?" I shout.

"Here." Ansel holds it up gingerly. I shudder at the sight of the gleaming metal weapon that holds so much destructive power. I know it's necessary though; if they're armed, we have to be too. Even with our super strength, we can't be weaponless. Who knows how many guns the guards have stored up or how long this fight may go on.

"By the way, we're not on Castor." Levi starts to explain, but Pippa interrupts him.

"We know already! So this is Pollux?"

There's no need to confirm, and no time. Ansel and Maude begin pounding on the metal door, shouting Ollie's name, and my dad's. Why hadn't Levi and I thought of that? If Ollie and my dad and the others are inside, maybe there's a chance they'll open the door.

I feel myself holding my breath as we all join in. Ansel and Pippa grab a nearby table and try ramming it into the door, attempting to knock it down with their excessive strength. But it doesn't budge. The alarm's still blaring, threatening to drown out our cries. "We're here," we shout, offering reassurance. "Not the guards. It's us. Maude, Theodora, Ansel, Pippa, Pru, Levi, and Emma!" But with each passing second, a lump forms in my throat. If I was wrong about this, and we're no closer to rescuing them, *and* we've pissed off Gravelle with our stunt...

That's when the door wrenches open.

Two guards stand in the entryway, aiming their guns right at us. One's on his comm device, alerting Gravelle that we're here.

But I'm not focused on the guards—I'm standing on tiptoe,

straining to see around them. And what I do see guts me. Behind them is a truly grim sight.

It *is* a cage. A cross between a pen, where farm animals are held, and an enclosure that's part prison, part zoo. It's dimly lit inside, and there's something dirty about it, but institutional at the same time. Sleek equipment lines the upper walls, where windows are noticeably absent. There is no natural light in this room at all. I gasp as I take in the full scene in front of me; it's like nothing I've ever witnessed before. Figures lie propped up against the cement-block walls, and a literal cage—like the bars of a jail cell—encloses the entire space.

I scan the faces of the people on the ground in desperation, looking for my loved ones. I see originals, including Jake and Archer, as well as some of the DNA parents. They look lifeless and emaciated. My stomach roils with nausea.

Ollie, is all I can think. *Dad*. Where is he? Where are they? Where's Jane?

"Gravelle sent us down here to visit our originals," Maude sweet talks one of the guards, or tries to, anyway, over the still-blaring sound of the alarm. "He wants us to see exactly why we're so much better than them. So much stronger and smarter."

"Lies," answers a guard, his finger trembling on the trigger of his gun. Before he can press it, Levi kicks the gun out of his grasp and tackles the guard. All hell breaks loose as Theodora, Ansel, and Maude take on the second one.

I rush past them, through the doorway to the perimeter of the room, scanning the bodies lying there. Their mouths are duct-taped, their wrists handcuffed to the metal bars of their cage. Every single DNA parent and original wears some kind of regulation burlap shirt and pants, tied at the waist with string. They're barefoot and thin, lying on coarse mats on the hard floor. I have to bite my lip so I don't get sick; Gravelle's been treating them like animals all these months. Worse. All I want to do is release them, but I can't. I'm not *inside* the cage, but merely on the outskirts of it. I couldn't free them if I wanted to.

Beside me, Maude is trying to pry the bars apart with her extraordinary strength, but they don't move. She's strong, but not strong enough to bend the thick metal.

"Emma!" I hear Maude scream. I glance behind me just in time to see three guards charging me. Maude's warning doesn't come soon enough. They grab me.

I struggle against them, but it's no use; I can't fight them all off. The next thing I know, a gun's being fired, two of the guards release me, and Pippa charges the third, who lets go of my arm. I flee, toward the far end of the cage.

"Emma?" says a voice. I squint into the dimly lit pen and see him standing there in front of me, wearing that same burlap uniform and gripping the bars of the cage from the inside, his eyes looking unfocused and confused.

It's him. It's really Ollie.

If I could, I'd fling my arms around him, not caring about anything but feeling him, solid, for the first time in months. He looks so frail, like he's barely eaten the last hundred days. My eyes roam over his face, that familiar face that's been my lifeline since we were kids. "I thought I'd lost you again." I choke out the words. I can't believe he's here, in front of me. Our only barrier is those bars.

"You didn't," he whispers, his eyes glistening with tears. I feel our connection even as the world falls to pieces around us. "You won't. Ever."

"Promise?" I breathe.

"Promise."

"I've got the keys," Levi shouts gruffly over the wail of the alarm, forcing me to wrest my eyes from Ollie's face. Levi runs to where I stand and begins fiddling with the padlock on the cage. "Glad you're all right, brother," Levi says, working hard on the lock. At the sound of that word—*brother*—I feel a pang of remorse, acutely aware of last night, and how Levi and I spent it together. I flush deep in my bones at the memory of it. Of how he made me feel. When Ollie's been in this *cage*, suffering so much. When I love him too. Maybe not in the same way. But I do.

There's no time to acknowledge what's happened or anything except this moment *right now*, getting out of here alive. Levi's opened the cage, and we rush inside to tend to as many of the DNA parents as we can. I scan the ground for my father—is he here? Everyone's so emaciated, it's hard to distinguish who's who. I gasp when I notice Frederica Leroy, usually so sophisticated, languishing on the ground, incapacitated next to Tessa, who is equally thin and unresponsive.

"What's wrong with everyone?" I shout to Ollie.

"Starvation, or nearly. Lack of water, fresh air. And the portal," he explains. "Every day, for hours on end. No one's been spared. I've gotten the least of it, since I'm his biological son. Everyone else…" he trails off, looking pained, like it physically hurts him to talk about it.

I finally spot my father, restrained in cuffs across the pen. When his eyes land on mine, I feel a rush of adrenaline and relief. I have to get him out of here.

"Dad," I shout, my heart raging in my throat. I run to his side, ripping the tape off his mouth.

Suddenly, the alarm stops its blaring, plunging the room into unexpected silence. The absence of that noise scares me. What now? Is this the end of the road? Are the guards going to lock me and Levi in this cage along with my dad and the others? My friends are streaming in, wielding guns—not to use, but to threaten—and shouting orders at each other to rip away the cuffs and drag the originals out of here. I spot Jane now, finally. She doesn't look as weak as the others, probably because she hasn't been here as long. My heart surges at the sight of her. She's alive.

"Get everyone to the perimeter of the building, using any means necessary!" Maude screams. "Then find the boats. We have to get off this island!"

I cry out for someone, anyone, to help my dad. Ansel moves up and swiftly yanks my father's cuffs, ripping him free, though the shackles still dangle from his wrists.

"Thank you," he mouths to Ansel, his voice raspy and weak.

"Lean on me," I say, and he complies. I half drag, half carry my father to the edge of the cage, where Pippa and Pru are holding the door open. Guards swarm in, and I try to count them. There are at least ten, maybe eleven, but I can't stop to check. I am singularly focused on getting my dad out of this hole. Ollie's next to me in an instant, lending a hand, and we manage to carry my dad outside the room and into the hallway. We prop him up behind some pipes that run the length of the corridor.

I hear shots being fired in the caged room, and my friends struggling, but I tune it out. I have to focus on my father. Right now, he is all that matters.

"Emma," my dad croaks, his voice sounding scratchy and raw. At least it's more audible now. I hope that means he's gaining strength.

"Save your energy," I beg him. "We need to get you out of this place. Gravelle has replaced you, but it's not too late to return you both to your lives—"

"So it's true then," Ollie says, recognition dawning on his face. "He installed Duplicates in our place."

I nod. "Yes. They've been given all your thoughts and memories. You were probably both implanted, without your knowledge, with a device that continuously transmits those memories straight to their brains—"

I'm distracted by Ansel and Madison Huxley hurrying past. She's in the regulation uniform, yelling something muffled about being completely traumatized, though she looks more robust than some of the others. Ansel must have freed her. Which reminds me. We haven't rescued everyone yet. There are still more people in that pen.

"We should go back," I tell Ollie. "The others—"

"Wait," my dad says, weakly. "Emma, I have to tell you something." Now's not the time—there are literally shots being fired around the corner—but something about the intensity in his eyes gives me pause. "Please," he croaks. "I know you're angry at me, Emma. You have every right to be. But you have to understand. When I lost you—when I lost *her*—I'd already lost your mother. I experienced more pain in that year than I thought was humanly possible. It nearly did me in. I didn't want to accept that Gravelle had copied her, because I worried that I'd never love you as much as I should. It turned out to be quite the opposite, Emma. I fell in love with you instantly and completely."

"Dad—" I say at the same time that Ollie says, "Mr. Chance—"

But he doesn't let us speak. "I was terrified that one day I'd lose you too, and that when that happened, I wouldn't ever recover."

"But why would you lose me?" I see Theodora and Maude marching past us, carrying two compromised DNA parents on their backs—Frederica Leroy and Zeke Choate.

"I wanted to tell you the truth, but who tells their three-year-old that she's a replacement for another girl? You don't put that kind of burden on a child. I told myself I'd confess it all to you once you were old enough to understand. But don't you see the impossible position I was in? Once you were old enough to handle the truth, you were also old enough—*are* old enough—to choose to leave me."

"But you're my dad. My family." I gasp when I hear another shot behind me. I'm so torn. I have to get my dad out of here. But the others—we can't leave them…

"But what about the Similars? You're almost eighteen

340

now, Emma. You could choose to live with them and leave me behind." This is more vulnerability than I've seen in my dad my entire life. Of course he's emotional. He's been locked up in this cage for months.

Before I can formulate a response, I hear a commotion behind me in the hallway. "Theodora!" a voice screams. Ollie, my dad, and I turn to survey the hectic scene, and that's when we see Theodora on the concrete floor, convulsing.

Maude's at her friend's side within seconds. The rest of us follow. I meet Maude's eyes, knowing it as fully as she does. It's the stealth virus. Gravelle keyed in those commands an hour ago, and now it's taking full effect. I watch, horrified, as Theodora's arms and legs thrash, her limbs flailing like they're moving independently from her body. Then she goes completely still.

"Theodora. Wake up. *Please.*" It's a voice I don't recognize. I scan the group until I see who's run up to lean over Theodora's prone body. The girl's long hair, unwashed and hanging in greasy clumps from months of confinement, shades her face. It's Tessa, freed from the cage, looking stronger than my dad and some of the others. "Help her," she cries out. "Somebody help her! She's not waking up," she pleads, accusing the guards who stand nearby. "What's wrong with her? What did you do?"

"I'm afraid it was what *she* did." Gravelle appears in the doorway, shielded by his own personal guards, looking like a parent forced to tame a wayward child. "I warned her. Defying me would force my hand. A deadly stealth virus has been activated in her DNA, Tessa. I hated to do it, but your Similar gave me little choice in the matter. Guards? Handle this."

Two guards march over to Tessa and yank her by her pony-tail to standing. I can tell it hurts her, but she only grimaces. "You are going to be sorry," she snarls at Gravelle. Then she bites one of the guard's hands. He yelps in pain. As punishment, the second guard ruthlessly jerks Tessa's head back by her hair. I hear a crack in her neck, and she cries out. "She's dying," Tessa sobs. "Isn't she?" The bitten guard holds a gun to her temple. "Is that it? Is she going to die?" Tessa rails at Gravelle.

"Yes and no," says another voice. I pivot my gaze to the end of the hallway to see who's approaching and pray it's someone from the Quarry.

But it's not.

I can finally see who's joining us, though it takes me a second to place him, here on Pollux, out of context. I've only ever seen him in person that evening in the park, back when the Duplicates first came to campus.

It's Albert Seymour. Ollie's uncle. Gravelle's half brother.

"What do you mean?" Tessa chokes, tears streaming down her face. "Yes and no?"

"I mean yes, the activation is fatal," Seymour answers, his voice even-tempered, showing little emotion. "But no, she's not *going* to die, because she is already dead. Guards, please take Theodora away. Her body is creating a distraction." The guards hoist Theodora unceremoniously onto their shoulders. Tessa screams, and the other Similars hold back strangled cries for their—for *our*—friend. Theodora. Who only ever wanted to be loved by the Leroys. Who came to Darkwood in search of a life, a real identity, and who was shortchanged every step of the way.

I bite back a sob. Ollie's hand is on my shoulder. I feel it and the comfort it provides, but I don't turn in his direction. This is all too much. If I look at his face, at the tenderness and shock written there, I will permanently crack.

Two guards drag a protesting Tessa away. Before they clear the door, Ansel delivers a kick to one guard's head, and Pippa knees the second forcefully in the groin. The guards release Tessa long enough for Ansel to grab her arm and drag her, wailing, down the hallway, in the opposite direction of where the other guards are taking Theodora. Tessa's cries can be heard the length of the corridor. It only takes a moment for one of the guards to right himself, closing in on Tessa and Ansel. Maude tackles him and wrestles for his gun.

I need to move. I know this. But I'm frozen to the spot. My mind is stuck on Seymour, on how he ordered those guards to dispose of Theodora's body. He called her a "distraction." It feels like the guards are carrying away a little piece of me too, along with Theodora's body. I think I know what that piece of me is: the hope Levi talked about last night. The kind that's so dangerous because once you let yourself believe in it, you can only be disappointed.

The scene around me turns frantic. My friends, enraged by Theodora's apparent murder, begin to organize. I hear Maude shout to the other Similars that she'll meet them downstairs at the library entrance. From there they'll head to the docks and board boats that can take us to the mainland.

A shot rings out. Maude's fired a gun, and a guard across from her crumples. She must have successfully nabbed it from him and shot him. There's a steel in her eyes I haven't seen before. She is not taking Theodora's death lightly. How could she? It's why she's willing to use the gun now. She's been pushed past the breaking point. It's now us or them. There is no other option.

I watch Maude march past the fallen guard, feeling like everything's happening around me in a dream. I'm rooted to the spot, unable to make my feet work. My brain can't order my body to move, not until I understand it—how Seymour could say those things about Theodora.

There can only be one explanation. He is not at all the man he has pretended to be.

I turn to face him, finally registering that his unassuming voice and appearance belies a cold-hearted and cruel interior. He's just as much of a monster as his half brother is. Maybe more. "You're part of this, aren't you?" I say. "You lied to us when you told us there were only three Duplicates. You knew about the others—of *course* you did. We were naive enough to believe you. But I should have known. You and Gravelle have been working together this whole time. Haven't you?"

Ollie grabs my hand, staring his uncle down. "It's true. Isn't it?"

"Interesting theory, Eden," Seymour answers, completely ignoring Ollie and focusing his steely eyes on me. He no longer seems like the slightly nutty professor I'd made him out to be in my mind. *The person he wanted you to see*, I tell myself. He'd projected a certain image, and we had fallen for it, hook, line, and sinker. Now, I can't believe I ever saw him that way, when his true nature is so abominable and staring me in the face, his mask removed. "You're as clever as they come, Eden, I'll give you that much. Of course, I already knew that, empirically, because I've studied your DNA at length. You are correct. I don't merely tolerate the Duplicates. They are the culmination of decades of hard work, research, and experimentation. They are, indeed, my crowning achievement."

EXPENDABLE

"EMMA, SAVE YOURSELF," my father's begging me over the shots that ring out. Ollie and I wordlessly hoist my dad to his feet.

"Can you walk?" I ask him as Pippa rushes by with a zoned-out Bianca on her back.

"Get everyone to the exits," Maude barks, wielding that gun. Now that she's shot a guard, the rest see her as a threat and avoid her path. "Most of the DNA parents can't walk," Maude tells me, pacing the floor with that weapon gripped in her hand. "Jaeger's lost too much blood. We can't waste any more time!"

I spin and see Jago carrying an unconscious Jaeger on his back.

"Jago's okay?" I ask Maude.

She nods, stepping in front of a guard to cut him off at the pass.

Archer also moves in, and one of his dads—Luis—hobbles next to him, leaning on his son for support. I note that all the parents seem far more compromised than their kids. Gravelle blames them for his expulsion twenty years ago and probably tortured them the most. I shake off that thought. We have only one priority now. Getting to the boats and off this island.

But first, Seymour. I feel an intense, boiling rage at this man who pretended to act ethically, but who deceived us all.

"You're a monster disguised as a scientist," I seethe. "You claim to be furthering knowledge for *good*…and yet, you're nothing more than a common thief. You've stolen lives that weren't yours to take!"

"I refer to it as bettering," Seymour explains. "The Duplicates are living these lives a thousand times better than any of *them* ever could."

"What does that mean?" my father demands, weakly. He tries to stand on his own but falters. Ollie steadies him.

"Dad," I say, worried about how fragile he is. I need to get him out of here.

"You want us to beg for our lives back," my father gasps, addressing Gravelle, who's been quiet up until now, silently observing. "Do you need us to say it? That we wronged you when we were kids? Is that what you want—an apology?"

"It's too late for that," Gravelle answers.

"Too late because you've replaced us. And you think your path to happiness is to watch us suffer, as our lives are taken over by imposters. How sad. And foolish."

"Nice words, coming from someone who never thanked me for gifting him with the impossible," Gravelle answers, indicating me. "A second chance at being a father."

"But I'm right, aren't I?" my father replies, his voice weak but his spirit intact.

"Enough." Seymour cuts in. "You're entirely missing the point. My brother's worldview is limited in scope. This isn't about petty revenge."

"Excuse me?" Gravelle looks murderous. "There's nothing petty about my agenda—"

"I've allowed you to believe that your master plan was of the utmost importance," Seymour interrupts, "and perhaps that was my first mistake. But we both know this is about far more than one-upping a bunch of influential families. The Duplicates— not the betas who first appeared at Darkwood, but these vastly improved models—are highly superior to their originals in every way. Thoughts and memories have been downloaded straight into their minds via receiver technology that I patented. Duplicates grow quickly, aging from birth to adulthood in as little as a year, bypassing the emotional messiness of childhood. They are free of disease, since they possess many of the capabilities that were built into *your* DNA, Eden. In the long run, they will actually *improve* humanity. If each and every person can be replaced with a more resilient, disease-free model, and all that's required to preserve a person's selfhood is to download the original's ideas, thoughts, and memories in the newer version... Isn't it obvious? Models can be periodically replaced and upgraded. Changes made, bad memories edited out and tweaked. And not only that. Duplicates will allow individual humans the ability to live *forever* by simply submitting themselves for upgrades at necessary checkpoints, with the new Duplicate seamlessly installed. It's revolutionary, isn't it?"

"Revolutionary?" Ollie looks at his uncle, disgusted. "Are you out of your mind? We were replaced without our knowledge or consent!"

"That's how it had to be, this time," Seymour explains. "Once the practice is widespread, everyone will request to be upgraded. I'll admit, that may take time. In the meantime, by replacing some very influential folks, I'll be able to spread my ideas widely, and in the right circles—via my Duplicates—so that I may put in place the proper legislation to proceed seamlessly with my plans."

"Let me get this straight," I say, still feeling like I'm in a dream. This can't be real. "Both of you," I indicate Gravelle and Seymour, "for different but complementary reasons, set out to replace all these people permanently with Duplicates. Oliver, my father, Bianca Huxley. Jane. Jaeger. You," I turn to face Gravelle, "for your own vindictive agenda. So you could watch the people who mistreated you suffer and see them beg for their lives back. And you," I turn to Seymour, "because you have some twisted authoritarian vision of replacing all of humanity with 'newer models' like software?"

"Visionaries have to act on humanity's behalf." Seymour shrugs. "It's never simple, but that is the only path to progress." I'm so enraged by Seymour's justification of his crimes, I could slap him. Of course, I don't, and I won't, not yet. We won't strike until it's the exact right moment.

"So what about the originals, then? They live here, indefinitely? Doomed to grow old, watching their lives unfold with imposters as the major players? Is that their life sentence, that live feed of their lives being hijacked?"

"My apologies, Eden. I can see I left out the most crucial detail of all," Seymour answers. "They won't live here indefinitely. That would cost us far too many resources. And what would be the point? The originals are entirely expendable. Once we confirm that we've permanently downloaded every last one of their thoughts, memories, and emotions, via their implants, we'll store that information securely on our server. And then, after they're no longer needed, we'll dispose of them."

I feel sick, like the floor beneath me is shifting. He wants to kill them all.

"Seal the perimeters," I hear Seymour instructing his guards on a comm device. "No one leaves." Panic rises in my chest. This is even worse than we thought. They're going to trap us in here. In moments, this entire compound will become our cage.

"Go," I say to Ollie, who hoists my father on his back and begins carrying him out. "Do whatever you have to do. Save my dad. Please." Ollie isn't nearly as strong as the Similars, and he's been here, compromised and wasting away in that pen, for the last three months. But adrenaline must be kicking in, because he's managing, and I'm grateful.

I can see now what I'd been too distracted to notice before. All hell has broken loose. Similars are fighting guards. Shots are being fired in every direction. I notice Jane Ward dragging herself to an exit and say a silent prayer that she makes it out of here alive. I'm instantly reminded of the cage, and I race back to it to see if anyone's still inside. We can't leave anyone behind—even if we die trying to save them. I could never live with myself if I knew that someone's parent or, God forbid, one of the originals was left here to die.

I scan the room, taking stock, and spot only one figure in the corner, cowering there, still shackled to the metal bars.

It's Jake Choate.

I am at his side in seconds. Summoning all my strength, I reach for his cuffs and yank them from the bars, not believing I can do it but knowing I have to try. I'm shocked to see that they come loose.

Jake gasps, grabbing my hand and standing, insecurely, on his feet.

"I owe you one," he moans, meeting my eyes. Then he runs, shakily, out of the room and down the hallway. I follow.

Maude has circled back and is advancing on Gravelle, murder in her eyes as she trains the gun on him.

"Would you kill your guardian so easily, Maude?"

"Would you kill your old classmates so easily? Your son, Oliver? And what about Levi? And Theodora…"

"Theodora shouldn't have defied me. I warned her, didn't I? As for everyone else, you know the answer, Maude. Ollie and Levi will be spared, to live here with me. So will you, Jago, and the others. You don't belong in the outside world, that's clear."

"But the DNA parents," she hisses.

"You heard my brother. We'll download every last thought

to use in a future upgrade. They won't be *dying*—far from it. They'll be some of the first humans to achieve immortality!"

Maude's expression is one of pure rage. She looks driven. Focused. Like she's never been more sure of anything in her life.

"That's a convenient way to justify murder. As for the Similars—we'll never stay here. *We'd* rather *die*."

And she fires the gun.

I watch, disbelieving, as Gravelle crumples. I don't wait to find out what happens after that, to see how hurt he is, or if— dare I hope for it?—he's dead. As I run at top speed down the hall to the stairs, I hear Seymour shouting at the guards to "unleash the Duplicates."

"Absolutely not," Gravelle barks, his breathing slowing and his voice growing raspy. "The Duplicates are far too valuable to be used as veritable bullets."

"They're blank slates," I hear Seymour protest. "They're entirely replaceable."

Their voices fade out as I push open the door to the stairwell, stepping over a fallen guard with blood pooled around his head to get past. I don't have time to consider all the death around me or to wonder if Maude dealt Gravelle a fatal blow. I have to move, before it's too late.

I can't wrap my mind around what Seymour meant. Unleash the *Duplicates*? The Duplicates aren't here. They're there, on the video screen, in their homes, posing as my friends and family.

But when I exit the stairwell onto the first-floor hallway of the compound, I understand.

It's like an army has been dispatched.

Bodies file into the hallway where several Similars are carrying DNA parents toward the library, aiming for that checkpoint, then the beach outside and the boats. But these aren't just *any* bodies. Streaming into the hall is another Madison clone. Another Tessa. Another Archer. Another Pru. These clones are all dressed alike, in some kind of uniform that's sleek and gray and built for fighting.

And now I understand. *These* are the Duplicates Seymour was referring to. They look like they're here for one reason, and one reason only.

To destroy us.

We've taken out enough guards to prove we're a formidable force. Several of us have guns, reluctant as we are to use them. But it's clear why Seymour wanted these clones unleashed. He needs soldiers. Ones who are soulless enough, with little to no concern for their own well-being, to follow his every order. And right now, his orders are to fight—even kill—us.

These Duplicates look singularly focused on their task—blocking us from leaving. Several move, swiftly and effortlessly, to the opposite entryway—the glass doors on the other side of the library that lead outside, to the shore—and plant their bodies in front of it. I wonder if that door has already been sealed on Seymour's orders, and if we'll ever get past the Duplicates who now stand guard.

"They're trapping us in," I tell Maude as she races past me.

"Then we'll fight them," she growls, just as a Madison Duplicate steps into our path. Even though she's here to fight us, I find myself enthralled by her eerily familiar face, exactly like

Maude's and Madison's, yet blank—a blank slate, as Seymour put it. My stomach wrenches at the thought of what her life must be like. So empty. So pointless, except to do Gravelle and Seymour's bidding.

"I'll help," a voice pipes up. It's the real Madison Huxley, looking more resolved than I've ever seen her. She grabs Maude's free hand, and mine, and together, the three of us encircle the Madison Duplicate in a human ring. There's no way for her to escape. She's blocked on all sides.

Across from us, Ansel and Archer fight off an Archer Duplicate who's wielding a blade of some kind. The Duplicate flings it at Archer's chest, but Ansel manages to catch the weapon in midair.

Seymour has armed them, I realize. *These really* are *soldiers.*

"She's got a knife!" I try to warn Maude and Madison, but too late. Our Duplicate, cornered as she is, slides a pocketknife from her boot and aims it straight at Madison's chest. Maude flings her body in the path of the knife, where it gouges her arm, instead.

"Maude!" I gasp at the sight of the handle sticking out of her upper arm, horrified.

"You bitch," Madison shrieks at the Duplicate as she jumps on top of her, clawing at the clone's face and hair. Thank God Madison's a track star. She actually has skills.

"I'm okay," Maude grimaces. Before I can stop her, she yanks the knife by the handle, straight out of her arm. Blood pours forth in a river, but Maude barely reacts. She rips a piece of cloth from her shirt and ties it around her arm in a makeshift tourniquet.

Then she steels herself for battle. "I'll help you," she grunts as she leaps to Madison's side and grabs the clone by the throat. The clone stops struggling—she can't fight the two of them together—and Maude ties her wrists with an electrical cord she rips out of the wall. When the Duplicate is bound, unable to hurt us, Madison turns her attention to Maude.

"You saved my life," Madison acknowledges, sounding like she's not quite sure she can stomach—or believe—those words. Yet she can't deny they're true.

Maude stands over the Duplicate, surveying her. "Wouldn't you have done the same for me?"

Madison doesn't have a chance to answer, and there's no time to celebrate this small victory, because three figures block our path. It's three Oliver clones, assuming a fighting stance and projecting an almost deadly vibe. My heart pounds in my rib cage, and I have to remind myself that these clones aren't Ollie. They are soulless. They are empty vessels. They watch us with a harrowing venom in their eyes that sends chills up and down my spine. After a nerve-racking standstill, Maude rushes at one of them, delivering a swift kick to his jaw. The clone staggers backward, his mouth full of fresh blood; he must have bit his lip after the blow. The second Ollie Duplicate is fighting Madison, who's grabbed him by the groin and is squeezing, hard. The third Oliver makes a move to pull a weapon from his shoe, but I don't let him reach it. I throw my entire body at him, full force.

He's better trained than I am. *Much* better trained. He swiftly wrenches my arm behind my back and holds me in a painful headlock. I'm starting to see stars when someone whacks him on the head with a piece of electronics, and the clone releases me.

I look up to see Levi taking on the Ollie clone.

"Go," he orders. "This one's mine." The three of us run, tearing across the library, where I see many of the DNA parents gathered. Most of them aren't functional and lean against the wall, either injured or too drugged to be able to fight. I panic when I see my own dad attempting to fend off two clones of himself, both eerily still, their emotionless faces like masks.

"Dad!" I rush toward him, pulling him away from the Duplicates. But they yank back. And they're strong. Maybe even stronger than me.

I summon all my strength. *You can do this, Emma. You might not be trained in fighting, but genetically, you're still a Similar.* I kick one Colin Duplicate in the gut with a satisfying jolt, then spin and throw my entire body weight at the other. Similars are fighting Duplicates all around me; the whole library is a mess of bodies and sweat and blood.

"Emma, no," my father cries. "Save yourself—"

"No." That's the last thing I'd ever do. I claw at one of the Colin Duplicates' faces, and Levi moves in to take on the other. When my father is finally free of their grasp, I beg him to run.

"Get outside the library doors. Find a boat." I grimace as a Duplicate yanks me back by my hair.

But Levi delivers a hefty blow to that clone's head, and he releases me. We share a look of triumph, but it's short-lived. Two guards approach Levi from behind, out of his sight. I see one guard raise a gun. The other steps forward, his body poised to attack.

"Levi!" I scream. His eyes widen and lock on mine for a split second before he spins, facing the guards. He assumes a fighting stance, but before he can attack, I hear a gunshot.

No. No, no, no.

I feel my heart leaving my body as I realize what's transpired. The guard has shot a bullet straight at Levi.

There's a blur of bodies and shouts and the sickening sight of someone crumpling to the floor. I can't look, I can't face this, and yet my feet carry me independently, without instruction from my mind, across the sun-glinted room to the heap on the cool marble.

It's not Levi.

It's my father. He's been shot.

"Dad?" I cry out, my voice sounding divorced from my body. "Daddy…"

I know what happened, now, even though I didn't see it. My father leaped in front of that bullet to save Levi's life. And he may have just ended his own.

I am at his side, a bird with broken wings, flitting next to him, pathetic. I feel stricken. I feel like I'm missing my voice and my limbs. A red spot blooms at his chest, making its way outward over his burlap shirt and onto the floor. "No, no, no…" I keep whispering. *No. No!*

My father tries to get up but is impossibly weak. So he stays where he is, on the floor, reaching for my hand. I grasp it with a muffled cry, tears pouring from my eyes, blurring my vision.

"I'm okay, honey. I'm okay," he finally says. I know he's saying this entirely for my benefit because he's my father, and parents always want to protect their children if they can, don't they? But I have to be the adult now. He needs me to comfort him, not the other way around.

A part of my brain reminds me the battle rages on around me, and we can't stop, not now, but nothing matters to me except my father's face and the hole at the center of him that I am helpless to fill. "I understand," I tell him, choking out the words. "I know why you never told me who I was. You were protecting me. You loved me too much to lose me."

"Good," he replies. I can tell it's painful for him to talk. That realization cuts a new cleft in my heart, already ripped wide open.

This is so sick. So wrong. Originals and clones shooting Duplicates who can't help it, who never knew any better. All this fighting and suffering, and for what?

"You're not expendable," I tell him, my voice sounding so raw and fierce I don't recognize it. "I don't care what they teach those other Duplicates, what memories they give them. They'll never replace you, not for me." I wish I had a pharma for him, for the pain. I wish I could rush him to the hospital. I wish I could do something—*anything*. But all I can do is hold his hand and watch as the world implodes around me.

Similars are still battling Duplicates, who seem to fall and rise again to fight with renewed purpose. At the doorway that leads outside, my friends are charging at the soulless clones with knives and guns. More guards stream in from the hall, some of them wearing ripped and bloodstained clothing. But my friends are too busy to notice; they're carrying an eight-foot table toward the exit, and I watch as it hovers midair. Then they charge forward, ramming the table straight into the doors, shattering the glass into a thousand pieces and climbing right over the felled Duplicates to get outside. Whatever was keeping those doors sealed couldn't seal the glass.

Similars begin carrying the weak DNA parents on their backs. But the Duplicates who haven't fallen are charging forward with an unwaning fervor. I see two Pru Duplicates rip Frederica Leroy off Ansel's back, flinging her to the marble floor, her head hitting with a resounding thunk. I am sickened by the savagery all around me. So pointless. So unnecessary.

"Stop," I say, at first only to myself. I'm sure no one else can hear me. So I raise my voice. "*Stop!* Everyone. Stop fighting! Stop killing each other! It isn't necessary! It doesn't have to be!"

A few Duplicates turn their heads to look at me. I feel myself gaining confidence, and intensity. If my father is going to die on the floor on Pollux Island, it can't be for nothing. *It can't.*

"Please. Listen," I hear myself saying. "We aren't the enemy. Neither are you," I tell the nearest Duplicate, a copy of Pru who looks at me, perplexed, like I'm one species and she's another. But she isn't. We're all humans, aren't we? We're all teens, some of us brought into this world for the wrong reasons. But we're here now, and we're the same. "Stop it," I cry out again, until the movement in the room slows. Some lower their weapons to stare at me. Levi holds a guard by the wrist but tears his eyes from the fighting to focus on me. So does Ollie. Pru watches me with tears streaming down her face, as a guard grips her by her hair. "When I first found out I was a Similar. A *clone*," I add, emphasizing the word for the sake of the Duplicates, wanting them to understand. They're watching me now. Listening intently. "I thought that word meant something. I thought being a clone was something I had to hide." I'm choosing every word carefully. I have to get through to them. I must.

I look around the library, at the spines of books glinting on the endless rows of shelves. I look from Similar to Duplicate and remind myself that we're all just kids. *High schoolers.* We didn't want this. We didn't ask for this. We didn't ask to fight and hurt and kill each other. My body floods with warmth, and it's like I can somehow *feel* what the Duplicates are thinking. I'm not getting individual thoughts like in the past, when I read Harlowe's and Ollie's and Jane's minds. This time, it's like I'm tuning into a staticky radio station, with bits and pieces of thoughts streaming in and out of my head.

The Duplicates' thoughts.

Fight them…

They only want to destroy us…

What we were built for…

The reason we exist…

No. That's not right. This isn't why they were created. Maybe it was the reason at first, but it shouldn't have been. It's all wrong.

I summon all of my mental strength to send my own thoughts back to them. I've never done this before. But it feels like if we're going to have any shot at getting out of here, I have to do this. I have to find a way to get through to them.

Focus, Emma.

I can make that static louder and stronger if I focus on it enough.

I block out everything that isn't the Duplicates and their minds. I think of what I want to tell them. What I need them to know. And things begin to sharpen. To clarify. It's like there's a string that connects my mind to the Duplicates', and without even understanding it, or how that could possibly be, I'm doing everything in my power to harness that connection and send the most positive, healing thoughts into their heads.

You don't have to do this. None of us do.

I think maybe it's working, because the Duplicates seem focused on me. Quiet. Even a little enthralled.

"You have so much to look forward to," I say to the nearest Duplicate, feeling myself smile even as tears streak down my face. I'm thinking of my dad, and how these might be the last words he ever hears me speak. I want him to know how much my life—hard as it's been—has been filled with joy. "There's so much wonder in the world you can still experience for the first time. And yes, there will be heartaches. And yes, there will be unbelievable highs. Like falling in love for the first time. And learning all the things about yourself, like what you love and what you hate. And most importantly, who you want to be. We're individuals. People who can't be molded and shaped and replaced and swapped like pieces on a giant chess board. I'm a Similar, but that doesn't define me. Just like being a Duplicate isn't the defining thing about you."

I look from one Duplicate to another, digging as deeply within myself as I can to try to influence their minds. Focusing on the positive thoughts I want to convey to them and praying those can supersede the destructive ones they've been programmed with.

"Please," I whisper. "Trust me. You don't want this. You don't have to *be* this."

One of the Duplicates—a clone of Pru—steps toward me, and I think she might be about to say something to me. I reach out my hand. Maybe I really can do this. Bridge the divide. Show them another way—

"Enough!" Seymour shouts. His voice cuts into the silence, breaking the spell that I've cast. The Pru Duplicate steps back from me. She lowers her hand. Her brow furrows. Then she turns back to the others.

I let out a choked cry.

Seymour has broken my link to them. He's cut the cord between me and them, severing our connection. For one moment, I thought I'd gotten through to them, gotten them on our side.

But if I did, the connection's gone.

They turn away from me, resuming their fight with fresh purpose. I feel empty, as though I've utterly failed everyone.

"Impressive speech, Eden, but you didn't fact-check it before delivery."

Gravelle stands over me and my father, holding on to his cane like a lifeline. He looks shaky but intact. I scan his body for bullet wounds but don't find any.

Didn't Maude shoot him? What happened? Why is this bastard okay?

"I don't know what you're talking about, and I don't care," I answer, watching my dad's face grow paler. His eyes are closed now, and his face looks ashen. His hand feels clammy in mine. Is this the end? I don't know if I can bear it.

"You aren't a Similar," Gravelle replies. "That's the part you got wrong."

"We've been over this," I say, resigned. "I know I am. And my dad confirmed it. Right, Dad?"

He nods, and I imagine that simple gesture is taking all the energy he has left. I feel bile in my throat, watching him slip away like this. Unable to do anything for him. I'm so furious and devastated that I can barely hold up my end of this conversation. I wish Gravelle would go away. What does he want from me? What fresh torture is he trying to inflict? In my peripheral vision, I see that the Similars have stormed out the blasted door and are successfully carrying DNA parents to safety. Guards line the floor, some injured, others dead. I know my friends had to use those guns. I know they hated every minute of it. But what choice did they have?

Then I see her.

She's standing there, amid the action and chaos, looking so much like me. Same brown hair. Same brown eyes. She walks into the room, right through the center of the fray, and faces me.

She is my exact copy. Another Emma.

She is me.

"You made a Duplicate of *me*?" I exclaim, reluctantly letting go of my father's hand so I can stand and get a better look at this girl. Her features mirror my own exactly, down to the last freckle and smile line. I'm drawn to her, feeling an instant connection.

But of course I do; she's my copy. "But why? I'm a Similar, not an original. You copied the originals, not us." I'm reeling, not understanding this at all. I feel like I'm in the bottom of one of those holiday snow globes, looking up at a world I can't make sense of. Is this how my friends felt when they faced their DNA twins? Because this Emma feels oddly like a *part* of me.

The other Emma takes a step toward me, and I brace myself, defensive.

She doesn't come any closer. She pauses where she is, five or six feet away from me, sensing my distress.

"I'm not here to fight you," she says, with a kind of fierceness I wonder if I possess too.

I hold up my hands in a gesture of surrender. "That's the last thing I want," I tell her.

"Good," she answers. "Because the only thing I care about is getting Ollie and Levi and my dad and my friends off this island. Where are they? Are they okay? Because if they aren't, I might seriously lose it—"

She stops midsentence, and I know exactly why. She's seen him now. She's noticed the heap at my feet. My father's body, lying there, barely breathing.

She crumples to her knees, a silent "no" trying to escape her lips, but all that comes out is a muffled, strained cry.

I feel her pain with every atom of my being, because it's the same pain as mine. This Emma—whoever she is—she has all my memories and thoughts and feelings. She is bearing this pain as acutely as I am.

I scan the room for my friends, for someone who can help

me make sense of this. Who is this girl? What is she doing here? My eyes land on Maude, who's carrying a wounded Archer on her back, and I snag her.

"I need the infrared light." Maude has it in her pocket and hands it to me, no questions asked. Then she moves off, full of purpose.

I kneel beside this other Emma, whose face is masked by tears. I don't think she even registers me next to her, so focused is she on my father. So I gently take her wrist and shine the infrared light on it.

No time stamp.

I grab her other wrist and shine the light there too.

Still no time stamp.

I look from this other Emma to Gravelle, who's still standing by, looking almost pleased at the total destruction and loss of life around him. How ironic that he stands here, unhurt, while the rest of us suffer. How ironic that Maude's gunshot didn't even wound him. How *unfair*.

"There are no numbers," I say to Gravelle, utterly bereft. I feel like he's watching me, observing how I'm going to react. I'm a player in his game, one he's orchestrated from the beginning. That's all I am to him, and all I'll ever be. "There's no time stamp. No batch, no lot. Every Duplicate has one. She can't be my Duplicate without it. And if she's not my Duplicate, then who is she?"

I stop short, suddenly understanding. Wishing I didn't.

You aren't a Similar, Gravelle had said a minute ago. *That's the part you got wrong.*

Feeling the sudden terror of someone who is walking alone at night and knows she's being followed, harboring that dread, I take the infrared light and shine it on my *own* wrist.

It's there, plain as day. The time stamp. On my arm.

002.34.

Batch two, lot 34. Which can only mean one thing.

I'm *not* a Similar. I am not who I thought I was, but not because I'm not the original Emma. I'm not even the Eden cloned from her.

I am a third version of myself. One grown on this island and implanted with all of Emma's memories. I am not recognizable to myself. And yet, I know the time stamp doesn't lie.

I am a Duplicate. 002.34, to be precise.

I am a number. A time stamp. A person created in a lab with no name, no parents, no family, no real life.

Nothing about my world will ever be the same again.

RESET

"I'M A DUPLICATE? But how? That's—that doesn't make *sense…*"

But it does make sense. And I know I'm fighting the truth. There's a second Emma kneeling next to me, and I have the time stamp on my wrist. She doesn't. There's no other way to explain this. Is there?

"Ah, recognition dawning," Gravelle purrs. "No, 002.34, you are *not* a Similar. You're a Duplicate."

I cringe at the term. 002.34. I am a nameless vessel with no identity. But how? *How?*

I stare at this other Emma, the *real* Emma. Only now do I realize she's not wearing the Duplicate uniform. How did I not see this five minutes ago? She's wearing the same type of clothes I am. Jeans, a T-shirt, and a hoodie. *My clothes.* I try to wrap my brain around this. If I'm a Duplicate, why do I feel so very much like *me*?

"But…but…" I begin, grasping at straws. "I remember every last detail about my life in Technicolor."

"So do the others." Gravelle shrugs. "How do you think they so easily took on their roles? Ollie seemed almost exactly like your best friend, didn't he?"

I spin on Gravelle, feeling like I've lost my footing and I'm being pitched down a mountain. "But I can't be a Duplicate," I say, my voice hollow.

"And why not? You're too special? You *are* special, 002.34, because the girl you were cloned from is extraordinarily so."

The scene around me is foggy. I can't focus on anything; my mind is a whir of desperate, spinning thoughts. I watch my friends return for more of the parents, shouting at each other to get on the boats. The shouts sound far off, even though I'm mere feet from the action. The world is a blur.

"You are special for a second reason, 002.34. You are my best Duplicate, my most perfect copy. Dare I say it: my pièce de résistance. Strong, brilliant, and able to read minds."

"But—but the activation," I sputter. "When I saw Ollie reporting back to you. I don't do that! I've never communicated with you—"

"Of course you have. Your activation time's in the dead of night. Three a.m. I had to be certain it was a time no one would run into you—you're so unpredictable in your patterns, 002.34.

But you absolutely communicated with me. I can show you the proof."

"But if I reported back everything I knew, I would have told you that I knew Ollie was a Duplicate!" The realization is horrifying.

"And you did. But I wasn't worried. You hadn't discovered my ultimate plan, had you?"

My heart sinks to my feet.

"What about our plan to go to the political rally, to protect Bianca and Jaeger?"

"I knew about that too." Gravelle smiles. "I'm pleased with how well the activation feature operated. Smoothly. Seamlessly. No bugs. No issues."

So I told him everything. I gave it all away. Our plans to travel to New York City and protect Bianca. My skin crawls with the thought that I was betraying us all, without ever knowing it.

I look down at Emma, who's bending over my father like she's in prayer. My dad's face is sweat-soaked. His eyes still closed. His jaw slack.

"But how..."

"How did I switch you? That was simple. When Eden paid me a surprise visit at the end of last year, I implanted a device in her brain, just like I did with all the DNA parents and originals, though it was harder with them; I had to send my ground crew to do that. The device transmitted all of Eden's thoughts and memories straight to you, like a wireless download. And it worked perfectly. While Eden was thrust into my portal, I simply switched out your body with hers, one for the other, allowing you to escape my island—all the while letting you believe you were her. Well, you *are* her, because what is identity, really? But semantics. She stayed on Castor Island with me for the summer and the entire school year, until she was transferred here to Pollux."

I look at Emma—not Eden, I'll never use that name—the real Emma, the Similar, to gauge her reaction. Maybe she already knows all of this. She's been here for nearly a year. That realization takes a chunk out of me. As much as I feel like I've been pushed off a cliff and can't find purchase, I can't imagine what it's been like for *her*. Held captive all year while someone else lived her life. She's rocking back and forth over her father, *our* father. If he dies, we'll share a twin pain.

I think I'm going to be sick to my stomach. I feel like I've been tricked out of everything I've ever relied on, fundamental truths like "the earth is round" and "the sky is blue." If Colin is *her* father, can he also be mine? What does this mean for *me*? Are my memories not my own? Is my entire life a lie, an even bigger one than I thought when I learned about the original Emma who died as a three-year-old? Am I even a person? Or simply a collection of data and memories and cells?

I'm snapped out of these despairing thoughts by Seymour. He's striding over to Gravelle as he surveys Emma, then me.

"She knows?" Seymour asks his brother quietly. Gravelle nods.

Seymour studies me like I'm one of his specimens. "I hope you realize how perfect you are, 002.34."

"Stop calling me that."

"You are my ideal clone. Strong and agile like a Similar, with an extra-special skill: mind control. Once we can make others exactly like you, and use this technique to copy some of the greatest and most powerful men and women in this country…"

"You'll have succeeded," I say, the words tumbling out of me and tasting like poison on my tongue. "So what now?" I face Seymour, forcing him to look at me. To really see me. "You kill her? Because she's my original, and therefore, she's expendable?"

I hear my father gasp.

"Dad," I croak. But when I search his face, there's no response. Emma meets my eyes, silent, and I know what she's not saying. He's dead. That gasp was his last one.

I look back up at Seymour, ready to rail at him, but he isn't there. Maybe he left—too much of a coward to stand there and face me. Or maybe a Similar has grabbed him and shot him. I hope so.

Staring back down at my dad's lifeless face, I focus all my rage and pain on Gravelle. "You sick bastard," I sob, letting myself open like a faucet, the tears for my father pouring out of me unchecked. "He was your roommate," I shout. If I thought I wanted Gravelle dead before, there's no contest now. I have never felt this much rage in my entire life. "He was kind to you." I shake. "He cared about you. And this is how you repay him?"

"I repaid him already, and then some," Gravelle responds. "I delivered Eden to him. Didn't I?"

I charge at Gravelle, bearing down on him, knocking his cane from his hand. Maude's at my side in an instant, pulling me off him.

"Save your energy," she tells me. "He's an old, sick fool…"

"I thought you shot him," I say through gritted teeth.

"I did," she answers quietly as I step back from Gravelle, watching him shakily reaching for his cane.

"Then where's the wound?" I demand.

I get my answer in moments, as three other Gravelles stride into the room and surround this Gravelle.

"I must have shot his Duplicate," Maude explains, her voice tight.

"You mean—"

"These aren't soulless, blank Duplicates. They're…"

Like me, I almost say out loud. Full of their original's thoughts and memories. But I hold it in.

I understand exactly who they are, *what* they are. They're an insurance policy for him. If one dies, there are more.

"It will be harder to eradicate me than you thought," the Gravelle in the middle of the circle says. *Our* Gravelle—or is he? He's got his cane back and is leaning on it. The ones who circle him don't hold canes, I now realize.

Which means *he's* our original.

"They can't protect you forever," I snarl as my friends arrive to flank me. "He's the one we want," I tell his copies. "So move out of the way."

My friends pounce. Jago thrusts a knife at one of the Gravelles. Ansel tackles a second clone. Levi approaches from behind, cutting another Gravelle off at the knees. But our Gravelle remains in the center, clumsily dodging the action with the help of his cane, protected by his copies.

I feel so much anger at this man. For killing my father and Theodora. For causing all this suffering.

I don't care about anything right now except hurting him as much as he's hurt all of us.

So I charge. Straight toward the circle of Gravelles who've formed a human shield around their leader. My friends are chipping away at that shield as they take each Duplicate down, one by one.

I find an opening. Crouching low, I push through the human barrier. Past the kicking and thrusting bodies to the real Gravelle—I'm certain it's him, the way they're protecting him at all costs—and knock the cane out of his hand. Then I tackle him, sending him to the ground.

Maude's at my side, handing me a knife. Sweating, tears springing from my eyes, I point the blade directly at his throat.

"You're afraid, aren't you," I whisper in Gravelle's ear. A Gravelle Duplicate tries to grab me, but Maude kicks him off. "It's not so fun being on this side of things," I add. "Is it?"

"Emma," says a voice. I turn to see the other Emma—the original one—calling out to me.

I give Gravelle's scarred face one last look and hand the knife to Levi, who has taken down two of the Gravelles for good, knocking them out, and is standing next to me.

"Throw him in the cage to rot," I instruct him.

It's what seems fitting. I won't kill him; I can't. But he deserves to suffer.

Just then, a shot rings out. I don't see the bullet hit him, but I see what happens afterward. Blood is spreading out of Gravelle's chest like a red-wine stain on the pristine floor.

The bullet struck him right at the center, the heart of him—if he ever had one. But who did this?

I scan the library, looking past the rows of vintage first editions, to see Jago holding a gun.

"That was for Theodora," he says quietly.

I feel myself deflating, in relief, in utter fatigue.

Gravelle is dead.

You are a Duplicate.

I walk past Gravelle's bleeding form—abandoned now by his copies—to find Maude at the doorway, stepping on a guard's chest and firing a gun at him. She hits his foot, aiming to impair but not kill him.

"What's going to happen when we leave here?" I ask her, a new realization dawning on me. "The Duplicates at home—they aren't just going to hand their lives back to their originals. They believe they are who they are." I know this more than anyone, but I don't say it out loud. "Even if we get all the originals safely home…"

Levi moves up, overhearing. "Who will ever believe that Bianca Huxley isn't who she says she is? That Jane Ward is an imposter? How will we ever restore the real parents back to their lives? What if no one believes us about the time stamps? We won't be able to force the Duplicates to submit to the infrared light. Everyone will think that *these* are the imposters. It will be nearly impossible to prove who they are."

Seeing Levi here, now, I want to acknowledge what just happened. My father jumped in front of that bullet to save the boy I love. But I'm in shock. I can't confront it, or this bombshell that

I'm a Duplicate. If I think about it for even a second, I'll crack. If I'm not Emma, but 002.34, does that mean everything that happened with Levi was a lie? Does that mean the feelings he had weren't really for me, but for the "real" Emma?

"What if..." Maude wonders out loud. "What if we could somehow reprogram them? The Duplicates, I mean."

"They aren't *robots*." I know I sound defensive, but I'm one of them. Of course, Maude and Levi don't know that. They've been so caught up in the fighting, they must not have noticed the other Emma near my father's body. Or if they did, they assumed she's another Duplicate, since this place is teeming with clones. They wouldn't have assumed that I'm the copy. And they didn't hear Gravelle reveal my true identity, I'm sure of it.

"Of course they aren't robots, but they've been brainwashed, haven't they?" Maude goes on. "A reset," she says, her wheels turning. "We have to get to the server room. Follow me." Maude leads me and Levi away from the ongoing fighting, up a back stairwell and down a set of corridors to another sterile white room, this one with a bay of windows overlooking the beach. The sight of the opaque blue water nearly brings me to my knees because of what it represents—our freedom. If we can get there—out of this building, to safety—and find a way off this island... I see some of my friends loading the weak DNA parents onto boats, far in the distance, and I'm thankful. I hope we all make it out alive.

But first, we have to try to reverse all the damage Gravelle and Seymour have done.

I survey the server room, which is filled with the most

high-tech computers, at least fifteen monitors, and other hardware I don't recognize.

Maude starts typing furiously on an elaborate keyboard. "If we can find a way to reset the Duplicates, back to their original state, the ones at home will abandon their roles."

Reset the Duplicates? Reset them so that they don't remember anything about their lives? So *I* don't remember anything about *my* life? The thought is so terrifying I feel the ground begin to spin beneath me.

Maude, oblivious to how this would affect me, goes on. "Gravelle's brain implants—we'll have to shut those down, make sure they stop transmitting...from fighting us."

"Can you really do all that?" I ask weakly. If I felt thrown off course by the idea of being a Duplicate, I now feel shaken to my very core. Dizzy, like if I don't grab hold of something solid, I might evaporate.

And yet, I understand why Maude is suggesting this, why it needs to happen.

Maude moves through a series of windows on the screen. I try to banish the pounding in my heart, focusing on the monitor. I can't make sense of what she's doing, but I understand the gist—she's hacking the system. "I've already gotten into the server that controls all thought management. I'm two steps away from hitting a central reboot. Holy cow!" she says suddenly, sitting up in her chair like she's being branded with a hot poker.

"What?" Levi asks. "What's wrong?"

Maude's shaking her head like she doesn't believe what she's seeing in the programming. "It's a fail-safe," she whispers. "Built into the code. If we reset the Duplicates, wiping their minds clean—"

"Which we have to do if we want to guarantee that the originals get their lives back," I remind her, my voice not revealing how utterly bereft I feel inside. I know it's what we have to do. But I'm going to lose my entire identity. My past, my present, and my future. I'll have nothing—no memories, no life. It's the most horrifying thing I can imagine, and I try to hide the tears that well in my eyes.

"If we go ahead with the reset," Maude keeps talking, completely unaware that I'm breaking inside, "this entire island explodes. Castor too."

I tear my mind away from my own fears long enough to process what Maude's just told us. "Wait. What are you saying? A bomb will detonate? More than one bomb?"

"Gravelle and Seymour must have set it up that way," she says, her face a mask as she tries to work through this. "If the authorities ever came to investigate, and they needed to erase all the evidence of what they'd done, they must have assumed this was the only way. To reset all the minds, destroy the islands—and all their research."

"It also means they anticipated *this*. What we're about to do right now," Levi adds.

"A fail-safe, like Maude said," I whisper. I'm only now processing the full repercussions of what that means. My eyes linger on the boats outside the window in the distance. The terror I feel at being reset begins to morph into dread, and, quickly, resignation. I know what I need to do. It's going to be painful, in more ways than one. But it's the only way. "Show me how to do it," I tell Maude, accepting that this *has* to happen this way. This is what I must do. It has to be me. I'm going to lose my mind anyway, aren't I? All of my memories, the thoughts that make me *me*—whoever that even is? Once the reset happens, I'll be an empty shell of a person. It's an incredibly scary thought—so overwhelmingly sad, really, that I try not to let myself go there. "I'll stay here and do the reset. You two need to leave before this bomb goes off. I want you far out in the water before I do it."

Maude looks stricken. "But why would we let you sacrifice yourself?"

"Because," I answer her. I choke back tears. "I'm a Duplicate. 002.34."

"*You?*" She looks lost, like a little girl. So uncharacteristically out of control. The bewildered expression on her face almost brings me to my knees.

And Levi—I've never seen such confusion and hurt on his face. I've never seen him entirely speechless.

"Yes," I answer, forcing my voice not to tremble. "That's what Gravelle was telling me just now, before I attacked him. Last year, on Castor Island, he switched us. I've been with you, and the real Emma, the Similar Emma, has been here. All year. She's downstairs right now, in the library, by my father's body. I swear I didn't know any of this until half an hour ago. I'm as shocked as you are."

I remember that I still have the infrared light, and I slip it out of my pocket, shining it directly on my wrist, illuminating my time stamp. I know Maude will want to see proof. She's too logical. Too skeptical. There's no way she'd believe me otherwise.

"I wish it weren't true. Believe me, I…" I steel myself. There's no time to waste. "Please, Maude. Show me what I need to do."

"But," Maude protests. As strong as she is, this is more than she bargained for. "But if you go through with the reset, we'll be erasing *you*. All of your unique thoughts and memories from senior year. They'll be gone…"

Like the night I spent with Levi. I meet his eyes, and we don't say it out loud, but we both feel it. We don't want those memories to die along with me. At least, I know I don't. But what choice do we have? He'll have to remember for the both of us. I'll live on in his mind.

"It won't matter, because I'll be dead," I answer her.

"No," she protests again. "I won't let you do it."

"It's the only way!" I have to make her see. I don't want this; of course I don't. I don't want to be reset. I don't want to die. "I could never live with myself if I let Ollie and Jane and all the others suffer like that, shut out of their own lives because no one believes they're who they say they are. We can't let Gravelle and Seymour win. We *can't*. If we do, this will all have been for nothing. My dad's death. Theodora's…" I don't say what's in the back of my mind: that I have no life to go back to, anyway.

"I'm with Emma," Levi declares softly. His use of my name guts me. He hasn't said 002.34.

I watch Maude as she takes it all in. She presses her hands to her temples, thinking, hard. Finally, she looks up at me, spent.

"You'll move through this series of screens," she says quietly.

"Follow the prompts to the three red buttons. Then the F7 command will appear. Press that, and the orange reboot button will pop up at the end of the sequence. Pressing it will reset every Duplicate, deactivate the implants in the originals and DNA parents, and signal the bombs to detonate." I commit everything she said to memory. I can't mess this up.

"Thank you." I breathe out. "Now, please. Both of you. Go. I won't do it until I know you're safely on the boats."

It's too painful to look at them. To think of the lives back home that they'll inhabit, while I stay here to die, alone. If I let myself go there, I'll never go through with this. So I don't. I keep my eyes on the beach outside the window. With relief, I see that even as the Similars keep fighting Duplicates and guards on the shore, many of them are escaping. Ollie is climbing into a boat with Pru and Jaeger. Thank God. Ollie's going to live. He's going to be okay. Ansel is helping Tessa and Madison into another one.

I position myself in front of the keyboard, ready to press the three red buttons like Maude instructed me, but waiting until I've seen all the boats take off into the water.

Then I hear the door slam behind me. Good. They've gone.

But someone's still here. I can feel it, the presence of someone else behind me.

I turn quickly in my chair. My heart swells in my rib cage when I see that it's Levi.

"She's gone," he says to me, his voice reassuring. "It's just us now. We'll wait until we're sure they're all safe, and then we'll do it—"

"Are you insane?" I say to him, my pulse threatening to bust through my veins. "You can't be here. You have to go. You can't die for me! I'm not even Emma. Not really. I'm a Duplicate—"

"So am I," he interrupts, his eyes pleading with me. Suddenly, they look so sad and vacant. "So am I."

I stare at him like I'm seeing a ghost. What is he saying? Is this a trick?

"I had no idea, either, until we got here, to Pollux, and I saw the evidence. My time stamp," Levi explains bitterly. "Just like yours. We were played, Emma, don't you see? Levi the Similar was on Castor this whole time, this whole *year*, with the Emma Similar. I was sent to Darkwood instead, and you and I…"

We were never who we thought we were.

The enormity of what Gravelle has done to us hits me like a blow to the chest. It's unthinkable. Levi was a Duplicate, this whole time? We both were?

I'm deep in my thoughts when I hear a gunshot.

Then the door crashes down.

Someone's kicked it in.

It's Seymour. Standing there, wielding a gun, and pointing it straight at me.

CONTROL

"HANDS OFF THE keys. *Now*," Seymour commands, pointing the gun directly at my head.

I don't lift my fingers from the keyboard. He has more to lose than I do. Which means I have to play this just right. "I know about the fail-safe," I tell him. "I know that all I have to do is hit the reboot button, and everything you've worked for—all your research, all your years of scheming—will be instantly destroyed."

"You wouldn't," Seymour says, his fingers still curled around the gun. "Kill yourself, to save a bunch of people who care nothing for you? Or you?" He swings the gun to point it at Levi. "I made you. I made you *both*. You are nothing but my creations, born less than two years ago in my lab and rapidly reared and trained. You are specimens. You are *nobodies*. Don't kid yourself that any of them care about you, because they don't."

Out of the corner of my eye, I see more chaos on the shore. My friends fighting with guards—ripping, clawing—and, in most cases, gaining the upper hand. One boat has taken off already into the water, with Ollie, Pru, and Jaeger on board, and I am grateful. I take stock of everyone I love—the Similars, the DNA parents, and the originals—and count them boarding the remaining boats. My friends are prevailing, downing guards right and left. They're jumping into the boats and escaping the island, which is what I need to see happen before I can go through with the reboot. But I scan the shore for Levi—Similar Levi—and don't see him. I can't move forward unless I know he's safe. I'll have to stay alive long enough, and stall Seymour long enough, to know for sure.

"Emma," the Levi next to me breathes, but I don't answer him. I close my eyes, focusing hard on Seymour, the Seymour I can see in my mind's eye, as hard as I've ever focused on anything. I picture his smug face. I remember him lying to us back at school. I think of all the pain and suffering he's caused these families, all for his own selfish gain, his misguided ideas of what "scientific advancement" really is.

And I hear his thoughts.

What's she doing? Why is she closing her eyes like that? Little brat, just like Eden, never happy with any of what we've given her—

I can control you, I think to myself. *I can stop you from pulling that trigger.*

Stupid, meddling mind-reading clone. I'll have no choice but to shoot her to bits. Shame, all that work destroyed for nothing—

You won't do anything to me. You won't shoot me. You won't stop me. Your brain controls not only your thoughts, but everything you do. I'm controlling you now, Seymour. Set the gun down.

I open my eyes to face him. I've never felt more powerful in my life. I'm not just reading Seymour's mind. I'm in charge. *I'm* deciding what he thinks and says and does. Seymour's still holding the gun, but he's not pulling the trigger. He sets it down. Levi gingerly picks it up.

You will walk to the computer, I think.

Seymour begins to shuffle his feet. He looks down at them, confused.

You will hit the three red buttons, I tell him.

He approaches the keyboard. I don't hear a single thought in his head, because he *can't* think independently. Not with me controlling him like this.

Doesn't feel good not being in charge of your own free will, does it? Doesn't feel good when your "creation" becomes your master.

Seymour presses the three red buttons. The F7 command appears.

On the shore, it's a frenetic, desperate scene as my friends nab the last boats and help the remaining DNA parents board them. I finally see Levi, stumbling out of the building holding a figure in his arms. It's Theodora. Her body is limp and unmoving. But he has her, and he's not leaving her here. Even if she is beyond reviving. I feel tears in my eyes for her. For Theodora. I wish I'd been able to tell her how much she meant to me. I also feel a deep kind of longing for Levi—the Levi I fell in love with last year, that Emma first fell in love with. I'll never see him again. And he'll never know how I really felt. I watch as he approaches a boat, resting Theodora inside it.

I turn back to Seymour. Levi's safe, and so are my friends, and it's time.

Now. Press the orange reboot button, I instruct him. *Do it.*

He doesn't hesitate, because he can't; I won't let him. He presses it.

I brace myself for the loss of everything I've ever known. My memories of Ollie. Of being his best friend and loving him all these years, of splitting sandwiches and watching films and staying up way too late scarfing down junk food and sharing our lives. My memories of the Similars, of my dad, lying lifeless on that cold, hard floor. And, of course, my memories of being with Levi. Of how he rocked my entire world and found a way to heal my scarred heart. I don't know how quick the process will be— the process of losing myself and my identity and every thought I've ever known. I hope it's not long and drawn out. I hope it isn't painful.

In moments, it all happens. An explosion erupts somewhere within the compound, and I'm knocked out of my seat. The room is buckling and trembling so violently, the floor literally rolling beneath me, that I can't stabilize myself. The chair is out of my reach, even as I try crawling over to it, thrusting my body forward to reach it. Seymour is on the floor, unable to grasp on to anything, since I'm still controlling his mind. He's rocked by the waves, powerless to steady himself.

The bombs have gone off. The entire room rattles as a string of mini-explosions hits, as labs and furnaces and everything else on this compound gets triggered by the initial blast. I climb back gingerly into my seat, finally able to grasp it, and glance hungrily out the window, expecting to see all the boats gone, the shore empty except for fallen guards.

I nearly keel over when I spot him. Levi's on the shore, crumpled in a heap. He's been hit. Debris is everywhere. This entire island is a powder keg, with destruction rippling across it in waves.

And I'm the one who triggered it.

"No," I cry out. "Levi, no!" This can't be happening. I checked before I ordered Seymour to hit that command. I *checked* on everyone! But especially Levi! I saw him leave the building and carry Theodora's body to that boat. *I thought he was safe.*

But you didn't see him climb into the boat himself, did you?

The Levi who is still here with me, Duplicate Levi, rushes to my side. We race to the window and watch, transfixed in our fear, as the other Emma huddles over the other Levi. Panic grabs hold of me with its unforgiving claws, and my eyes are glued to his prone form. *Please let him be okay. Please let him and Emma get off this island.* I let out a choke of relief when he starts to move his arms and legs, and eventually stands up, seemingly unharmed. Levi and Emma scramble for the last boat, and Emma's already pulling the cord to start the engine, as smoke begins to billow out from the front doors of the compound and flames overtake the library. The thick black smoke makes its way into that beautiful building, the one filled with scores of irreplaceable books. In minutes, they will burn to ash.

I let out a sob. Levi's okay. So is Emma.

Duplicate Levi grabs my hand and squeezes it so hard it hurts, and we hold on to each other for dear life as one last explosion rocks us, toppling us to the floor.

I'm ready, I think to myself. I clamber to my feet and watch the other Emma settle into the boat next to Levi, resting her head on his shoulder as the island burns. Everyone I love has left the island now for good, and I know that with this one, last act, I'll free the Duplicates at home and facilitate the return of the DNA parents and originals to their old lives. Ollie and Jane will get their lives back. So will Levi and Emma. It will be worth it, to die.

Smoke is billowing into the room through the open door. I begin to cough, and so does Seymour, who's still powerless to speak or move of his own accord. The coughing is involuntary. But he can't flee the fire. He must stay here with us, and die. I consider releasing him from the hold I have over him. But what if he found a way, later, to reverse everything? To fly away in the copter and undo the reset? I can't take that chance.

I will control you to the end, I think. *It's what you deserve.*

"Levi," I say, because it's the name that must feel the most real to him. He's as much Levi as I'm Emma. He and I meant something to each other this year, in a way no one else will ever know, or understand. What he and I had, it has to have mattered. I have to believe that it did.

The room has stopped shaking, and Levi pulls me close to him, presses his lips to my cheek.

"Before it happens," he breathes into my ear. "Before we forget it all…"

"I'm scared," I admit to him.

"Me too," he answers back. "I don't want to leave this life. I don't want to leave you," he says, his voice so tender it almost kills me to hear it. "Not before we've gotten a real chance to live it. But maybe it's better this way, if we forget. When we die—we won't know, will we?"

"We could throw a chair through the window," I tell him, tasting the salt of tears in my mouth. I hadn't even realized I'd been crying. "We could jump..."

Levi doesn't answer me, and I know we're thinking the same thing: jump to what life? In moments, we won't even know who we are. Would living like that—with no thoughts, no identity, no way to survive—even be worth it? That thought is scarier than letting the smoke overtake us. Much scarier than dying here, together, knowing we did everything we could for the people we love.

"It was always you, Emma," he chokes. I can't answer him. It hurts too much to talk.

So we stand there, holding each other. I smell the smoke that's right outside the door, and in a few minutes I walk to it, to open it. The doorknob is scalding, and I snatch my hand away. A wall of thick, black fumes stops me from leaving. I don't want to walk through that. I don't know what might greet me on the other side. White-hot fire? Flames that would burn my flesh?

It's a strange sensation, losing all of one's memories and thoughts and feelings. It starts out small. I feel vaguely foggy, like someone's drugged me. Thoughts flit in and out of my head, but they are mere musings. They linger like flies, buzzing around my consciousness. I hope my friends are safe. I don't remember why I wish for this, but I do. I know I love the boy who's sitting on the floor next to me, holding my hand. We've ducked down low, because that's what you do in a fire. Isn't it?

I look down at my own hand, threaded through the boy's. Whose hands are these?

Why am I coughing so violently?

Oh. There's smoke billowing through the door.

I look at the man splayed on the floor, also coughing fitfully. I know this man isn't good. But why? And what has he done?

The smoke is overwhelming, so I lie down on the floor, gasping for the last clean air, and curl myself into a ball.

The boy lies down next to me. We're still holding hands, linked until the end.

I try to think of something comforting to carry me through this, but when I grasp for a memory, something to hold on to—there's nothing there.

HOME

TWO WEEKS LATER, we're home. Home is Darkwood—with its relentless gossip and impossible standards, its in vitro meat and freezing dorms, and the old abandoned pump house that's something straight out of a nightmare. It's the place where I fell in love with Levi junior year, where Ollie and I spent so many afternoons before that, lying on our backs on the grass, dreaming. I've missed it so much that my longing for it all is still a gaping hole in me, one it will take months to fill. Every time I walk into the dining hall, or my dorm room, I think of her—my Duplicate—and wonder what my senior year, *her* senior year, was like.

I was on Castor Island for nearly a year. Away from Ollie

and Pru and the Similars and my father. I lost a year of my life because I was Gravelle's prisoner. The only thing that made it remotely tolerable was Levi.

He was there with me, on Castor. We didn't know it in the beginning, and those first few weeks were a specific kind of hell, finding myself trapped on the compound with Gravelle, all alone without a soul but the guards in sight. I was so lonely—so desperate to escape. I quickly learned how futile my efforts were. Every time I tried, the guards thrust me into the portal. So I resolved to wait, pacing my stark room, slowly going mad. Gravelle made sure I had plenty to do to keep me busy. Textbooks and coursework would arrive at my room each day—including a syllabus—and assignments would appear on a tablet, with pop quizzes and homework I worked on well into the night. I never lacked for schoolwork to keep me occupied. Leave it to Gravelle to make sure I wasn't "missing" my senior year—even though I was, in every other sense of the word.

Then we found each other. Gravelle wanted it to happen, of course. He sent me to the library on a research assignment, and that's when I saw him there. It nearly leveled me to learn that Levi was trapped on Castor too. I felt a conflicted kind of joy at the sight of him. Elation that he was there, with me, and I could touch him and hold him and feel his warmth underneath my fingertips. I was also bereft, because I thought he'd been freed. Every moment he was there with me was a moment he was a prisoner. I didn't want that for him. I didn't want that for us. I would have taken back my secluded imprisonment in a heartbeat if it had meant he could leave.

Of course, Gravelle had other plans. He dealt out our punishments slowly. First, he informed me about my past. That I was—*am*—a Similar. That took me weeks to comprehend and even longer to accept. But it was only the first blow. When Gravelle informed me and Levi that DNA copies of us had been sent back to Darkwood, to stand in as us and live our lives for us, we were wrecked. He told us that we'd be living on Castor, with him, for the rest of our lives. He told us that the Duplicates believed they were us, and not to bother trying to escape; we never would.

As much as it pained me that Levi was trapped right by my side, he quickly became my oxygen, my air. It had only been a few weeks since that night we spent together in Bar Harbor, and every cell in my body longed to be with him. Not only because we were all we had, but also because he understood me in a way that no one else had, or ever would. He was the one who talked me off the ledge when I learned I was a Similar. He had known, he told me. I was angry at first—outraged—but that knee-jerk anger eventually morphed into understanding, and I knew why he'd kept it from me. Everything about his life had been so twisted, so cruel. He was sparing me from that. He had tried to, anyway. After that, every chance we got, we found a way to see each other. Some days it was only for minutes. Some days longer. Kissing each other, our bodies pressed together like magnets, it all felt so crazy when we thought of our lives, of what we were losing, of the enormity of it all. And yet, it felt so necessary and right. When I wasn't studying, I spent my waking hours engineering ways to end up in his path, and he in mine. I spent most of my sleeping hours dreaming that one day we'd be able to be together, and not as prisoners. This was a coping mechanism. One I used, at least in part, to numb the pain I felt over being separated from Ollie, and my father, and Pru. The idea that I might never see them again was too much to bear.

Eventually, Gravelle moved us to Pollux. I don't know his reasons, I only know it's where he was training the Duplicates. I never saw them once while I was there. They were hidden from us, kept in the lower part of the compound, which we didn't have access to. I certainly never saw my father or the other DNA parents and originals once they arrived on the island. I had no idea they'd all been replaced, just like me and Levi, not until the guards grew lax one day—the day the islands exploded—and Levi and I escaped our restricted area, only to discover the entire compound was in tatters, and my friends were fighting the guards and Duplicates and Gravelle and Seymour.

Our Duplicates—mine and Levi's—died saving all of us. Resetting all the clones back here at home and "releasing" them from their duty to follow Gravelle and Seymour's orders. Duplicate Levi and Emma had to reset themselves to do it—and I can imagine that they were terrified. But they did it anyway. They destroyed the islands, and all that research, ensuring no more Duplicates could ever be created again.

Before we escaped in the boats, I visited my father one last time, in the library where he lay, dead, and where he later burned. I kissed him and slid his wedding ring off his finger. The ring's on a chain around my neck, with my Darkwood key. When I graduate, I'll give the key back. But I'll never take off the ring.

Once the bombs detonated, Levi and I made it into a

motorboat where we watched Pollux Island burn, the orange and yellow flames licking at a building that had once been beautiful. Ollie was safe, and Pru, and everyone else I loved, except Theodora. Her death split me apart. It was so unfair. So senseless. As we crossed the choppy water to our freedom and Levi took over the controls of the boat, my eyes became so heavy that I fell asleep on his shoulder.

Some of us went home, not to Darkwood but to our real houses. Pru and Pippa traveled with Jaeger to the farm. Tessa to her mother's apartment. Ansel and Archer to the de Leons'. Ollie and, yes, Levi, to Booker and Jane's. I hoped this would be Levi's chance, finally, to make amends with his DNA family.

I insisted on flying back to San Francisco on my own. I needed to go through my father's things. I needed time alone, to process. It had been him and me for so long; that's how it had to be in the days following his death. Just me, with my memories of him. It's painful accepting his last year with me wasn't with me at all. My Duplicate had conversations with him I'll never be privy to. I missed so much in a lifetime where he and I had so little. So little time, so little understanding. At night, I lie awake imagining what she might have said to him. Ollie tells me my father died in an act of love, to save Duplicate Levi, and his distance all those years stemmed from his deep-seated fear of losing me. I hold on to that like a lifeline. It's all I have. My father's memorial will be this summer. I need time to plan, to think about what I want to say in his eulogy. I'm not ready to officially say goodbye. Not yet.

We are back at school, and Jane has been reinstated as

headmistress. Duplicate Jane, along with the other Duplicates who were rebooted, have abandoned their roles and are searching for their real identities, as individuals. Many of them have expressed how directionless they feel—and all of them are, in a way, displaced. Jaeger has invited them to live on his farm, and some have found temporary homes, oddly enough, with their originals. I don't know what the future will hold for them, but I make a promise to myself to help them figure that out, as soon as I graduate.

The blank Duplicates from Pollux didn't survive. Victims of the explosion, they didn't make it off the island. I am deeply sad about that, but I know there was no alternative. The real Gravelle died of his gunshot wound. Seymour perished with my Duplicate and Levi's clone, passing out from smoke inhalation before being consumed by flames.

As for the DNA parents, most have a new lease on their old lives, having been away from their families and jobs and homes for months. Madison has credited Maude with saving her life. And, since Ansel's heroic rescue of Madison from the cage, the two have started up a relationship of sorts. They were recently caught kissing in the science lab when Madison was visiting for the weekend. I don't know whether to laugh or cry at the idea of them as a couple. I hope it means that Madison's really changed.

Our private memorial for Theodora is scheduled for tonight, on the shore of the lake. Ollie, Levi, Ansel, Maude, Jago, Pru, Pippa and I will celebrate her life. It will just be us there, those who knew her best...and Tessa. She's been so broken up by her Similar's death, she's come back to Darkwood with us and has been sleeping on the floor by Theodora's empty bed, paying tribute in her own way to the girl who had the potential to be like a sister, but whom she never got the chance to really know and love.

Ollie meets me before the memorial for Theodora in the courtyard outside Cypress. We haven't talked much since we got back, but I've felt his unconditional support in the wake of my father's death. I hear him walking up and turn to watch him ambling toward me, his hands stuffed deep in the pockets of a light wool coat. I missed Ollie so much last year, it hurt like a cracked rib. Being with Levi, falling so deeply for him while we were on Castor, didn't lessen the pain I felt at being separated once more from my best friend. We were robbed of our junior year together, and then we lost our senior year too. I'll never get those years with him back, and it's a pain that still haunts me.

"Hey," he says, folding me into his familiar chest, where I burrow in and let myself relax for the first time since I've been back at school.

"Hey," I answer, pulling back to look at him, to study his face and promise I'll never take him for granted, ever again. "You look like you've eaten a burger or two."

"My mom's been feeding me nonstop since we got back." He smiles. "Burgers, lasagna, chicken curry, chicken potpie…"

"And the editing? How's that going?"

"Let's see. Eight hundred hours of footage, and I think my bot's going to kill me. I have him weeding through it twenty-four-seven. I put together a highlight reel. I think it's ready for public consumption, but you'd better take a look at it first."

"I'll watch it tonight. Two, maybe three a.m.," I answer, and we both know I'm not joking. I used to stay up all night thinking of him. Then Levi. Now, it's my dad's face I see when I try to close my eyes.

"Okay, but don't give me *too* many notes, because I already sent the highlight reel to NYU," Ollie says slowly, like he's gauging how I'll respond.

"And?"

"And they have a spot. For me. Next year." He laughs, and the sound is so joyful and right, I want to grasp on to it and never let go.

"How could you not lead with that?" I smile now too, running up to hug him again, and we do a sort of awkward and wonderful happy dance together before settling down and wandering over to the wall that faces Dark Lake. I lean on it, looking out.

"Oxford's sorting out whether I've been accepted or not," I say as I scan the lake. "Harlowe really screwed me, or my Duplicate, I guess I should say, but luckily Duplicate Emma's grades and scores were top-notch, and with Jane vouching for me and explaining what Harlowe did, they're going to see what they can do. Good thing Gravelle forced me to study nonstop when I was his prisoner," I say through gritted teeth. "Or I wouldn't even deserve to be going."

"Are the others—"

I cut Ollie off, understanding him before he even finishes. "Maude and Jago are going too. And Levi. Oxford was always the place they wanted to go to blend in, and I...I..."

"It's where you belong too."

"I didn't even apply there. My Duplicate did, on my behalf. That's not how she saw it, of course, but it's what happened. And now, it just feels…right? Ollie, I—"

"No, Emma. Don't. Please don't feel like you have to make some kind of sweeping grand gesture right now."

"I don't do grand gestures. Do you know me at all?"

Ollie laughs. "What was I thinking? Of course you don't."

"I don't know if I'm the same person I was two years ago. I don't know if I'm the same person I was two months ago," I say, trying to explain myself but feeling like I'm coming up short. "I know being a Similar doesn't define me. But now, with my dad gone… I'm really alone."

"And so are they." He doesn't say, *and so is Levi*, but I know he's thinking it. We both are. Ollie is and always will be my past. But Levi is my future. Not because I'm a Similar and can't be with Ollie because he's not. But because Levi was always the one. And Ollie will always be my best friend.

"Maude and Pippa and the others, they told me about a lot of what I missed senior year. But so much of it—it feels like someone else's life. Like some other girl lived it. Which is, I guess, what happened. To both of us," I add, remembering that Ollie and Levi's lives were hijacked too.

"There's only one thing I regret from this year," Ollie says, his gray eyes shining so bright I want to live in them indefinitely and bottle up that "usness" that's so precious and only ours.

"What's that?" I ask breathily.

"That the Emma I kissed wasn't you."

Those words set every atom of my being on fire. I know I'm

not in love with Ollie, not like I am with Levi. But still, I *do* love him, in a way that's only mine and his. And in that moment I feel so much for him—for all the pain we've both suffered—that I don't respond. I simply let him pull me close. He needs this—this one kiss—and maybe I do too.

His hands cupping my face, Ollie gently leans toward me and presses his lips to mine. It is tender and sweet and sends tingles up my spine. It doesn't mean what it could, in some other life, a parallel world where we got to be together. Maybe Ollie wants it to; I don't know. For me, it's a kiss that means something singular, in this moment. It means we are Emma and Ollie, solidified in space and time, and no one can ever take that away from us again. In a way, this kiss is its own sort of goodbye, to what might have been between us. To the road we won't ever take.

When we break apart, I position myself in the crook of Ollie's arm, where it's warm and familiar. He shifts his gaze across the courtyard, pulling the collar of his coat up in a way that tugs at my heartstrings and makes me, for just a minute, wonder what it would have been like, what it *could* have been like, had we not been best friends since third grade. Had we met somehow differently, under other circumstances. Had Levi never come to Darkwood.

"Walk down with you to the lake?" Ollie smiles.

I nod and accept his hand, and we start down the path that will lead us to Theodora's memorial.

◇─┤ ├─◇

The memorial is everything it should be. Mostly the Similars talk, and Pru, Ollie, and I listen, as they share stories of Theodora as a child, and how she loved drawing. I think back to the first time I ever really noticed her. How lovely her handwriting was. It's such a tiny detail, barely anything. The truth is that I wish I'd known her better, and now I'll never have that chance.

Tessa asks the Similars for permission to speak. She talks about the first two weeks of the summer before last, when Theodora first arrived at her home on Central Park West, and how thrilled she was to finally have someone to confide in. Someone who would understand her. Someone who could be her confidante, the sister she'd always wanted but thought she'd never have. "I understand now why she did it," she says. "Why she uncovered my dad's crimes. Even my mother understands. So I guess what I really want to say is, I'm sorry, Pru, that you got caught in the middle of my breakdown. That's all."

After the memorial, we scatter. Some of us go back to the dorms, others go to walk along the beach. Everyone's talking about graduation next month, and colleges. We already knew Madison would be heading to Stanford after this gap year campaigning for her mom. Pru and Pippa modestly tell the others that they're Harvard-bound, which makes me happy. Ollie and Ansel are both heading to NYU, where Archer goes, though Ansel wouldn't be caught dead in the drama department and plans to study history and anthropology. Even Jake's heading off to UCLA to play soccer. Tessa will join the first years at Dartmouth.

My friends walk back up to campus, but I turn the other way, toward the water. I'm standing on the shore of the lake when someone calls my name. I turn to see Levi there, the moonlight glinting off his too-long hair, and now, in the glow of the evening, my pulse quickens to what feels like a possibly fatal rate. He is here. I am home.

"Levi," I say, closing the two feet between us in one fell swoop and crashing right into him, my lips landing on his, my arms grabbing his shirt, and a feeling of complete *want* rising from my belly to my cheeks. He responds, kissing me hard and hot and fast, and as I sink into him, trying to press every bit of surface area of my body to is, I know, in an instant, how right, and wonderful, and *final* this is. Levi is who I want; it has always been him. I will always love Ollie unconditionally, but Levi is *mine*.

When the kiss finally breaks, I burrow my head into the spot under his shoulder that feels like it was built for me. Wordlessly, he traces a finger down my cheek, and we take in the night: the lake, the crisp air, the sliver of a moon.

"I love you, you know." It's not the first time I've said it, but even so, it shocks me every time I do. The old Emma, the one who started her junior year a broken wreck, had no idea how to love anyone. I was always so afraid I'd lose anyone I got close to. But Levi and I went through a year no one else will ever understand. We are bound to each other, and only a year so wrong, on so many levels, could make this—us—so right.

We spend the late hours of the night lying on the sand, looking at the stars. For the first time I can remember, I feel a certain kind of contentment, being here with him, right where I belong. There were days on Castor, months when I thought we'd never have this. Knowing now that we have real futures, together—it's still hard for me to believe.

"I think about them all the time," I tell him. I mean Duplicate Emma and Levi. We're only graduating because they went to our classes, applied to colleges, lived our lives for us. It isn't fair that they had to die. I'll never stop mourning the lives they had to give up.

"How could we not?" Levi answers.

The next morning at breakfast, we're greeted with a presentation on the view screen. It's Ollie's highlight reel. The film, even in its nascent stage, is brilliant, not that I'm biased or anything. It tells the story of everything that happened on Pollux Island, and one thing is overwhelmingly clear: the Similars stopped Gravelle and Seymour from implementing their plans—plans that would have been catastrophic for so many Darkwood families, and the rest of the world. And they risked their lives to do it.

When the credits roll, Ollie gets a standing ovation from most of the student body. Harlowe sulks in a corner, and a smattering of students seem skeptical, others bored. But the majority of the kids at our school, including Ivy and Graham, jump to their feet, full of admiration. Especially for Ollie, who showed them the truth.

We sit together for the very first time. *All* of us. Me, the Similars—and their originals. Tessa and Madison, who seem to be on campus a lot these days. It's almost like they're looking for an excuse to hang out with us. I don't know if I'll ever get used to that. Archer's eating with us too, here during NYU's spring break. He's never looked happier to be back at school. And, of course, Ollie and Pru, who sit on either side of me, with Levi across the table. I catch Levi's eyes as we stand, clapping, supporting Ollie in this moment that feels big, bigger than any of us. I smile, because I think I finally know who I am now, or who I might become, anyway. I think I might like her.

ACKNOWLEDGMENTS

A giant, over-the-top, group hug thank-you to everyone at Sourcebooks who has supported this series from day one. I can't thank you enough for your enthusiasm for Emma, Levi, Ollie, and the Similars. Annie Berger, I am so lucky to have gotten the chance to collaborate with you on this book—your insights have been so sharp and spot-on, and I could not have made it to the finish line without you. (Thank you for talking me down off the overplotting ledge!)

To the Sourcebooks team: Beth Oleniczak, Mallory Hyde, Valerie Pierce, Ashlyn Keil, Heidi Weiland, Steve Geck, Cassie Gutman, Michelle Lecuyer, and Sarah Kasman—*thank you*. You are superstars at what you do, and just in case I haven't said it enough already, I appreciate it all. To Nicole Hower, who designed the most dark and deliciously twisty cover imaginable for this book and *The Similars* paperback: thank you! And huge thanks to Robin Macmillan for an image that so perfectly encapsulates the Darkwood vibe.

Thank you, thank you, to my agent, Sasha Raskin, whose dedication and early support made this series a reality when it was just a fever dream in my head. You're the best.

Stephen Breimer, Leigh Brecheen, Matt Sadeghian, Chloe Pisello, David Martin, Jazmine Hill, Alexandra Kundrat, and everyone on Team Similars at Avalon: you know how amazing you are. Thank you.

Barry and Felicia Ptolemy, thank you for the book trailer that launched a thousand ships. You are both visionaries.

Gretchen Koss, thank you for your belief in me and my books!

Ansley Fones, you are my web diva/genius—what would I do without you?!

To my family—Mom, Dad, Jessica, and Nicholas—thanks for never tiring of my weird hypotheticals and for appreciating the way my brain works. Love you all so much. Ray, Sonya, Amy, and Jacob: you've been there from the beginning, and I can't thank you enough for your eternal support.

To my friends who are like family: Bill Hanson, Winnie Kemp, Stephany Gabriner, Victoria Frank, Celeste Oberfest, Alexa Gerrity, Nidhi Mehta, Tammy Camp, Wayee Chu, Allison Manzari, Jackie Ankumah, Lyndsay Lyle, Lauren Belden, Caitlin Crawford and Andy Lurie, my JCC moms (you know who you are!), Live Oak moms (ditto!) and the HBS ladies (of course!)—thanks for years of pep talks, for buying books in bulk, for bolstering me, and for being the best friends anyone could ask for. Bill and Winnie, your critiques and feedback are literally what made this book what it is. Prolific-4-evah. And special thanks to my SMS classmates (go turkey), my Stanford friends and our community in SF: you're all the best.

Laura King, you *are* family to me; no one else on the planet could do what you do for my kiddos, and I am so grateful.

Several of my author and writer friends have been lifelines to me through this journey: Danielle Paige, Jill Lorie Hurst, David Kreizman, Lillian Clark, Natasha Ngan, Yangsze Choo, and Allison Raskin, thanks for being my therapists and spirit animals.

And thank you to Kimberly Hamilton, Cody Harris, Sarah Lacy, and Alli Deeter for organizing book clubs and events, and for introducing *The Similars* to new readers—so appreciated!

To Ethan: because of you I can tell wild stories, and that is everything. Thanks for years (years!) of letting my mind wander to those worlds, and even being a little bit proud of it, and me. You are the best dad, friend, soul mate, and cofounder of the Kurz crew, and you make me laugh more than anyone—still! To Leo and Quincy: Yes! I get why *Captain Underpants* is so, so funny. Dav Pilkey is a genius, and reading is the best! I love you both so much, and no, I probably won't stop writing, but I promise I'll find a way to *also* pick you up from school (sometimes).

To every book blogger, BookTuber, bookstagrammer, reader, librarian, teacher, and bookseller who has read, reviewed, championed, or snapped a pic of this series: THANK YOU. And to every single reader who has reached out to me—you are what makes this all worthwhile.

ABOUT THE AUTHOR

Rebecca Hanover is a television writer, sandwich lover, and young adult author. She earned a bachelor of arts from Stanford University in English and drama and was awarded an Emmy for Best Writing as a staff writer on the CBS daytime drama *Guiding Light*. Rebecca lives in San Francisco with her husband, Ethan, and their two sons. Follow her online at rebeccahanover.com.

FIREreads

#getbooklit

Your hub for the hottest young adult books!

Visit us online and sign up for our
newsletter at FIREreads.com

 @sourcebooksfire

 sourcebooksfire

fireeads.tumblr.com